ONCE A F

KATE HARDY

CHALLENGING THE NURSE'S RULES

BY
JANICE LYNN

MILLS &
BOON

Kate Hardy lives in Norwich, in the east of England, with her husband, two young children, one bouncy spaniel, and too many books to count! When she's not busy writing romance or researching local history she helps out at her children's schools. She also loves cooking—spot the recipes sneaked into her books! (They're also on her website, along with extracts and stories behind the books.) Writing for Mills & Boon has been a dream come true for Kate—something she wanted to do ever since she was twelve. She's been writing Medical Romances™ for Mills & Boon for over ten years now. She says it's the best of both worlds, because she gets to learn lots of new things when she's researching the background to a book: add a touch of passion, drama and danger, a new gorgeous hero every time, and it's the perfect job!

Kate's always delighted to hear from readers, so do drop in to her website at www.katehardy.com

Janice Lynn has a Masters in Nursing from Vanderbilt University, and works as a nurse practitioner in a family practice. She lives in the southern United States with her husband, their four children, their Jack Russell—appropriately named Trouble—and a lot of unnamed dust bunnies that have moved in since she started her writing career.

To find out more about Janice and her writing visit www.janicelynn.com

ONCE A PLAYBOY...

BY
KATE HARDY

For Sheila, my wonderful editor—who puts up with a lot
(and always takes out the reindeer!)

First published in Great Britain 2012
by Mills & Boon, an imprint of Harlequin (UK) Limited.
Harlequin (UK) Limited, Eton House, 18-24 Paradise Road,
Richmond, Surrey TW9 1SR

© Pamela Brooks 2012

ISBN: 978 0 263 89195 9

Harlequin (UK) policy is to use papers that are natural, renewable and recyclable products and made from wood grown in sustainable forests. The logging and manufacturing process conform to the legal environmental regulations of the country of origin.

Printed and bound in Spain
by Blackprint CPI, Barcelona

CHAPTER ONE

'So you're doing static cycling on a flat surface, and swimming?' Serena asked.

'Yes,' George said.

'Does it hurt?'

'No.' And it wasn't a complete fib. George could do the swimming and static cycling bits of his exercise programme without any problems. But he'd pushed himself a bit too far this week, thinking that he could start the last phase of his treatment a little bit sooner than his body was really ready for it.

She raised her eyebrow. 'How about the truth?'

'It is the truth.'

Serena folded her arms. 'George, I know it's driving you crazy not being able to do everything you could do before the accident, and you want to get your life back yesterday, but it's going to take time until you're completely fit again. You did a fair bit of damage to your thigh and your wrists—and, remember, it takes up to six months for a broken femur to heal, plus there's all the soft tissue damage surrounding it.'

And that wasn't the only damage he'd done to his body, George knew. Though he wasn't thinking about *that* particular issue right now. He sighed. 'OK. If you must know, I tried running, a couple of days ago. Through chest-deep water, so it wasn't weight-bearing.'

She raised her eyebrows. 'And?'

'It was absolutely fine.'

'If I had my way,' Serena said, 'my patients would be banned from looking up *anything* on the internet.'

He coughed. 'How did you know that's where I read about it?'

'Because you didn't get that advice from me or from Bruno. Your last lot of X-rays were fine—your bones are stable and they're healing nicely—but you really can't run before you can walk. Literally.'

'I realise that now.' Much as he hated to admit it.

She sighed. 'What else did you do, George?'

'Tried it on land. Not very far,' he added swiftly.

'But it hurt.' It wasn't a question.

'A bit,' he admitted.

'I'd say it's your quads, by the way you walked in.' She shook her head. 'What am I going to do with you, George?'

'I used to hear that a lot. At school as well as at home,' he said.

'Why does that not surprise me?' She rolled her eyes. 'Do you mind if I take a closer look and check that you haven't done any real damage?'

'Sure.' He paused. 'Does this mean taking off my clothes?'

'Well, it's a bit tricky to judge muscles through a layer of material.' She gave him an amused smile. 'Let me know when you're ready.'

He still felt slightly self-conscious about stripping in front of her. Which was totally ridiculous. Apart from the fact that Serena James was his physiotherapist and this wasn't his first session with her, George had stripped in enough bedrooms—and other places—not to feel in the slightest bit awkward at taking his clothes off in front of a woman. Especially as this wasn't even a full strip; he'd still be wearing underpants and a T-shirt.

But he appreciated the fact that Serena had turned her back while he removed the hated tracksuit bottoms, leaving him a little bit of dignity. He'd already put up with more than enough during his recuperation. He'd hated feeling so dependent. And he was so, so ready to have his life back again.

If that meant he had to take this last phase just a little bit more slowly, then he'd have to learn to be patient. Even though taking things slowly felt as if it was killing him. He really loathed living life at a snail's pace. For him, it wasn't living, it was existing. And there was a huge difference between the two.

'Ready now,' he said, and she turned to face him.

Her hands were gentle as she probed his leg and felt the muscles. And although Serena's movements were completely asexual, a physiotherapist's touch rather than a lover's, as she moved her head George caught the scent of her shampoo. Like sun-warmed, ripened strawberries. And all the blood in his head rushed south.

Oh, hell. He'd better start thinking of something else—such as how much repairing the roof at Somers Hall was going to cost this year and all the regulations that they'd have to comply with—or he was going to embarrass both of them.

Or was he? Did Serena feel this weird connection between them, too? And, if so, what would she want to do about it?

He glanced at her left hand. No ring. OK, so the lack of a ring didn't mean that she wasn't in a committed relationship, but he had the feeling that Serena James was the kind of woman who believed in marriage and would want that gold band on her finger. Which in turn meant that he was completely the wrong kind of man for her. He didn't do commitment. Ever. If his mother's behaviour hadn't cured him of that idea, Rebecca certainly had.

'There's some tightness in your muscles here and here.' Serena demonstrated by touch. 'I can give you some different exercises to work on these, and that will help.'

'Thanks. And I promise I'll do the exercises every day, for as many reps as you tell me to.'

'And you'll also promise me that you won't overdo it,' she said firmly, folding her arms and looking him straight in the eye.

He smiled. 'Would I overdo it?'

'Considering that you ended up this way in the first place because you had a fight with a cliff and lost, my vote would be for yes.'

He loved the teasing glint in her green eyes. And he liked Serena James. Either she didn't know he was heir to Somers Hall and the barony, or she didn't care, because she treated him as if he were just an ordinary patient. George appreciated her being so down-to-earth and practical with him.

She turned away again to give him time to replace his tracksuit bottoms. This was the kind of clothing he never wore outside a sports field, preferring designer denims or made-to-measure suit trousers; the accident had done a fair bit of damage to his sartorial style, too, because jeans still didn't feel comfortable on his broken leg. Dressing properly again was another thing he was looking forward to.

'OK, I'm decent again,' he said with a smirk.

'So why do you do it?' she asked as she turned back to him.

'Do what?'

'All the dangerous sports.'

He shrugged. 'My brother says I'm an adrenalin junkie.'

'Is he right?'

'I enjoy the rush of extreme sports,' he admitted. 'I guess it's just a way of getting rid of tension.' And it meant he didn't have time to let himself think too deeply about anything.

'And you can't think of a safer way of getting rid of tension?'

At this very moment, he could. Not that he was going to embarrass her by telling her exactly what was in his head. Or the fact that it involved her. 'Powered paragliding isn't unsafe,' he parried instead.

'Says the man with a broken femur and two broken wrists.'

'Which are almost healed,' he reminded her. 'I was wearing a helmet, and I'd done all the training. I just happened to be thinking about something else at the same time as a gust of wind caught me, and by the time I realised what was happening it was too late to avoid the cliff.'

She raised an eyebrow. 'It must've been quite something on your mind to distract you that much.'

It really was. As in whether he was really his father's son. For a normal family, it might not have been so much of an issue, but for the Somers family it had had a lot of legal ramifications. Such as who was the real heir to the barony, and what would happen to the estate and the entailment. Absolutely life-changing things.

Luckily the DNA tests had proved that his mother

had been completely wrong in her beliefs, and that George and his younger brother Ed were indeed David Somers's legitimate sons. But, before they'd done the tests, their mother's diaries and letters had given George some seriously bad moments, worrying about what was going to happen to his family.

And it had brought him low enough to wonder about whether he'd still be part of them, if it turned out that he was actually the by-blow of one of his mother's many lovers instead of his father's son. Which again was ridiculous; he knew that his father, stepmother, brother and sisters loved him as much as he loved them.

But that was because they were his family. That meant they were practically obliged to love him. And they did.

Except for one person.

Zara Somers had been able to walk away from him and Ed without a second thought when George was six years old, and she'd acted as if her sons didn't exist from that moment on until the day she died. No matter how ridiculous George knew it was intellectually, emotionally the doubts were always there and he couldn't quite squash them. Would his girlfriends, like his mother, be more interested in his social standing, not seeing him for who he really was beneath the label?

He'd risked it once. He'd fallen for Rebecca at university; and he'd been so sure that she saw him for who he was and loved him anyway.

How wrong he'd been.

His background hadn't attracted her; it had pushed her away. She'd said she couldn't cope with living in a goldfish bowl as the future wife of a future baron; and even though he'd said the barony stuff was just a label, she'd claimed it was what made him who he was and it couldn't be separated. He'd even offered to give it up for her; but that still wasn't enough for her. She'd given him his ring back. *I love you too much to make you unhappy.*

And then she'd walked away for good.

George had made quite sure from then on that he was the one to leave. Which was why he kept all his relationships short and sweet and very far from serious, nowadays.

'Yes,' he said.

Serena flushed at his curtness. 'Sorry. I mean, I saw the stuff in the papers.'

So had most of the country. The gossip rags had had a field day when the news had leaked that David Somers's heirs might not be who they thought they were.

'I didn't mean to pry or spread gossip,' she added.

He believed her. And it wasn't her fault that his mother had been the way she was. Or that Rebecca hadn't been able to see past her own insecurities and take a chance with him. 'It's OK. And you haven't upset me. I don't mind talking about it.' And it was true, now. The DNA test results had been conclusive and had put paid to all the rumours. Then Ed had announced his engagement to Jane, and the press had been utterly charmed by his brother's Cinderella bride. 'Anyway, it's all done and dusted now. I won't let myself get distracted in the future.'

'You're actually going back to doing that parachute thing?' Serena looked surprised.

'Powered paragliding,' he corrected. 'Sadly, no. The whole family ganged up on me and made me agree to sell the rig. And my consultant said I can't go skiing again until the pin's out of my leg.' He grimaced. 'So I guess I'm going to have a very, very boring year, limping everywhere and being grumpy with everyone because I'd much rather be doing something else.' Something with enough speed to let him leave all his self-doubts behind. Something that meant he didn't have time to sit still and think.

She smiled. 'I'm sure you can find something to keep yourself amused.'

Some*one* would be a better idea. And she happened to be standing right in front of him. He had a feeling that Serena James could distract him beautifully; even though she wasn't his usual type, there was something about her that really grabbed his attention.

'How are your wrists?' she asked.

'Better. I can manage without the splints now. And I've got pretty much the full range of movement back, thanks to the exercises you gave me.' He gave her a rueful smile. 'You have no idea how much I'm looking forward to being able to drive myself again.'

'Taxis that bad, are they?'

'They are when they're being driven by your little sisters, and the fare is a whole journey's worth of nagging.'

She laughed.

'You're supposed to be sympathetic,' he said.

'I am.' She was still smiling. 'But I'm just imagining you being bossed around by a woman.'

'My sister,' he corrected. 'Bossy isn't the half of it. The oldest one's the scariest barrister I've ever met—you just don't answer Alice back. Ever. The middle one's an architect and threatens to gag me with gaffer tape if I dare suggest she modifies her driving slightly so she doesn't scrape my car, and the baby just switches to speaking Latin if you try to talk her into letting you do something!'

Serena laughed again. 'I bet you charm all three of them into doing everything you ask of them.'

Fair point. It was what George did with women. Charmed them. With two exceptions—ones he didn't usually let himself think about—women tended to agree to what he wanted.

And right now he wanted *her*.

Serena had a beautiful mouth—a perfect rose-bud. She wasn't wearing a scrap of make-up, but she really didn't need any. She had a fresh, natural beauty. Flawless skin that made him itch to touch it, feel how soft it was under his fingertips. And he couldn't help wondering what that mouth would feel like against his own.

'So you think I'm a shallow, charming playboy? I'm hurt,' he said, batting his eyelashes at her. 'Deeply wounded.'

'Sure you are.' That glint of amusement was back in her eyes.

'Oh, but I am.' And the suggestion was too much for him to resist. 'And, as you're the one making me feel bad right now, Serena, maybe you should be the one to kiss me better.'

She simply smiled at him. 'I'm afraid that's not part of the treatment, Mr Somers.'

He noticed that she'd switched back to formality with him. Well, it was his own fault for being too pushy. Time to backtrack. 'I apologise for teasing, Ms James— or should that be Mrs?'

'Ms is fine.'

Which still didn't tell him whether she was mar-ried—or at least committed elsewhere. Though he had a feeling that she wasn't. A feeling that wasn't based on any actual information: simply his gut instinct. And his gut had rarely led him wrong in the past. Only with Rebecca, and that had been his fault for wanting what she couldn't give him.

Serena took him through all the exercises, and he concentrated on making sure he got them right.

'Good. I think we're done for today,' she said.

'See you on Thursday? Or are you going to make me see Brutal Bruno instead, to teach me a lesson for being cheeky with you today?'

'Bruno's as gentle as a lamb,' she protested.

'Not with me, he isn't,' George said feelingly, re-membering his first sessions with the physiotherapist while he had still been in hospital. Once the painkillers had worn off, the movements had hurt like hell. Not that he would've admitted to any of it. He'd wanted to be out of hospital with his independence back. Like yesterday.

'Oh, you big baby.' She laughed. 'I'll see you on Thursday.'

He'd see her on Thursday.

Funny how that made the whole physiotherapy thing seem bearable.

Serena was still smiling as she wrote up the notes.

George Somers was just too gorgeous for his own good.

Another time, another place, and she would've been tempted to take him up on his offer of kissing him bet-ter.

But...

She couldn't afford to be unprofessional. She needed this job, and getting too friendly with your patients was the quickest way to risk ending up in a sticky situation and with a disciplinary charge on your records, at the very least.

Plus she knew that George Somers was the kind of man who never dated anyone more than a couple of times. He didn't do serious relationships. His picture was in the press with a different woman practically every week—usually a tall, skinny blonde—and having two broken wrists, a broken leg and concussion hadn't seemed to slow him down in the slightest. He was the last kind of man she wanted to get involved with. And why on earth would the heir to a barony—a man who'd dated supermodels, according to all the newspapers—be in the slightest bit interested in an ordinary woman like her?

And then there was Ethan. Her son's needs came first and they always would, as far as she was concerned. End of story.

So, much as Serena found George Somers attractive, she knew he'd better remain a patient and only a patient. She couldn't afford to offer him anything else.

She looked at her appointment schedule. Her next patient was another of her favourites, Lisa Miller, who'd been suffering from whiplash for the last six weeks and whose range of movements was responding beautifully to treatment. Serena smiled and went over to the door to call her in.

When Serena had finished her session with the patient after Lisa—an elderly lady who was recovering from a hip replacement—she took a break, just long enough to gulp down a cup of coffee in the staff kitchen.

Jess, one of the other physiotherapists, was already there, leaning against the worktop. 'The kettle's just boiled. Want a coffee?' she asked, taking a mug out of the cupboard and waving it at Serena.

'Thanks, Jess. That'd be great.'

'So how was Mr Hot?' Jess asked, making the coffee and then handing Serena the mug.

'Mr Hot?' Serena asked warily.

'Your first patient this afternoon.' Jess grinned and fanned herself. 'I can't believe you didn't know who I meant. He's *seriously* gorgeous.'

Serena didn't dare reply to that, in case her words were too revealing. The last thing she needed was for her colleagues to think she was lusting after one of her patients.

'Is he single?'

'No idea,' Serena fibbed. 'Anyway, I thought you were engaged?'

'I am, but I'm not dead. I can still look. And he's something else.' Jess rolled her eyes. 'I can't believe you don't know anything about him. I mean, if I was single and one of my patients was that hot, I'd want to know everything about him.'

'There is such a thing as patient confidentiality,' Serena said dryly.

'True.' Jess gave her an irrepressible smile. 'You know, if he *is* single, you could always ask him out.'

'Of course I can't! He's my patient.'

'Only until his treatment's finished,' Jess pointed out. 'And then there's nothing to stop you getting to know him better.'

Serena played her trump card. 'Ethan.'

'You know your parents would babysit like a shot if you asked them.'

That was true. But Serena's mother already picked the little boy up from school every afternoon and kept him entertained until Serena had finished her shift; Serena felt she was taking quite enough from her parents as it was, without asking for more.

Jess patted her arm. 'Serena, I know you're a brilliant mum and you're a great physio—you've taught me such a lot over the last year—but there's more to life than work and being a single parent. You hardly ever go on team nights out. When was the last time you had some fun?'

Serena lifted her chin, stung. 'I have plenty of fun with my son.'

'I know you do, but that's not what I meant. When was the last time you did something just for *you*, went out with someone on a date?'

'I'm happy with my life the way it is,' Serena protested.

Jess raised an eyebrow. 'Are you?'

Serena didn't answer that.

'Try to make some time just for you,' Jess said softly. 'Because you're important, too.'

'Yeah.' Serena added cold water to her coffee and gulped it down. 'I'd better dash. I don't want to get behind with my appointments.'

Though, as she left the kitchen, she knew she was being a coward, not facing up to Jess's questions. When was the last time she'd gone on a date? Not since she'd been going out with Jason, Ethan's father.

But that didn't mean she wanted to go out with George. She'd already dated one heartbreaker who'd let her down, and that was more than enough for her. She'd learned from her mistakes, the hard way. It wasn't something she intended to repeat.

CHAPTER TWO

GEORGE lay flat on the floor with his legs stretched out in front of him. Then he raised his bad leg thirty centimetres from the floor and traced a T-shape in the air, just as Serena had taught him.

Serena.

He closed his eyes as he repeated the exercise, seeing her face in his mind's eye. That beautiful, beautiful mouth. What would it feel like against his skin? He tipped his head back, imagining her mouth teasing a path down his throat; then lower, down his sternum, and lower still, over his abdomen. Her hair would be loose and brushing against his skin, soft as silk, its coolness in sharp contrast to the heat of her mouth.

He blew out a breath.

This really wasn't sensible, fantasising about his physiotherapist like this. Especially as she'd made it quite clear that she wasn't interested in him. Serena James wasn't the type of woman he normally dated. She wasn't one of the tall, rail-thin blondes who graced his arm at parties. She had light brown hair that most people would describe as 'mouse', she couldn't be more than five feet four inches tall, and she had definite curves. Glorious curves that he ached to touch. To mould with his palms. To caress and tease until she was as full of desire for him as he was for her.

He knew what his bossiest sister would say. Alice would roll her eyes and say that he wanted Serena precisely because he knew she was out of reach. Because she was one of the first women in years who'd resisted him.

Worse still, he knew that was probably true. Serena James was a challenge. She intrigued him. And he found it hard to resist a pretty face and the chance to have some fun.

If he had any sense, he'd ask if he could see Bruno instead of Serena to finish off the rest of his treatment.

But the idea of seeing Serena again on Thursday was too much for him.

Serena smiled at George when he walked in, and heat arrowed down to his groin.

Down, boy. This is meant to be professional, he reminded his libido.

'So you've been doing the exercises I suggested?' she asked.

'Yes.'

'*Just* the exercises?'

He gave her his most charming smile. 'Why wouldn't I?'

'Because you're the type to push yourself too hard,' she said softly. 'What did you do, George?'

She could read him like a book. He wasn't sure if that intrigued him more or worried him. Most people were happy just to see the surface; Serena clearly looked deeper and he had a feeling that she saw what most people missed about him. Which in itself was dangerous. Apart from his family, he didn't let people get that close.

'I tried driving at the weekend. On private land, so there wasn't a risk to anyone else.' Odd how it felt important to tell her that. Normally, he didn't give a damn what people thought about him. But what Serena thought... For some reason, that mattered. And he'd rather not start analysing why.

She raised an eyebrow. 'Did it hurt?'

'No. I realise I'm not quite ready to drive in London again, yet,' he admitted, 'but now I've got a benchmark to work with. And it really helps, knowing that I'm not going to be dependent on the girls and Ed—my brother—for what already feels like for ever.'

She examined him, then made him go through the full range of movements just to the point of pain. 'That's good. Your range has improved hugely over the last few weeks.'

'Thanks to you.'

'And you, for sticking with the exercises. A lot of people struggle and some of them just give up.'

'Not me. I want my independence back, and if that means sticking to an exercise programme, then the exercises take priority over everything else every day,' George said.

She smiled. 'Actually, you've done well. I think you're ready for the last stage.' She gave him more exercises; even as George concentrated on her instructions and making sure he was doing everything correctly, to get the maximum benefit from the movements, he couldn't help looking at her.

And he caught her looking back at him. Specifically, at his mouth.

All his senses immediately went on full alert. Was she thinking about it, the same way he was? What would she do if he kissed her?

He had a feeling that she'd retreat into formality again. She'd panicked enough at his last appointment, when he'd suggested she kiss him; he was pretty sure that actually doing what he'd suggested would send her running in the opposite direction.

But next week was his last appointment. He didn't have time to wait and coax her round to his point of view. He was going to have to make his move then, or lose the chance of seeing her again—for good.

On Monday morning, Serena put George through his paces again.

And then it was over. He was signed off. No more physio.

No more seeing her, unless he asked her out now. He'd thought about it all weekend. On paper, it was ridiculous. She wasn't his type and he was pretty sure he wasn't hers. Yet she intrigued him too much for him to let it go. 'That was my last appointment,' he said.

'I know. You've done very well.'

'I brought you these, to say thanks for all the work you've done on my wrists and my leg. And for being patient with me. I know I haven't exactly been the easiest of clients.' He produced a flattish square box, slightly bigger than a CD case; it was wrapped in thick burgundy-coloured paper and tied with a gold gauzy ribbon.

She shook her head. 'I'm sorry. I can't accept gifts.'

'Rules and regulations?' he asked.

'They're there to protect patients.'

'And staff, I guess.' To make sure that nobody could claim that a therapist had taken advantage of a vulnerable patient and extorted expensive presents from them. He could understand that. 'Pity. It isn't a diamond tiara or anything like that,' he said, just to reassure her. 'It's just something small.' The kind of thing he'd take to the hostess of a dinner party.

She looked embarrassed. 'It's very kind of you to think of me, Mr Somers, but I'm afraid I really can't accept anything.'

He put the box on her desk. 'Serena. Look at me,' he said softly.

Looking at him was a mistake. Those blue, blue eyes. That beautifully shaped mouth. Serena could barely tear her gaze away from it.

'Serena,' he whispered.

And she knew in that second that he was going to kiss her.

In the name of common sense, she should back away. Or at least turn her head aside so he ended up kissing her cheek and not her mouth.

But she couldn't move. It was as if some invisible force was holding her in place. Making her wait for the moment when he finally kissed her.

George's lips brushed against hers ever so gently; to her surprise, his kiss wasn't demanding and forceful, but sweet and light and coaxing. Tempting.

Back away and tell him you don't do this.

But her common sense was drowned out by the way her lips were tingling. She wanted more. Lots more. Right now.

As if he could read her mind, he touched his mouth to hers again. And again, his mouth nipped gently at her lower lip, inviting and inciting. The next thing she knew, her fingers were sliding into his hair, his arms were wrapped tightly round her, and her mouth was opening under his. Inviting the kind of kiss she hadn't shared with anyone since Ethan's father.

And even that had been a pale, pale imitation of the way George was kissing her. The way his mouth promised as much as it demanded, giving as well as taking. Her blood felt as if it were fizzing through her veins. And her temperature was most definitely spiking.

He broke the kiss and stroked her face. 'Serena. I knew it would be like that between us,' he said softly.

Hot. Intense. *Perfect*.

'I've wanted to do that for weeks.'

She'd wanted it, too. But it couldn't happen. She dragged in a breath and took a step away from him; not that it made much difference. They could've been standing at opposite ends of Wembley Stadium with thousands of people jammed between them, and she'd still be spine-tinglingly aware of his presence. 'We shouldn't have done that, Mr Somers,' she said shakily. 'You're my patient.'

'Actually, I'm not,' he pointed out. 'That was my last session. My treatment's over. So we're not patient and therapist any more. We're just you and me. Two ordinary people. There's no reason why we can't do whatever we want.' He stole another of those sweet, mind-drugging kisses. 'I'd like to see you outside work, Serena. Will you go out with me?'

She shook her head. 'I can't.'

'You're involved with someone else?'

This was her cue to tell a little white lie. She knew instinctively that George Somers was an honourable man. He wouldn't push her if he thought that would mean she'd be unfaithful to her partner. All she had to do was say yes. One tiny little word.

But her mouth wasn't playing ball. 'I'm single.'

'So what's the problem?'

How could he not see it? 'We're from different worlds. Seriously different. You're the son of a baron. You mix with royalty.'

'*Minor* royalty,' he corrected. 'Not that often. And most of whom I find pretty tedious, to be honest.'

'And celebs.' She'd seen the pictures in the gossip rags that clients left in the waiting room. George Somers didn't date ordinary women like her. He had a taste for tall, skinny blondes with incredibly short skirts and teeth so white and even that it was obvious they'd spent a fortune on cosmetic dentistry.

He shrugged. 'My world isn't all glitz and glamour. And if you don't want to go to a showbiz party, that's fine by me. I can think of plenty of other things I'd rather do with you.'

Heaven help her, so could she. And it made her skin feel too tight. 'I can't believe we're having this conversation.'

'I'm just an ordinary man, Serena.'

That absolutely wasn't true. There was nothing in the least bit ordinary about George Somers.

'I find you attractive.' His eyes glittered. 'And, from the way you kissed me back just now, I'd say it's completely mutual.'

It was. She did find him attractive. Which was a huge problem. Help. It had been so long since she'd been out with anyone that she couldn't even remember how to play the dating game. She'd only make a mess of this.

'I have a child,' she blurted out. 'I'm a single mum.' And then she felt ashamed of herself for using Ethan as an excuse. As a shield. Her son deserved more than that.

'OK. I can understand that you want to protect your

child—it's not fair for a kid to get attached to an "uncle" who isn't going to stick around,' George said.

He understood that?

'Which isn't me suggesting that you have a string of men parading through your life, either,' he added.

She felt the colour rise in her cheeks. So he didn't think she was an easy conquest, either.

'If anything, I get the impression you've gone completely the other way and you don't normally date anyone. But having a child doesn't mean that you can't see anyone, Serena. It doesn't mean that you can't have a little fun in your life.'

Exactly what her colleague Jess had said. She pushed temptation away. 'I'm a working mum. I need to spend my free time with my son.'

'Of course you do. But you need a little time for you, too,' he said softly. He leaned forward, closing the gap between them, and brushed his lips against hers. Almost as if he was promising that nobody was going to get hurt by this.

'Have lunch with me on Tuesday,' he said, his voice soft and incredibly seductive.

'I c—' she began, and he pressed the tip of his finger lightly against her mouth, not letting her refuse.

'I know you have patients to see, Serena, and you need to stick to your schedule at work. If you're busy on Tuesday, we can make it another day. But we're going to have lunch together next week. *Just* lunch. You, me, and—' his eyes crinkled at the corners '—hopefully a little bit of sunshine.'

How could she possibly resist an invitation like that?

'Thank you,' she said.

'Are you vegetarian? Is there anything you really don't like or are allergic to, foodwise?'

'No to all three.'

'Same here. Which makes life simpler. Good.' He took a card from his wallet and scribbled a number on the back. 'That's my mobile. So I'll see you on Tuesday at midday. If that's a problem, text me with an alternative. My schedule's reasonably flexible at the moment.'

Her fingers touched his as she took the card, and it sent a shiver of desire all the way through her. Crazy. She'd managed to keep the attraction in check while he was her patient. Now he wasn't her patient any more, all bets were off. And her mouth was still tingling from that kiss.

He took the box from her desk and handed it to her. 'Right. Now, this isn't a gift from a grateful patient, so it isn't covered by the rules and regulations. This is just a very small, no-strings gift from me to you.'

She stared at him. 'Why?'

'Because I think you'll like it. And I like putting a little bit of sunshine into people's days.' There was a glitter of something she couldn't read in his eyes. 'And it's not for sharing, Serena. I meant it when I said it was just for you.'

'May I open it now?'

'No.' He smiled. 'Wait until I've gone.' He stole another kiss. 'Until Tuesday.'

She sat down at her desk as he closed the door behind him and untied the ribbon.

His gift turned out to be a small square box of the most exquisite dark chocolates. From Fortnum and Mason: the poshest grocery store in London, and quite possibly the poshest store in the world. That one small box of chocolates had probably cost him half as much as a whole week's grocery shop for herself and Ethan.

She'd never, ever been given something so decadent.

How had George known that she loved dark chocolate? Or had it been one of the little things they'd chatted about during the weeks of his treatment, and he'd actually listened to what she'd told him?

When Serena took the lid off the box and saw the chocolates nestled in dark brown frilled paper, and spied a crystallised violet on top of one smooth, dark, sinful chocolate—her absolute favourite flavour—she couldn't resist taking it and biting off a corner. The bitterness of the smooth, rich chocolate was the perfect foil to the sweet floral fondant inside, and it took her breath away.

Shockingly, it also reminded her of kissing him. Of the sweetness of his mouth in that sinfully dark kiss. She knew that she'd always associate violet creams with kissing George, from now on.

And she really needed her head examined. Had she really agreed to meet him for lunch, next week? Had she really let him kiss her until she was dizzy?

All the same, she finished the chocolate, then put the lid back on and slipped the box into her handbag before texting him to say thank you.

This isn't a gift from a grateful patient... This is just a very small, no-strings gift from me to you.

Maybe.

But would they be able to say the same about lunch?

CHAPTER THREE

SERENA just about managed to concentrate on her patients for the rest of the afternoon, and then went straight to her parents' house to collect her son.

'Mummy!' Ethan flung himself at her, wrapping his arms round her legs and hugging her tightly. When he released her, Serena knelt down so she was at his level and could hug him back properly.

'Did you have a nice day at school, darling?'

'We played football. It was brilliant.' He beamed at her. 'And I drawed you a picture. Nanna made basghetti for tea. I helped stir the sauce.'

Serena ruffled his hair; the fact that her five-year-old still couldn't quite say the name of his favourite food still made her heart melt. She looked up at her mother. 'Thanks, Mum.'

'I've made a huge panful, so you're staying to tea tonight. Don't argue,' Carolyn said with a smile.

Serena smiled back, grateful that she wouldn't have to cook dinner tonight. 'You spoil me, Mum. Thank you.'

'Can I help Granddad with his puzzle?' Ethan asked.

'Of course you can, gorgeous boy.' Serena kissed him before releasing him, and the little boy sped away to join Serena's father.

'So how was your day, love?' Carolyn asked, bustling around.

'OK.' Serena tried for brightness, not wanting her mother to know how ruffled her usual composure was.

'How was it *really*?' Carolyn asked.

Serena frowned. 'How do you know it wasn't OK?'

'The same way that you know if Ethan's had a tough day at school. Mother's instinct,' Carolyn said. 'Except I've had a few more years to hone mine than you have. What happened?'

Serena went to the doorway to check that Ethan was busy with her father, then quietly shut the door so he wouldn't accidentally overhear her conversation. 'I was asked out on a date.'

'That's great. We'll babysit,' Carolyn said immediately.

Serena shook her head. 'Not an evening. Lunch.'

'So you don't need a babysitter.' Carolyn shrugged. 'Well, lunch is still nice. And it means you won't feel guilty about taking time you feel you ought to spend with Ethan.'

Guilt. Yes. That was exactly it. 'I can't do it, Mum.'

Carolyn looked puzzled. 'Why not?'

'He was my patient.'

'Was?' Carolyn asked.

'His last treatment was today.'

'Then, as he's not actually your patient any more, there's nothing to stop you seeing him, is there?' Carolyn pointed out.

Serena bit her lip. 'What about Ethan?'

'If this man's asked you out to lunch, then—assuming it isn't a weekend—Ethan will be at school.'

'No, I mean...' She grimaced. 'It feels wrong. Dating someone.'

'Does he know about Ethan?'

Serena nodded.

'And is it a problem for him?'

'No. He was pretty sensitive about it,' Serena admitted.

Carolyn gave her a hug. 'Not all men are like Jason, you know.'

'I know.'

'And you haven't dated in—well, since Jason.'

Seven years ago. That was the last time she'd been out with a man who wasn't Jason. Jason had walked out on her almost two years after their first date; in the five years since then, she hadn't dated at all. She sighed. 'That's half the problem, Mum. I don't know *how*. I don't know the rules of dating any more.'

'I don't think they've changed that much,' Carolyn said gently. 'Just be yourself and it'll be fine.'

'It won't work, Mum.'

'How do you know, if you don't give it a chance?'

'We're from different worlds.'

Carolyn spread her hands. 'And?'

'I'm not really his type.'

'He wouldn't have asked you out if he didn't like you for who you are,' Carolyn pointed out. She stroked Serena's hair away from her face. 'Love, you give Ethan everything he needs and you're a great mum. But you need to make some time for yourself as well. Between Ethan and work, there's nothing left for you. And that isn't healthy.'

Jess had said the same thing. Did her father and the rest of her colleagues think that, too? Serena wondered.

'Do you like him?' Carolyn asked.

That was the tough question. And Serena certainly wasn't admitting that George made her heart miss a beat every time she saw him. Or that he'd completely melted her common sense with just one kiss. She could barely admit that to herself.

Carolyn smiled at her silence. 'So you *do* like him. Otherwise you wouldn't have mentioned a word about it to me.'

Serena had no answer to that. She knew it was true.

'So I take it you're going to have lunch with him, then?'

'No. Yes. I don't know.' The whole idea of it had her lost in confusion.

'What's the worst that could happen?' Carolyn asked.

That she'd fall in love with George and he'd let her down. That he'd break her heart, the way Jason had. That he'd walk out on her when she needed him most.

As if the whole thing had been perfectly readable on her face, Carolyn patted her hand. 'The whole world won't suddenly go down with the plague if you have lunch with a man, love.'

'I guess not.'

'You might discover that you don't have anything in common and he's really boring. Or you might discover that he's actually really nice and you'd like to see a bit more of him. But the only way you'll find out for sure is to go and have lunch with him.'

It was tempting. So very, very tempting.

And Serena had nearly a week to think about it. A week where George Somers and his beautiful mouth occupied every moment when she wasn't busy with a patient or with her son. And even then she was guiltily aware of drifting off into a daydream when she was supposed to be concentrating on writing up her notes. Especially as it took her nearly a week to finish the chocolates, they were so rich—and every single one of them made her think of kissing him. Of the way he'd scrambled her brains.

But in the end, on the Monday morning, she chickened out. As much as she wanted to see George again, he was just too dangerous for her peace of mind. She texted him at the beginning of her shift. *Thank you for the offer of lunch tomorrow, but I'm afraid I can't make it. Serena.*

She gave no excuses, leaving him no opening for negotiation. And she deliberately didn't give him an alternative, as he'd suggested.

Dating George Somers was a lovely daydream. But the reality would be something else. It could get complicated. Messy. So it was better not to start something they couldn't finish. Much more sensible; and Serena was always sensible, nowadays. There was no way she'd let her little boy be caught in the middle of any emotional upheaval. He was too important.

Thank you for the offer of lunch tomorrow, but I'm afraid I can't make it. Serena.

George stared at the message. He knew it was probably for the best. She was right in that they were from different worlds—and, the last time he'd tried dating someone not from his world, it had ended in misery for both of them. So he'd be better off just forgetting her.

Except he couldn't.

That beautiful mouth haunted him. A couple of kisses just weren't enough. He wanted to see those gorgeous green eyes glittering with laughter. And he wanted to feel her mouth on his again, explore her sweetness. Bring her out of herself and see just who she was behind her shell.

The sensible side of him knew he ought to leave it well alone.

The reckless side of him couldn't possibly resist the challenge.

Serena always kept her phone off while she was at work; if there was an emergency at school, she knew that the teachers would ring through to Reception and her colleagues would pass on the message immediately. She switched her phone on again when her shift finished, and there were no beeps to say that she'd received any messages.

Oh.

So George hadn't bothered replying to her text.

She stifled the faint ache of disappointment. Well, she'd been proved right. George hadn't been that interested. Or maybe he'd been having second thoughts, too, and realised that she just wasn't right for him; in which case her message must've been a welcome relief for him. And this feeling of being let down…well, that was plain ridiculous.

This was all for the best. She knew that.

But Serena still felt out of sorts the next day. It made her cross with herself; though she wasn't sure if she was more cross with herself for being a coward and ducking out of the date in the first place, or for being light-headed enough to think that someone like George Somers would really want to date someone like her.

So she coped with it the way she always did, by throwing herself into work. Her first patient, Janet Riley, was a new patient and suffered from Parkinson's.

Serena introduced herself with a smile. 'Your consultant has sent you to me so I can assess your balance and mobility. I'm going to do something called a Berg test, which looks at a range of different movements—well, it's called a test, but it isn't anything that you'll pass or fail. What it does is to help me see which things you find easy to do and which movements you find more difficult, so I can recommend support where you need it. It'll be part of your annual assessments from now on, and today's results will be a benchmark so we can see how and where things change, to make sure you get the right help you need.'

'I'm fine, really. I don't want to make a fuss,' Janet said.

'You're not making a fuss,' Serena reassured her. Though she knew where Janet was coming from. She didn't like making a fuss, either. And she hated the fact that she still felt so thrown by George. That she was still wishing she'd been brave enough to have lunch with him, even though at the same time she knew she'd done the sensible thing.

She took Janet through the fourteen different tests. Moving from a sitting position to standing was a problem; Serena made a note for the occupational health team to look at the chairs at Janet's home to see if they needed to be raised to make standing up easier, as well as possibly installing grab rails for the bathroom and toilet. Janet clearly also found it difficult to turn and look behind and to place an alternate foot on a stool—stairs might also need looking at, Serena noted. And retrieving an object from the floor took more effort and time than was comfortable for Janet.

'We have group exercise sessions here especially for people who find balance a little tricky. I think you'd benefit from them,' she said. 'The exercises will help with your balance, strength and suppleness.'

'But I've only just been diagnosed,' Janet said.

'That's a good time to start,' Serena said with a smile, 'because it means we can keep you going at this level for a lot longer. We have several groups, all at different levels, so you won't feel like the odd one out. Just come along to the first one and give it a try,' she coaxed.

Janet bit her lip. 'I don't want to make a fuss.'

'You're not making a fuss,' Serena reassured her again. 'And the big thing is that it'll help you keep your independence.'

Something that Serena herself valued highly—and something she'd find incredibly difficult to give up. Carving out a successful career as well as bringing up her son as a single parent meant that she was used to being in control. Having to lean on someone else now would be unthinkable.

Janet looked thoughtful. 'So I won't have to get people to do things for me.'

Just as Serena had hoped: this was the key. Janet needed to feel independent. 'Exactly. It'll give you a chance to do more things the way you want to do them.' She smiled at the older woman. 'And then you won't have to bite your tongue and feel ungrateful when someone does something for you and they don't do it to your standards.'

Janet looked relieved. 'So it's normal to feel like that? I've felt so mean-spirited.'

'It's perfectly normal. I'd be the same,' Serena reassured her. 'So will you give it a try?'

Janet nodded.

'Great.' Serena booked her in for the session, wrote out an appointment card for her, and then wrote up her notes before seeing her next patient.

Lenny Rivers had a Colles' fracture of the wrist. The same injury as George; and Serena was cross with herself for thinking of him. She forced herself to be calm and patient as she explained to Lenny, 'I need to check the movements of your shoulder, first, as it can be damaged by a fall on the hand. Has your arm been in a sling?'

'Not as much as it should've been,' Lenny admitted, looking faintly guilty.

She smiled. Given that his arm hadn't been kept that immobile, his elbow wouldn't be a problem. 'Let's have a look.' She examined him gently; the colour of his skin looked fine and there was no abnormal swelling, so he was healing nicely. 'Your skin's a bit dry, but that's really common after you've been in plaster. If you use a gentle moisturiser or baby oil on your skin, that will help get rid of the dryness. Have you been in any pain?'

'Not really.'

'Good. You might find you do get some swelling, so if that happens all you need to do is elevate your arm a bit, maybe put an ice pack for up to fifteen minutes, four times a day. Though make sure the ice isn't straight against your skin, or you could burn it,' she warned.

'It feels a bit strange with the plaster off,' Lenny said. 'I'm a bit scared to use it, in case I hurt it again.'

'I can give you a splint to help support it for the next couple of weeks,' Serena said. 'It will help you rest your wrist, but won't restrict your movements.'

She recorded the rotatory movements of Lenny's forearm, his wrist flexion and extension, and his finger and thumb movements. She could remember doing this with George; thinking of him made her heart sink. How stupid she'd been to think that George had been serious about wanting to see her. He was a playboy. She would've been a temporary distraction for him—and that wasn't what she wanted. Though she didn't want a serious relationship, either—because that would mean putting her trust in someone. And how could you trust a playboy not to let you down?

Forcing thoughts of George from her mind, she talked Lenny through the exercises. 'I'm going to give you a leaflet with all the exercises and the advice I've given you today. The exercises are illustrated by photographs, so that'll help you remember how to do them,' she explained. 'You need to do ten reps of each, three or four times a day.'

'Before every meal and then just before bed?'

'That sounds about perfect.'

He smiled. 'I'll do the first reps now, as it's lunchtime.'

Yes, lunch that she was going to be spending on her own, at her desk. Which was her own fault; but it was better than the alternative. That she would've looked forward to lunch with George and he would've stood her up.

She wrote up Lenny's notes, then checked her phone quickly before she went to the hospital canteen to grab a sandwich, and was shocked to see a text from George.

Even if you have back-to-back patients, you still need a break. I'll bring lunch with me and wait for you in the waiting room.

What?

She stared at the phone, horror-stricken. He hadn't replied to her text, so she'd been certain that he'd lost interest in her.

But it seemed that George was planning to meet her at work, completely ignoring her refusal.

Help. No way could George Somers sit in any kind of room without drawing attention to himself. He could be quietly reading a book or something, and women would still be staring at him. He had that kind of presence. If he was in the waiting room right now, he'd stand up to greet her the second she walked in.

People would notice.

People would *talk*.

The last thing she wanted was people gossiping about her. She just had to hope that George wasn't already there. Especially as the time-stamp on the text told her he'd only just sent it.

She had to force herself to walk slowly into the waiting room, not to run in panic. To her relief, George wasn't waiting there. She headed out past the reception desk and was just about to take her phone out of her bag and call him when she saw him walking down the corridor towards her.

CHAPTER FOUR

'Hi.' George's smile made Serena's knees weak. 'Busy morning?'

'Yes.' She dragged in a breath. She really hadn't been expecting this. 'George, I texted you. I said I couldn't make lunch.'

'True. But you didn't give me an alternative date or tell me why you couldn't make it.' His eyes glittered. 'So I guessed that you were actually free, but you'd panicked at the idea of having lunch with me and you'd chickened out.'

She had to admit it. Even though it was embarrassing and made her feel like a gawky teenager instead of a sensible thirty-year-old. 'Yes,' she muttered, feeling colour flood into her face.

'Just as well I'm brave enough for both of us, then,' he said lightly. 'I brought some lunch. I thought we could have a picnic in the park opposite the hospital.'

She noticed then that he was carrying a small wicker basket and a blanket. This clearly hadn't been a spur-of-the-moment decision to grab a couple of sandwiches, some fruit and a drink from a shop and then head out into the sunshine. To bring a wicker basket—the sort that looked as if it contained proper cutlery and crockery, as well as food—meant that he must have planned this. 'You brought a picnic?' Stupid question. It was *obvious*. But she didn't know what else to say.

He shrugged. 'It seemed like the best solution, in case you were short on time.'

And it also made it difficult—practically impossible—for her to refuse to have lunch with him now.

'How long have you got until your next appointment?' he asked.

'Just over half an hour.'

'OK. That gives us five minutes to find a nice spot, twenty minutes to eat, and five minutes to walk back so you're not late for work.'

She appreciated the fact that he took her work seriously and wasn't expecting her to play hooky just to indulge him. But all the same... 'George, I know this is really rude of me, and I'm sorry about that, but I just don't understand why you're here.'

'To have lunch with you. As we agreed last week.'

Until she'd backed out. 'But why *me*?' That was what she couldn't understand. She didn't belong in his world. 'Apart from the fact you date a different woman every week, I'm not exactly your type.'

'Firstly, I don't date anywhere near as many women as the gossip rags make out; and, secondly, when it comes to you being my type, allow me to be the judge of that.' He gave her another of the knee-melting smiles. 'You intrigue me, Serena.'

'Because I turned you down, and you're not used to that?'

'You're a challenge, you mean? There may be a little truth in that,' he allowed, his eyes crinkling at the corners. 'And I like the fact that you're straight with me. But mainly you just intrigue me. I think there's more to you than meets the eye, Ms James. And I want to find out if my theory about you is right.'

'What theory?'

'Have lunch with me, and I might tell you.'

But that wasn't her only worry. 'The paparazzi follow you about, don't they?'

'Only at parties,' he said. 'A few of them followed me to my physiotherapy sessions. But, as soon as they realised what was going on and they weren't going to get any juicy gossip or photographs because my life is incredibly quiet and slow and boring right now, they stopped following me. So don't worry—your picture isn't going to be splashed all over the gossip rags tomorrow.'

'Sorry.' She bit her lip. 'I'm just used to…well, a more ordinary life.'

'No problem. So, shall we go and have some lunch?'

They found a quiet spot in the park; he spread out the blanket and gestured to her to sit down. Even though they were in a public place, this felt oddly intimate. As if it were only the two of them in the park, even though it was the middle of London and the park was full of people enjoying the late summer sunshine.

George opened the basket and removed two plain china plates. Then he looked up and caught her smiling. He gave her a questioning look. 'What?'

'I've never met anyone who actually owns a proper picnic basket, let alone one that contains real crockery. Wow.'

He smiled back. 'Picnics are more fun if you do them properly.'

'So you made the picnic yourself?'

'No. Though I did I choose the food myself,' he said. 'I happen to know a very nice deli. That probably sounds disgustingly lazy, but I should perhaps warn you that I'm a bit challenged in the culinary department. My brother says I'm the worst cook in the universe.'

She laughed. 'Anyone can make a sandwich, George.'

'Don't bet on it.' He laughed back. 'Next time, I'll make them myself and see if you can tell the difference.'

Next time. Her smile faded. 'George. This is really sweet of you to treat me to lunch, but...' She needed to be kind about this, but she also had to be honest. She needed to be fair to both of them. 'I don't think there ought to be a next time,' she said gently.

'Why not?'

'Because I'm a single mum. I'm not really in the market for a relationship.'

'Seeing me doesn't have to involve your child,' he said softly. 'Do you have a boy or a girl?'

'A boy.' Guilt at turning George down, when he was being so sweet, nudged her into adding his name. 'Ethan.'

'That's a nice name,' George said. 'How old is he?'

'Five.'

'So he's at school. Well, you and I are simply having lunch together and, right now, Ethan doesn't need to know anything about me. And he definitely doesn't need to worry that I'm trying to push his dad out of the picture.'

Serena blew out a breath. It warmed her that George was clearly thinking of her son's needs, but she couldn't let him labour under that misconception about Jason. 'Ethan's dad isn't actually in the picture.'

George said nothing, just waited.

She gave in and told him the rest of it. 'Jason couldn't cope with being a dad. Especially as Ethan was a colicky baby. He left us when Ethan was six weeks old.

I gave him his engagement ring back, and he hasn't seen Ethan or me since.'

'That's tough on you.'

In some respects, she hated that Ethan was missing out on a father's love. He didn't have a dad to play football with him in the park or teach him to ride his bike or do any of the mad, exciting things that dads did with their children. But he had a grandfather who was more than willing to do all those things, and a mother and a grandmother who loved him to bits and were there to kiss scraped knees better and give him a hug when he needed one. So they didn't need pity. She and Ethan were doing just fine. 'I don't regret Ethan for a minute. He's the light of my life.'

'And he's lucky to have a mother who loves him as much as you obviously do.'

That sounded personal. Then she remembered what she'd read in the paper: that George's mother had walked out on him when he wasn't much older than Ethan was now. 'Sorry. I didn't mean to bring up bad stuff for you… About your mum, I mean.'

'You haven't. I grew up with a mother who loved me. Just because Frances isn't my biological mother, it doesn't make her any the less my mother.' He shrugged. 'She's the one who was always there when I had a bad day at school or a nightmare at three in the morning. She's the one who listened to me and then made everything all right again with a hug.'

Just as Serena did for Ethan, and she hated it when her son came home in tears, all upset and angry because someone had been unkind to him in the playground. The idea of George as that same kind of vulnerable little boy needing a hug brought tears to her eyes. 'Sorry. Now I'm being truly wet.'

'Not at all. But today was meant to be about having fun—and right now I think things are getting a bit heavy for both of us, so we need to take a deep breath and change direction.' He took her hand, drew it to his mouth and pressed a kiss into her palm before folding his fingers over it.

The cherishing gesture made the lump in her throat even bigger.

'Don't apologise,' he said.

'How did you know I was going to apologise?' she asked, feeling the colour flood into her face.

'As you've apologised three times already in the last five minutes, let's call it an educated guess,' he said dryly. 'We need to set some ground rules. Starting with no apologies being necessary, OK? We're still getting to know each other. We're bound to find the odd sore spot while we're talking. It won't be a deliberate attempt to hurt each other.'

'OK.' She looked straight at him. 'What are the other ground rules?'

'You're not in the market for a relationship. That's fine, because neither am I.'

'Don't you have to…well, settle down and marry someone suitable?'

'To keep the title going, you mean?'

'Yes.'

That was the big question. The one he was trying not to think about. The crash had left him with some less visible injuries; and, given the results of the test he'd had last week, he'd made very little progress in healing. It was looking more and more likely that he wouldn't be able to provide his family with an heir. Which meant that the whole issue of finding a suitable bride and settling down was something he could push to the back of his mind for a bit longer.

He shrugged. 'Hopefully Dad will live until he's a hundred so it won't be an immediate issue.'

'Uh-huh.'

'I'm not looking for forever, Serena,' he said quietly. 'Not right now. I'm just enjoying the present.'

'Feeling lucky to be alive?'

That was exactly how he was feeling; and he appreciated the fact that she understood that. 'Obviously it's not the first time I've ever had an accident. There's always a risk when you do the more physically demanding sports. But it's the first time I've been in such a serious crash. And it's the first time I've been banged up for weeks and weeks and weeks. The first time I've had to rely on other people so much.' And he'd hated every second of it.

'And it gave you too much time to think?'

'Way too much time.' And he didn't want to go into those thoughts. They were too dark, too much, and he'd rather just ignore them and enjoy the sunlight. Maybe he was a coward, locking everything away in a box in his head marked 'Do not open'—but what was the point in going over and over things he couldn't fix? He was caught between a rock and a hard place. Women either saw him in terms of his title—and no way was he settling for someone like his mother—or, like Rebecca, they saw him for himself but didn't feel they could fit into his world.

'Right now, I need time out. Some fun. I think you do, too. So you and me—this is all about having a good time. No pressure, no seriousness, and it's most definitely nobody else's business. Oh, and just in case you were wondering, I only date one person at a time. So any pictures you see in the papers of me with my arm round someone will have been manipulated by the editors purely to sell copies of their gossip rags. So do you think you can stop panicking now and relax with me?'

It was easy for him to say, Serena thought. She hadn't dated in years, she didn't have a clue what she was doing, and George... She had a nasty feeling that George could really break her heart if she let him close. OK, so he'd been up front about this thing between them being just fun. But that was from his point of view. If he could make her that dizzy with a single kiss, almost a week ago, what would happen if she spent more time with him? What would happen today? What if he kissed her again?

As if he guessed at her fears, he said softly, 'I'm not going to pounce on you, Serena. I'm not expecting you to have sex with me in the middle of the park. Today's about getting to know each other a bit more, having a bit of fun. I get the feeling that you don't get a lot of time for that.'

'That's your theory about me?' She grimaced. 'Everybody seems to be saying that to me, this past week,' she said ruefully. 'I must be coming across as the most humourless person in the world.'

'No. You come across as very serious and professional, but you also have a twinkle in your eye and during our appointments you gave as good as you got, teasing me back. That's what intrigues me. You want to know my real theory about you?'

'Yes.' She really did.

'I think there's a woman inside you who knows how to have fun, but you're keeping her locked up. And I'd like to know what would make you let her out.'

'As I said.' She sighed. 'Humourless.'

'No, that's not what I said. You're being too hard on yourself. Let's have lunch.' He took out two glasses—proper glasses, not plastic ones, she noticed—and poured in what looked like freshly squeezed orange juice, topping up the drinks with sparkling water. 'This was the nearest I could get to a non-alcoholic Buck's Fizz,' he said.

She was touched that he'd recognised she needed a clear head for the rest of her shift and wouldn't want to drink wine. 'Thank you. That's lovely.'

'To the beginnings of a new friendship,' he said, lifting his glass.

'I'll drink to that. *Just* friends,' she felt compelled to add.

'Good friends,' he said with a smile.

The sandwiches—at least, she thought they were sandwiches—were all wrapped neatly in greaseproof paper. He'd definitely gone to a posh deli, Serena thought. 'What's in the packets?'

'I was hoping you'd ask that.' His eyes crinkled at the corners. 'Close your eyes.'

'Why?'

'So you can take a bite and guess.'

Oh, help. This was a dangerous game. And hadn't they just agreed to be friends? This was more like the kind of game lovers played.

Clearly her worries showed on her face, because he said softly, 'Relax. This is going to be fun.'

What could she do but go along with him and close her eyes?

The bread was gorgeous, soft and full of grains and seeds. There was a distinct peppery taste, mingled with something sweet with a hint of fieriness, and something juicy.

'So what do you think?' he asked.

'Rocket, prawns and sweet chilli sauce?' she guessed.

'Excellent. You've just earned your first sandwich. You can open your eyes now.'

A neatly cut triangle—with a bite taken from the apex—sat on the plate in front of her.

'That's quite some deli,' she said.

'It certainly is. And I have to admit to buying my lunch from there, most days.' He brought out some bowls and set them on the blanket between them; one contained tiny plum tomatoes, one contained batons of cucumber, one contained plump black olives, and the last one contained some kind of dip. 'Aioli,' he said. 'Help yourself.'

'This is such a treat. I was just going to grab the nearest sandwich in the canteen—probably boring cheese and pickle. Thank you,' she said, finishing the sandwich and dipping a cucumber baton in the aioli.

'Ready for the next sandwich?' he asked.

'Sure. Do I have to close my eyes again?'

'I'm afraid so.' He, too, dipped a cucumber baton in the aioli and ate it while he waited for her to close her eyes. 'Tell me what you think.'

'The bread's denser on this one. It tastes almost smoky. Rye bread?' she asked.

'Yes.'

'Some kind of meat, and I think coleslaw. And...is that cheese?'

'Swiss cheese and pastrami. It's a Reuben sandwich,' he said. 'Traditionally it'd be sauerkraut, but I like mine with coleslaw.'

'I've never eaten a Reuben sandwich before. Though obviously I've heard of it—it's a classic New York deli sandwich, isn't it?'

'Sure is,' he confirmed. 'Do you like it?'

She nodded. 'Very much.'

'Good. Now for number three. Close your eyes again.'

This she recognised instantly. It was her favourite Christmas sandwich—and also the last thing she'd expect to eat in September. 'Brie, bacon and cranberry sauce. I *love* this. Especially when it's toasted.'

He was smiling as she opened her eyes.

'I can't remember the last time someone made lunch into a game like this,' she admitted. 'Except maybe for me pretending that the mush on a spoon was an aeroplane, to get Ethan to eat it when he was a toddler.'

'Aeroplane. Hmm. I'll remember that.'

'I bet you've flown a plane yourself, haven't you?' Given his accident and what he'd told her during physiotherapy sessions, she knew that George liked doing dangerous things.

'I have a pilot's licence, if that's what you're asking.' He laughed. 'Ed's always telling me that I'm trying to be James Bond.'

'He might just have a point.' And George was every bit as good-looking as the actors who'd played James Bond. More so, Serena thought, and the idea of him in a dinner jacket and bow tie made her very glad she was sitting down, because her knees went weak.

When they'd finished the sandwiches and the veggies, he made her close her eyes again and made an aeroplane noise as he swooped whatever it was towards her mouth,

She took a bite and delicious tartness exploded in her mouth. 'Raspberries. Gorgeous.' She couldn't resist teasing him. 'Would these be from your Scottish estate, Lord Somers?'

'I'm not actually Lord Somers—that's my dad.' Eventually it would be him. But he really didn't want to talk about his background. It had ruined things with Rebecca; OK, so he wasn't intending to make this thing with Serena permanent, but he didn't want the barony thing getting in the way with her, either. He smiled to take the sting from his words. 'And we don't have a Scottish estate.' He shrugged. 'And that's all boring stuff. Let's not talk about that. Tell me about you instead.'

'You already know everything. I'm a mum with a five-year-old son, I'm a physiotherapist and I love my job.'

'So, between work and your son, you don't have a lot of spare time.'

'Exactly.' She was glad he understood that.

'Are you close to your parents?'

She blinked. 'Of course I am. And I owe them tons. My mum picks up Ethan from school for me every afternoon and looks after him until I pick him up after my shift. And she and Dad look after him in the school holidays, when I'm working.'

George looked thoughtful. 'So if you had an evening out, your parents would babysit?'

Like a shot. Her mother had already offered. And Serena still felt guilty. 'I don't like to ask too much. I know he's their only grandchild and they love him to bits, but they already do so much for me. I don't want to take advantage and expect them to look after him when I'm not working.'

George didn't think that Serena was the sort to take advantage. But clearly she was going to use the babysitting angle as an excuse not to see him in the evenings.

Fair enough. He could work with that. If anything, it gave him more of a challenge to be inventive. 'So we'll have to stick to lunch dates.' For the time being. 'Do you normally get half an hour for lunch?'

'Forty minutes, sometimes.'

'And do you ever have afternoons where you finish early? I was thinking, maybe we could go ice-skating. There's that new rink that's just opened.'

'You,' she said, 'are *not* going ice-skating. Not with a pin in your leg. Even if you're up to Olympic standards in a skating rink!'

'I'm not up to Olympic standards,' he admitted. 'And you're probably right.'

'I'm *definitely* right. And I really don't want to see you hurt yourself again by overdoing things before you're properly healed.'

He took her hand and kissed the back of it. 'Thank you. For caring.' He glanced at his watch. 'I need to go. I'll walk you back.'

She looked like a rabbit in headlights. Frozen. Scared. And yet he knew she'd enjoyed their lunch together. He'd seen her laughing, seen the dimples in her cheeks. She'd just forgotten how to have fun for herself, and he planned to remind her how to do that.

'You don't need to walk me back to the department,' she said, her eyes wide.

He raised an eyebrow. 'So I'm going to be your dirty little secret, then?'

She blushed spectacularly. 'No. It's just…' She looked awkward. 'I don't mean to be horrible, but the hospital has a very lively grapevine, and I'd rather not be its favourite subject.'

He imagined she'd already been there, when Ethan's father had walked out on her. People speculating about why he'd left, and who else was involved. Pitying glances, whispered gossip. She must've hated it. So he wasn't going to make a fuss about this. 'No problem. See you Friday?' he suggested. 'If it's not raining, we can have another picnic. If it's raining, then we'll have to find a café to shelter in.'

'I need to check my duty roster.'

It was the excuse he'd been half expecting since she'd mentioned his father's title. Rebecca, all over again. What an idiot he was. He forced himself to give her a casual smile. 'Sure.'

'I, um, did enjoy lunch.'

Not enough to repeat it, though. And he had a pretty good idea why. 'Me, too,' he said. He leaned forward and kissed her cheek. Serena's skin was soft and smooth, and he itched to yank her into his arms and kiss her properly; but she was already antsy, and he wasn't going to make a fool of himself. 'See you,' he said coolly, and walked away without looking back.

CHAPTER FIVE

SERENA knew she'd pushed George away. Which was stupid. He'd suggested having fun, not for ever. And she *had* enjoyed lunch. It had been nice to be treated as just herself, for once—not as a physiotherapist, a colleague or Ethan's mum, much as she loved all those roles. George had seen her for who she was.

And she knew perfectly well that she was free on Friday at lunchtime. She was free *every* lunchtime. She'd chickened out, and she was cross with herself for being so ridiculous and making a big deal out of it.

All the same, it was later that evening when she texted George. *If you're still free on Friday, I'll bring the picnic. Same time, same place?*

George stared at the text. He really hadn't expected that. Either Serena hadn't been making a feeble excuse—she really *had* needed to check the roster—or she'd had time to think about it and decided that maybe she'd enjoyed his company and wanted to see him again.

And now she was asking him to lunch—*and* saying that she was providing it.

That kind of independence was refreshing. Most of the women he'd dated would've been quite happy for him to continue making all the effort—to be the one to bring the picnic or book a table at some little bistro, and most importantly to foot the bill. Serena clearly believed in taking turns. He liked that. And it made her a little more than just a challenge; that need for independence was something he could identify with, too.

Sounds good. See you Friday outside the department, he texted back.

At midday on Friday, George loitered in the corridor outside the physiotherapy department, waiting for Serena. Hopefully none of the other staff would come out for their lunch break, see him there, and make the connection; mindful of what Serena had said about the hospital grapevine, the last thing he wanted was to make life awkward for her at work.

Several people that he assumed were patients walked past; and then Serena came hurrying out, clutching a bag. 'Sorry I'm late,' she said.

He smiled at her. 'Not a problem.' He knew that she couldn't walk away from a patient, the way that someone with an office job could walk away from their desk. If a patient's treatment became complicated or they needed a little more time, then of course she had to stay longer. 'I didn't mind waiting.'

'I didn't think about bringing a picnic blanket,' she said as they walked into the park. 'S—'

'Hey, you're not allowed to say the S-word,' he cut in, realising that she was just about to apologise.

She gave him a rueful smile. 'Ground rules, hmm?'

'Absolutely.' And he planned to add another one this afternoon. One he thought they might both enjoy.

They found an empty bench, and she set a bag between them. 'This isn't posh deli food,' she warned as she took a plastic box from the bag and unclipped the lid.

'So you're going to feed me cheese and pickle sandwiches from the hospital canteen?' he teased.

'That's for me to know and you to guess. Close your eyes, and then you can tell me what you taste.'

There was a twinkle in her eye; the serious professionalism she usually hid behind was definitely starting to melt. Clearly she'd enjoyed the game he'd played with her last time and wanted to take a turn at it herself. Smiling back at her, he closed his eyes.

'Ready? First one.'

He felt something cool against his lip, then took a bite. 'Cheese and pickle,' was his verdict. But not quite the kind of sandwich he'd expected. 'In flatbread.'

'It's not just any old pickle, I'll have you know. That's my mum's tomato chutney, made with the tomatoes she and Ethan grew in our back garden this summer.'

Home-made. Family. The thing he wanted and fought against at the same time, because the whole thing was so messed up. He could see how settled and secure Ed and their father were, and it tempted him to think about settling down himself. But then again, the one time he'd tried that it had backfired badly. He'd been so sure he'd picked the right woman—the bright, clever girl he'd met at university who saw him for himself. He'd taken her home, knowing that his family would make a fuss of her and make her feel welcome.

But taking her to Somers Hall had changed things. It had brought out all kinds of issues he hadn't even thought about. Rebecca couldn't cope with the differences between their lives, and she'd said she couldn't take the pressure—pressure he didn't even begin to understand because he really couldn't see it. How could she be pressured when he was by her side, protecting her?

And nothing he could do or say would change her mind. She'd walked out on him. Unlike the gold-diggers, she'd been genuine—but she'd still walked out on him. Because the barony, as always, got in the way.

He pushed the thoughts away. That wasn't what he and Serena had signed up for. This was all meant to be about *fun*.

He switched back into charm mode. 'Do give my compliments to your mother. It's very nice,' he said.

The next sandwich—again in a wrap—was a flavour he was more familiar with. 'Bacon and avocado. And I think there's rocket in there, too.'

'Excellent. You get a gold star for taste-testing,' she said.

He smiled. 'I'm a bit too old for stickers. Is there an alternative reward?'

'That depends what you have in mind.'

Which told him he wasn't going to get what he really wanted. Not yet. Serena was the one woman who seemed immune to his charm and saw right through his flirtatiousness. George tapped his cheek and gave her a winsome look. For a moment, he thought that Serena was going to go back into her shell and back away from him again. But to his relief she smiled, leaned over to him and kissed his cheek.

This close, he could smell the strawberry scent of her shampoo again, and it made his body tighten. Crazy. He was used to dating women who doused themselves in expensive designer perfume. And yet the simple fruity scent of her shampoo turned him on far more.

To distract himself—and because he did actually

want to know what made her tick—he asked, 'So what made you become a physiotherapist?'

'My best friend at school had cystic fibrosis,' she said. 'She needed physiotherapy when the sticky secretions started to block her lungs, to clear the mucus. Her physiotherapist taught her parents how to do it. She taught me how to do it, too, so if Kelly was staying over at our house and had a bad night, I could do the physio for her. I felt awful at first, hitting my friend on the back and making her cough up stuff, but she told me to think about it as making her better and helping her breathe.' She shrugged. 'I guess that's what really started me thinking about physiotherapy as a career, and when I looked into it I liked the idea of having such a wide range of patients, and being able to help with so many different conditions.'

'So, apart from treating idiots like me who don't pay attention to what they're doing and hurt themselves, what sort of things do you do?'

Serena was pleased that George was showing an interest in her job. Given that his brother was a doctor, she was even more pleased that George hadn't asked her why she hadn't become one too—as if any other role in medicine wasn't as valuable as a doctor or surgeon. She'd done well enough in her A-levels to have the grades to study medicine at university, but she'd already known that physiotherapy was the area she wanted to work in and she'd opted for the specialist course. 'Well, every day is different. I could be treating anyone from a toddler who's had an operation for clicky hip and needs to learn to walk again, through to someone with whiplash or a bad sprain, or someone older who's developed a condition that affects their mobility and balance. Most of the time, I work on a one-to-one basis, but sometimes I work as part of a bigger team from different disciplines, helping someone whose condition is a bit more complicated.' And she loved every second of her job.

'How long have you been a physio?'

'I qualified when I was twenty-one. I spent three years in the department as a junior, and I was just about to qualify as a senior when I fell pregnant with Ethan.' Another reason why Jason hadn't been happy. Ethan hadn't been planned, and Jason had said that the timing was all wrong—that the baby was a mistake and would get in the way of her promotion. He'd even suggested that she should have a termination. So she really should've known that she wouldn't be able to rely on Jason to support her once the baby was born. He hadn't really wanted to be a dad in the first place, much less to a 'difficult' baby; Ethan's colic had given him the perfect get-out, and he'd taken it immediately. 'My career went on hold for a little while, because I took six months off after Ethan was born.'

'You're a senior physiotherapist now?' George asked.

She nodded. 'I'm getting to the stage where I need to think about where I want my career to go next. I've been doing some teaching work within the department, and my boss suggested that I could maybe consider doing a day a week teaching undergraduates in the physiotherapy course at the university linked with the hospital.'

'Is that what you'd like to do?'

'Yes and no.' She wrinkled her nose. 'I enjoy teaching; but I also like working with patients and I'd really miss that if I didn't do it. But if I can do some part-time teaching and some part-time practice, that would be the best of both worlds.' She smiled at him. 'Thank you. I've been mulling things over and trying to work out what I really wanted to do, and you've helped me get that straight in my head.'

'You really love your job, don't you?' he asked.

'Absolutely. And the best bit is signing people off.'

He looked surprised. 'How come?'

'Because that's when I know I've done my job properly. I signed off a patient last week who just wanted to be able to take a bath—she had osteoarthritis and she just couldn't manage getting in and out of the bath, but she didn't like showers and didn't want to be forced into having a walk-in shower installed instead. But we've been working together on her mobility and some exercises to help reduce the pain, and last week she was finally able to get into the bath and out again without help. When I first met her, she was quiet and—well, withdrawn. But her confidence has really blossomed, and I love that my job can make that kind of difference to someone's life.'

Wow. She really, really loved her career, George thought. Whereas he'd been marking time—despite what he'd told his brother Ed, he found the barony and the estate a burden and he played his role there because it was his duty.

'What about you?' she asked.

He looked at her. 'How do you mean?'

'Well, I know you're the heir to the barony and everything that goes with it, so you probably never got a choice in what you wanted to do with your life.'

She could say that again. The barony was like a shackle round his neck. He couldn't shirk his duty and he'd never let his family down; but how he wished sometimes that things were different. That he was just an ordinary man who had an ordinary life and could choose what he wanted to do instead of having to live up to centuries of expectations.

Not that he was going to dump any of that on her. He hadn't even talked about it with Ed, who was pretty much the closest person to him in the world. Ed had guessed at it, earlier in the year, and even offered to take over the reins and give George his freedom—but it wouldn't have been fair to make his brother give up his vocation. No. The burden and the price were his alone.

He just shrugged and switched on his best smile. The one that deflected all questions.

'If you could do anything you like, what would you do?'

So Serena realised he didn't actually have a choice in what he did. If he'd been free to choose what he did with his life, he would have done something different. And it spooked him slightly that he was actually having a proper conversation with Serena—something he never did with the women in his life, since Rebecca, with the exception of his stepmother and sisters. He never let *anyone* that close.

But she'd asked. She sounded interested. So maybe he'd tell her some of it.

'I might've been a professional skier,' he said. 'Or maybe a stuntman.'

She raised an eyebrow. 'Something dangerous.'

'*Controlled* danger,' he said. 'Risks that have been properly thought through. So I'd get the adrenalin rush of doing extreme sports, but the chances of hurting myself would be minimised. And nobody would have to worry.'

'Stunt people still get hurt,' she pointed out. 'I treated one who'd cracked his spine, last year.'

'But that was one accident in how many working

days? The odds of serious injury are low, if you've trained properly.' He gave her a rueful smile. 'But sadly I had to cross that off my list of suitable occupations.'

'So what do you actually do, as the heir to the estate?' she asked.

He shrugged. 'I guess I'm a spoiled playboy.'

She shook her head. 'You're more serious than everyone thinks you are. There's more to you than just the party boy who poses for the paparazzi.'

'I'm glad you think so,' he said, keeping his tone light but meaning it. Since the accident, he'd had a lot of time to think about his life, and he wasn't entirely happy with what he saw.

'So what does it mean for you, running the estate?'

Duty. At the expense of love.

But whining wouldn't change things, and plenty of people had it worse than he did. He'd keep this light. Chatty. 'You wouldn't believe how much it costs to maintain an old pile. We already do wedding packages, but I'd love to expand on that and do other events. I'm trying to persuade Dad to do an annual extravaganza for Bonfire Night—fireworks with music—so at the moment I'm looking into what we'd need to do to set it up and how far in advance any licences need to be organised. Obviously it's too late for this year, but we could maybe do something in the summer.'

'And you'd be the one to set off the fireworks?' she asked dryly.

He laughed. 'Actually, the big professional displays are all set up by computer and triggered by switches. It's not like the boxes you'd buy for a home garden display and light at arm's length with a taper—and, yes, before you ask, I *was* a bit disappointed when I found that out.'

She smiled. 'I bet your family was relieved, though.'

When George had first suggested it, his father had panicked and asked Ed to talk sense into him. Which had only served to increase George's determination to do something to put his own stamp on the estate management. To bring something new to the barony. Something more than helping Frances set up the wedding packages, more than expanding the farm shops into something that supported local businesses too. That had been extending plans that were already there; he wanted to innovate. To make a difference. Do something to make the sacrifice he'd made worthwhile.

'Dad's just about stopped thinking that I'm going to turn his rose garden into a bonfire—at least, that's the family joke. But I wouldn't take risks with anyone else's safety.'

'I know you wouldn't.' She looked thoughtful. 'Actually, those big displays to music can be really magical. Especially if it's by a lake.'

'Sadly, we don't have a lake.' And creating one in the grounds would probably be a step too far, even for him. 'But we do have a field next to the house that we could use as the firing and drop zone.' All they'd have to do was mow it. He'd checked it out so he knew there weren't any rare species of plant at risk; it was just an ordinary field and there would be no difficulties with using it.

'What sort of music would you use?' she asked.

He threw the question back at her. 'What sort of music do you think I like?'

'Dance?' she suggested.

He laughed. 'At thirty-four, I'm a little bit too old for that.' And it was one of the reasons why he'd stopped clubbing, a year or so back. He loathed the music they played.

'Indie?' she guessed.

'Warmer. Keep going.'

'Um…'

'Classic rock,' he said, taking pity on her. He hummed the first few bars of Queen's 'Don't Stop Me Now'. 'That song could've been written especially for me.'

'And a half,' she agreed with a smile. 'So that's the sort of thing you'd use?'

'Actually, I'd use classical music for a display. I suppose the obvious one would be Handel's *Music for the Royal Fireworks*. But I'd like to use something more dramatic—like the *1812 Overture*.'

She looked thoughtful. 'You'd need really split-second timing for Tchaikovsky. If you're serious about this, I could ask Dad for some advice on a playlist.'

George blinked. 'Are you telling me your dad's a pyrotechnician?'

Her eyes glittered with amusement. 'No, he's a music teacher. Actually, he's the head of music at the local high school.' She looked proud, and George remembered her saying that she was close to her parents.

And if her father was a music teacher… 'So I'm guessing you play an instrument—to grade eight standard, too.'

She nodded.

'Piano?' he guessed.

'And the cello.' She smiled. 'Dad taught me the piano. He's teaching Ethan, too. It was so cute that my son played "Happy Birthday to You" to me on the piano for my birthday.'

'Did you ever think about being a professional musician?'

She shook her head. 'I do it just for fun—it relaxes me.'

So that was what she did for fun. Given his own lack

of musical ability, George was intrigued. How would she look when she played? Would she close her eyes, losing herself in the music? Would she let her barriers down? 'Would you play for me, some time?'

She looked wary, and then her face cleared. 'Sure. Do you play anything?'

'No. There's a piano in the library at the Hall, but I didn't really have the patience for lessons,' he admitted. 'Especially when it meant practising scales.' He grimaced at the memory. 'I think I lasted a month before I put a frog in my piano teacher's pocket and she refused to teach me ever again. Though, to be fair, I probably wouldn't have done it if I'd known she had a phobia about frogs. I would've got a hairy plastic spider or something, instead.'

'The poor woman. How old were you?'

'About six.' The lessons had started about a month after Zara had walked out. His father had obviously hoped that music would help to distract his eldest son from the loss of his mother, but it hadn't worked. Especially as the piano teacher had flirted with his father—or tried to. David hadn't been interested; though George had worried that she'd come in and take over from his mother, and then push him and Ed away from his father. He'd wanted the woman to go away. And if she wouldn't go away, then he'd wanted her at least to stop making him sit perfectly still and do the same thing over and over and over again.

'What was worse? Doing something repetitive, or sitting still?' Serena asked.

Was it that obvious, or did Serena just understand him more than most people? 'They were both as bad as each other.' He grimaced. 'I can pick out the odd tune with my right hand, with a lot of mistakes, but that's about it.'

'Does anyone else in your family play?'

'Alice. She's actually pretty good, so she's in charge of Christmas carols. Which she loves,' he said with a grin, 'because it means she can boss everyone about.'

Serena rolled her eyes. 'I'm sure your sister isn't anywhere near as bossy as you claim.'

'No. She's much worse.' He laughed. 'So I take it you listen to a lot of classical music, then?'

'A mixture, really. It depends on my mood. Sometimes I listen to one of the pop stations on the radio— and sometimes it's the blues. Dad brought me up on the stuff. He plays guitar as well as piano. Actually, I don't think there's an instrument he can't play.'

'Blues,' George said thoughtfully. 'That works for me, too. Especially on Friday night, when I'm chilling out.'

Then panic slid through his veins. What was he doing? Thinking that he had some common ground with her dad, imagining talking to the guy over a beer and starting to bond with him as he got closer to Serena—it wasn't going to happen. It hadn't happened with Rebecca's parents; they'd been too aware of the social differences between them and put extra pressure on their daughter, unable to see that he loved her for herself and wasn't just amusing himself at her expense.

And why was he thinking about love, anyway? He didn't want a relationship. Not right now. 'I'd better get you back to work.' And then he ruined any attempt at cool by adding, 'Have lunch with me on Monday?'

She smiled at him. 'I'd like that. Same time?'

'Great.'

He helped her pack up the picnic, and then walked

with her to the edge of the park. 'I was thinking. We need another ground rule,' he said.

She looked puzzled. 'What kind of ground rule?'

'I think we should institute a kiss goodbye,' he said with a smile.

'Sure.' She raised herself onto tiptoe, clearly aiming to kiss his cheek. George moved at the very last second, so that her mouth connected with his mouth rather than his cheek.

It was the softest, sweetest touch on his lips. And it made his mouth tingle.

She pulled back, colour blooming in her face. 'Um.'

'Serena.' He cupped her cheek, and dipped his head so he could brush his mouth against hers. Tiny, tiny kisses, and his lips felt more and more sensitised with every single one, until she slid one hand into his hair and started kissing him back.

When he broke the kiss, his pulse was hammering and his head was swimming.

Wow. This was a first. He'd never responded to anyone like this before—even Rebecca. And it scared him and intrigued him in equal measure. What was so different about Serena James that made him feel this way? Was it because she was a challenge, because she saw through all his flirtatiousness and charm? Was it because he'd met a woman he could actually have a deep conversation with? Or was it her independence that resonated with him, echoing his own need to be independent?

He could see that she was scared and intrigued, too. Her pupils were huge and her cheeks were flushed—and yet there was a hint of fear in her eyes. Was she scared that they were already taking this too fast?

So, surprisingly, was he.

He strove to sound casual. 'See you Monday. Have a nice weekend.'

'You, too.' She lingered for a moment, and George wondered if she was going to kiss him again. But she clearly changed her mind—running scared?—and smiled instead. 'Bye.'

He watched her walk away, then jammed his hands in his pockets and walked in the opposite direction. But all afternoon he just couldn't settle. He could really do with something to burn off the adrenalin fizzing through him. Except everything he'd normally do was off limits, because he knew either his leg or his wrists would let him down. Pushing himself too hard now would mean having to wait even longer until he was fully fit, and he'd had enough of waiting.

In the end, he speed-dialled a number on his mobile phone.

'Alice Somers.'

He loved his sister's crisp, no-nonsense tone. 'Hi there, bossy-boots. Are you busy?'

'It's the middle of Friday afternoon, Georgie-boy. Normal people are at work at this time of day.'

'Well, I'm not normal.' At least, he wasn't tied to a nine-to-five job. His work tended to be project-based. 'Friday's also the day when most people leave early,' he said, hoping that he could tempt her into doing exactly that.

She sighed. 'You're bored, aren't you?'

'No.' Just out of sorts. Wanting things he couldn't have, and cross with himself for wanting them. 'Right now, I need to feel the wind in my hair. And, much as it pains me to admit it to you, I can't quite manage driving my car in London yet.'

'Ah. So you need a chauffeur.'

'Yes.' And he needed company. Someone who could deal with his restlessness and wouldn't give him a hard time.

'What if I scrape your car?' she tested.

'Then I get to borrow Bea's gaffer tape to stop you nagging me. For a whole month,' he shot back.

She laughed. 'We can have the top down?'

'We can have the top down,' he confirmed. 'And we can go wherever you like.'

'The seaside, I think. And we'll eat junk food on the beach. Actually, we'll make it Brighton, so we can do all the thrill rides.'

Just what he needed. Just what he would've loved to do with Serena, except he knew she wasn't free to go with him—and right now he wasn't ready to pitch into a family situation and offer to take her little boy with them. He didn't think she would be too happy about him meeting Ethan, either. So this was the next best alternative. Alice, much as he teased her about being bossy, understood him; and, best of all, she was quick enough that he didn't have to spell things out for her.

'That,' he said softly, 'is exactly why you're my fa-vourite sister.' That, and the nights he'd sat up with Ed when she'd had meningitis at the age of two, reassur-ing his eight-year-old brother from the lofty age of ten that, yes, Father Christmas would bring their baby sis-ter home and everything would be perfectly all right— even though he'd been just as terrified as Ed that baby Alice might actually die in hospital. He'd silently prayed his heart out when Ed was asleep and promised never to ask for anything ever again, if only their baby sister would come home safely. 'Though if you tell Bea or Charlie I said that, I'll deny it for the rest of my days,' he added swiftly.

She laughed. 'OK. I can't get off early, but I'll come straight over to yours from work. And I'll text you if I get held up.'

'Great. Love you, Ally.' She, like the rest of his family, was safe to say those words to.

'Love you too, Georgie-boy.' She paused, and her voice gentled. 'Hang on in there. I know it's been hard for you, but you'll be back to normal soon.'

'I know.' Except right now he felt as if normal would never happen again. And, even if it did, what did he have to offer a woman like Serena—a woman who clearly loved her son and might want a bigger family, too? That was something he definitely couldn't offer her without a lot of complications and a great deal of potential heartbreak. Right now, Ed was the only person who knew about that situation, and George had sworn him to secrecy. 'Thanks. I'll see you later.'

And hopefully, by the time his sister turned up, this restlessness—and this crazy yearning for something that he knew just wasn't him—would have gone.

CHAPTER SIX

'GOOD weekend?' George asked as Serena walked out of the hospital with him.

'Fine, thanks.' She smiled. 'It was a glorious day, yesterday, so we spent it at the park. How was yours?'

'OK.' George gave her a sidelong look. 'What's your view on funfairs?'

She looked surprised. 'As a physio? They're definitely not for people with back or neck problems, because it's so easy to make a condition worse.'

'I meant you personally.'

She shrugged. 'They're OK. As long as I don't have to go on the roller-coaster.' She raised an eyebrow. 'Which I imagine would be the first thing you'd queue up for.'

'If it's a fast one, yes.' He smiled. 'The best one ever I've been on had a triple loop in the middle.'

'That's my idea of a nightmare. I think I'm happier walking round the hoopla stalls and eating doughnuts.' She looked at him. 'Why do you ask?'

He shrugged. 'Just wondered.' If she didn't like thrill rides, whisking her off to the fair for the evening wouldn't be a good idea, after all. 'I talked my bossy sister into driving me to Brighton on Friday night and we did all the rides on the pier.'

Serena smiled. 'And she nagged you all the way from London to Brighton?'

'Something like that. She doesn't often get me sitting still for long enough to nag me.'

'Sitting still drives you crazy, doesn't it? And you need the adrenalin rush you get from extreme sports.'

'Well, yes,' he admitted. Though he'd also noticed that he could manage to sit still with Serena. And that was a very good reason why he really ought to make this his last lunch with her. This was their third date— and three dates was his limit, right?

Except they were taking this a lot more slowly than he had with previous girlfriends, so this didn't actually feel like their third date.

'I could teach you some breathing exercises, if you like. Ones that could help you relax a bit.'

What would help more, George thought, would be if she kissed him properly. Right now he couldn't stop looking at her mouth. Remembering how it felt when her lips were on his. Wanting to taste their softness again.

If he asked, he knew she'd say no. What she was offering was breathing exercises. Relaxation stuff that would just leave him antsy. 'So what's that, meditation?' It came out slightly grumpier than he'd intended, and he winced. 'Sorry.'

'George.' She took his hand and squeezed it. 'Everyone's different. Everyone has their own way of dealing with things.'

And he knew he used adrenalin to help him avoid thinking about emotional stuff. If he didn't sit still, it meant he didn't have time to think. 'I guess,' he said again.

'The roller-coaster didn't work, did it?'

'It helped. But not quite enough,' he admitted.

She leaned over and kissed him softly on the lips, her mouth warm and soft and leaving him aching for more. Much more.

He blinked. 'What was that for?'

'Because I think you needed it.' She stroked his hair back from his forehead. 'You're too hard on yourself, you know.'

If anything, George thought, he wasn't hard enough on himself. 'Sorry. I'm a bit out of sorts today.'

'Want to talk about it?'

He shook his head. 'I'm fine. Really,' he fibbed. Right now he couldn't explain this unsettled, yearning feeling to himself, let alone to anyone else. And, even though he was pretty sure Serena wouldn't break his confidence, he didn't want to talk to her about this. Because she was part of the problem. 'Come on. Let's take a walk while the sun's still shining, before you have to get back to your shift.'

'Sure.' And, to his pleasure, she twined her fingers through his as they walked through the park. Funny how just holding her hand made his world seem brighter. That in itself should have him running for cover. But he just liked being with her.

Despite knowing he should cool things off, George fell into the habit of having lunch with Serena three times a week. She was gradually opening up to him, and she'd lost that wary expression in her eyes when she looked at him. Although she still wouldn't let him walk her back to the department, she seemed happy enough to walk hand in hand with him in the park.

And then there was the day they walked over to the pond. The sun was shining, she looked adorable, and he couldn't resist pulling her into his arm. 'Dance with me?' he asked.

'I can't dance,' she protested.

'Sure you can. Just follow my lead.' He began humming the intro to a Michael Bublé song, and then started to dance a foxtrot round the pond with her as he broke into the first verse.

For a moment, she resisted; then, to his relief, she relaxed and followed his lead. Just as he'd reassured her, she could dance perfectly well; George thought she was a natural. Being musical, Serena understood rhythm and picked up the slow, slow, quick-quick slow tempo immediately. And he could imagine dancing with her properly at a ball; she'd be wearing an off-the-shoulder dress, and he'd be able to dip his head and kiss the soft curve of her neck until she lifted her head, offering him her throat…

Then he became aware that she was talking to him.

'Sorry. I didn't catch that.' Though he wasn't going to admit why he hadn't been paying attention and what he'd been fantasising about.

'I said, I didn't know you could sing like this. You have a lovely voice.'

'Thank you.' He wasn't ready to let her go, and kept dancing with her; and she simply smiled and let him do it, not seeming to mind that people were watching them and smiling.

Now Serena was letting him bring her out of herself, George realised that she was even more amazing than he'd suspected. He'd never taken it this slowly in the past, but he was really enjoying dating Serena. And, when they finally managed to spend a night together, he had a feeling that it would be incredible.

He reined his thoughts back sharply. Was he crazy?

This was temporary. Normally by now he would have ended it, not wanting his girlfriend to think that there might be any future in their relationship. It scared him to think that that he'd been seeing Serena for three weeks now and he still wasn't ready to end it. What was wrong with him?

He must be crazy. He knew relationships didn't work for him; she wasn't Rebecca, but there were enough similarities for him to think what an idiot he was, setting himself up for her to walk away. And she *would* walk away—she'd been hurt and found it just as hard to trust as he did. He should just end this now.

But.

He wanted to watch her blossom just that little bit more. And for that he needed more than a snatched lunch break.

On the following Wednesday, George said, 'I've been thinking. Is there any chance we can swap lunchtime this Friday for the evening?'

'I…' Serena looked wary.

He leaned forward and stole a kiss. 'Please?'

She sighed. 'All right. I'll ask Mum and Dad if they can babysit. But, whatever you've got in mind, you need to be clear on the fact that I'm going halves with you.'

'Not necessarily.' George knew that she was a single mum and money was tight, and he had no intention of wrecking her budget. 'Serena, if I take you out to dinner, there won't be any strings attached. I'm not the kind of man who expects a woman to go to bed with him just because he's taken her out for the evening and maybe bought her dinner.'

Her face turned fiery red. 'I didn't mean that. I know

you're not. But I'm used to my independence. To paying my own way.'

He coughed. 'You mean, you're not used to dating.'

'That's unfair, George.'

It was also true, and both of them knew it. Though he knew he'd strayed over a line. And he'd hurt her, though he hadn't intended to. 'I'm sorry.'

She raised an eyebrow. 'I thought one of your ground rules was "no apologies"?'

'Sometimes rules need to be broken.' He gave her a wry smile. 'OK. We'll go halves.'

'I know I'm being awkward, but I'd rather we didn't go to any glitzy parties, either.' She bit her lip. 'I just wouldn't fit into that kind of thing.'

'Actually, you would. You have brilliant people skills.'

'But I wouldn't feel comfortable in that world,' she said softly. 'All the showbiz stuff—that's a million miles away from my real life. I haven't even treated any celebs at the hospital.'

He stole another kiss. 'OK. How about we go to the cinema? And maybe go for an ice cream afterwards?'

'An ordinary cinema? Not a posh red carpet première or anything like that?' she checked.

'An ordinary cinema,' he promised. 'Just you and me.' An ordinary date. And how weird it was that he was looking forward to something so simple far more than the glitzy parties he was usually invited to.

She smiled. 'Thank you. I'd like that. But I'll pay for my own ticket, OK?' she added.

'I understand you like being independent, but you can take it a bit too far, you know.' He rolled his eyes. 'Just for the record, am I allowed to buy you some popcorn or an ice cream?'

'We'll see.'

He'd just bet she said that to her son when she didn't want to come out with a straight 'no'. It was frustrating; yet at the same time he found it endearing. He laughed. 'I like you, Serena. I like you a lot.'

'I like you, too.' She looked suddenly shy. 'And I'd better get back to work.'

All the same, she let him kiss her goodbye. For long enough that her lips were ever so slightly reddened when he let her go, and he was aching to carry her to his bed.

He strove for cool. 'See you Friday. I'll pick you up.'

'I'll meet you there. *If* my parents can babysit.'

He was learning when to push her and when to hold back; this was definitely a 'hold back' moment. 'Of course. Call me,' he said, and then yanked her back into his arms for a final kiss goodbye. Just so he could see her eyes sparkle.

That evening, Carolyn raised one eyebrow when Serena walked in. 'I don't need to ask. You had a good day. And a very nice lunch, I'm guessing.'

'Yes.' Serena felt the colour flood into her face. Was it that obvious that George had kissed her silly? 'Mum, can I ask you a huge favour? Would you and Dad be able to babysit on Friday evening, if you're not already doing something?'

Carolyn looked pleased. 'So your lunch dates have been going well?'

'It's early days. And it's just the cinema. Maybe an ice cream afterwards,' Serena added.

'Of course we'll babysit,' Carolyn said. 'It'll do you good to have an evening out.'

* * *

Though Serena couldn't quite share Carolyn's confidence or shake her doubts. Was she doing the right thing? The more time she spent with George, the more she was discovering that she liked him. He was good company, he made her smile, and he was sexy as hell.

Which made him dangerous. She couldn't afford to risk her heart again. Not with Ethan in the equation. She didn't want her little boy to get hurt, either.

Not that George had ever suggested that things between them were going to get that serious. He'd said right from the start that this was just for fun. She sighed. She really ought to lighten up and just enjoy it. This was just an evening out, between friends.

Who was she trying to kid? This was a *date*. And she didn't have a clue what to do.

She managed to take refuge in work, with her first patient the next morning needing an assessment for multiple sclerosis. It was the kind of appointment she really enjoyed, setting baselines for her patient's current physical condition once she'd analysed their movement, strength, muscle tone, co-ordination and feeling, and then setting some achievable goals to reach. Keeping busy meant that she didn't have to think about George.

And she was aware of how ironic that was: George did exactly the same thing. He kept himself busy and never sat still so he didn't have to think about his emotions, either.

But then it was Friday evening, and her nerves all came rushing back. It took her ages to choose what to wear, and she took more care than usual with her hair and make-up.

She caught her breath as she walked towards the cinema where they'd agreed to meet and saw George waiting outside, leaning against the wall and checking something on his mobile phone. He really was gorgeous. And he was attracting second glances from every woman who passed, from teenagers right through to grandmothers. Though that was hardly surprising; he reminded her of one of the actors who'd played James Bond, with that thick dark hair and those piercing blue eyes. Not to mention his beautifully shaped mouth...

She pulled herself together. Just. This was her first night out with a man in years, so of course she was going to be a bundle of nerves. She just needed to get used to dating again, that was all. And she knew George wasn't going to pressure her into anything she wasn't ready to do. Even though she was pretty sure he usually ended up in bed with his girlfriends on the first night, she was aware that he was different with her. And not because he wasn't attracted to her—the way he kissed her told her that the physical attraction was mutual. Maybe his enforced slowing down after his accident had made him take things a little more slowly in other areas, too.

'Hi, there,' she said softly as she walked up to him.

'Hi.' He leaned down to kiss her, his eyes crinkling at the corners. 'You look lovely.'

'Thank you.' He was probably just being polite, she knew—she was an ordinary single mum, not the kind of glamorous woman he usually dated—but the compliment still made her feel warm inside.

He tucked her arm through the crook of his. 'So are you still being impossibly independent, or will you let me treat you to the show?'

'Independent,' she said. She softened her words with a smile. 'But I'll let you buy the popcorn.'

'That's progress, I suppose,' he said. 'What would you like to see?'

'I really don't mind.' Just being here with him was enough, right now.

'I'm guessing the gory action movie wouldn't be top of your list.'

'No.' Though she'd bet it was at the top of his. She couldn't help smiling at the thought.

'How about the girly rom-com?' he suggested.

'Not if you'd hate it.'

He leaned down to whisper in her ear, 'I could put up with the most tedious girly rom-com in the world if you'd let me hold your hand all the way through it.'

She laughed. 'Now you're making me feel like a teenager.' All gauche and excited at the idea of hand-holding. If he could make her feel like this over something so innocuous, then heaven help her when she eventually went to bed with him...

Help. She shouldn't even be thinking about that. Now she could really do with a cold shower. Or a fan. And this wasn't part of their deal. They'd agreed to be friends.

Except there had been kissing.

So they *could* be friends and a bit more...

The idea slid insidiously into her head, and made her blush even more.

George simply kissed her swiftly on the mouth, took her hand and led her to the queue to get their tickets. The butterflies in Serena's stomach were doing elaborate cartwheels by the time they found their seats in the auditorium. And they increased even more when George drew her hand up to his mouth, pressed a kiss into her palm and then laced his fingers through hers again.

The film starred one of Serena's favourite actors, but she couldn't concentrate on the film or the plot. What she was really aware of was the way George was holding her hand. As if it was something precious, something to cherish. *As if she was special.*

It would be so, so easy to let herself fall for him.

And so, so stupid to risk her heart getting broken again. This was just for fun, she reminded herself. And they *were* going to have fun.

They shared an ice cream sundae in a nearby café afterwards, until George dropped his spoon.

'I'll catch the waitress's eye and ask her for another,' Serena said.

He caught her hand. 'There's no need. We can share.'

Something in his expression gave him away. 'You dropped your spoon on purpose, didn't you?' she asked.

He blew her a kiss. 'That's for me to know and you to wonder.' He filched the spoon from her hand and fed her a spoonful of ice cream, making her lean forward, then handed it back and gave her a sultry look. 'Time for you to do me.'

Her temperature spiked at his words. She had the distinct feeling that he was talking about more than just feeding him ice cream and the idea of being skin to skin with him sent desire curling through her veins. 'Behave,' she breathed, and was cross with herself at the husky tone in her voice. Oh, great. He'd know exactly what effect he had on her now.

He gave her an irrepressible smile. 'Tut, Ms James. I'm not the one with the naughty mind. I simply meant that it's my turn for a spoonful of ice cream.'

'That's the biggest, fattest lie I've ever heard,' she retorted.

He grinned. 'I could make you take that back.'

'Just admit it.'

His gaze went hot. 'OK. So it had a double meaning.

Guilty, m'lud.' His lowered his voice. 'And right now I'd be a lot happier eating this ice cream in bed with you.'

Oh, the pictures that put in her head.

And it silenced her, temporarily.

He just gave her the wickedest, wickedest smile. As if he knew exactly what he was doing to her, and he was doing it on purpose.

For that, she smeared the ice cream at the side of his mouth.

He licked it off. Slowly. And raised an eyebrow at her. 'Do I get to do this to you now?' His voice deepened. 'And I think I should be the one to lick it off, too.'

If he carried on like this, she was going to start hyperventilating. 'George,' she whispered, wanting him and yet terrified of wanting him at the same time.

He took the spoon back, and moistened his lower lip. 'Just as well we're in public. So I'll behave. But I'm thinking about it, too. What we'd be like together.' He leaned over to kiss her briefly across the table, then fed her a spoonful of ice cream.

Hot male and cold, sweet vanilla.

It made Serena's senses spin. And, with every spoonful, her desire grew hotter and hotter. Judging by the way his pupils were absolutely huge, it was the same for him.

Tonight…

Could they?

Would they?

When they'd finished, George paid.

'I owe you half,' she said as they left the café.

'I think I can just about afford to buy you half an ice cream sundae,' he said. 'And, just for the record, it didn't come with any strings attached.'

Ah. So he wasn't expecting her to go to bed with

him tonight. She wasn't sure if she was more relieved or disappointed. But she couldn't just ignore the fact that he wasn't pushing her. That he was trying to take things at her pace. 'Thank you,' she said.

He laced his fingers through hers. 'Don't feel awkward about it, Serena. We're...' He paused, as if not sure what to say. 'Friends,' he said.

Again, she wasn't sure whether to be more relieved or disappointed. Being friends meant that she could keep her heart intact. But being friends also meant that she had to tamp this desire down and resist the temptation to act on it.

'I enjoyed tonight.' He gave her a sidelong look. 'I think it's the first time I've really been able to relax since my accident.'

And that was a huge admission for a man like George. Her heart melted, and she tightened her fingers round his. 'I enjoyed tonight, too. I can't remember the last time I went to the cinema and it didn't involve an animated film.'

'Maybe we can do it again some time.'

Was he being polite, she wondered, or was he just trying not to pressure her? 'That'd be nice.'

He saw her safely home and kissed her goodnight on the doorstep—a warm, sweet kiss that had Serena tingling all the way down to her toes. And how easy it would be to take it that little bit further. To let the spark grow into a flame.

'Would you like to come in for a coffee?' she asked, half hoping that he'd accept and half-hoping that he'd refuse.

It would be so, so easy to say yes.

George glanced at Serena's house. An ordinary family home—unlike the ancestral pile that was his. An ordinary family.

Like Rebecca's.

And although Serena wasn't Rebecca, he was pretty sure that some of the same issues would surface if he let himself get much closer to her. He was used to being under constant scrutiny; she wasn't. He was used to dealing with people from all social backgrounds; despite her work, she wasn't. And in the end his background would get in the way.

He didn't do relationships, and she'd told him the same. Coming in for a coffee meant meeting her parents, because they were babysitting; and meeting each other's families just wasn't part of this thing between them. They'd had fun tonight.

And it was stupid of him—and greedy—to want more.

'I'll see you later.' He stroked her face. 'Sweet dreams.' He kissed her again, then waited until she'd unlocked the front door before striding away.

Sweet dreams. No, they weren't going to be sweet, Serena thought ruefully. After what he'd said to her over the ice cream, her dreams were going to be X-rated. And she was going to have to be very, very careful not to fall for George and let him break her heart.

CHAPTER SEVEN

THE following week, George asked Serena to go to a gig with him on the Thursday night. 'It should be a good night,' he said. 'There's an up-and-coming blues guitarist playing. I've seen him a couple of times, and I think you might like him. And, best of all, it's in a small place, so we'll actually be close enough to see him playing.'

Serena looked slightly worried. 'Is it the sort of place where the press would follow you?'

'No. The press still think I'm this boring guy with a limp who doesn't do anything exciting.' He flapped a dismissive hand. 'They're not interested in me right now. Don't worry, you're not going to end up on the front page of the tabloids.' He smiled at her. 'So will you come with me?'

'If Mum and Dad don't mind babysitting.'

'I'm happy to treat them to a night out in return,' he said. 'Dinner at their favourite restaurant, maybe?'

She shook her head. 'You really don't need to do that.'

'I know. But I'd like to. To say thank you.'

She said nothing, but he could practically read it on her face. She'd noted that he was happy enough to buy her parents dinner, but he'd ducked out of meeting them.

And she clearly wasn't impressed at the idea of buying dinner for people you hadn't even met.

Well. There were limits on this thing between them. It was for fun, not a relationship. They'd agreed that right from the start. Meeting her family would be a step in the wrong direction for both of them.

This absolutely wasn't a relationship.

'Let me know later tonight. If you can make it, I'll get tickets,' he said. 'And, no, you're not paying. You're indulging me and keeping me company. It's my idea, so it's my bill.' He took her hand and kissed it. 'Got it?'

She smiled. 'Got it. But I can buy you a beer, right?'

'We'll see,' he said, mimicking her words to him about letting him buying popcorn or an ice cream.

She texted him later that evening. *If the offer's still open, my parents can babysit.*

Good. He texted her back, *Great. I'll pick you up at seven.*

As he'd half expected, the reply came back: *No need. Meet you there. Let me know the address.*

But if he pushed her over the independence issue, it might make her back into her shell. He wanted to tempt her out further. To see if music did the same thing to her that it did to him. He wanted to see her eyes sparkle with pleasure and a genuine smile on her face.

Even in jeans and a black sweater—clothes that would look casual and almost scruffy on anyone else—George looked stunning, Serena thought as she walked round the corner and saw him standing outside the club where he'd arranged to meet her that evening.

'The man in black, hmm?' she said, trying to keep it light. Though her voice was husky, and she was pretty sure it showed all over her face how gorgeous she thought he was.

'Indeed.' He picked her up, swung her round, then kissed her until she was dizzy. 'Good evening.'

How could he manage to sound so cool and calm after that? she wondered. But she followed his lead and kept it casual. 'Good evening.'

He kept his arm round her as they walked into the club, and it made her feel warm inside. As if he were making a statement that she was his girl. Crazy, because that wasn't what they'd agreed to. But tonight she felt like a million dollars, being with him.

'Would you like a drink?' he asked.

'Yes, but I'm paying for yours as well as mine,' she insisted.

He kissed her briefly. 'If it makes you happy, then fine—you can buy me a beer.'

'Good.' She kissed him back. 'This is going to be such a treat. Thanks for asking me to come with you tonight. I can't remember the last time I heard live music—well, apart from the school performances, because we always go to those to support Dad.'

'You might hate this,' George pointed out.

She shook her head. 'Apart from the fact that I love the blues, you said you've seen this guy play before. If he wasn't any good, then you wouldn't have bothered coming to see him again, right?'

He smiled. 'Right.'

She bought them both a beer from the bar, noting that it was served in plastic cups—obviously for the audience's safety, in case someone dropped a glass in the middle of a crowded concert—and walked with George through to the room where the support band was already playing. He was right about it being a tiny venue, and she loved the intimacy of the room. It was perfect for seeing a band.

Before the main act started, George manoeuvred her right down to the front. 'This way, we get a good view.' He stood behind her with his arms wrapped round her waist, pulling her back against his body. 'And I won't let anyone push you further forward into the stage. You're perfectly safe and you won't get squashed.'

'Thank you.' She hadn't expected him to be so thoughtful—not being particularly tall, she would only have had a view of the audience's heads if they'd stood further back. And the way he was holding her made her felt so cherished.

The roadies did a quick sound check after the support band had finished, and then the guitarist they'd come to see walked onto the stage, to enthusiastic applause. The first song was a standard blues number, which Serena enjoyed; and then he started singing something she assumed was one of his own compositions. A song about being lonely.

It caught her on the raw; she *had* been lonely, since Jason had walked out on her. Much as she adored her son and she knew she could always rely on the support of her parents and close friends, she missed the intimacy of living with someone. Of falling asleep in the arms of the man who loved her. Of being loved as an equal partner.

The song made her loneliness slam home.

Except George was standing with her right now, with his arms wrapped round her. Cherishing her. The slow, heavy beat of the music made her so aware of the feel of his body against hers, the strong and steady beat of his heart, his cheek pressed against hers with the slightest, slightest prick of stubble, and a rumble in his chest as he sang along to the song—clearly it was one he knew well. The speakers were too loud for her to be able to pick out George's voice properly, but she could remember him singing along while he danced with her through the park and she knew he had a great voice.

The guitarist segued into a fabulous version of the old Nina Simone standard 'Feeling Good'. And right now Serena did feel good. She was enjoying the music but, even more, she was enjoying being so close to George. Even though the room was crowded, the intimacy of the venue made it feel as if it was just the two of them in the room.

She closed her eyes and leaned back against him; and then he moved so that he was kissing the curve of her neck. The feel of his mouth teasing her skin made her shiver and want more. She arched back, twisting her head so that she could kiss him. The moment his mouth found hers, she was lost, completely oblivious to the people around them and the guitarist on the stage. All she was aware of was the way George was kissing her, his mouth hot and demanding. His arms were wrapped tightly round her, jamming their bodies together, and she could feel his arousal pressing against her. He was just as turned on as she was, and she knew that right now they both wanted the same thing. To fulfil the desire that had been building between them from the very first moment they'd set eyes on each other. The desire they'd both suppressed for too long.

When George broke the kiss, his eyes were dark and intense as he looked at her and mouthed her name. Serena pressed one hand against his cheek. She was so, so tempted to suggest that they forget the rest of the gig and go straight back to his place. Right now, she desperately wanted make love with him. To be skin to skin with him. To let him take her over the edge—and to enjoy doing exactly the same for him, watching his eyes change as he climaxed.

But her parents were babysitting her son, she had work in the morning, and she knew that if she threw caution to the wind and made love with George tonight, it would break down the last barrier and she'd fall for him. Hard. She couldn't let herself do that. Couldn't open herself up to the risk of him breaking her heart.

As if the struggle showed in her face and he understood, he bent to kiss her again, his mouth light and undemanding, then moved so that he was standing behind her again with his arms wrapped round her waist. Just holding her, letting her know that he wasn't going anywhere, and he wasn't going to pressure her into anything she wasn't ready for.

Serena had to blink away the tears.

Especially as the guitarist started singing another old classic, 'Piece of my Heart'. How very, very appropriate the lyrics were.

At the end of the gig, George asked, 'Did you enjoy it?'

'I loved it,' she said honestly.

'Me, too.' He paused. 'Serena.' His pupils were huge. 'You make me ache. I want you.'

The huskiness in his voice stoked the desire deep inside her. She dragged in a breath. 'I want you, too,' she admitted.

He kissed her swiftly. 'Come home with me.'

Where she knew he'd make love to her, ease the ache and make her feel amazing. She swallowed hard. 'I want to say yes. I really, *really* want to say yes.'

'But?' he asked softly.

She bit her lip. All the reasons that had stopped her

earlier rose up to haunt her. 'I can't,' she whispered. 'I've got work tomorrow, and there's Ethan—my parents are babysitting and it isn't fair on them to come home late.' And especially not to roll up tomorrow morning, with just enough time to grab a shower and take Ethan to school before she went to work.

Spending the whole night with George just wasn't an option.

And a quick tumble in his bed wouldn't be enough for her. Or for him, given the expression on his face right now.

'OK. I'm not going to rush you.' He brushed his mouth lightly against hers. 'Though it's going to happen between us, Serena.' His voice deepened, became husky with desire. 'I want you, you want me—and it's going to happen. One day. Very, very soon.' He punctuated every phrase with a kiss, and her knees went weak.

'But for now, I'll take you home.'

'I can—' she began.

'I know you can look after yourself. I know you're perfectly capable of seeing yourself home. But indulge me for now, will you?' He kissed her again. 'I'm not ready to say goodnight, not just yet.'

Neither was she. These extra snatched minutes together were precious.

He hailed a taxi, settled her in the back, then climbed in beside her.

All the way back to her place, he held her hand. Neither of them said a word. And she didn't dare look at him, because she knew the longing and the desire would be too much for her and she'd make a real fool of herself. It would be all too easy to throw herself at him. To kiss him with abandon, uncaring that the taxi driver could see them.

And that just wasn't her.

George insisted on getting out of the taxi and seeing her to her front door. At the front gate, he kissed her lingeringly, seeming not to care that the cabbie's meter was still running on the taxi and his bill was going to be enormous.

And she still wasn't ready to say goodnight. Though there was one way she could keep him with her just a little longer… 'Do you want to come in for a coffee or something?' she asked when he broke the kiss.

Just what she'd asked when George had taken her to the cinema.

And, given that Serena's parents were babysitting, saying yes meant meeting her family.

He'd said no last week. Was she merely being polite, he wondered, or was this her way of saying she was ready to move on to the next stage of a relationship? That she was prepared to arrange a sleepover for her son and to spend the entire night in his arms?

Though she'd backed away from the suggestion of going back to his flat tonight, even for a little while. He'd seen in her face that it had been a struggle for her and she'd wanted to go with him—to let him scoop her up and carry her to his wide, wide bed and make love to here until they were both sated—but at the same time she hadn't been quite ready to move this thing between them forward. She still had doubts that held her back.

Besides, they'd agreed up front that neither of them was in the market for a relationship. And having sex would definitely change things between them. For her, sex wouldn't be casual; and he had the nastiest feeling that, for once, it would be the same for him, too. That it wouldn't be like it had been with his other girlfriends, simple physical pleasure with no strings. That he was risking stepping into the same territory he'd had with Rebecca. Making himself vulnerable.

Meeting her family.

It was a step George hadn't intended to take. Been there, done that, been burned.

But maybe, just maybe, it was the right thing to do. And he had social skills. He could be polite and charming. 'OK. I'll just go and settle up with the cabbie.'

'Let me know how mu—' she began.

He cut her off by kissing her. 'No. You don't need to go halves on the fare. And don't argue.'

He paid the cabbie, then followed her into the house.

As Serena closed the front door behind them, a door to what he presumed was the living room opened, and two middle-aged people stood there.

Serena introduced them swiftly. 'Mum, Dad, this is George. George, these are my parents, Carolyn and Mitchell James.'

'Lovely to meet you,' he said, shaking their hands.

'Did you enjoy the gig?' Mitchell asked.

'Yes, thanks. It was fabulous,' George said with a smile.

'You would've enjoyed it, Dad,' Serena said. 'He did "Feeling Good" and "Piece of My Heart".'

'That takes me back. Those used to be part of my band's set,' Mitchell said.

'You were in a band?' George asked, surprised. 'Serena told me you're the head of music at school and you play quite a few instruments, but she didn't say you had a band.'

'He was lead singer and rhythm guitarist,' Carolyn said. 'We met when I went to see his band play, back in my student days.'

'We did mainly blues covers,' Mitchell explained. 'Though I did once write a song for Carrie.'

'And your band played it at our wedding,' she said, looking misty-eyed.

'It's brilliant. I'd get Dad to play for us now, but I don't want to wake Ethan,' Serena said. She looked anxiously at her parents. 'Was he all right tonight?'

'He was absolutely fine. He went to bed like a lamb, got me to read the Little Wolves story twice, and fell asleep halfway through the second time,' Mitchell reassured her.

'Good.' Serena looked relieved. 'I'm making coffee, if everyone wants some?'

Somehow they all ended up congregating in the kitchen, which George swiftly realised was the heart of Serena's house. There was a scrubbed pine dining table in one corner of the room with four matching chairs, her fridge was covered in a child's drawings held to the door by magnets, and there was a plastic sheet on the wall filled with photographs that were obviously of her little boy. Pictures of them together, mother and son. Pictures of him with her parents. And the love was so clear on their faces. Though he could see it first-hand, too, in the way Serena's parents acted towards her.

'Do have a biscuit, George,' Carolyn said, opening a tin and offering it to him.

Serena glanced round from the kettle and raised an eyebrow. 'Mum, I didn't have anything like that indoors. Have you been spoiling Ethan again?'

'Grandmother's privilege,' Carolyn said, at the same time as Mitchell said, 'No, they're babysitter munchies,' and they all laughed.

'Come and sit down,' Mitchell said, pulling out a chair for George.

George was torn between wanting this and wanting to run. This wasn't what he'd signed up for. He wasn't brave like Frances, his stepmother, able to step in and heal a broken family. He couldn't take the place of Ethan's father. And Serena was vulnerable—even more so than he was, deep down. What the hell was he doing here?

Yet he really, *really* liked her. He knew she'd fit right into his family. Frances would love her; Alice would approve; Ed, Bea and Charlie would take to her immediately; and David would be quietly delighted that someone had finally made his oldest child think about settling down.

But George had learned one particular lesson the hard way. *Don't get too close.* His mother had been able to walk out on them because the title hadn't been enough for her. And Rebecca had walked out on him, too, because the title had been too much for her. And, although he'd denied it at the time, he'd come to realise that she'd been right in her insistence that you couldn't separate the man from his background. There just wasn't any middle ground.

He needed to back off. Though he had to find a nice way of doing it. A way where he wouldn't hurt Serena.

But for tonight he could be with her, pretend just for a little while that he was a better man than he really was. He summoned up a smile, sat at the table, took a biscuit and chatted to her parents. He drank the coffee that Serena gave him. He even rested his arm along the back of her chair as they talked; somehow it felt right, felt comfortable.

'So what is it you do, George?' Mitchell asked.

George was pretty sure that Serena's parents knew exactly who he was and had already checked him out online. But at least they were giving him the benefit of the doubt, rather than assuming that he was exactly how the press portrayed him, and he appreciated that. Rebecca's parents hadn't afforded him that same courtesy. 'I work in the family business—mainly supporting my father, and working on my own projects that benefit the estate. And, if I get my own way on my current pet project, we'll be doing events with music and fireworks at the hall next year.' He smiled. 'Serena tells me you might be able to suggest some good playlists for the music, Mitchell.'

To his relief, the ploy worked; Mitchell didn't probe any more into whether he was a suitable prospect for his daughter, and George had a thoroughly enjoyable discussion with him about music.

Then he glanced at his watch. 'Sorry, it's getting late. I ought to go and let you all get some sleep.'

'We'll give you a lift home,' Mitchell said.

'Thanks, but I'm fine with a taxi.' He smiled at them to soften his refusal.

'Come to lunch on Sunday,' Carolyn offered.

Help. This was going way too fast for him. He hadn't expected to like Serena's parents this much. Or for them to warm to him, either.

But he knew from experience that this wouldn't work. He couldn't get any closer. 'It's so kind of you to offer,' he said, 'but I'm afraid my parents are expecting me in Suffolk on Sunday. Dad and I will be talking all day about roof repairs and boring everyone stiff,' he added, just in case Serena's parents were expecting him to extend an invitation to Serena and Ethan. He really wasn't ready to take them to Suffolk. It would raise all kinds of expectations in his family. Expectations he knew he couldn't fulfil.

'Another Sunday, then,' Carolyn said.

'That'd be lovely.' And George knew he'd make sure he found another reasonable excuse, so as not to hurt them.

On the taxi back to his flat, George brooded. Serena's family was lovely. He'd just bet that her son was a total sweetheart. Having a partner—someone to support what she did at work, to back her up in parenting, to share the good times and the bad—would be the icing on the cake for her. Making them into a proper family.

But George knew he couldn't be that person. He couldn't make it a perfect family with a little brother or sister for Ethan. At least, not without a lot of medical intervention; and even then there were no guarantees that it would work. The accident had almost totally wrecked his chances of having children of his own. He'd put off settling down and producing an heir—and now there was a very good chance it was too late.

He pushed the thought away, not wanting to think about how much he'd let his family down. The test results weren't getting any better, so it was time he worked out how to tell them the truth.

And as for Serena...

Maybe he needed to end this now, before before they both got hurt.

He really, really had to stop wanting what he just couldn't have.

CHAPTER EIGHT

For the next two weeks, George managed to keep it light with Serena. Though it grew harder and harder to stop when he was kissing her goodbye. He couldn't help remembering the desire in her expression when she'd kissed him at the concert. And when she shyly suggested that maybe they could have dinner together on the Saturday night... He had a feeling that dinner wasn't all she had in mind. It was a big deal for her to offer a Saturday night. How could he resist?

'Mummy, who's George?' Ethan asked on the Saturday morning.

Serena froze. 'Someone I know from work.' Which was true, as far as it went; she had met George at work. 'Why?'

'Nanna said you were having tea with him tonight. Are you having basghetti?'

'No, darling.'

Ethan's face fell. 'Oh.' He bit his lip.

Serena scooped him onto her lap. 'If you'd rather I didn't go, darling, that's fine.'

He shook his head. 'But if you go out for basghetti, I want to go, too.'

Serena had to take a moment to digest that. Ethan

clearly didn't have a problem with the idea of her seeing someone—but it seemed he wanted to feel part of what was going on.

George had been careful to say right from the start that seeing her didn't have to involve her child. Ethan clearly wanted to meet George, but how would George feel about meeting Ethan? Maybe she'd sound him out tonight. Ask him if he'd like to meet her son.

'Maybe next time,' she hedged. 'I love you, Ethan.'

He beamed at her. 'I love you too, Mummy, all the way to the stars and back.'

A lump rose in her throat: a phrase from one of Ethan's favourite bedtime stories. This was something she'd never jeopardise. But George had met and liked her parents. Hopefully it would be the same with her son.

The phone shrilled, and she kissed the top of Ethan's head. 'I'd better get that. Do you want to find a storybook for me to read you in a minute?'

The next morning, George answered the phone, a little surprised that Serena was calling him. 'Hi. How are you?'

'I'm fine, thanks.' She sounded awkward. 'I'm so sorry. I'm going to have to call off tonight. Mum's got a migraine; they tend to go on for a day or so, and it's not fair to ask her and Dad to look after Ethan when she's not well.'

'Of course.' And he couldn't even dragoon one of his siblings into babysitting for them. Apart from the fact he wasn't ready to admit to his family that he'd been seeing someone, Serena hadn't met any of them. He was pretty sure she wouldn't let a complete stranger look after her child, even if he could vouch for them.

Though he was shocked by how disappointed he felt at not seeing her tonight. He'd been looking forward to a quiet romantic evening with her.

'I, um, was thinking,' she said. 'Maybe we could both take Ethan to the park this morning, instead. We could have lunch out; there's a nice café on the other side of the park.'

He could say no. Back out. Tell her that he didn't do family stuff under any circumstances.

But his interest was piqued. He'd met her parents, and they clearly hadn't tried to put her off him, because now she was actually willing to let him meet her son. So did that mean she would let him into her life?

And was that what he really wanted? To be part of her life, part of her family?

'George?'

'Sorry. I was wool-gathering. Um.' He had to make a decision. Fast. Back away? Or take a risk and see where it took them?

Adrenalin won. 'Shall I meet you at yours?'

'That'd be good.'

'Great. Give me half an hour to do some stuff here, and then I'll be straight over.'

'OK. See you soon.'

And he could actually hear the smile in her voice. A smile he could see in his mind's eye; a smile that made him melt.

His common sense was telling him to back off, but George ignored it. He wanted a day with Serena. The sky was a deep autumn blue, the air was crisp, and it was the perfect kind of day to wander in the sunshine.

He drove over to Serena's, because he knew then he'd have to concentrate on the journey and he wouldn't have time to think about whether he was about to make the biggest mistake of his life. When he rang the doorbell, he felt ridiculously nervous. He'd never had that much to do with kids, apart from his siblings, so he didn't have a clue what to say or how to act around Ethan.

But then Serena answered the door and he saw the tension in her face. She'd clearly believed he'd have second thoughts and wouldn't turn up, or would call her with some feeble, badly thought-out excuse. And no doubt she was just as nervous as he was, wondering how he and Ethan would get on.

'Hi. These are for you.' Awkwardly, he handed her the flowers. It was the first time he'd ever bought her flowers; he hadn't wanted to make her feel ill-at-ease by going over the top and buying half the stock at the local florist's, so he'd chosen a simple yet pretty bouquet in rich autumn shades.

She looked thrilled, and he was relieved to discover that he'd judged it just right. The bouquet was big enough to make her feel special, yet small enough not to be overwhelming.

'Thank you, George. They're absolutely lovely.'

Her eyes were shining, and all he wanted to do right at that moment was hold her. Kiss her. Tell her...

No. He wasn't ready to say those words. Not yet. Admitting to himself that he was even thinking it was tough enough.

'Come in,' she said. 'I'll just put these in water.'

He followed her into the kitchen. A little boy was sitting at the table, drawing.

He'd seen the photos in the kitchen before, but actually meeting Ethan was something else. The little boy looked very like Serena, with those same stunning green eyes, though his hair was darker and a mass of curls rather than Serena's very straight light brown hair.

Ethan had the same serious expression as his mother, and George wondered for a moment whether the little boy's smile would be as rare and as sweet as Serena's.

'Ethan, this is my friend George. Granddad can't come to the park with us today because Nanna isn't feeling very well and he wants to look after her, so George is going to come to the park with us instead,' Serena explained.

Help. What did you say to small boys? Especially ones who were giving you a look of pure suspicion? George fell back on formality. 'Hello, Ethan.' He held his hand out across the table.

The little boy shook his hand solemnly. 'Hello.'

'What sort of things do you like doing at the park?'

Ethan thought about it for a moment. 'Playing football.'

George nodded. 'Sounds fun. I like playing football, too.' He gave Serena a quick glance, checking that she wasn't going to nag him about his leg if he played football with her son.

The sweetness in her smile made his knees weak. If Ethan wasn't here, right now he'd be kissing her until they were both dizzy. And then he'd be carrying her off to her bed.

But her son was here. And his thoughts were completely inappropriate in this situation.

He forced himself to concentrate on the little boy. 'There's only one thing—I don't actually have a football.'

'I do,' Ethan said. He slid down from the table rushed off, presumably to fetch his ball.

George looked up at Serena, noting that the tension in her face had eased.

'Are you sure you don't mind coming to the park with us?' she asked softly.

No, he wasn't sure at all. This might be the worst idea he'd ever had, because right at this moment he felt incredibly mixed up. He really wanted to do this; yet at the same time he wanted to get in his car and drive away as fast and as far as he could.

Part of him was terrified at the idea of getting close to a ready-made family; and then there was the shocking, unexpected feeling of seeing Serena and her son together—the realisation that he'd never have that bond with anyone because he couldn't have children of his own. 'Sure,' he fibbed. 'Um, I'm afraid I didn't think when I drove over. My car's a two-seater. Can we take the Tube to the park, or do you want me to call us a taxi?'

'Neither.' She smiled again. 'We're within walking distance.'

'Of course you are.' And now he felt even more stupid. Hell, he didn't do this sort of thing. He didn't have a clue where to start. Schmoozing the press, racing someone down a double black diamond ski run, charming people who came to visit the Hall—those were all things he was good at. But knowing how to give a little boy a fun day out was way outside his experience. He couldn't even draw on his own past, because he had no idea whether the sort of things he'd done as a child were still fun for the kids of today.

'I'd better get you a visitor permit for your car, so you don't get a parking ticket.' Serena took a pad from a drawer and filled in the top sheet quickly, then tore it off and handed it to him.

'Thanks.' By the time George had stuck it inside his windscreen, making sure it was visible to any passing traffic wardens, Serena and Ethan were ready to go and she was locking the front door behind them.

'Is that your car?' Ethan asked as George closed the passenger door.

'Yes.'

'It's like James Bond's car.' He frowned. 'Are you James Bond in disguise?'

'No.' Though George was amused by the description. Was that what Serena had called him? 'Do you like cars?'

Ethan nodded. 'Mummy doesn't have a car.'

'Because we don't need one. We can take the Tube wherever we need to go,' Serena said.

'Does your car have an ejector seat?' Ethan asked, peering at it.

Just the kind of question he would have asked, at Ethan's age. 'No. It doesn't have any rockets, either, which is a bit of a shame. It'd be fun to make it go really fast.' George paused. 'Do you like James Bond?'

'Granddad does. He's got a book with all the cars in.'

Oh. So that was how Ethan knew about the cars. George had been pretty sure Serena wouldn't let her son watch the Bond films, not at five years old. And Granddad might like Bond's cars, George thought, but he definitely wouldn't approve of Bond—or anyone like Bond—dating his daughter. He needed to be very careful here.

'Come on, Ethan. Let's go to the park,' Serena said.

They walked to the park in near silence, with Ethan holding his mother's hand tightly. Serena chatted a bit, but George didn't have a clue what to say; and Ethan, now they were away from the car, was almost silent. Was he normally this quiet? George wondered. Or was the little boy a just bit shy with strangers? Or, he thought, feeling slightly sick, did Ethan resent George being with them and taking his mother's attention away from him?

There was no way could he ask that question tactfully.

But he made an effort to chat to the little boy. 'What's your favourite football team?'

'Chelsea.' Ethan paused. 'Granddad likes Chelsea.'

Ethan clearly adored his grandfather. Having met Mitchell James, George was pretty sure it was mutual. And he really didn't understand how Serena's ex had been able to walk away from a little boy who would've hung on his every word, made him the centre of his world. God, if *he* had a child...

He pushed the thought away. Now wasn't the time. And he needed to get the little boy talking to him. Now. 'Do you like ducks?'

Ethan nodded.

'Is there a pond at the park?'

'No.'

'I know a park with ducks. And swans. Maybe we could go and feed them some time.' He almost suggested driving there this afternoon. But there wasn't room for all three of them in his car. Besides, even if there had been room, George didn't think that Serena would be too happy about her son being driven around in a vintage car that had barely any of the safety equipment that was standard in modern cars.

Right now, he knew he was making a real mess of this. He gave Serena a quick glance. But she looked approving, so maybe he wasn't doing quite as badly as he thought.

Finally, they reached the park. George kicked the ball around a bit in the field, making sure he didn't kick the ball too hard and Ethan could stop the ball and kick it back, and the little boy seemed to come out of his shell a bit.

Maybe he was just a little bit shy, like his mother, and once he got to know George a bit better he'd relax with him.

'Time for a break,' Serena said eventually. 'Shall we go to the café for some lunch?'

'Yay!' Ethan looked positively animated; this was clearly a favourite treat.

Serena found them a table next to the window. 'What would you like, Ethan?' she asked.

'Basghetti, please.' He beamed at her, then confided shyly to George, 'Basghetti's my favourite.'

George was utterly charmed by the mispronunciation. And it shocked him to the core; since when had he found children cute? But Serena's son was incredibly sweet. Which wasn't too surprising, given what his mother was like, though George hadn't expected to be so drawn to the little boy. And he pushed back the sudden yearning. This was crazy. Having children had always been something in the 'some time, doing my duty' category.

'I like it, too,' George said. 'I think I'll have the same.'

Ethan looked pleased.

'Let's make it three plates of spaghetti,' Serena said. 'What shall we have to drink?'

'I'll go and order,' George said when everyone had chosen. 'And this is my treat, because you've treated me to a really nice morning in the park, OK?'

He could see the war in Serena's eyes; he knew she needed to feel independent, and yet she clearly didn't want to argue with him in front of her son. So he stood up and, making sure that Ethan couldn't see his face, blew her a kiss. Just to let her know that he understood and there were no strings attached to his offer. He was doing this because he wanted to do it, not because he had any ulterior motives.

Finally, she gave him a smile. 'Thank you. That's very nice of you.'

He went up to the counter to order spaghetti and apple juice for three. It felt weird, being part of a family group like this. He didn't want to analyse his feelings too closely.

'Your little boy's adorable,' the woman next to him in the queue said. 'He has your hair, doesn't he?'

Not at all. Ethan wasn't his. And the chances were, he would never have children of his own. Something he'd stuffed into a box marked 'Do not think about', and now he was forced to open it and realise that, actually, it was a big deal and actually, yes, he did want to be a dad. He took a deep breath and pushed it all back into his mental box, but the lid didn't fit properly any more.

But he smiled politely back at her and said, 'Thank you. Yes, he's a sweetheart.'

'How old is he?'

'Five.' Thank God he knew that. Otherwise he would've had to bluff.

'That's a lovely age.'

'Yes, it is.' And it was the age when, if your heart broke, it never quite mended again. He'd learned that one the hard way, too.

Even though Ethan and Serena seemed to enjoy their spaghetti when it arrived, George couldn't enjoy his. He felt too antsy. And he could feel himself putting the barriers all the way back up. He couldn't help it; this situation was pressing all of his buttons. In some respects, everything he wanted was within his grasp. A ready-made family. And he actually felt a weird sense of belonging with them.

But. If he let himself get too close to them, it could all go so badly wrong. The closer he got, the more he'd have to lose. All the same, he faked a smile and did his best to chat nicely over lunch.

On the way out of the café, his mobile phone rang.

He glanced at the screen and then at Serena. 'Do you mind if I take this?'

She spread her hands. 'Sure.'

He spoke rapidly into the phone; Serena tried not to listen in, but she couldn't help hearing him say at the end of his conversation, 'That'd be great. OK. See you tomorrow. Love you.'

Love you. Words she hadn't expected to hear from George. And how ridiculous that she suddenly wanted to hear them said in her direction. She must be crazy.

She didn't think he was talking to another woman. He had told her that this thing between them was exclusive, and the man she'd come to know was very far from being a cheat and a liar.

'Who was that?' she asked casually.

'Ed.'

His *brother*? She raised an eyebrow. 'Wow. You don't often hear men telling their brothers they love them.'

He shrugged. 'Well. I do. We've been through a lot together.'

And clearly his brother was a safe person to say those words to, she thought. George was definitely close to his family, and he'd seemed to get on well with her parents. He was a little more wary with Ethan, but maybe he just wasn't used to kids. And she was obviously hoping for way too much from today.

'Time to go home, I think,' she said. 'Before it gets really cold and dark.'

On the way back, they stopped at the playground. George made the effort to push Ethan on the swings and spin him on the roundabout. It felt so strange, being part of a family group like this. He would never have thought of spending a day with Serena and her son at the park, and he was surprised by how much he was enjoying it. He also had a nasty, creeping feeling that this was what he really wanted out of life. To be part of a family. The centre of it. But if he asked Serena to make a life and a family with him, she'd have to give up so much. It was too much to ask. And it wasn't fair to dump his problems on her.

Then he spotted the giant slide at the end of the playground. There was a man going down it with a little boy on his lap. Both of them were grinning broadly and yelling, 'Bogeys!'

'That looks amazing,' he said as they walked closer to it.

Serena shook her head. 'Not for me.'

Of course. She didn't like thrill rides. But George noticed that Ethan was looking longingly at the slide.

Then Ethan said, 'Granddad takes me down that.'

Oh. So the slide wasn't strictly out of bounds for the little boy, then. George looked at Serena, and mouthed, 'Trust me?'

He saw panic flash across her face, and mouthed, 'I won't let him get hurt. I promise.'

The slide was slightly damp from the autumn air, and his coat was a slippery fabric that would make the surface super-slidey. This, he thought, was going to be a fast ride. The kind of adrenalin rush he'd really missed since his accident. And something that would distract him from his thoughts. Just what he really, really needed right now. And, as a bonus, Serena's little boy would enjoy it, too.

'Ethan, would you like to go down the slide with me?' he asked.

Ethan looked at his mother, clearly torn between wanting to go on the slide and yet not being entirely sure of George.

'You can, if you want to,' Serena said.

So Serena would trust him with the most precious thing in her life. George felt as if someone had just wrapped a fist round his heart and squeezed it. How could she be so generous, when he was so selfish?

'This is going to be fast. Do you yell something when you go down the slide with Granddad?' he asked the little boy.

'No.'

'Well, when I go skiing, I yell "whoo-hoo". Well, obviously I don't yell it out loud in the mountains, because I don't want to cause an avalanche, but I yell it inside my head. There isn't any snow here, so we can yell it out loud if you want to.'

Ethan thought about it, then nodded.

He climbed up the steps, holding Ethan's hand to make sure that he didn't fall. No doubt his grandfather did exactly the same. And this was what his father ought to be doing. The kind of thing his own father had done, when he was this age. Serena's ex had no idea what kind of treasure he'd thrown away.

George sat at the top of the slide and settled Ethan safely on his lap, wrapping his arms round him to make sure he was secure.

Serena was waiting for them at the bottom, looking really worried.

Well, he could prove to her that he did have a responsible side. Sort of.

'Ready? One, two, three—whoo-hoo!'

Ethan echoed the yell, and George launched them down the slide. And it was fantastic, really fast. He hadn't had a rush like this in months. Not since just before he'd hit the cliff.

'That was brilliant,' Ethan said at the bottom, his eyes glowing with pleasure.

'Shall we do it again?'

The little boy nodded enthusiastically.

'Come with us,' he said to Serena, holding his hand out to her.

She shook her head.

George clucked at her and flapped his arms as if they were wings, but she didn't rise to the bait of him calling her a chicken.

'You're missing out, you know,' he said softly. 'It's fun.' More than he'd ever imagined. What an idiot he'd been to push away the idea of fatherhood when he'd had the chance. Duty, indeed. It would've been the best thing in the world. 'Come on, Serena. Join us.'

She just folded her arms and shook her head obstinately.

'OK. Your loss. Come on, Ethan.'

The second time was better still.

But, the third time they went down the slide, George could see that they were going to land awkwardly. He needed to keep a tight hold on Ethan to keep him safe, but at the same time he didn't dare risk landing on his bad leg. Just in case he set his progress right back to the start. He shifted slightly to protect his bad leg; his other foot hit the sandy floor first, hard, and it felt as if flames were licking up his leg. Oh, great. Clearly he'd done some damage on the impact. Probably a sprain—though no way was he going to admit it to Serena and hear her say, 'I told you so.'

'Can we do it again, please?' Ethan asked.

If he hadn't hurt his ankle, he would've been happy to do this all afternoon. 'No, I think three times is enough. And your mum's been standing around waiting for us. She must be cold.' He ruffled the little boy's hair. 'Time to go home.'

Somehow he managed to walk back to Serena's house without limping, even though every step made him want to catch his breath.

'I'll make us all some hot chocolate. Do you want to stay for dinner?' Serena asked.

Yes. He did. But Ethan had gone quiet on them again on the way back to the house. Was he tired out from all that running around, or had he had time to think about things and just didn't want George around?

George could still remembered what it felt like to be around that age and have people come in and try to take your parent's attention away. His piano teacher hadn't been the only woman who'd liked the idea of being the next Lady Somers, and he'd hated the way they'd simpered over his father, meaning that his father hadn't been able to spend time with him and Ed.

Ah, hell. With the best intentions in the world, this wasn't going to work. And George wasn't going to drag a small boy through the same misery he'd been through as a child.

'No, I'd better go. There are some things I promised to do for my dad before tomorrow.' It was a fib, but it was designed to protect them rather than hurt them.

He said goodbye, forcing himself to sound light and breezy and smiley. But driving back to his place hurt like crazy. George was really limping by the time he got to his flat. As soon as he got indoors, he took off his shoes and socks and gingerly felt his ankle; it was really painful to the touch and had already started swelling. OK. He'd sprained his ankle enough times in the past to know that all he needed was an ice pack and to put his foot up to make the swelling go down.

Though, on the down side, it meant he was forced to stay still. When he was still, he couldn't avoid his thoughts.

Today had been amazing. His world had been rocked to the core because he'd finally worked out what he wanted.

But today had also been everything he couldn't have. He couldn't make a family with Serena. He couldn't give her a little brother or sister for Ethan. And her little boy had been so wary of him, even after they'd had fun on the slide. Didn't they say that children always saw through you? Ethan had clearly worked out that George wasn't the right one for his mother.

And now George knew what he had to do. The right thing, for all of them.

He dragged himself off the sofa and grabbed his mobile phone.

There was a message from her waiting for him. *Thanks for today. Really enjoyed it. So did E.*

George wasn't so sure.

He knew he'd enjoyed it. Too much. But he just couldn't do this. Be part of a family. A family that he could break apart again all too easily when they knew what he really was. Wasn't that why Zara had walked out on them? And not just her: for Rebecca, his title had got in the way of love.

He'd survived them abandoning him. He wasn't sure

the same would be true if he let himself get close to Serena and Ethan and they abandoned him. There was too much at stake. Too much to lose. He needed to get out before any of them got hurt any more

But, God, how was he going to tell her?

When you ripped off a plaster, you had to do it hard and fast to make it less painful. This was the same thing. He had to be straight with her. And he needed to do it right now.

Sorry. Can't do this any more. Wish I could be different.

He stared at the message for a long, long time before he finally sent it. And then he went to drown his thoughts in the bottom of a bottle of vodka.

CHAPTER NINE

SORRY. Can't do this any more. Wish I could be different.

Serena stared at the screen. Was she really reading this, or had she fallen asleep and was having some kind of nightmare? She flicked out of the message and back in again, just to check; but it still said the same.

She couldn't believe this. The day she finally decided to trust George, to let him into her life and let him meet her son—that was the day he'd decided to end it between them.

By text.

Without even giving her a proper reason.

This was like one of those teenage moments where the boy who'd just dumped you said, 'It's not you, it's me,' to make you feel better about it. Except this didn't make her feel any better. It made her feel as if the bottom had just dropped out of her world.

She was shocked by how much it hurt. And in a way it was worse than Jason's betrayal. At least she'd been prepared for Jason walking out; she'd known from the start that he wasn't keen on the idea of being a father and she'd come to realise that he wasn't going to change his mind. And then the weeks of sleep deprivation that came with a colicky, screaming baby had made them both scratchy enough to have that final fight.

But this—this was completely out of the blue. They'd had such a nice day together at the park. OK, so George hadn't stayed for dinner, but she already knew that he spent most Sundays in Suffolk and she'd heard him talking to his brother, making arrangements for the day. She'd just assumed he'd meant it when he'd said that he had something to sort out for his father before he went to Suffolk, not that he was giving her the brush-off.

Then again, maybe she'd seen what she wanted to see—that there was more to George than being a shallow playboy. Maybe she'd been completely wrong. Maybe the gossip rags were right about him, after all.

Miserable and feeling sick, she went to check on Ethan. Her little boy was asleep and looked so peaceful. The complete opposite from the turmoil ripping through her heart, she thought wryly. She dragged in a shuddery breath, bent down to kiss his cheek, then slowly walked downstairs.

She'd been such a fool to think this thing between her and George was changing, growing. That it was starting to mean something to him, the same way it meant something to her. Clearly it hadn't. She'd just been a distraction for him. Someone to take his mind off the fact his mobility was limited while he recovered from the accident.

And now it was over.

Serena slept badly that night. Her eyes felt as if they were full of sand, the next morning, gritty and painful from the tears she'd cried in the night.

Ethan was sitting at the kitchen table, drawing, when she finally dragged herself downstairs. He looked up at her and smiled. 'Mummy! I drawed you a picture. It's you, me and George in the park.'

She could've wept.

'It's lovely, darling. Thank you.' She hugged him. 'I'll put it here on the fridge.' Where it would remind her never to be so stupid again and open her heart to the kind of man who would just let her down.

'And I drawed one for George.'

She couldn't dampen her little boy's enthusiasm by telling him that George had dumped her. 'Thank you. I'm sure he'll love it. I'll take it to work and give it to him,' she fibbed. Lying wasn't something she'd normally do, but she had no other choice unless she was prepared to hurt Ethan.

She'd spent five years being so, so careful, protecting his feelings from any hurt. And now she'd made a huge mistake that was going to have repercussions for him, too. She hated the fact that she'd been stupid enough to introduce her son to someone who had no intention of sticking around. She'd been such an idiot to fall for George. Like Jason, he just wasn't going to be there for her. Clearly she had rubbish judgement when it came to men.

Still, as hard as it was, she'd learned her lesson now.

She was better off on her own.

It was a miserable week. Serena grabbed a sandwich from the canteen every day and ate it while doing paperwork, to keep herself occupied and stop remembering those wonderful lunchtimes with George. She didn't even know the real reason why he'd dumped her, but she sure as hell wasn't going to be needy and ask him. It was over, and that was that.

'You're quiet,' Jess said in the middle of the week, during her morning break.

'Just tired.' And it wasn't a total fib. She hadn't slept properly all week. She'd been too miserable.

'Anything I can do?'

'No. I'm fine, honestly.' She faked a smile that she hoped Jess wouldn't question. 'And I'd better get back to my patients.'

Some of her regular patients had noticed that she was quiet, too. And so had her mother. Though Carolyn hadn't pushed her to talk about it. She'd just given Serena a hug and said, 'I love you.' And it had been touch and go for Serena not to burst into tears.

She pulled herself together as she called in her next patient, Jennie Roberts.

'I wasn't expecting my doctor to send me to a physiotherapist to treat my lymphoedema,' Jennie said. 'I mean, I've got the compression sleeve, and I know it'll take time for the swelling to go down.'

'The compression sleeve will help, yes, but I'm going to teach you something called simple lymphatic drainage,' Serena explained. 'The exercises will help you get the fluid out of the tissues and make your arm feel more comfortable. Then just keep wearing the sleeve, keep checking your skin, and go back to your GP if you see any problems.'

She taught Jennie some deep breathing exercises to help relax her, then showed her how to massage herself to help stretch the skin downwards from just below her ears and down into the hollows of her neck. 'Then you need to do some circular upward massage of your skin on the armpit of your left side—your right side is fine.' She worked through the massage technique with Jennie, then showed her how to massage the skin on her chest and abdomen upwards to her armpit. 'Finish off with some more of the deep breathing exercises, and do this every day, and you'll start to see a difference,' she said with a smile.

Maybe that was what she needed to do, too, she thought ruefully. Deep breathing, think about anything other than George, and do it every day until she started to see a difference. It would take time—a long time—but she'd do it.

George knew he'd done the right thing. He'd told himself that over and over and over again.

So why did it feel so wrong? Why did he miss Serena so much? Why did his lunch taste like ashes instead of sunshine, the way it had when he'd been with her?

He had to stop moping, move his life forward and make some plans for the estate, he told himself out loud.

But it didn't stop him missing Serena. *Desperately.*

Several times each day he nearly called her.

But he knew it would be the wrong thing. Because he couldn't offer her what she needed most. He knew he just wasn't enough. So he had to be fair to her. Leave her in peace. Let her find someone who deserved her and Ethan. Because he wasn't that man.

On the Thursday afternoon, Serena left the department and saw someone who looked like George walking down the corridor towards her. She shook herself. How stupid was she, thinking she saw him in places when it obviously wasn't him at all?

As she drew closer, her skin prickled.

It really was George.

And he was limping

Close up, he looked terrible, with deep shadows under his eyes. Was it because of the pain, or was he feeling bad about the way he'd dumped her?

He gave her an awkward smile. 'Hello.'

'I didn't expect to see you here.' She forced herself to be polite, even though she wanted to push him into a puddle for being so selfish and so stupid—and she was still angry with him for dumping her by text without even telling her what she'd done to make him change his mind about her. 'Are you back here for more physiotherapy?' Obviously he'd booked in with someone else, not with her.

'No. I was here for some other tests.'

'You were limping.'

He shrugged. 'I guess.'

She frowned. 'Have you hurt your leg again?'

'I'm fine.'

Then she realised that he hadn't been favouring the leg she'd given him treatment on and a really nasty thought hit her. 'Did you hurt yourself at the park on Saturday?'

He blew out a breath. 'Nothing much passes you, does it?'

'I can't book you in for treatment. If you need physio, you'll need a referral from your family doctor.' But guilt slammed into her. She shouldn't have taken him to the park, or at least not let him play football with Ethan or go on that wretched slide. Otherwise he wouldn't have hurt himself. She blew out a breath. 'If it's really hurting, I could take a look at it. Not *here*, obviously.'

'I don't deserve that.' He reached up and stroked his thumb underneath her eyes. 'You have shadows here. Did I do that?'

The gentleness of his touch almost made her cry. She lifted her chin. 'Don't flatter yourself. I'm not losing any sleep over you.' Even as she spoke, she knew he could see perfectly well that she was lying.

'I've missed you, Serena.' he said softly. 'I've missed you like hell. And sometimes I wonder if I'm the most stupid man in the universe.'

She'd missed him, too. Desperately. 'I can answer that. Yes, you probably *are* the most stupid man in the universe.' They'd had such potential, and he'd cut it off. Without telling her why. Her anger boiled over. 'You didn't even have the guts to dump me face to face.'

He sucked in a breath. 'I'm sorry. I didn't mean to hurt you.'

'You didn't. I'm absolutely fine,' she lied, lifting her chin and trying her best to fake it. 'It wouldn't have worked between us anyway. Better to end it now than let it drag on and get embarrassing.'

'I…' He sighed. 'Be happy, Serena.' He turned away, but not before she'd seen the pain in his eyes. Emotional or physical? She couldn't be sure. And it cut her to the quick.

'George, wait. You're in pain.' And, even though he'd hurt her and he'd let her down, she couldn't see him limp away. Not when she could do something about it. Being bitter and angry and resentful—that wasn't who she was. She *helped* people. Even if they'd hurt her, the way George had done.

'I'll live,' he said dryly. 'I'll call my GP tomorrow.'

'Tomorrow's Saturday. You won't get an appointment until next week, and you won't get a referral for however long after that.' She shook her head. 'Let me help you.'

He was silent for a long, long moment. Then he nodded. 'Thank you.'

'I need to sort something out first. Excuse me a second.'

She grabbed her mobile phone from her handbag and called her mother. 'Something's come up at work. I'll ring you when I'm on my way home. Sorry to ask, but can you give Ethan his tea for me?'

'Of course I can, love. Is everything all right?'

'It's just a patient who needs some help.' That much was almost true; George was an ex-patient, and he needed help. 'Everything's fine.' But that last bit was a total fib.

'Well, you can have dinner with us when you're done,' Carolyn said.

'Don't wait to eat with me, Mum,' Serena said hastily. 'I don't know how long I'm going to be. I'm happy to grab a sandwich or heat something through later. And thank you. I really appreciate you picking up the slack for me. I owe you.'

She ended the call and slipped her mobile phone back into her handbag, then looked at George. 'Is your place closer than mine?'

'Yes.'

'OK. I'll treat you there.'

She followed him in silence onto the Tube and then up the road to his flat. It was in a very exclusive-looking apartment block, which overlooked the river so it obviously had a huge price tag attached. And she noticed that his limp was worse as he walked up the stairs.

His flat turned out to be very much a bachelor pad. There were no feminine touches whatsoever. Everything was monochrome. He actually had white carpets; talk about high maintenance when it came to cleaning. She'd be worrying all the time in case Ethan spilled a glass of blackcurrant over the carpet and the stain wouldn't come out. This most definitely wasn't a child-friendly place.

She noticed that his TV was glossy, state-of-the-art stuff. George was clearly a man who loved gadgets, and she'd just bet that he updated his equipment the second it went out of date. His priorities were a million miles away from hers. He was a playboy who didn't have to care about anything other than his own gratification, and she needed to remember that.

'Can I get you a coffee or anything?' he asked.

'No, I'm fine.'

'I appreciate the offer of help,' he said. 'Especially as it was my own fault. I could see I was going down the slide too fast, and I tried to protect my bad leg.'

'So you took all the impact on your good leg.'

He nodded. 'I think I sprained my ankle.'

'Why didn't you tell me at the time?'

He shrugged. 'Because I'm an idiot, I guess.'

And because he'd been panicking, perhaps, thinking that she was trying to make him part of her family and start a real relationship with him? Emotionally, George was a disaster area. A complete mess. She knew he had commitment issues; he was a player, not the kind of man who'd settle down. A completely unsuitable prospect. So she had to be fair to him: half this mess was her own fault for not being realistic and for wanting more than they'd agreed.

'Where do you think the best place would be to look at my ankle?' he asked. 'The kitchen? The living room?'

The bedroom, so he could lie down. But that would be too much for her to handle. 'The living room's fine.'

He pulled the curtains and switched on the overhead light. 'OK. I know the drill. Jeans off, so you can look at my leg.'

She felt colour seep into her face and was furious with herself. This was a professional thing, not a personal one. She was a trained physiotherapist and she needed to act like one, not like a starstruck fool mooning over a man who'd made it very clear that there was no place for her and her son in his life. 'Actually, no.' Embarrassment made her voice a little more crisp than she'd intended. 'It's your ankle, so you don't need to take off your jeans. Just roll up the leg of your jeans to the knee and take off your sock.'

He did so, and she examined his ankle. 'There's some swelling and bruising. You obviously hit it fairly hard.'

'Yes.'

She bit her lip. 'Sorry.'

'Hey. It wasn't your idea to go down the slide. You said it was a bad idea, and I didn't listen. This is all down to me.'

Maybe. 'Is the swelling better than it was, or worse?'

'Better,' he said.

'Hmm. I need to see you walk. Can you walk across the room for me, and back again?'

She just about managed to keep it professional, not letting herself think of how that bare leg might feel tangled with hers, and watched his gait.

'OK, you can sit down now. You haven't broken anything, but you've damaged your ligaments.' She shook her head. 'You really should've gone to see your GP before now, to get treatment.'

'It felt like a sprain, not a break.'

'And you're the expert?' she asked caustically. 'Ligament damage can cause you real problems if it's not treated properly. You'll need to do some exercises to get your mobility back, though you must keep it gentle.'

'What do you suggest?'

'You can start by moving your foot up and down, as if pressing on a car pedal.'

'The accelerator, in my case?' he asked wryly.

She couldn't suppress a brief smile. 'Something like

that. Now circle your foot in a clockwise direction.' He did so. 'Now anticlockwise. Does it hurt?'

'A bit,' he admitted.

'Then you *must* take it steady. Don't force it, or you'll make things worse. You need to stretch your Achilles tendon without putting weight on it. The easiest way is to loop a towel under your foot and use it to pull your toes towards you. Just keep the reps gentle,' she instructed. 'Do a couple of minutes of those exercises at a time. You can do some heel and toe walking, too—a minute walking on your toes, then the same on your heels, then alternate heel and toes. Oh, and writing the alphabet in the air with your big toe is good, too.'

'How often?'

'Four times a day,' she said. 'Until you're better. So.' She shrugged. 'That's you sorted.'

'Thank you. It's more than I deserve.' He rolled down his trouser leg.

'I'd better go.'

'Serena.' He stood up and placed one hand on her shoulder. 'I'm sorry.'

'Me, too.' There was a huge lump in her throat. They could've been so good together. But he'd chosen to walk away from her. Just like Jason. She couldn't help the question. 'Why did you dump me?'

'Because I'm not good for you.'

She grimaced. 'I *hate* that. It's like when a teenage boy says "Oh, it's not you, it's me", to try and make the girl feel better—it doesn't work. She still feels dumped. And miserable.' Just how she'd been feeling since Saturday night.

'I'm sorry,' he said again.

She shook her head and blinked the tears back. 'Why do I get involved with emotionally constrained men?'

A muscle in his jaw tightened. 'I'm not your ex.'

'No, but you walked away from me completely out of the blue. I thought we'd had a nice day together. I thought...' Her voice faded. She wasn't admitting to *that*. How wrong she'd been, thinking that maybe George was starting to care about her, the way she'd started to care about him.

'I have...issues,' he said.

'And you won't talk about them.'

He sighed. 'No.'

'Then how on earth do you think you're ever going to resolve whatever those issues are, if you won't talk about them?'

'I have no idea.' He wrapped one arm round her waist and rested his cheek against hers, the way he'd stood with her at the concert. He didn't say another word; he just stood there, holding her close.

Serena had no idea which of them moved first, but then she was in his arms properly, and he was kissing her.

She knew they shouldn't be doing this—that this was a really, really stupid thing to do and it had no future whatsoever—but she couldn't help herself. Desire flickered through her veins, making her head spin.

When he broke the kiss, he was shaking. 'Serena, I know this isn't fair, but I want you more badly than I've ever wanted anything in my entire life.'

She knew that feeling.

This was her cue to be sensible. To say no and walk away.

She opened her mouth to say it, and the wrong word came out. 'Yes.'

CHAPTER TEN

GEORGE dipped his head and kissed Serena lightly. 'I'm so glad you said yes,' he said softly. 'Or I might just have imploded.'

Yeah. She knew that feeling. And even though she had huge, huge doubts about whether this was the right thing to do, there was no way she could stop herself. She *needed* this.

He took her hand and led her out of the living room, down the corridor to his bedroom. It overlooked the river, she noticed, and the lights from the buildings along the bank were reflected in the dark water. She'd just bet it looked amazing first thing in the morning, with sunlight sparkling on the river.

He kept hold of her hand as he closed the curtains and switched the bedside light on. His bed was huge, with deep pillows and a fluffy duvet and a wrought-iron frame.

'Don't look so worried,' he said.

She dragged in a breath. 'You should probably know that it's been a while since I last did this.'

'It doesn't matter. But if I do anything that makes you feel uncomfortable, just tell me and I'll stop,' he said gently. 'Right now, all I want to do is to make you feel good. To give you pleasure. Lots and lots of pleasure.'

He traced the outline of her lower lip with the pad of his thumb, and her lips parted automatically.

She wanted him so much, she was actually quivering with need.

He undid her shirt slowly, button by button, stroking every centimetre of skin he uncovered. 'Gorgeous,' he whispered, and pushed the soft cotton off her shoulders. 'Your skin's so soft, so touchable. You're beautiful, Serena.'

She flushed. 'Right now, I don't feel it. I'm wearing serviceable underwear.' Beige and plain. Sensible knickers. How bad could this get?

He frowned. 'You've lost me.'

'The first time for you and me, it was meant to be the pretty stuff, all lace.' Except she'd never had the chance to wear it for him. And it definitely wasn't the kind of stuff she wore to work. She was thirty years old, sensible and *boring*.

He smiled and brushed his mouth against hers. 'You still look gorgeous to me, lace or no lace. But, since you obviously have issues about your underwear, the best thing we can do right now is to get rid of it.' He stole another kiss. 'And let me tell you that the idea of having you naked and in my bed *really* works for me.'

He unclipped her bra and let it drop to the floor. She shivered as he cupped her breasts and teased her nipples with the pads of his thumbs. Her skin was tingling; she wanted so much more than this. It must've shown in her face, because he stooped to kiss the hollow of her collarbones; then he moved lower, took one nipple into his mouth and sucked. She gasped and slid her fingers into his hair, urging him on.

Then she felt him flinch and pulled away. 'George. Your leg.'

'I'm fine.' He sucked in a breath. 'Or I will be, once I'm inside you.'

His words sent a kick of desire through her. That was what she wanted, too.

Except, right now, it wasn't equal. 'I'm naked to the waist, and you're…' Fully clothed. Practically unruffled. Not even a button out of place.

He smiled. 'I'm entirely in your hands. Do what you will with me.'

How could she resist an offer like that?

George was wearing a plain white shirt. Expensive designer stuff, no doubt, so she resisted the temptation to rip his shirt open and undid the buttons carefully. She untucked his shirt from his jeans, revealing his muscular chest and flat abdomen. She couldn't resist skating her hands over his pecs and down over his stomach; it made his lips part and he gave a sigh of pure pleasure.

And what a thrill it was to know that she could affect someone as gorgeous as George Somers in this way.

'Serena. You drive me crazy. I need you now,' he said fiercely, and dragged her back into his arms, kissing her.

She had no idea who finished undressing whom, but when he finally stopped kissing her she realised that they were both naked.

'I would do the caveman thing,' he said, 'but…' He grimaced, and looked down at the bruising round his ankle.

Yeah. She'd love him to do the caveman thing, too, pick her up and carry her to his bed. But the physiotherapist in her woke up. 'That's totally not a sensible thing to do when you've got a sprained ankle. And I'm not exactly a featherweight, either,' she said wryly.

'You're definitely not fat, Serena. But I'm glad you're all curves. Glorious curves. I love your curves.' He slid his hand down her sides, moulding the flats of his palms to her curves. 'Delicious. You feel so good. And, just in case you're in any doubt about how much I want you...' He kissed her again, drawing her close to his body and pressing the flat of her palm over the left side of his chest so she could feel how his heart was thudding.

She was actually making his pulse race.

He pulled the duvet aside and patted the sheet. 'Just pretend I carried you, OK?'

Macho to the end. Serena couldn't help smiling as she sat down and lay back against the pillows.

Wow. Lying on his mattress was like floating. The pillows were the softest and deepest she'd ever touched, and his sheets were incredibly soft.

His hands were soft, too, and very sure as he lay beside her and touched her. He slid one hand between her thighs; his finger skated along her sex and the action made her shiver.

'Do you like that?' he asked softly.

She nodded, barely able to speak.

He did it again, and again, until she felt completely boneless and closed her eyes, giving herself up to the pure pleasure of his touch.

She felt the mattress give, and opened her eyes to see him standing in the middle of the room. Had he changed his mind? Was that why he'd left the bed?

Again, the question must've shown on her face, because he said softly, 'We need a condom,' and retrieved one from his wallet. He ripped the packet open and slid the latex along his shaft.

And then he climbed back onto the bed, shifting so that he was kneeling between her thighs. There was a sparkle in those beautiful blue eyes.

'Now, where were we?' he asked huskily.

In answer, she reached up to kiss him.

'That's better,' he said when she broke the kiss. 'Look at me, Serena.'

His eyes were dark and intense with passion. She couldn't help a gasp of pleasure as he fitted the tip of his penis to her entrance and pushed, filling her completely.

'OK?' he asked softly, concern etched into his face.

She nodded. 'OK. Very OK.'

He smiled. 'Good.' He began to move, then, stoking the pitch of her desire with every thrust, taking her closer and closer to the edge. She closed her eyes again, focusing on the pleasure he made her feel.

But then she felt his muscles tense and opened her eyes. 'George?'

'I'm fine.'

She knew he wasn't being completely honest—and why. 'Is your leg hurting?'

'I'm fine,' he repeated.

She knew he wasn't. She reached up to kiss him. 'Don't be brave on my account. And especially not for this.' She stroked his face. 'Not when I have a better idea.'

His eyes narrowed. 'A better idea?'

'Lie down,' she whispered.

The tension in his face vanished as he eased out of her. 'I do believe, Serena James, that you might just be a bad girl under all that brisk professionalism.'

Being a bad girl.

She could do that. Right here, right now. Because she wanted George more than she'd ever wanted anyone in her whole life.

He rolled over and lay back against the pillows. She straddled him, slid one hand between them to position him more easily, and gently lowered herself onto him.

'Oh, now that's good,' he breathed. 'Seriously good. You feel amazing.'

Encouraged, she tightened her muscles round him.

He groaned. 'Better still. And what a view.' He reached up to play with her breasts. 'Your skin's so soft.'

She splayed her hands against his chest, enjoying the feel of the scattering of dark hair against her fingertips. He was gorgeous. And all hers. Right here, right now.

And then she was coming, harder and faster than she thought was possible.

As her muscles tightened round him, he sat up, wrapped his arms round her and held her close, his mouth jammed over hers to swallow her cry of pleasure. She felt the answering surge of his own climax. And there was no more need for words; they simply held each other and let it all wash over them.

When Serena had climbed off him and he was about to deal with the condom, George looked down. 'Oh, hell.'

'What?'

'The condom. It broke.' He grimaced. 'I'm sorry.'

Her eyes went wide with worry. 'The condom broke? Oh, my God. I'm not on the Pill or anything.' She swallowed hard. 'I'd better call into the nearest pharmacy and get the morning-after pill.'

'Whatever happens, I'll stand by you,' he said awkwardly.

She shook her head. 'I don't need anyone to stand by me. I managed just fine with Ethan.'

Not that she'd had a choice in the matter, George knew. Her fiancé had decided that he couldn't cope with being a father and had simply left her to it.

He wanted to tell her this was different. He wanted to tell her that he *wanted* to stand by her. Right at that second, he could imagine their child—a little girl with his own dark hair and Serena's stunning green eyes—toddling after Ethan in the gardens at Somers Hall, the way that his little sister Alice had always toddled after him.

Christ, he wanted this so much that it was like a physical pain. And it scared him spitless.

Except it wasn't going to happen. Not like this.

And he owed it to Serena to tell her the rest of it. To give her the reassurance she needed.

'Actually, there's a very good chance that you won't need any support whatsoever,' he said carefully, trying to keep his tone as neutral as possible. No way did he want her to guess his feelings about this.

'What? Why?' She looked completely confused.

'Let me deal with this, and I'll explain.' He went to the bathroom and dealt with the broken condom. Even though he didn't dawdle, he discovered that Serena was almost fully dressed again when he went back into the bedroom; she was sitting on the bed, buttoning up her shirt.

And he was buck naked. Not good.

He grabbed his jeans and pulled them on. It wasn't perfect, but it'd have to do.

'So what did you mean just now?' she asked.

He took in a deep breath. This really wasn't the time and place he'd intended to have this conversation with her. But, in the circumstances, he didn't have a choice. 'Shall I make us some coffee?'

She shook her head. 'I need to get home.'

And he couldn't stall any longer. He sighed and sat on the bed next to her. 'OK. We didn't actually need the condom just now.' And he had to say the words. Out loud. The words that took away his future. 'I can't have children naturally. At least, not without a great deal of medical intervention.'

She stared at him. 'Why not?'

'When I hit the cliff.' He closed his eyes for a moment, but he couldn't block it out. He still had the occasional nightmare about the moment of impact; could still hear that sickening thud, feel the pain ripping through his body. 'It wasn't just broken bones. The impact was on my testes, as well. It's damaged my fertility. That was why I was at the hospital today. I'd had more tests, to see if the situation had changed.'

She waited, saying nothing.

'And it hasn't.' He swallowed hard. 'So the bottom line is, if we produced a baby because of this, it'd be a miracle.' He might as well spell it out for her. 'Actually, we could make love every day without any protection for the next three years, and it'd still be a miracle if you fell pregnant.'

'Your fertility's that low? Oh, George.' She looked shocked, and then sympathetic. 'I'm sorry. That's rough on you.'

It would be rough on anyone. But for someone who was supposed to produce an heir, the future seventeenth Lord Somers... Yeah, it was rough. George still hadn't quite come to terms with it. The thing he'd been putting off, thinking that he had all the time in the world... and now it turned out that he didn't. That, when it came down to it, he'd failed.

'I don't need your pity,' he warned.

'It's not pity. It's sympathy. I don't know what to say right now.' She blew out a breath. 'Except I think we might both need this.' She slid her arms round him and held him close.

He appreciated the hug. She was right. He really needed the warmth of her arms round him.

But he couldn't duck out of the issue. He had to be fair to her. 'So where do we go from here?' he asked.

She pulled away and was silent for a long, long moment, then shook her head. 'I don't know. What happened just now—it probably shouldn't have. We're not together.'

Because he'd been an idiot. He'd panicked and dumped her, instead of talking it through with her. Would she give him another chance? 'We could be,' he said.

She shook her head. 'Don't start something you can't follow through, George. It's not fair to any of us. You're not looking for a relationship.' She dragged in a breath. 'I think it's best if I go now. And I—I'll be in touch. To let you know about…consequences.'

He already knew there wouldn't be any consequences.

And this was it.

It was over.

She was walking out on him. And he knew from experience that there was nothing he could say to make her stay. Nothing he could do, except watch her leave.

Nothing.

CHAPTER ELEVEN

SERENA walked back to the Tube station, concentrating on putting one foot after the other. But when she was sitting down on the train, she had time to think. To wonder. Had she been unfair to George? He'd looked absolutely devastated when he'd told her that he couldn't have children.

Was that the real reason why he'd pushed her away on Saturday? Because he thought she wanted more children, and he wouldn't be able to give them to her? Or was it because she already had a child, so spending time with a child who wasn't his, and knowing that he would never have children of his own, felt like rubbing salt in the wound?

The more she thought about it, the more she wondered.

Should she have given him more of a chance?

OK, so he was the one who'd dumped her, but it hadn't made him happy. Far from it. And she wasn't happy about the situation, either. She'd missed him.

Maybe she should've put her pride aside and gone to see him on Monday, then asked him to look her in the eye and tell her that he didn't want her. Because she was pretty sure he wouldn't have been able to do it. Given what had just happened between them, she was absolutely convinced that he wanted her as much as she wanted him.

But would being with George make either of them happy?

She knew what she wanted. A man she could rely on. Someone who'd love her all the way back. Someone who'd love Ethan as much as she did despite the fact that he was another man's child. Someone who'd support her career and not expect hers to come second to his all the time.

Could George tick all those boxes?

More to the point, did he want to?

And what did he want from a life partner? Did he even want a life partner?

There were too many questions; and she was too tired and too miserable to come up with any answers.

She called in to the pharmacy on the way to her parents' house to buy the morning-after pill, just to be sure. Sensible Serena. Ha. What she'd just done with George had been very far from sensible. And it had changed things between them. What she'd thought was all done and dusted was all up in the air again; and she had no idea how things were going to settle.

When she walked into her parents' kitchen, Carolyn smiled at her. 'Hello, love. Is everything OK with your patient?'

'Sure,' Serena fibbed. And now she felt really bad. She really had intended just to treat George's injuries. To keep it platonic and professional. But neither of them had been able to keep their hands off the other. And there was no way she could possibly tell her mother the truth: that she'd shirked her responsibilities to her child so she could go to bed with George. Guilt slammed through her. How could she have been so reckless? And so unfair to her parents and her son?

'Let me get you something to eat,' Carolyn said.

Serena shook her head. 'Thanks, but I'm not really hungry, Mum.' That was true. Guilt had taken away her appetite. 'I'm just a bit tired.' That was an excuse, and she hoped that her mother couldn't see straight through it. 'Plus I really ought to get Ethan home. It's getting on for his bedtime, and he's got school tomorrow.' She hugged her mother. 'Thanks for looking after him for me. And I'm sorry for making everything last-minute.'

'These things happen. Are you all right?'

'Sure I am,' she fibbed. 'Just tired.' And heartsick. And wondering what George was doing right now. And cross with herself for being so pathetic.

She took Ethan home and settled him to bed. Then she read through the leaflet of the morning-after pill before gulping it down with a glass of water. There was a long list of side effects; she just hoped that she wasn't sick within the next three hours, or it wouldn't work. Though, according to George, she probably wouldn't need it anyway because he was practically infertile.

She woke in the night, feeling nauseous and with a stomach ache. Well, she'd half expected some side effects. She sat up for a while, sipping a glass of water, until she felt better. Part of her wondered what George was doing now. Was he awake, too, thinking about what had happened between them and wishing that things were different?

But, then, it was really none of her business. They weren't together any more. He'd let her walk out of his life. Once her period had started and she could tell him for definite that he was off the hook, she'd never see him again. Except in the pages of the gossip magazines, squiring his usual tall, rail-thin blondes.

And why did that hurt so much?

George could still smell Serena's perfume on his pillows, even though he'd changed his sheets and pillowcases.

Oh, great. He wasn't going to get any sleep in his bed, that was for sure. Because he wouldn't be able to stop thinking about her, every time he turned over and smelled her perfume.

In the end he dragged himself over to the sofa in the living room, ran through a set of the physiotherapy exercises Serena had taught him, then switched on his games console and loaded up one of his favourite games.

Except that didn't help, either.

It wasn't as if he could go and do one of his usual thrill-seeking things to keep his mind occupied—not with a pin in one leg and a sprain in the other ankle. Which increased his frustration even more. He was stuck, with nothing to do except think. And brood.

George was out of sorts for the whole of the next day. He couldn't settle to anything.

Don't start something you can't follow through. Serena's words echoed in his head.

She had a point. And he hadn't exactly followed through, had he? He'd let his experience with Rebecca get in the way. He'd let Serena walk out without fighting for her. Without giving them a real chance.

Serena wasn't Rebecca. She was older; she had different life experiences and a different family background—one that was supportive and loving rather than judgemental. Yes, there were huge differences between his background and hers; but that didn't necessarily mean they wouldn't be able to find some sort of compromise. He liked her family. He was pretty sure she'd like his.

And, now he thought about it, she'd seemed to understand about the barony thing. She'd realised that it felt as if it took all his choices away. Maybe, just maybe, she understood him. Maybe, just maybe, this was his chance to have a real relationship—not the short, sweet but ultimately unsatisfying flings he'd had over the last few years.

He'd been the one to back away. Which meant that he had to be the one to see if they could fix this.

He glanced at his watch. With any luck, by the time he got to her house, Ethan would be asleep and he could speak freely with her. Find out how she felt. Find out if they had a chance. Determined, he pulled on his shoes, locked his door behind him, and left for the Tube.

Serena's phone beeped.

Odd. She wasn't expecting a text. She picked up her phone and flicked into the messaging screen.

It was from George. She frowned. Why was he texting her?

She opened the message. *Is Ethan asleep?*

It was an odd question. Or perhaps he wanted to call her and was checking first that she was free to talk. She couldn't think that they had anything to say to each other, but she texted back, *Yes.*

Her phone beeped again. *Good. I'm at the front door.*

What? At *her* front door? Right now? But why was he here? Surely they'd said everything last night?

Not quite believing it, she walked to the front door and opened it. George was standing there.

'What do you want?' she asked.

'To talk to you.' He sounded wary, and there was tension in his face.

She shook her head. 'We said it all, last night.'

'No, we didn't. Not by a long way. Can I come in?'

Serena swallowed hard. She knew this could end up being a huge mistake. But that tension in his face was on the edge of pain. And, God help her, she still wanted him.

'All right.' She stood aside and let him come in. 'Do you want a coffee?'

'No, I'm fine.' He paused. 'Did you manage to get the morning-after pill?'

She nodded grimly. 'I took it last night.'

'I read up on it today. It's not always effective. It depends where you are on your cycle.' Then he grimaced. 'Not that you probably needed it, in any case.'

'Why are you here, George?'

'Because...' He took a deep breath. 'Serena, I've behaved incredibly badly towards you, and I'm sorry. You're right about me being emotionally constrained. I don't even always tell Ed everything. He practically had to drag it out of me about the DNA stuff—and even then, I probably wouldn't have said anything if I hadn't had the accident.' He sighed. 'You're right. I should talk about my issues.'

'Is that why you're here? To talk to me about them?'

'No. I'm here because I miss you. I...' He shook his head, looking dazed. 'Since I was twenty, I've always kept my relationships short and sweet.'

'We agreed that we weren't having a relationship. Just fun.'

'It's turned into more than that for me,' he said softly.

'A lot more. I'm not being arrogant, but I think it's the same for you, too.'

Yes. It was. Though she wasn't quite prepared to admit that yet.

'I don't exactly have a good track record, and it spooks the hell out of me that I actually want a relationship with someone. I hate this feeling of not having a clue what I'm doing. I know you've been badly hurt before and I don't want to let you down, the way your ex did.' His eyes were dark with sincerity. 'I know I'm probably going to make a complete mess of things, because—well, this isn't how I normally do things. But I know one thing without any doubt whatsoever. Hurting my ankle means I've been stuck in one place and I've had time to think about what I really want from life. I want a proper, grown-up relationship.' He took a deep breath. 'And I want it with *you*. I'm miserable without you, Serena. I need you in my life.'

She lifted her chin. 'I come as a package.'

'I know you do. That isn't an issue.'

'Isn't it?' She looked him straight in the eye. 'Did you back off because of Ethan?'

George knew he had to be totally honest with Serena about this, if they were to stand a chance. 'Yes and no. No, not because I didn't want to be bothered with him or because I've got any ridiculous hang-ups about taking on someone else's child—neither of those are true. You already know I grew up with a stepmother, and Frances is brilliant.' He shook his head in wonder. 'How the hell she put up with me when I was a stroppy six-year-old, I'll never know. I was horrible. But she persevered with me, and I'm glad she did.'

'That was the no. What about the yes?'

He blew out a breath. 'I've never talked to anyone about this. Ever. Even to Ed.'

'Then maybe it's time you did.'

'You're right. Will you let me hold you while I talk?' He bit his lip. 'Oh, I hate sounding so needy. That isn't me but with you, I feel grounded. I can be still.'

'And that scares you too, doesn't it?' she asked.

'Not half as much as your perception,' he admitted. 'It feels as if you can see right through me.'

Her expression softened. 'Come and sit down. Talk to me.'

George followed her into the living room. If he was going to be sensible about this, he'd sit next to her on the sofa. But that wasn't enough. To hell with being sensible. If he was going to let those words come out, he needed her in his arms. He scooped her up and settled her on his lap. 'That's better.'

'So why did you back off from Ethan?' she asked.

'Because I could see myself in him. I was in that same situation, the child of a single parent, and I hated all the women who tried to hit on my dad and become the next Lady Somers after my mother walked out. It wasn't just that piano teacher—there were loads of them, at Ed's nursery and my primary school, all batting their eyelashes at him and trying to get his attention. And I was about Ethan's age when it happened, so I've got a pretty good idea how he must feel about me barging in on your lives.'

'Not necessarily.' Serena shook her head. 'Firstly, you didn't hit on me in front of him, like those women did on you. I told him you were my friend. And, secondly…' She wriggled off his lap.

Panic flooded through him. 'Serena?'

'There's something I need to show you. Something

you need to see. Give me a second.' She went over to her handbag, took out a folded piece of paper, then handed it to him.

It was a child's drawing—clearly Ethan's—of three stick people, a slide and a swing.

'That's us at the park,' she said softly. 'He drew one for me; it's on my fridge. And then he drew one for you. So I think that gives you a pretty good idea what he thinks. If he didn't like you, he wouldn't have drawn you in a picture—and he certainly wouldn't have drawn the three of us together in a picture for you.'

George's eyes were stinging. 'He drew a picture of us for me.' He couldn't quite take this in. 'The three of us, in the park. I…' He shook his head, trying to clear it. 'When did he do this?'

'The morning after you texted me. I got up to find him drawing at the kitchen table. And then he gave me that for you.'

Guilt slammed into him. How wrong he'd got this whole thing. 'He drew a picture of us for me,' George said again. But he really couldn't get his head round this. He'd found it next to impossible to open his heart to anyone taking his mother's place. How could Ethan possibly be OK with someone planning to step into his absent father's place—or, worse still, threatening his own place in his mother's heart?

He needed to explain this to Serena. Somehow. 'Kids see things differently. I didn't want Ethan to feel that I was trying to take his place in your heart. I didn't want him to feel pushed out, the way I'd felt pushed out when I was his age.'

She stroked his face. 'George, that was never in question. Of course you can't take Ethan's place in my heart.

But don't you know that love stretches? That there's room for more than one person?'

He couldn't answer that.

She shook her head. 'For goodness' sake. You're the oldest of five. Your family didn't start loving you a bit less every time another baby came along, did they?'

'No. That isn't what I mean. I'm...' He sighed. 'I told you I was no good at this stuff.' He gave her a bitter smile. 'I'm going to go down in history as the feckless baron in our family. Reckless.'

'For how long have your family been barons?' she asked.

'A few hundred years.' He shrugged. 'Dad's the fifteenth baron.'

'Then I bet there are people in your family history who really *were* feckless. Who squandered a fortune on cards or what have you.'

He smiled, despite himself. 'Scientific experiments, actually—we have a Victorian forebear who thought himself an inventor, though he didn't actually have a clue, and he practically emptied the coffers. And then there was a great-grandfather who lost a lot in the Wall Street Crash.'

'Do you play the stock market?'

He shook his head. 'I don't do cards, either. Or casinos. They bore me.'

'So your recklessness is limited to throwing yourself off mountains, driving a vintage car too fast with the top down, and...' She smiled and sat back on his lap again. 'There are worse things you could do, George.'

It was the best cue she could've given him. He could get past this lump in his throat caused by her little boy's drawing. He could be George the Entertainer, the way he usually was, making everyone smile and at the same time deflecting any views into his soul. Smiling, he launched into a falsetto version of 'There Are Worse Things I Could Do'.

She raised an eyebrow. 'I didn't have you down as a *Grease* fan.'

'I'm not. Anyway, how did you know that's from *Grease*?'

'Dad and the head of drama put on a production at school every year. They alternate between *Grease*, *Oliver* and *Joseph*, so over the years I've got to know all the songs pretty well,' she explained. 'So who's the *Grease* fan?'

'Alice. It's her guilty pleasure.' He rolled his eyes. 'She makes me take her for her birthday every single year. In London, if it's playing; otherwise I have to find out where it is on tour and book tickets there.'

She smiled. 'For someone who's meant to be so bossy and scary, it sounds to me as if your sister has a real soft side.'

He smiled back. 'She does. Though she'd skewer anyone who suggested it.'

'So what do your other sisters make you do?'

He wasn't sure he liked where this was going, and parried it with a question of his own. 'What makes you think they nag me into anything?'

'Because I think you have a soft side, too. And I think you love your family very, very much. And I think that if anyone suggested that to you in public, you'd put on your best aristocratic drawl and pretend that you were completely bored and above all that sort of thing.'

Panic skittering through him—how had she managed to know him so well?—he drawled, 'Whatever.'

It didn't put her off the scent at all. 'So what do you do for your other sisters' birthdays?'

He sighed. She really wasn't going to give up, was she? He could try to sidetrack her, but she'd come straight back to this and ask again. He gave in. 'For Bea, it's the best art exhibition of the year in London. It's officially her birthday treat, but she likes going to the very first day of the exhibition, even if it's not actually on her birthday.'

'And I bet you use every contact you have to make sure you get that ticket.'

He did. Though wild horses wouldn't drag that admission from him.

'What about your youngest sister, the one who speaks to everyone in Latin?'

'Charlie likes a weekend up in Northumbria, walking along Hadrian's Wall. If it's snowing, so much the better.'

'And Ed?'

'Lunch in Paris.' George smiled. 'It always involves Michelin stars. He refuses to admit it, but he's such a foodie.'

She chuckled. 'Says you.'

He spread his hands. 'I don't mind admitting I like good food. I just don't happen to cook it myself.'

Her next question floored him. 'What do they do for your birthday?'

He didn't want to answer that. Instead, he kissed her.

'George, don't try to put me off. You said you'd talk to me, and I'm holding you to that.' She looked him straight in the eye. 'What do they do for you?'

He shrugged. 'I don't celebrate birthdays.'

'Why not?'

'I guess I'm like Peter Pan. I don't want to grow up.'

She didn't look as if she believed a word of it. 'Why do you push your brother and sisters away?'

He frowned. 'I don't push them away. I just don't do birthdays.'

'How old were you when it happened?'

Panic lanced through him. How could she possibly know? 'I have absolutely no idea what you're talking about.'

'Something happened,' she said. 'You had a really, really horrible birthday. And you were small when it happened. That's why you don't celebrate. Because it brings back the bad memories.'

'I…' His throat closed up.

'Was that when your mum left?'

He blew out a breath. 'Hell. Are you sure you're in the right job? Newspapers would pay you millions to ferret out stuff for them. Or are you a reincarnation of the chief Spanish Inquisitioner?'

'I'm taking that as a yes.' She leaned forward and kissed him. 'It sounds to me as if your mother was a very, very unhappy woman. Maybe she was ill. Because I would walk barefoot through flames for Ethan. I can't imagine anything that would ever, ever make me leave my son—not unless I wasn't in my right mind. It'd be like tearing out my heart and throwing it away. And to leave you… George, she must've been ill. That's the only reason why she could've done it. Especially on your birthday.'

He shook his head. 'She was looking for something that Dad, Ed and I couldn't give her. We weren't enough for her and she didn't love us. She only married Dad for the title. I know she was unhappy.' He sighed. 'And then she went from lover to lover, always looking for something she couldn't find. She never settled with anyone.'

Much like himself. And that was another thing. He was Zara's child. He'd inherited fifty per cent of her genes. Supposing this restlessness was genetic? Supposing he made a family with Serena and Ethan and he got bored and dumped them—hurt them the way Zara had hurt him, Ed and David? Panic flooded through him.

Serena held him close. 'It wasn't *you*,' she said softly. 'She left because she was unhappy. Not because you weren't enough.'

'You scare me,' he said. 'You see right into my head.'

'You're not the man you think you are,' she said. 'Or the man you try to make everyone think you are. Do you want to know my theory?'

'No,' he said with resignation, 'but I have a feeling you're going to tell me anyway.'

She nodded. 'You're a man with so much love to give. And you're scared of giving it in case the person you give it to throws it away, the way your mother did. Even though you're clearly very close to your family, and you go to huge lengths to make their birthdays special, you put yourself in the background because underneath it all you think you won't be enough for them. And that's why you won't let them make a fuss of you.' She paused. 'And that's why they all nag you. Because they love you and it drives them absolutely insane that you won't let them close.'

'I do let them close. I tell them I love them, and they know I mean it. You heard me say it on the phone to Ed.'

'But when they say it back to you, George, they know you don't believe them.'

He could hardly breathe. She'd arrowed in on absolutely everything.

'You're enough for them, George,' she said softly. 'They love you for who you are. They worry about you because you're always doing something dangerous, because you can't sit still. And I think you can't sit still because you fear that, if you do, you won't like what you see.'

'I already know I don't like what I see.' He looked away. 'I told you, I have a reckless personality. I spend my life schmoozing.'

'No. You're gorgeous, George. You like having fun. And you like making other people have fun. You put sunshine into people's lives. You listen to people and you take notice—like with those chocolates you gave me. That's what you said when you gave them to me— that you liked putting a little bit of sunshine into people's days. I think that's what your vocation is. Making people have fun.' She stole a kiss. 'You know what? You won't go down in history as reckless. Not at all. You'll be the Sunshine Baron.'

He felt as if something was cracking inside him. 'Serena, I want you so much. And I'm terrified that I can't be the man you want me to be.'

'How do you know you're not that man already?'

'Because.' *Tell her about Rebecca.* Except he couldn't make the words come out.

'Because what?' she prompted gently.

'There was someone.' He swallowed hard. 'Someone I fell for. At university. She wasn't from—well, my world.' Just like Serena wasn't. 'But I loved her and I thought she loved me.'

'What happened?'

'I took her home. I thought she'd enjoy the New Year ball my parents always throw. But Rebecca hated it.' He sighed. 'I guess some of our set asked too many questions—who her parents were, where she was from, that kind of thing. I told her to ignore them because it wasn't any of their business and it didn't bother me.'

'But it bothered her?' Serena asked softly.

George nodded. 'She felt that people were judging her. Not my parents—my family's great. But I guess we're part of a wider social set. And she said she couldn't give up her life for me. I wasn't asking her to do that—of *course* I wasn't, I'm not so selfish that I'd ignore her needs—but she refused to compromise.' He blew out a breath. Could Serena compromise? Or would she, too, feel that he was expecting her to give up everything for him? 'I told her the baronial stuff was just a label and I was just a normal, ordinary man, but she said you couldn't separate it out—the baronial stuff was what made me who I am.'

'Fair point,' Serena said.

So it *was* an issue for her, too. 'Maybe,' he said carefully. Where was she going with this?

'I'm the daughter of two teachers. That's part of who I am,' she said softly, stroking his face. 'And you're the son of a baron. You grew up with—well, privilege, I guess.'

He grimaced. 'That's what she said. She said she loved me too much to make me unhappy, and then she walked out on me. She wouldn't even let me drive her home or back to Oxford or wherever she wanted to go; instead, she insisted on getting a taxi to the station.' And how shocked and hurt he'd been. How could you tell someone you loved them and then leave them? It'd felt as if she'd been making excuses. She'd changed her mind about wanting to be with him. *It's not you, it's me.* 'When term started again...well, she made it clear she didn't want to see me any more.'

And here he was about to take that same risk again. With someone not from his world. With someone who was older, wiser, stronger—but someone who still might not be able to cope with all the razzamatazz.

'How old were you?' she asked gently.

'Twenty.'

'Young enough for it to feel like the end of the world. I'm sorry she broke your heart.'

'It happens. You had it tougher than I did.' He sighed. 'It just feels that the barony stuff always gets in the way. Women either see me as a ticket to a glamorous life, or they think they can't fit in. There doesn't seem to be anything in between.' He gave her a bleak look. 'I'm over her.'

'Are you? You haven't got involved with anyone seriously since then, have you?'

'No, but I stopped loving her a long time ago.' He sighed. 'But that's not the real issue, not any more. There's something more important than that. I can't give you a family, Serena. I can't give you a brother or sister for Ethan. Not without a hell of a lot of medical help, and even then there's no guarantee that it'll work—I know people who've put themselves through several rounds of IVF and it's destroyed them, all the waiting and the longing and the hope and then absolutely nothing at the end.' He gritted his teeth. 'I absolutely will *not* put you through that.'

She stroked his face. 'Ask me what I want you to be.'

He couldn't. It felt as if his throat was filled with glue. He hadn't been enough for his mother to stay; and he hadn't been enough for Rebecca to see past the baronial circus. How could he be enough for Serena?

'Ask me, George,' she said softly.

'I'm not that brave,' he admitted.

'You can jump off cliffs and throw yourself down double black diamond ski runs and go on the fastest, scariest roller-coasters—things it would scare me spit-less to do—but you can't ask me one little question?'

He couldn't say a word.

She took his hand, pressed a kiss into the palm, curled his fingers over it. 'Then I'll tell you anyway. First, just so you know, I couldn't care less about a title or what have you. Yes, that's a part of you—but only a small part.'

He couldn't quite believe what she was saying. What she was offering. Was he hearing things because he wanted this so much?

'I want you to be *you*,' she said softly. 'Yes, I admit, I'd prefer not to have my heart in my mouth every time you do something thrill-seeking—even the slide in the playground terrified me, so heaven knows how I'll feel about you launching yourself down a difficult ski run on some impossible mountain—but I know you need the adrenalin rush. I'd rather be there when you do the mad stuff, worrying myself sick about you, than to see you with your wings clipped, trying to be something you're not and hating the life you've been stuck with.'

Worrying herself sick. And he knew he'd already hurt her. If he had a lump in his throat at Ethan's pic-ture, how must she have felt? Especially as the little boy had drawn it the morning after *he* had broken it off between them. 'I let you down.' Just as his mother had let him down. If that was who he was, then he had the potential to hurt Serena even more. And he'd rather cut off his right arm than do that.

'I let you down just as much,' she said softly. 'I knew you had issues about commitment, and I still pushed you into something you weren't ready for—something that made you panic and push me away.'

A tear leaked down her face, and he brushed it away with the pad of his thumb. 'Don't cry.'

'Says you.' She rubbed her thumb gently across his eyelashes. 'Your eyes are wet, too.'

'I know,' he admitted. 'And I never cry. Ever.' At least, not since his mother had walked out. And the night when Alice was two and he thought his little sister might die in hospital. 'I can't explain how I feel right now. I don't have the words. I just—I want to crack a joke or do something wild. Fly a plane, tackle the surf in Hawaii, ski down the hardest slope in the world.'

'Like a bird in a cage,' she said. 'I don't want to trap you.'

And that was the weird thing. He wanted to run—but, more than that, he wanted to stay. 'You're not trapping me.' He dragged in a breath. 'Will you give me another chance? This scares the hell out of me, but I want to make a go of it with you, Serena. I want a proper relationship, where we go out together on dates and we don't care who sees us. And I don't mean just with you. I want days out with Ethan, too. I want us to take him to the zoo and the aquarium, to see the dinosaurs and the big blue whale at the National History museum, to go swimming and to the park. I want us to do all the fun things that families do together.' He moistened suddenly dry lips. 'I might not be much good at it at first, but I'll pay attention and I'll learn. And, until I learn, I'll do my best to get it right.'

'Your best will be enough. *You're* enough, George.'

He knew right then that he loved Serena. He wasn't ready to tell her that, yet—he'd already opened more than enough of his heart up to her tonight—but he loved her. And he was going to make this work, whatever it took.

CHAPTER TWELVE

THE following evening, Serena invited George over for pizza with Ethan. It was much earlier than George usually ate his evening meal, but he was willing to make the change to accommodate the little boy. And he was surprised by how much fun he had, teaching Ethan how to draw a cartoon dog.

He talked Serena into playing the piano for him. Just as he'd thought, she played beautifully.

'Now I really need to put that pizza in the oven, or we'll starve,' she said, smiling.

'Mummy tells me that you play the piano, too,' George said to Ethan.

The little boy nodded. 'I played "Happy Birthday to You" on her birthday. And Granddad taught me a new song last week.'

'Would you play it for me?' George asked.

Ethan beamed, and played 'Twinkle Twinkle Little Star'.

'That was great.' George clapped. 'Can I sing along with you next time?'

'Come and play.' Ethan shifted up on the piano stool and patted the seat beside him.

'I can't play,' George said.

'I'll teach you. Granddad and me play a special one together.' Ethan grinned. 'I'll show you what you have to do.'

Serena listened from the kitchen as George and her son bonded over the piano keyboard. Ethan taught George a simple four-note phrase. 'You do it starting on that key, then that one, then that one, then that one,' he said, showing George what to do.

'OK,' George said, and did as he was instructed.

'Now I'll put my bit in,' Ethan said. 'You start.'

There was a lump in Serena's throat as she heard them harmonise 'Heart and Soul', George doing the bass while Ethan did the melody. She leaned on the door jamb, watching them play together.

'That was beautiful,' she said when they'd finished.

'High five,' Ethan said, putting his hand up for George to clap. 'Granddad gives me chocolate buttons when I play stuff right. I haven't got any chocolate, but I'll get Mummy to buy some for you some next time.'

'I'll hold you to that,' George said with a grin.

Eating together in the kitchen really made it feel as if they were a family, Serena thought. And when she caught George's eye, he didn't look trapped. He looked *happy*.

At work the next day, Serena was able to sign off Lisa Miller, her patient with whiplash. 'This is my favourite bit of my job,' she said. 'Obviously I'm sad to say goodbye to my patients—especially the ones I've been treating for a while—but when I sign them off I know I've done my job properly. I've helped them and they're in nowhere near so much pain.'

'You've made the treatment bearable,' Lisa said. 'I'll miss you.' She hugged Serena. 'Thank you for all you've done.' She smiled. 'You look really happy. Is it your birthday or something?'

Serena smiled back. 'No.' Though it felt like her birthday and Christmas rolled into one. She and George had agreed to make a real go of their relationship, and Ethan seemed to have taken to George. All felt really *right* with the world.

When she'd finished writing up her notes, she went to grab a hot drink from the staffroom.

'Perfect timing,' Jess said, waving a mug at her. 'Coffee?'

'Thanks.'

'Obviously you've worked it out with the mystery man, then,' Jess said.

Serena blinked in surprise. 'How come you know about that?'

Jess spread her hands. 'I worked it out for myself. You stopped going out for lunch and grabbed a sandwich at your desk for a week, and when you didn't think anyone was watching you looked really sad. Bruno and I were planning to drag you off to the canteen today and feed you chocolate until you told us what was wrong. Except it's obviously not wrong any more.'

'No. It's fine,' Serena said softly.

'Good. I'm glad it's worked out. I hated seeing you unhappy and not being able to do anything to help.'

For a second, Serena almost told her friend that she was dating Mr Hot, but right now she was still getting used to the idea. So she just smiled. 'Yes, I'm happy.'

And for the next ten days it was great. She saw George every evening, and on both Saturdays they spent the day as a family, taking Ethan to the aquarium on the Saturday when it rained, and to feed the ducks at the park near George on the Saturday when it was dry. George even skipped a Sunday in Suffolk to have lunch with her parents, and charmed her mother with flowers and her father with some seriously good wine.

Though as time went by Serena noticed that George still hadn't introduced her to any of his family. She knew that all his siblings lived in London, so it would be easy enough to arrange; so what was holding him back? OK, so it had gone wrong with Rebecca; but did this mean he thought she wasn't going to fit in to his aristocratic life, either? She'd been full of bravado when she'd told him that his title didn't matter. It didn't, to her; but his social set had clearly not been impressed with the idea of him being involved with a commoner all those years ago. Would it matter to them—or George's family—that he was getting involved with a single mother who'd made a total mess of her past relationships? Did they stand a chance?

But every time she tried to bring it up in conversation, George simply changed the subject and stonewalled her. And every time her worries grew just a little more.

When Serena checked her list at work the next morning, she sucked in a breath. She must've blocked this one from her subconscious. Of all the days to have a new patient with this condition…

But this family needed her help. She had to put her personal feelings aside.

She forced herself to smile as Samantha Pritchard brought in her three-year-old daughter Izzie. 'Hello. I'm Serena.' She could see that Samantha was very, very close to tears. 'Can I get you a glass of water or any-thing?'

Samantha dragged in a breath. 'Thanks, but I'm fine.'

She didn't sound it. Serena crouched down to Izzie's level. 'Hello, Izzie. How would you like to have a look in my special toybox and find something to play with while I talk to Mummy?'

The little girl looked delighted. 'Yeah!'

'Here you go.' She took Izzie over to the corner where she kept the toy-box for her younger patients; once the little girl was settled, she turned back to Samantha. 'Talk to me,' she said gently.

Samantha dragged in a breath. 'There's never been anything like this in our family, and her older brother is just fine, so I had no idea that Ian and I were carri-ers.' She swallowed hard. 'Izzie had the heel prick test when she was born. The doctors said they weren't happy so they did a sweat test, and her salt levels were way higher than normal. They scraped some cells out of her cheek to do a genetic test and then...' She dragged in a breath... 'They said Izzie had cystic fibrosis. But she didn't really have any symptoms as a baby. She had a few colds, but babies get colds, don't they?'

'Of course they do,' Serena said gently. 'And some-times symptoms don't appear until later in childhood.'

'Then she had a bad chest infection last week and she couldn't get her breath.' Samantha looked over towards her daughter to check that she was busy with the toys and not paying attention to her words. 'I was terrified she was going to die,' she said in a lowered voice.

'It's scary, the first couple of times it happens,' Serena said. 'But we can do a lot to help clear that sticky mucus and stop it happening again. I can teach you how to loosen it, and I can show you some games that'll help improve Izzie's breathing and make her lungs work more effectively.'

'Do you treat a lot of patients with CF?' Samantha asked.

'I do,' Serena said, knowing that she needed reassurance. 'Plus my best friend—' she changed the tense quickly, not wanting to open such a recent wound for Samantha '—has CF. Actually, that's why I became a physiotherapist. I learned how to do Kelly's physio when we were at school, so I could help her. When Izzie grows older, you'll be able to teach her friends how to do it, and her teachers at school as well.'

Samantha looked thoughtful. 'Does it hurt? I saw these videos on the internet…'

'No, it doesn't hurt. And if you can help to make a game of it when they're little, it isn't so scary for them. What happens is that the mucus gets thick and sticky and block some of the little tiny airways in her lungs—that means that her lungs aren't working quite so effectively and it's hard for her to breathe. The physiotherapy helps to loosen the mucus so she can cough it up instead of it blocking her airways. You might only need to do it once or twice a day for, say, ten minutes at a time, when Izzie's well, though if she gets an infection she might need it more often and for a longer session.' Serena paused. 'How long ago did she last eat?'

'Breakfast. About an hour ago.'

'That's great—she needs to be lying with her head down for this, and if you make sure you do the therapy at least an hour after she's eaten, she's less likely to be sick and get scared,' Serena explained. 'Ready to do the first bit?'

Samantha nodded.

Serena squeezed her hand. 'Hang on in there. You're not hurting her, you're helping her. Just remember that, OK?'

'OK.' Samantha bit her lip.

'Wow, Izzie, you've done that whole puzzle. That's great,' Serena said, crouching next to the little girl. 'We're going to play some games now. The first one is a special way of patting your back, and then we're going to have a competition to see who can blow a snowball the furthest. Can you do that?'

Izzie nodded enthusiastically.

Serena got her to lie on her tummy with her head down, and showed Samantha how to give firm pats to Izzie's back to help her cough up the mucus. Samantha was hesitant at first, but Serena gently guided her into the way to give Izzie the most help, and by the end of the session Samantha's confidence had grown.

'Now we're going to play some games,' Serena told Izzie.

'The snowball?'

'The snowball,' Serena confirmed with a smile. She looked at Samantha. 'The idea is to help her with her deep breathing. I'll show you the most popular ones, and if you do each of them three or four times in a session, and do it every day, it'll really help. I'd recommend keeping a special toy box just for these games.'

Samantha nodded. 'Sounds good to me.'

Serena took two cotton-wool balls from her desk drawer. 'Two snowballs,' she said to Izzie. 'I'm going to hold one on each hand, and we'll see who can blow them the furthest, you or Mummy.'

'Me, me!' Izzie said, beaming.

Serena knew that Samantha was letting her daughter win, but the whole point of it was for Izzie to have fun with her physiotherapy so she'd keep it up. 'You can do it as football, too—put the cotton-wool balls on a table, have an empty box at the end for a goal, and blow through straws to see who can score the first goal.'

'Jordy can play football with me,' Izzie said.

Samantha smiled. 'Yes, he will.'

'Windmills are good, too. Oh, and do you like blowing bubbles, Izzie?' Serena asked.

Izzie nodded enthusiastically.

'They're good, too. Let me show you a special way to make the bubbles even bigger. You take a deep breath in, then make your mouth into the shape of an O, then a big breath out.' She demonstrated, then looked at Samantha. 'Gradually make it longer and longer breaths. And it's fun to blow bubbles through a straw into a glass of water. Do you like painting, Izzie?'

'She loves it,' Samantha said.

'Have you ever tried putting a blob of paint onto a sheet, then blow at it through a straw? It makes excellent pictures.'

'And it helps her breathing, too,' Samantha said.

'Absolutely. I'll give you a sheet of suggestions, just in case you get home and you worry that you've forgotten a couple of the things we talked about.'

'Thank you so much,' Samantha said.

Serena smiled. 'It's what I'm here for.' And she was relieved to see that Samantha looked a lot less worried when she and Izzie left.

Though, as she wrote the notes up, she thought again of Kelly. Two years. How quickly they'd gone.

She'd arranged that her mother would keep Ethan for a little longer that day, giving Serena time to call in at the cemetery after her shift. Kelly's parents had clearly already visited that day, because the vase on her grave was filled with fresh freesias.

Serena had brought a pot of bright yellow gerbera daisies, as vibrant as her best friend had been. 'Two years. It feels like two minutes and half a lifetime, both at the same time,' she said. 'I miss you. And I wish you were still here now. I'd so love you to meet George.' She dragged in a breath. 'You'd like him. He's not like Jason. OK, he's complicated and he's not perfect, and he made me really unhappy when he bailed out on me—you would've wanted to push him in a puddle. But at least he'll admit when he's made a mistake and he's willing to compromise and make things work. He's great with Ethan.' She swallowed hard and laid her hand on the gravestone. 'I miss you, Kel. But you still live on in my heart. You always will.'

She'd just about managed to stem the tears by the time she picked Ethan up from her parents', and she gave him an extra cuddle and a second story before bedtime that night. And then she sat looking through old photograph albums. Herself and Kelly at school, when they'd been the same age as Ethan. As teenagers. At Kelly's wedding, when she'd been chief bridesmaid. At Ethan's christening, with Kelly holding her godson, looking proud.

Her phone beeped, and she glanced at the screen; the text was from George. *If you need to talk I'm here, even if it's 3 in the morning xxx*

It was an odd message to send, because she hadn't told him about today being Kelly's anniversary. How had he known something was wrong?

She called him.

'Are you OK?' he asked.

'Yes—well, no,' she admitted. 'How did you know?'

'I spoke to your mum. I had a funny feeling when you said you were doing something tonight and you were so cagey about it. And she told me about Kelly.' He paused. 'Sorry. Today must be really hard for you.'

'It is,' she said with a sigh. 'I thought it would get easier after the first year—the first birthday and Christmas without her and the anniversary of her death—but it hasn't. Kelly was such a great godmother to Ethan, so full of fun. And she was my best friend since we were toddlers. I miss her horribly.' She swallowed hard. 'I had a three-year-old patient with CF today. I guess it caught me on the raw a bit.'

'Do you want me to come over?'

'No, I'll be OK. I just want to be quiet and look through my old photos and remember the good times.'

'OK. But if you change your mind, all you have to do is just pick up the phone. I'm not going anywhere,' George said.

There was a lump in her throat. He understood that she needed space, but he was making sure that she hadn't backed herself into a corner. And he was making sure that she knew he was there for her.

'Thank you. I'll see you tomorrow, OK?'

'OK.' For a second, before he put the phone down, she thought she heard him whisper, '*I love you*.'

That was crazy. She knew he wasn't ready to say those words to her yet. It might be a long, long time before he was ready to say it. Maybe she should be the one to say it first; but, on the other hand, she didn't want him to feel pressured. He needed to come to terms with his feelings in his own time. He needed to learn to trust that she wouldn't be like his mother or Rebecca.

'And this is when I could really do with a bottle of wine, a girly chat, and a laugh with you,' she told the photograph of Kelly. 'You'd put me straight. And him. But we'll get there.'

It would just take a little time.

CHAPTER THIRTEEN

At the end of the week, Serena felt the familiar dragging ache of her period starting.

Meaning she definitely wasn't pregnant.

She'd expected that; but what she hadn't expected was to feel so upset about it. Disappointed. As if she was missing something.

This was crazy. She and George were still at the early stages of their relationship, and he'd told her that having children with him would mean an awful lot of medical intervention with no guarantees of success. She couldn't be broody. She couldn't want a baby. She just *couldn't*. It wouldn't be fair on anyone.

And yet...the feelings had crept into her heart before she'd been aware of it. Taken hold.

She wanted George's baby. Something that she knew she just couldn't have.

She forced herself to smile at work and pretended that nothing was wrong; but then the last patient on her list before lunch was Owen Parsons, a computer programmer she'd been treating for RSI.

'Your range of movement has definitely improved,' she said when she assessed him. 'How's the pain?'

'Better. But it needs to be completely gone in five months.'

'Why five months?' she asked. 'Are you starting a new job?'

'You could say that, in a way.' He beamed. 'Beth and I—we've been having IVF. And it's finally worked.'

IVF. The only way that she and George would be able to have a baby; and the one thing that George was adamant he would never do. 'Congratulations,' she said, meaning it even at the same time as it made her ache with longing for something she couldn't have. 'I take it this wasn't your first try?'

'Third,' Owen said. 'It was gruelling on Beth—I'm the one with the problem, not her, and I felt so guilty about putting her through all that emotional and physical upheaval, especially when it didn't work.'

'Wasn't it a strain on your relationship?' It was none of her business and nothing to do with his treatment, but she couldn't help the question. Because that was what George believed, and she needed to know if it was true.

'Yes, it was a strain. But it made us stronger, and I think we're closer now because of what we've been through together,' Owen said. 'We agreed this would be our last try and we'd think about fostering or adopting if it didn't work, but we've been so lucky. We've got to sixteen weeks, the scans say the baby's doing fine, and now Beth's showing...' He grinned. 'Well, we just want to tell the whole world how happy we are.'

'I don't blame you,' Serena said. 'That's fantastic news.'

And if only she had some fantastic news to tell George, this evening, instead of the truth.

George arrived just before dinner, as they'd agreed. He'd clearly been enjoying himself in the children's section of a bookshop and had found a book about a cat that lived with six different owners on the same street. He read it to Ethan while Serena was busy with dinner and got Ethan to pick out some of the words and letters, careful to give the little boy praise when he got it right and correcting him gently when he didn't.

He was a natural father, she thought. And, for someone who claimed he didn't know what he was doing, he was making an amazing job of bonding with Ethan and doing fatherly things with the little boy.

After his bath, Ethan asked for the cat story again. This time Serena and George read it together, each of them doing the voices of different characters, with Ethan cuddled between them.

George would be so good with a baby, she thought. If only.

As soon as Ethan was asleep and she came back downstairs, George said, 'Tell me what's wrong.'

'How do you know anything's wrong?' she fenced.

'Because your dimples have gone.'

She shook her head. 'I don't have dimples.'

'Actually, you do, and they're very cute, but don't change the subject.' He wrapped her in his arms. 'Whatever it is, I'm here.'

'A problem shared is a problem halved, you mean?'

'No. That's what Ed always tells me, but sharing a problem only makes the other person miserable, too.'

Well, that was telling her. She shut up.

He stroked her face. 'But I get what Ed really means: if you don't share the problem, the other person will be more miserable because they know something's wrong and you aren't telling them, and it makes them feel helpless.'

She sighed. 'There isn't a good way to say it.'

'Don't try to sugar it, then. Just tell me.'

She swallowed hard. 'My period started today.'

He was expecting it—of course he was. He knew how far the odds were out of his favour. Plus Serena had taken the morning-after pill. Of course she wasn't pregnant.

But he was still shocked by how disappointed he felt.

She didn't look thrilled about the situation, either.

Oh, hell. He knew that this was exactly what it would be like if they were to have fertility treatment. Hope rising with every cycle they tried, and then crashing down again when the treatment didn't work. He really couldn't put her through that.

'Shouldn't you be relieved?' he asked.

'I don't know.'

Panic lanced through him. Oh, no, no, no. It sounded to him as if she wanted a baby. And that was something he just couldn't give her.

She leaned her head against his shoulder. 'I mean, I knew I wasn't going to be pregnant. I took the morning-after pill.'

'And I'm pretty much infertile.' Saying it aloud hurt, but he had to be honest with her. For both their sakes.

'Are you relieved?' she asked.

'Yes,' he lied.

But he felt the tiny shudder run through her. Ah, hell. He owed her honesty, at least. 'And no.' He blew out a breath. 'I never thought I wanted children. I thought it was going to be a duty, something I had to do for the family. It's only now it looks as if I can't have them that I realise what I'm missing. Don't they always say you don't know what you've got until it's gone?' He moved so that he could kiss her. 'I wish it could be different. I wish I could say to you, OK, let's make a real commitment to each other and start trying for a baby, a little brother or sister for Ethan. But the only way we can do that is with IVF. You're the one who'd bear the brunt of it. You're the one who'd have to have all the injections and the invasive physical stuff. It isn't fair to you. Especially as we can't guarantee it'll work.'

'Actually, I saw a patient today who's been having IVF treatment,' Serena said. 'It finally worked on their third cycle and, now his wife's sixteen weeks and showing, they feel confident enough to tell people. He said it was difficult at times, but even the tough stuff brought them closer together. So maybe,' she said softly, 'we shouldn't rule it out completely.'

George was shocked by how much that idea made him yearn for a child. Yet he still felt it wouldn't be fair to put Serena through it.

He kissed her again. 'We have each other. And Ethan. And our families. Right now, that's enough for me. Wanting anything more would be greedy.'

But all the same, it was there in his heart: a little glimmer of hope.

Maybe.

One day.

The following week, George got a phone call from Alice.

'Our receptionist reads that horrible mag.'

She didn't have to tell him which one. *Celebrity Life*. Which he sometimes thought should be renamed *The Bane of George Somers's Life*. 'And?'

'According to them, my big brother is a reformed character these days. He never goes clubbing. And the rumour is that he's thinking of settling down.' She paused. 'Is there anything you want to tell me, Georgie-boy?'

'No, m'lud.'

She groaned. 'George. You're impossible. Are you seeing someone?'

'I'm not in court and I'm not under oath. I don't have to answer that.'

'I'm your sister so, yes, you do,' she corrected swiftly. 'Are you? And is it serious?'

'No comment.'

'You're not denying it. Hmm. Therefore it's true. OK. Bye, sweetie.'

Uh-oh. When Alice called anyone 'sweetie', it usually meant trouble. He tried calling her straight back, but her phone was engaged.

Right. First things, first: he needed to see exactly what *Celebrity Life* had said about him. He was in the newsagent's, buying a copy to find out what mischief the gossip rag was making, when his mobile phone rang.

He glanced at the screen. Just as he'd half expected, it was his brother. 'Yes, Ed?'

'I'm under orders to make you spill the beans.'

He sighed. 'Alice is speculating.'

'When Alice speculates, she's usually right,' Ed parried. 'So when do we get to meet her?'

'When I'm ready. And not before.' He'd made that mistake before. He wouldn't repeat it.

'We only want to know that she's good to you. And might I remind you that you met Jane before any of the others did? *And* you called me "Tarzan".'

That clearly still rankled. George stifled a grin. 'What do you expect? I was recovering from anaesthetic when you brought her to meet me.'

'You did it after that. And you got Dad doing it.'

George just laughed.

Ed's voice softened. 'Just tell me she's good to you.'

'She's not one of the blonde clothes-horses. Will that do?'

'No.'

George sighed. 'Can't you lot just be patient?'

Ed hooted. 'That's rich, coming from you.'

'She's nice. You'll like her. And I promise I'll let you meet her soon.'

'You're just getting used to the idea that you want to be with someone for longer than three dates, hmm?' Ed asked.

'Something like that.'

'OK. I'll back off.'

'Thanks.' George paused. 'Ed, can I ask you a favour?'

'Sure. What?'

'Will you swap cars with me this weekend?'

There was a stunned silence at the other end of the line. 'You want to swap cars with *me*? Why?'

'Hey, this is a great offer. You get a vintage soft-top for a whole weekend and I won't even check for stone chips when you bring it back.'

'Why?' Ed repeated.

George knew he wasn't going to get away with anything less than the truth. 'Because my car's a two-seater and yours is sensible.'

There was another pause while Ed digested his words. 'Hang on. You want a sensible car with more than two seats. Does she have children?'

'One.'

'Right. And you're going to Suffolk.'

'I haven't asked her, yet. But probably. And you are *not* to come. Neither are the girls.'

'You're banning us from coming home?'

'This weekend, yes.'

'You lot all descended on Suffolk when I first took Janey home,' Ed reminded him.

'I know, and I'm the biggest hypocrite in the world. But I want to ease her in gently.' He didn't want her overwhelmed, the way Rebecca had been. 'I promise you'll be the first to meet her, after Dad and Frances.'

Ed laughed. 'I'd love to be a fly on the wall while you explain that to Alice.'

'Ed. Really.'

'OK. I'll stop teasing. Let me know where and when you want the car, OK?'

'I will. Thanks. Love you.'

'Love you, too. Even though you're the most infuriating, impossible...'

George laughed. 'I've heard it all before. But I'm becoming a reformed character.'

'That,' Ed said, 'is the best news I've heard all day. Call me. And put Alice out of her misery.'

'Nope. That's your job,' George said, and disconnected the call.

He bought the magazine and flicked through it. The society column was speculating that George was reformed, citing that he never went clubbing any more. It claimed to have heard a rumour that he'd been seen out with the same woman more than three times in a row. And then it speculated about what kind of woman would catch the future sixteenth Lord Somers...

George rolled his eyes. What a load of tripe. But he knew that he needed to talk to Serena about this. Right now, she'd be with a patient, so her phone would be off—not that he'd call her at work unless there was a huge emergency. Instead, he texted her. *Call me as soon as you're free. Need to run something by you.*

She rang him at lunchtime. 'What's up?'

'Can I meet you after work and we can get a coffee in the hospital canteen or something?' he asked.

'Is anything wrong?'

'Nothing to worry about. I just need to run something by you, that's all. Can you ask your mum if you can be twenty minutes late picking Ethan up tonight?'

'OK.'

George was sitting in the waiting room, reading a magazine, when Serena finished her shift

He stood up and smiled as she came towards him. 'Have you had a good day?'

'Yes.' Though she'd been worrying about what exactly he wanted to discuss with her.

'Let's go and grab that coffee.'

She found them a table in the canteen while he bought the coffee. When he came over to their table, she noticed that he still had a magazine under his arm. 'What's that?'

'What I wanted to talk to you about.' He set down their coffees, then opened the magazine and handed it to her.

She read the article, and her heart sank. She looked up at him. 'So the paparazzi are going to be on my tail now?'

'Possibly,' he admitted, 'but hopefully not.' He paused. 'I didn't see anyone following me here, but if they did they'll assume that I'm here for some treatment.'

She blinked. 'You mean they know about…?'

'They know I broke my wrists and my leg, because they saw me on crutches and in plaster.'

At least they didn't have any idea that his fertility was under question. 'So what does this mean?'

'For us? It means they think I'm about to become immensely respectable. Which in turn means they'll stop following me, because I won't be interesting enough to sell copies for them.'

'Uh-huh.' And if they found out he was seeing her... she could imagine they'd have a field day. The baron's heir and the single mum. Right at that moment, she had a very good idea of why Rebecca had bailed out on him. She didn't fit into his world.

And then there was Ethan. Serena could cope with the snobs laughing at her, but if they said a word about Ethan...

'You look as if you're about to turn into a wolf,' he remarked.

With an effort, she pulled herself together. 'I was just thinking. They can say what they like about me—and I guess they won't be very nice about me—but if they follow Ethan...'

'And take his photo? They won't. There's a code of practice, and if photographers break that code of practice—especially if they take photographs of a child, and even more so if they're secret photographs without parental consent—they know they'll end up in court and it won't be nice.' He smiled. 'My scary sister is very, very good in court. They all know that, and they're not going to take the risk of letting her skewer them.'

'OK.' She blew out a breath.

'And there's no reason for them to be vile about you, either,' he said.

'I don't come from your world.'

'I thought you said it didn't matter?' For a moment, his eyes were filled with panic.

'I'm not Rebecca.'

'I know. Sorry.' He paused. 'I know I haven't asked you to meet my family yet.'

'Uh-huh.' She tried to keep her voice neutral and not show how hurt she'd been by that.

'It's not because I don't think you're suitable, if that's what you're thinking.'

She gave an awkward shrug. 'Apart from the fact I'm a single mum, wouldn't they expect me to come from some…some family with a double-barrelled surname and a huge country estate? My family's just normal.'

'Your family's lovely. I like your parents very much,' George said. 'As for mine—remember, Dad was a single parent when he met Frances. Neither of them will judge you. They like kids, so they'll probably make a huge fuss of Ethan. And the dogs will be thrilled at having someone who won't get bored with throwing a ball for them. I haven't asked you to meet them before because I wasn't ready. I am now.'

'Because the press has forced your hand?' she asked.

'Yes and no. I've been thinking about it for a while, actually.' He paused. 'Do you have plans for the weekend?'

She shrugged. 'Probably the park, if it's not raining, or maybe making cookies and having a mammoth painting session.'

'How about a trip to Suffolk?' he asked tentatively.

She blinked. 'To meet your family?'

'Yup. Well, Dad and Frances. And then we'll meet up with the others separately, in London.'

'Separately.'

He rolled his eyes. 'Not because any of them will think you're remotely unsuitable. Trust me.'

'Why separately, then?'

'You're an only child. Do you have any idea what it would be like to have four incredibly nosey siblings—actually, five, if you count my favourite sister-in-law-to-be—descending on you?'

'Well, no,' she admitted.

'Exactly. *En masse*, they can be a bit overpowering.'

'I guess you know them best, seeing as they're your brother and sisters.'

'I do. And I want you to see them at their best. Which means separately, at first.' He smiled. 'By the way, it's Bonfire Night this weekend. I thought maybe we could go to a display in Suffolk—well, as long as Ethan doesn't mind the noise?'

'I forgot it was Bonfire Night. No, he likes fireworks—we usually have a box of fireworks in Mum and Dad's garden.'

'In that case, would they mind me stealing you this weekend? We could always have a belated bonfire night with them afterwards.'

She liked the fact that he'd thought of them and come up with an alternative to include them. 'OK. That'd be nice.'

But her voice wobbled slightly, and he reached over and took her hand. 'Stop worrying. It's all going to be just fine. We'll go down on Saturday morning and come back on Sunday evening. If you really hate it, we can come back early. But I'm hoping you'll like Suffolk.'

That she wouldn't react the way Rebecca had re-acted?

'It's...well.' He smiled. 'You'll see when we get there.'

CHAPTER FOURTEEN

'WHAT happened to your car?' Serena asked on Saturday morning when she followed George outside to put flowers and chocolates in the back of his car.

'I swapped cars with Ed for the weekend. I needed a sensible family car for us, and he and Janey can go and have some fun in mine.' He laughed. 'I've even promised not to check the paintwork minutely when I get it back.'

She smiled at him. 'Boys and their toys.'

'I restored that car myself, I'll have you know. I spent hours on it.' He gave her a rueful smile. 'I did think about maybe making it into a business and restoring vintage sports cars, but when you put that much work into something it's impossible to let it go to someone who might not look after it properly. And I don't want to end up with a vintage car collection gathering dust in a barn somewhere. I just want something I can enjoy driving.'

'Uh-huh.'

'And you can get family cars that are enjoyable drives.' He smiled at her. 'Not quite so much fun as mine, but I can compromise when I have to.'

He secured Ethan's child seat to the rear seat of the car and double-checked it. 'Right. Ready when you are.

Oh, and I should've checked with you earlier—is Ethan OK with dogs? He's not allergic or anything?'

'No, he's not allergic, and he loves dogs.' Serena gave him a rueful smile. 'The only reason we don't have one is because I'm out at work all day and it wouldn't be fair.'

'Good. I'd better warn you that we have three. They're loud, but they're all good-natured. And if he makes a fuss of them they'll adore him.'

The drive down to Suffolk only took an hour. When George pulled into the driveway and Serena had her first glimpse of Somers Hall, she thought it breathtaking: a huge redbrick building with stone mullioned windows and a narrow tower at each corner, each capped with a leaded domed roof.

'It's a castle!' Ethan said, sounding thrilled.

'Sort of,' George said, 'though we don't have a moat or a drawbridge.'

'It's gorgeous,' Serena said. 'A real stately home.' Though, at the same time as admiring it, she felt slightly intimidated by it. This was so far removed from the kind of place her parents and her friends lived in. But she couldn't turn and run, the way Rebecca had. She couldn't hurt him with her insecurities. 'How long has your family lived here?'

'About five hundred years,' George said.

'And it's open to the public?'

'The garden is, on Wednesdays and Saturdays plus whatever national garden open days Dad wants to do. Plus we do wedding packages. And, as my figures stack up and Dad will have to give in to common sense when I tackle him about it this weekend, we'll start doing fireworks displays next year.'

'I love fireworks,' Ethan said. 'We have fireworks with Nanna and Granddad in the garden.'

'We're going to see some really big fireworks this weekend,' George promised. 'And then we'll have the ones in the garden with Nanna and Granddad, OK?'

'OK,' Ethan said, sounding pleased.

Serena unstrapped Ethan from his car seat while George fetched their cases.

Three dogs came rushing out to meet them, barking and wagging their tails madly, with a man and woman walking at a more sedate pace behind them.

George put the cases down on the gravel and crouched down. 'Ethan, I have three beasties here who are just dying to meet you and have you make a fuss of them. This is Pepper the chocolate Labrador, Wolfgang the Westie, and Hattie the setter.'

'Pepper, Wolf…' Ethan stumbled over the names.

'Wolfgang,' George said. 'Or you can call him Wolfie. Or just say "Here, boy" and he'll come and sit next to you.'

'Pepper, Wolfie and Hattie.'

The dogs responded to their names by licking him. Ethan gave a gurgle of delighted laughter and made a fuss of them all.

George straightened up. 'Serena, these are my parents, Frances and David. Frances, Dad, this is Serena.'

Frances greeted her with a hug; David was a little more cool and formal, merely shaking her hand.

Please let them like her. For George's sake.

Rebecca had hurt George badly. Knowing that she, like Rebecca, wasn't from their world, would they expect her to do the same? Would they already be wary of her?

Oh, lord. She hadn't expected to be hit by a rush of insecurity like this.

'Come in and have some coffee. You must be gasping. And I hope George warned you about the dogs,' Frances said.

Serena smiled. 'He did.' Frances didn't need to know it had been totally at the last minute.

'Good. Welcome to Somers Hall,' Frances said, and shepherded her into the kitchen. 'George, can you take the bags up? You're in the East Wing.'

'Will do.' George gave Serena an encouraging smile. Ethan was still busy making a fuss of the dogs.

Frances said softly, 'I wasn't sure whether to put you in the same room with George or not. I'm afraid I erred on the safe side and put you in separate rooms next to each other, though there is a connecting door.'

Serena felt herself flush. 'Um. I'm sorry. It's awkward.'

Frances shook her head. 'It's not awkward. Just... Well, this is new for us. You're the first person he's brought home since...' She stopped, wincing.

'Rebecca.' Who'd felt that she didn't measure up. What would his parents think of her and Ethan? She came from a totally different background. Then there was the fact that she'd fallen for Ethan's father and made a real fool of herself. All her doubts and insecurities came rushing back. Which was crazy—George had already reassured her that his family would like her. He wouldn't have brought her here if he thought there would be a problem. So why did she feel so nervous?

Frances looked surprised. 'He told you about her?'
Serena nodded.

Frances's face was filled with relief. 'I don't actually know what happened between them. George tends to clam up and refuse to talk about things—he's worse than his father. But I do know she hurt him badly.'

And Serena could read the plea on Frances's face. The same that would be on hers one day, no doubt, when she first met her son's partner. *Don't hurt him.*

'I don't have blue blood or anything,' she blurted out.

Frances smiled. 'Neither do I. That didn't make a difference to David, and it won't make a difference to George.'

'And I'm a single mum.' She might as well get everything out in the open.

'It's good to have children running round the house. That's what the house needs. It's a family home,' Frances said softly. 'Not just a stately pile.'

'It's beautiful. Though George says the roof eats money.'

Frances rolled her eyes. 'Tell me about it.'

'But he was also telling me about his ideas for the firework display. The hall would be the perfect backdrop.' Then she bit her lip. 'Sorry. It's not my place to say that.'

'Actually, love, it's good to know that George has someone willing to bat his corner and support his ideas.'

Was Frances just saying that to be nice? Or did she really mean it? Serena knew that her worries were ridiculous, but meeting his family was turning out to be incredibly daunting. She had no idea how to address his parents or whether to curtsey or anything. George hadn't told her a thing. She was finding it tough enough at the age of thirty; how would she have coped at Rebecca's age?

Frances made coffee, gave Ethan some apple juice, and settled Serena at the kitchen table. 'Did you know

George has banned the girls and Ed from coming to lunch tomorrow?'

Serena sucked in a breath. 'Why?' Did he think his brother and sisters wouldn't accept her?

'Probably because he doesn't want you to feel crowded. They can be a bit full-on. But I should warn you, none of them intend to take the blindest bit of notice. I've already had texts from all of them this morning, asking what you're like, and I'd better warn you that they're all intending to turn up and meet you.'

'Oh.' Serena swallowed hard. What if they didn't like her?

Her worries must have shown on her face, because Frances said, 'They'll love you.' She patted Serena's hand. 'Don't worry. I won't let them interrogate you.'

Serena wasn't so sure that Frances could hold that much sway. 'George says Alice is scary.'

Frances hooted. 'Rubbish. They all adore him, and he knows it.' She sobered. 'I worry the most about him out of all my children. Well, I don't need to tell you what it's like, being a mum and worrying about your child.'

And that was when Serena realised that Frances meant what she said. She clearly thought of George as hers, and even more than that she loved him for who he was. It was a common bond, one that could grow. Provided Serena was brave enough to be honest. 'You're right. And I get why you worry about him. He'll do things for you all, but he won't let you do things for him. And he lives life at a million miles an hour because he's scared to stop and think. He doesn't like himself. The sad thing is, he can't see himself for who he really is.'

Frances sighed. 'You're so right, there. I take it you know about Zara, too?'

'Is that his mother? He's never actually said her

name. But, yes, he's told me a lot of things.' Serena grimaced. 'I think she did him a lot of damage. As did Rebecca.'

'But you're healing him. I think you and Ethan—you'll be good for him.' Frances gave her a perceptive look. 'And he might just be good for you.'

'He's a good man.'

'I know. And I'm not going to ask you if you love him. Because you wouldn't be here if you didn't.'

'Oh, I love him,' Serena said softly. 'It's a question of whether he'll let me.' And whether he'd ever trust her enough to love her back.

Though her doubts grew during the day. George barely seemed to meet her eye. Although she joined with him in championing the fireworks idea when he talked to his father, he didn't sling an arm round her shoulders or hold her hand or even smile at her.

Here, on his home territory, he'd gone distant. Even though he kept his promise to take Ethan to the firework display in the next village that evening—and Ethan loved it, especially as he sat on George's shoulders throughout—he was polite and cool when he kissed her goodnight. And the connecting door between their rooms remained firmly closed that night. She lay awake for hours, so sure that he'd come to her—and then wondering whether she ought to take the initiative and go to him. Or had he changed his mind about her, now he'd seen her in his real environment? Did he think she wouldn't fit in, the way Rebecca clearly hadn't?

This was where it had all gone wrong last time, George thought. He'd been so careful to keep it low key this time round—to bring Serena and Ethan to meet his parents, not on a weekend where there was an event at the hall or some kind of over-the-top social do where she'd feel judged by a horde of strangers—and yet he couldn't help worrying. Would she be able to cope with Somers Hall, knowing that in years to come he'd need her to help her run the house and host the parties?

All he wanted to do was walk through that connecting door and hold her. Sleep, holding her to his heart.

But he guessed that she'd feel awkward and embarrassed at the idea of spending the night in his arms under his parents' roof. Especially as this was the first time she'd met them.

And so he stayed where he was. Lonely. Brooding. Missing her.

Serena spent a bad night. Alone and awake, with too much to think about and worry about. In the morning, she packed her bags. She loved George, but she had to face facts. Maybe he'd been so badly hurt by Zara and Rebecca that he just wasn't capable of love any more. He was never truly going to be able to openly love her back.

After breakfast, once she'd helped wash up, she placed her hand on George's arm. 'Can we have a quick word?' she asked quietly.

'Sure.' He led her out into the corridor. 'What is it?'

'I need the number of a taxi firm.'

George stared at her, not quite able to process what he was hearing. He'd been here before. Please, no, not again. Ice trickled down his spine. 'A taxi firm? Why?'

Serena swallowed hard. 'I've packed our things, and if I get a taxi to the station then Ethan and I can get a train back to London. Can you apologise to your parents for me? Make up whatever story you need to spare their feelings, but I think it's best if I leave now.'

No, no, no. This was all going horribly wrong. He'd thought Serena and Ethan were getting on well with his parents. They fitted in. 'Why?' The question came out as a whisper.

She was shaking. 'Because this isn't going to work.' She sounded close to tears.

It was happening all over again.

He was going to lose her.

Unless he did something drastic. Given how he'd failed with Rebecca, he didn't have a clue what to do or say. He just wanted this all to stop. Now. Before it was too late. 'Don't go, Serena. Please don't go.'

He'd thought—hoped—that they'd grown close over the last few weeks. She understood him. He'd told her things he hadn't told another living soul. He loved her, and he thought that she might just love him back. Had he got it so badly wrong?

'Serena, I—'

But then the front door open and the dogs streamed through the corridor, barking and wagging their tails as people started walking towards them.

Oh, for pity's sake. Talk about bad timing. And why were they all here, crowding them and making the whole situation a hundred times worse? George stared at his siblings, horrified. 'What are you lot doing here? I asked you to give me space.'

'And miss out on meeting the first woman you've brought home since I was thirteen? No chance, Georgie.' Alice ruffled his hair. 'Hello, Serena. Lovely to meet you. Seeing as George doesn't have the manners to in-troduce me, I'm Alice. He's probably told you I'm the bossy one.'

'Because you are,' George said through gritted teeth.

'Stop arguing and let the poor girl talk.'

Anguished, George mouthed '*Sorry'* at Serena.

She looked slightly overwhelmed, but then smiled at Alice. 'Actually, he told me you're a *Grease* fan.'

'Really?' Alice looked surprised, then pleased, and introduced everyone swiftly. 'This is Bea and Charlie, our little sisters. This is Ed, my older but obviously not oldest brother, and Jane, his fiancée.'

'Hello,' Serena said politely.

'Don't worry. You'll survive the interrogation,' Jane said, 'even when the girls get the spotlights out.'

'Oh, you fibber! We didn't get any spotlights out for you when Ed brought you home for the first time,' Alice said, laughing.

'Are you quite sure about that?' Jane teased.

'Absolutely,' Bea said.

'And we need coffee,' Charlotte added, ushering everyone in the direction of the kitchen.

George caught Serena's hand. 'Sorry about this. I had no idea they were coming. Look, please stay. I'll drive you home straight after lunch and I promise we'll talk,' he said urgently.

Serena bit her lip. 'OK.'

'If they get too much, just say so and I'll shut them up,' George said. 'Because you're—'

'Unhand that poor girl right now and get in here,' Alice called, cutting off his words.

'We'd better go,' Serena said.

And her eyes were full of misery. Had he done that to her? He hated himself for that.

'Your father's in the library,' Frances said as George and Serena joined the others. 'Why don't you all go through and I'll bring the coffee in?'

'I'll help,' Serena said.

'No need, love.' Frances smiled at her and shooed her off with the others.

In the library, Ethan looked longingly at the piano. 'Me and George play together,' he said shyly.

Alice patted the piano stool, then lifted the lid. 'Come and show us, Ethan,' she said. 'I'd love to hear you play. And then maybe I can teach you a little bit, too.'

'Can we?' Ethan asked, looking up at George.

George glanced at Serena; at her nod, he joined the little boy on the piano stool.

'I can't believe you're actually sitting at the piano, George.' Ed raised his eyebrows. 'Did he tell you what he did to his poor piano teacher when he was six, Ethan? He put a frog in her pocket.'

'That's probably 'cause she didn't give him chocolate buttons for doing it right. I'm his piano teacher now,' Ethan said proudly, 'and I give him chocolate buttons and a star sticker when he's played well.'

George gave his brother a warning look; Ed's eyes sparkled with amusement, but he made himself look serious for the little boy's sake.

'Shall we show them what you learned, George?' Ethan asked.

'Absolutely, Teacher,' George said with a smile. 'Count us in.'

'Remember you do the first bit twice. One, two, three, four…'

They played 'Heart and Soul' together. George looked over at Serena. She'd know the lyrics to the song, he was sure. Would she realise that he was playing for her? That he meant it? That he loved her, heart and soul?

His siblings took over then, and he didn't get a chance to talk to her again until after lunch, when Bea was teaching Ethan how to build a house of cards, and Ed and Alice promised to go and find the old wooden train set in the loft so they could set up a complicated track in the library.

'Ethan's fine and happy. We need to talk. Come with me,' George said quietly, and slipped out of the library with Serena. He found her coat in the hallway and helped her into it before bundling into his own coat. 'First of all, I'm sorry about my family barging in like this,' he said as he closed the back door behind them.

'They're lovely,' Serena said.

'Well, I think so, but I'm biased. Though right now I'm wishing them all back in London. I didn't want to crowd you. I didn't want to make the same mistakes I made with Rebecca, making you feel overwhelmed.' He sighed. 'Serena. I don't want to you to go. I... Look, I'm not usually lost for words, but right here and now I just don't know what to say. You're obviously upset and I don't know why. I know I *ought* to know why, but... I'm just not good at this relationship stuff.'

'I'm really the first woman you've brought here since Rebecca?'

'The first,' he confirmed. 'Serena, please don't go. I...' He dragged in a breath. 'Come with me. I want to show you Dad's rose garden.'

'Why?' Serena looked utterly mystified.

'I always thought I was good with words, but when it's really important for me to get it right, they're letting me down. I need props.' There was a single red rose blooming on one bush, and he picked it.

'George, that's the last rose in the garden—you can't do that!' Serena said, sounding scandalised.

'Sure I can. And Dad won't mind. It's in a good cause.'

'How do you mean?'

He dropped to one knee. 'Serena, I...I belong with you and Ethan. I know you were worried that my family wouldn't accept you, but they do. They already love you. Not as much as I do, because that's not possible.'

Serena stared at George, hardly able to believe what she'd heard. 'You *love* me?' Her voice came out as a cracked whisper. She'd so desperately wanted to hear those words from him, but she'd thought he'd never be ready to say it—that he couldn't love her.

'I love you,' he confirmed. 'And Ethan. I've had a lot of time to think about what I want, and coming here with you just confirmed everything I was starting to believe. I don't want to do all the thrill-seeking stuff any more. I don't need to. I realise now I did it partly because I tried to fill a hole in my life and partly because I was running away from all the emotional stuff. But now I know what I really, really want.'

Serena waited, desperately hoping that he wanted the same thing that she did.

'I want you and Ethan to be my family officially. I want to be there with you, supporting your career every step of the way. I want you by my side, the way you've been this weekend when you batted my corner over the fireworks. I want to help you bring Ethan up and be a real father to him, the best father I can possibly be. Unfortunately the entailment thing means he won't be able to inherit the barony or the hall, but as my son he'll inherit everything else I own. He'll be *mine*. Frances taught me a long time ago that biology doesn't matter, but being there does. And I'm going to be there for him, Serena. Right by your side.'

Her eyes filled with tears. 'Oh, George. The way you were yesterday—I thought you'd decided I didn't fit in. That was why I was going to leave. Because I love you and I didn't think you could love me—and I can't go through another relationship where my partner's heart and soul aren't involved.'

'But mine are,' he said. 'Didn't you know that when I played the song with Ethan?'

She shook her head. 'I thought you'd already decided you'd made a mistake.' She bit her lip. 'You stayed in your own room last night.'

'Because we're under my parents' roof and I thought you might feel too awkward—just as I would be if we stayed with your parents.' He gave her a crooked smile. 'I should've said. Or at least come in and seen you and kissed you stupid, and then told you we were going to do it the old-fashioned way. But I'm rubbish at words—well, where you're concerned I am. I'm sorry you thought it meant I'd changed my mind about you. I haven't. I was working out when and how to do this— and I'm making a mess of this. Not helped by that lot descending on us—and I really didn't want you to feel overwhelmed and crowded. I know I'm babbling but I need to tell you. Everything. I probably ought to have a diamond in my pocket to do this, but I thought you might prefer to choose a ring with me. So I hope this rose will act as a very temporary measure. Oh, and by the way. Your parents approve. I asked them last week if they'd mind me proposing to you.'

What? She stared at him in shock. They hadn't breathed a word to her.

'I can't offer you a complete bed of roses.' He looked wryly at the rose he was holding. 'What I can offer you

SAVE UP TO 25%

Subscribe to Medical today and get 5 stories a month delivered to your door for 3, 6 or 12 months and gain up to 25% OFF! That's a fantastic saving of over £40!

MONTHS	FULL PRICE	YOUR PRICE	SAVING
3	£43.41	£36.90	15%
6	£86.82	£69.48	20%
12	£173.64	£130.20	25%

As a welcome gift we will also send you a FREE L'Occitane gift set worth £10

PLUS, by becoming a member you will also receive these additional benefits:

- FREE Home Delivery
- Receive new titles TWO MONTHS AHEAD of the shops
- Exclusive Special Offers & Monthly Newsletter
- Special Rewards Programme

No Obligation - You can cancel your subscription at any time by writing to us at Mills & Boon Book Club, PO Box 676, Richmond. TW9 1WU.

To subscribe, visit
millsandboon.co.uk/subscriptions

MILLS & BOON

M2I17

is something I didn't think existed any more, but since meeting you I've discovered it does. My heart.'

His heart. There was a huge lump in her throat. Didn't he know he was offering her everything she wanted?

'I love you. Will you marry me, Serena? Be my wife, my love—and share your child with me? Make us a family?'

'Yes. Absolutely yes.' She accepted the rose from him.

He got to his feet and kissed her. Soundly.

'You're everything I want, George,' she said softly. 'Everything.'

'And you and Ethan are everything I want.' He kissed her again. 'Let's go and tell the others. I think we might just have a party to arrange...'

EPILOGUE

Three years later

GEORGE sat on the edge of Serena's hospital bed, holding their newborn son.

'This is the absolute icing on the cake. I can't believe I have two boys now—Ethan and little Harry.' He looked at her. 'I'm so proud of you. And thank you. You've given me everything. And you're right. I don't love Ethan less now Harry's here. I…' He shook his head and smiled. 'I didn't quite believe you, but it's true. Your heart really *does* expand.'

'I told you so.' Serena's eyes filled with tears. 'We've been so lucky, George. I know you said that this was going to be our last cycle of IVF and if it didn't work, we weren't going to put ourselves through the wringer any more.'

'Because we didn't need to,' he reminded her. 'The heir stuff wasn't an issue any more. Hopefully Dad will be around until he's a hundred in any case, but if I didn't have an heir the barony would pass from me to Ed, or his son.'

'Even so, I wanted your baby. A little boy with your gorgeous blue eyes.' She stroked her tiny son's cheek. 'And he's definitely got your mouth.'

He laughed. 'Expect this baby to be very, very loved. I remember how much I adored having my sisters toddle after me, even though I claimed at the time how annoying they were, and Ethan's going to be thrilled at having a baby brother. And our parents are going to love being grandparents a second time over.'

The Somers family had all taken Ethan to their hearts, and Ethan had been happy about changing his surname to George's the day that his mother married George.

'Not to mention all the visitors you're going to get from the physio department, cooing over him. I'm under strict instructions to take a photograph and go by the department to show them on my way out, or I'm toast. And, yes, I'll send photos to your old department in Hampstead, too.'

'Good. I do miss them since we moved here last year.' They'd waited until Ethan was about to start middle school before moving to the East Wing of Somers Hall, so the change of schools would be easier for him. 'But my new colleagues are great, too.'

He leaned over and kissed her. 'Life doesn't get any better than this, Mrs Somers. Well, actually, it does. Because we've got all the milestones to go through together. The first smile, the first tooth, the first step— oh, and not to mention Ethan's first driving lesson in nine years' time...' He looked down at his son. 'And I do believe right now it's going to be the first nappy change. Seeing as you've done all the hard work so far today, this one's mine.'

Serena laughed. 'I'm not going to argue with you. I love you, George. And you're right. Of course we're going to have rough days, like everybody else. But we know we'll be able to get through them, because we're together. A family.'

'A family,' he echoed. 'I love you, too, Serena.' He stole another kiss. 'Now, and for the rest of our days.'

* * * * *

Dear Reader

Life sometimes forces us in new directions whether we want to go there or not. When nurse Joni Thompson's heart and career are left in tatters by the man she loves, she starts over in Bean's Creek, North Carolina, making a new life for herself, determined never to give another man control over her life.

Only she can't resist Dr Grant Bradley's smile—nor his touch. But so long as she's the one making the rules and they stick to them her heart and job will be safe…right? Too bad the dashing pulmonologist is playing by his own set of life rules—rules that leave her heart vulnerable. But what's a girl to do when he steals her breath and demands she give him her all?

Hope you enjoy Joni and Grant's story, and the Bean's Creek crew.

I love to hear from readers. Please e-mail me at janice@janicelynn.net to let me know what you think of Joni and Grant's story, or just to chat about romance. You can also visit me at www.janicelynn.net, or on Facebook, to find out my latest news.

Happy reading!

Janice

CHAPTER ONE

"THERE is just something about that man that makes my uterus want to come out of retirement."

Intensive Care nurse Joni Thompson's gaze jerked away from the IV pump she was programming to gawk at the eighty-plus-year-old skeleton of a woman lying in the hospital bed. Mrs. Sain had severe chronic obstructive pulmonary disease and was unfortunately a frequent flyer in the ICU when she lapsed into hypercapneic respiratory failure.

Joni didn't have to ask who her patient referred to. Apparently, even little old ladies two tiptoed steps from death's doorway weren't immune to his charm.

Dr. Grant Bradley, pulmonologist extraordinare.

Okay, so the man had it all. Brains, beauty, body.

Not that she'd noticed.

Much.

Oh, yes, much perfectly described how she'd not noticed Grant.

She'd not noticed much about his sky-blue eyes. Or much about his broad shoulders that couldn't be hidden beneath his standard hospital-issue scrub tops that perfectly matched those thickly lashed intelligent eyes. Or much about his narrow hips, and she just knew if she could pull his scrub pants tight to his body, he'd have a butt not worth much ado as well.

But his smile was what she'd not noticed the most much.

His smile lit up his face, dug dimples into his handsome cheeks, and made his beautiful eyes dance with mischief. The man's smile did funny things to her insides.

She closed her eyes and willed Grant out of her head yet again. Seemed like the longer he worked in Bean's Creek, the more she had to forcibly exorcise the man from her thoughts.

"It's his smile, you know."

Had Mrs. Sain read her mind or what?

Joni gawked at the white-haired woman fanning her face as if she really was having a full-blown hot flush brought on by a sudden surge of Dr. Grant Bradley-is-Hot hormones.

"When that man smiles it's as if he knows your every secret." Mrs. Sain's fanning increased, gaining good rhythm for a person in her frail condition. "As if he knows you're thinking about him, and he likes being the center of your attention." A soft sigh escaped thin, pale lips as her eyes closed. "Reminds me of my Hickerson."

Joni smiled at the woman's reminiscing of her late husband. Her patient often mentioned the devilishly handsome man she'd spent more than sixty-five years married to.

Was Mrs. Sain right? Was it Grant's smile that made him so irresistible? Joni considered the cocky sideways grin he frequently flashed her way. The man smiled exactly as if he knew what she was thinking and his arrogant self liked it that she wanted to rip off his clothes and lick him from head to toe and all in between.

Definitely all in between.

He expected no less than that reaction from women. Why would he?

The man was a god when it came to the opposite sex. Women of all ages fell over themselves vying for his attention, vying for one of those half-cocked grins to be just for them.

No, he wasn't a god, more like a tempting devil crooking his finger to lure women to the dark side.

Biting back a frustrated sigh, Joni shook her head at her still fanning—although rapidly losing momentum—patient. The woman had been on a vent less than forty-eight hours before. If Joni didn't know better she'd swear the IV fluid must have contained youth serum. Or one hundred-proof estrogen. Joni really liked the spunky older lady who somehow always managed to bounce back no matter how ill she was at time of admission.

"Not that he looks at me like that, mind you. But I've seen how he looks at you." Mrs. Sain placed her weathered hand on Joni's arm. "I think he may be a little sweet on you."

"I think your oxygen must be dropping because you obviously aren't thinking straight," Joni snorted, winking to soften her words because she'd been a bit more brusque than she'd meant to. Honestly, she just couldn't deal with Grant being "a little sweet" on her. She had her once messy life all straightened out. She didn't need Dr. Steal Her Breath throwing a curve into her life plan.

Mrs. Sain didn't appear in the slightest concerned about her oxygen levels, just laughed at Joni's remark and patted her arm with thin, clubbed fingers.

Trying her best not to react so she didn't encourage Mrs. Sain's current train of thought, Joni listened to the woman's heart and lungs. She noted the steady click of the woman's pacemaker and the coarse rhonchi and expiratory wheezing heard bibasilarly in both lungs anteriorly and posteriorly. As horrible as the woman's lungs sounded, they were still much improved from even the day before. Hopefully her breathing would continue to improve so Grant could discharge her back to the assisted living facility where she resided.

Grant sweet on her? Only in Joni's secret late-night fantasies was a man like Grant sweet on her.

No, that wasn't true. For some unknown reason Grant was interested in her. Although he'd seemed a bit standoffish with her at first, for the past few weeks he'd found reasons to seek her out, talk to her, touch her arm or hand, to make eye contact and smile that wicked smile at her.

He had asked her out.

For this weekend.

She'd immediately turned him down. Not that he'd accepted that. No, the great Dr. Bradley had told her to think about it because they both knew she wanted to go out with him as much as he wanted her to say yes.

Ha! Who was he to say that she wanted to go out with him?

How much did he want her to say yes? Why?

If she had said yes, go where?

He hadn't even told where their supposed date would have been. Most likely the hospital's Hearts for Health fundraiser.

The last thing she wanted was to go to a hospital event and be lumped into the category of Dr. Bradley's latest bedroom babe.

No matter how long she thought about his question, no matter how tempted she might be, her answer wouldn't change.

She knew all about men like Grant. They played the field then moved on, leaving havoc in their wake. Grant was no different. Hadn't he already made his way through a good portion of the single population at the hospital?

Okay, so technically she only knew of a couple of hospital employees he'd been linked with during the few months he'd been in Bean's Creek, but there were probably more, right? It wasn't as if she was privy to his social calendar, but she imagined the man never lacked for female company.

She imagined lots of things in regard to Grant.

So okay, he was interested and, truth be told, she thought about him a lot. Too much really. But she wouldn't be changing her mind about going out with him. She knew better. Had learned that lesson the hard way years ago.

Dr. Mark Braseel had taught her well.

"I think you might be a little sweet on him, too."

Mrs. Sain's words had the effect of hot lava dropping onto Joni's face. Was her annoying fascination with the man that obvious? How long had she been in a think-ing-of-Grant daze? No wonder he'd asked her out. He probably thought she was an easy score to add another notch to his proverbial macho-man belt.

No, thank you. Been there, done that. Not ever walk-ing down that painful road again regardless of how much Grant might tempt her. Some scars ran too deep to risk reopening.

She met Mrs. Sain's curious gaze, held it without blinking. "You couldn't be further from the truth."

Which was true. None of her thoughts about Grant

were sweet. If she were on that hot-blooded man, well, let's just say she wouldn't be sweet. Uh-uh, no way. She'd be a wildcat.

Hello! Where had that come from? Her? A wildcat?

She laughed out loud at the mere thought of her being wild, period. Not her. She was the perpetual good girl. The one and only time she'd stepped outside her good-girl shoes she'd paid too high a price.

A stab of pain pierced her chest and she blinked away the moisture that stung her eyes at the memory of her life's biggest mistake. She'd been so gullible, so stupid. No way would she ever let a man deceive her like that again.

"Now, Mrs. Sain, let's get back to important things. Like your health." She bit the inside of her lower lip, tasting the metallic tang of blood. Telling herself to get a grip, she refocused on the IV pump settings. "I'm so glad that your lungs are holding their own. Although they are still weak, you're doing wonderful to be so soon off the ventilator. Your saturations are staying in the low nineties."

"Only because of this." Mrs. Sain gestured to the nasal cannula that provided a continuous flow of concentrated oxygen. "But I'm not going to complain because at least I'm breathing without that tube down my throat."

"What are you not complaining about?" the subject of their earlier conversation asked as he invaded the room.

Invaded was the right word.

When Grant stepped into a room he encompassed and overwhelmed everyone and everything, all without putting forth any more effort than just existing. The man exuded charisma. Life could be so unfair.

"My oxygen." Mrs. Sain beamed at her doctor, encompassed and overwhelmed and obviously once again considering bringing her female organs out of retirement.

Grateful that her patient hadn't elaborated on what they'd been discussing, Joni tried to keep from looking directly at Grant. Keeping her gaze off his gorgeous face proved impossible. In mere seconds she was watching him grin at Mrs. Sain before he placed his stethoscope to her, carefully auscultating the crackling sounds the shallow rise and fall of her frail chest made.

Whatever his flaws might be—and she was sure he had a few even if she'd yet to really discover what they might be other than that he was a playboy—the man was an excellent doctor, one Joni would like on her side if her lungs ever failed.

Hello! Her lungs were failing right now, clearly not bringing in enough oxygen because when he looked up and their gazes met, she'd swear she felt…something. Something hot and intense and so powerful that she had to look away. Had to.

Because she felt encompassed and overwhelmed and as if her own uterus was doing cartwheels, wanting to come out of the self-imposed retirement Joni had forced her body into after Mark.

Because she felt as if she needed that ventilator her patient had not so long ago been weaned off.

She closed her eyes, sucked a deep breath into her starved lungs, touched the raised bed railing to ground herself to reality.

"Joni," Grant acknowledged her presence. Or maybe he wanted her to look back up at him. Or maybe he thought she was about to pass out. She didn't know. She didn't look or faint. Thank goodness.

Okay, so there was a little something-something between them. A little something-something that was hot and intense and quite potent. She had felt it the first time she'd laid eyes on him. Yes, she had caught him looking at her several times as well, but she'd decided he must be trying to figure out why she was always looking at him.

When he was distracted, she did look.

Look? More like let her eyes feast on him, soaking up every morsel of his eye-candiness. Which meant she was quite pathetic and not nearly as immune to his charms as she liked to think. Then again, maybe she was just trying to figure out what it was about the man that messed with her head when she'd been getting along just fine all these years without once being tempted to get involved in another relationship.

"You sure got quiet." Mrs. Sain practically cackled with her delight. Definitely, her eyes held a knowing sparkle and an *uh-hum, I knew* it gleam.

Suppressing a smile in spite of her inner turmoil, Joni shook her head at the older woman who'd come so far in such a short time. "You sure talk a lot for someone who was just taken off a vent a couple of days ago. Shouldn't you be quiet? Save your voice?" she teased.

Her eyes not losing their twinkle, the older woman attempted to take a deep breath into her diseased lungs. She only managed to bring on a coughing spell that lasted a full minute and had both Grant and Joni leaning her forward to beat on her back before she calmed and nodded. "You should spend some time with me when I'm not hacking up a lung."

Glad the coughing spell had ended, Joni thought she'd like spending time with this feisty woman very much. "I'd love to."

Grant said something from behind Joni. She couldn't make out his words, but then he spoke clearer, louder to his patient. "You keep improving the way you have over the past forty-eight hours and you're going to blow this joint in a few days."

Mrs. Sain's scarce eyelashes batted coyly at Grant. "You make house calls, Doc?"

Joni suppressed an eye roll. Grant just grinned at the feisty woman.

"Only when I have a nurse to chaperone me. Gotta have someone around to make sure I behave." He winked conspiratorially at his patient. "Maybe we can convince Joni to accompany me to check on you."

Mrs. Sain seemed to think that a brilliant idea. Joni just gave a noncommittal answer, finished logging in the data she'd collected, then skedaddled out of the hospital room before the two had her committing to something she'd regret—like making house calls with Grant.

She paused outside the closed door, took a deep breath. Phew. What was it about the man that got her so flustered?

Why ask a question she knew the answer to?

Everything about Dr. Grant Bradley flustered her—and apparently every other female on the planet.

"You are going to the Hearts for Health benefit on Friday, right?" Samantha Swann asked as she clocked out via the hospital time-keeping system on the nurses' station desktop computer.

"You know I am." Joni replaced her best friend at the computer, typed in her information, clocked out, then logged off the program. "I'm volunteering with the cake walk for an hour."

The North Carolina hospital was committed to being

involved within the community, playing an active role in helping out when needed. Hearts for Health was co-sponsored by the hospital, hospital employees, and local businesses to provide assistance to families with health-care needs within the community, whether that need was for transportation back and forth to doctors' appointments or for assistance with excessive medical expenses. Joni wholeheartedly believed in the organization and often volunteered a helping hand. Friday night was a fundraising event that involved a barbecue dinner, games, and a raffle for various items donated by local businesses.

"I'm selling tickets at the front door. Vann is stopping by about the time my shift ends. We'll look for you so we can all grab a bite to eat together."

Vann had been Samantha's significant other since they had been fifteen. He'd asked Samantha to marry him at least a dozen times, but Samantha had turned him down each and every time, stating that they really shouldn't ruin a perfectly good relationship that way. As Joni couldn't name a single happily married couple, she tended to agree with her friend.

"Sounds great." She gathered her purse and turned to go, colliding into Grant.

He reached out, steadied her, smiled down at her even as she pulled away from him. How long had he been standing behind her? Had he been listening to she and Samantha talk? Why was her heart clamoring its way out of her chest? Not because his body had felt strong and solid against her. Not because in that brief moment before she'd jerked back, a zillion electrodes had sparked to life within her. Not because he'd smelled so good she'd wanted to fill her lungs with the musky scent of him.

Samantha smiled at Grant. All the nursing staff liked him. Most couldn't say enough ooey-gooey things about him.

"Is there something I can help you with before I go?" Samantha offered, despite the fact she had clocked out, doing a fairly good imitation of Mrs. Sain's earlier eyelash batting.

"No. Thanks, though." His gaze briefly touched on Samantha, then shot right back to Joni. "Can I speak with you?"

Her heart rate zoomed from banging against her ribcage to an all-out pinball machine ball ricocheting hard throughout her chest cavity. She was pretty sure her rhythm would send a cardiologist into panic, too. No way was the fluttery thump-thump in her chest anywhere near normal. Maybe she should make an appointment with Vann.

"I guess so," she squeaked, sending a desperate don't-leave-me glance toward Samantha, who proceeded to bat her lashes again, wave, and do just that. Great. Some best friend.

With a friendly nod he said goodbye to Samantha, then turned the full force of his attention onto Joni. Never had eyes been bluer or more intense. Never had a grin been more lethal. "If you're ready to go, I'll walk you to your car."

Grabbing her bag, she nodded, keeping her gaze anywhere but on him. She didn't point out that his car would be in the physicians' parking area and nowhere near hers. Neither did she point out that she was perfectly capable of walking herself to her car and that she'd been doing so for the five years she'd worked at Bean's Creek Memorial.

"What do you want to talk about?"

"Why did you say no when I asked you out?"

They asked at the same time.

Although her feet kept moving at a normal pace, the urge to run shimmied up her spine. Every fight-or-flight protective response flared strong within her body. "That's what you wanted to talk about?"

"Not really."

Surprised by his answer, her gaze cut to him. "Pardon?"

"No, I don't really want to talk about a beautiful woman saying no when I ask her to go out with me. I'd really like to forget that ever happened." He grinned sheepishly.

Joni tried to ignore the way her own eyelashes threatened to flutter at him calling her beautiful, at the impact of that smile.

"But," he continued, "I do want to understand why you said no."

Did he have all night? Because explaining her reasons could take that long if she told him the truth. If she told him about Mark, about her mother, about her fear of addiction, about how she was determined to keep her eyes focused on her career.

"Does my reason matter?" she asked instead.

"Obviously, or we wouldn't be having this conversation."

Good point. "You aren't my type."

"Male?" His eyebrows waggled in a Groucho Marx imitation.

She rolled her eyes heavenwards and kept walking.

"Good looking?"

She bit the already sore spot on her lip. The man was really too much.

"Smart?"

This time she snorted, fighting to keep from smiling. She did not want to smile. Lord knew, he didn't need any encouragement.

"Really hot in bed?"

Stopping in mid-step, Joni turned to gawk. "Seriously?"

"Seriously." The way he said the word left her in no doubt that he really was. No doubt her Egyptian cotton sheets would blaze if his naked skin ever brushed against them.

"Let me show you."

There went the smile. The one Mrs. Sain had so accurately described. The one that was making her want to say, Okay, show me, O Lucifer.

"That's not what I meant," she said instead, shaking her head, mostly because she wanted to shake loose her crazy thoughts. She was not the kind of woman who had sex with a man just because he was self-professedly "really hot in bed". "I was referring to your question in the sense of did you really just say that? Not as in 'Are you really hot in bed?'."

"Yes to both." His grin kicked up another notch, digging dimples deep into his cheeks and making laugh lines appear at the corner of his eyes. Oh, yeah, the man was Satan personified, tempting beyond belief.

"And so humble, too." She was stronger than this, better than this. Turning away from his potent smile, she began walking toward the elevator again, knowing her peace of mind lay with getting far away from him as quickly as possible. "My answer is no to both."

"Why?" he asked, easily matching her step for step.

Because you are too much like the man who broke my heart.

Because if I let you close you will break my heart, too, and I'm not ever going through that again.

Now, where had that come from? She didn't usually wear Mark as a protective shield. She usually didn't have to. No man tempted her to veer from the path she'd chosen for herself. She had responsibilities, to herself and to her mother.

"You have to ask that after what you just said to me?" she replied flippantly, not liking it that her thoughts had turned to her past. "I'm not interested, Dr. Bradley. Go be God's gift to women with someone else."

His smile slipped a little, and he sighed. "Am I coming on too strong? Is that the problem?"

Taking a deep breath, she tried a different tactic. "We both work at the hospital. You shouldn't be coming on at all."

"There aren't any hospital rules against employees dating. I checked."

Why didn't that surprise her? "I'm sure you did, several dates ago," she bit out with a little more snarkiness than she'd intended.

His brow arched. "Oh, really?"

Heat flooding her face, Joni shrugged. "I just meant that I know you've gone out with a few hospital employees."

"You know that?" He looked intrigued by her response, which she found very irritating. Everything about the man irritated her.

"I know."

His lips twisted with amusement, annoying her further. "Who is it I'm supposed to have gone out with?"

Hot faced, Joni named the women who had been linked with him. She wanted nothing more than to race the rest of the way to the elevator and escape him.

They took several steps in silence before he said, "You know I sponsored a team in the golf tournament, right?"

No, she hadn't known that. "What golf tournament?"

"The one the Lions' club is putting on next month."

She vaguely recalled hearing something about the event, just hadn't paid much attention as she knew next to nothing about golf. "Oh." Then she frowned. "What does a golf tournament have to do with our conversation?"

"It's a co-ed tournament." His smile was lethal. "Do you know who my teammates are?" He punched the elevator down button.

She shook her head, waited for the elevator doors to slide open, and stepped inside the car, wishing by some miracle he wouldn't follow her.

Along with the hospital's medical director, he named the two women who she'd been told he was dating. The two women she'd just named.

Was he saying he hadn't dated either? Or that he'd just dated them due to the contact they shared with being teammates for the golf tournament?

"You are the only woman I've asked out on a date since I've moved to Bean's Creek."

Her heart spit and sputtered in her chest.

"You don't need to tell me any of this," she began, not quite sure why they were having this conversation or why his response made her want to throw her arms around his neck and kiss him. "For that matter, why are you telling me? What you do outside the hospital is of no consequence to me."

"See," he mused, pressing the door closed button and holding it in. His gaze held hers, refused to let her do anything more than stare back into the twinkling blue. "That's the problem. I want what I do outside the hospital to be of consequence to you."

CHAPTER TWO

SINCE when had Grant become so desperate that he had to corner a woman in an elevator to try to convince her to go on a date with him? Since when had he had to try to convince a woman to go out with him, period?

Since Joni had said no to him and he'd realized the curvy, auburn-haired beauty wasn't going to change her mind.

He'd wanted to ask her out the moment he'd arrived in Bean's Creek and met the always-smiling ICU nurse. Unfortunately, he'd learned a hard lesson about jumping into a relationship too fast. He'd wanted to be sure before he asked anyone out in Bean's Creek. To make sure he wasn't dealing with anyone mentally unstable or with addiction problems. He couldn't deal with another Ashley in his life. He'd had too much unfinished baggage to settle prior to starting a new relationship.

So he'd put his personal life on hold while he established his new practice, resolved the relationship issues he'd left behind the best he could under the circumstances, and now that he was ready to move forward, to embrace his new life, Joni had said no.

Which left him wondering why.

He'd have to be blind, deaf, and dumb not to know that she was interested in him. As interested in him as he was in her. A volatile chemistry sparked between them that threatened combustion on contact. He wasn't wrong about that. Which left what reason for her to say no?

Not that he was all that, but women didn't usually turn him down flat. Especially women who looked at him the way Joni looked at him. Had any woman ever looked at him that way? With such yearning in her eyes? He didn't think so. Which still didn't resolve the question of why she'd turned him down.

"Have I done something to offend you?" He couldn't think of anything specific, but maybe he'd inadvertently stepped on a toe or something. Maybe he should offer to rub her feet to make amends. He'd use any excuse to touch her.

She arched a brow, but didn't quite meet his eyes, more like stared at his ear or maybe a stray strand of hair. "Other than tell me you were hot in bed?"

"That offended you?" She wasn't a prude. He'd heard her laughing and cutting up with the other nurses and patients. Joni had a great sense of humor, even if she rarely gave him a direct glimpse of it. As a matter of fact, he was the only person she didn't smile at.

"Obviously, it didn't bowl me over," she pointed out, taking a step back and pressing firmly against the elevator handrail.

"Obviously." Grant regarded her long and hard and made a quick decision. "So tell me what would."

Her startled gaze shot to meet his head on. "What would what?"

"Bowl you over."

Her gaze lowered, her long lashes shading the lovely dark green hue of her eyes. "I don't want to be bowled over."

"Perhaps not, but humor me. What would it take for a man to win your interest? No, not a man, for me to win your interest and for you to go on a date with me?"

Her cheeks flushed a bright shade of pink, splotching her creamy skin that was otherwise only marked by the spattering of faint freckles across her nose. "Let it go, Grant. I'm not going to date you."

His brow mimicked her earlier movement. "Because I'm not your type?"

"I do recall mentioning that only minutes ago." She shot visual daggers at him.

Fine. He wasn't so egotistical that he thought every woman wanted him. Only he knew Joni did. So why was she being so adamant that she didn't?

"What is your type?" he questioned, determined that if she wasn't going to date him he at least wanted to know her reasoning. "No one seems to know."

Her lips pursed. "Have you been checking up on me?"

He'd asked, put out feelers to make sure she wasn't involved with someone, to make sure she was free for him to ask out, to make sure no one raised red flags about her as a person. "Yeah, I guess I have, because I did ask around at the hospital."

She exhaled with an annoyed huff. "Great. Now everyone will know."

"Will know what?"

"That you asked about me." Her expression screamed, Duh!

His confidence was ebbing fast, as was his reassurance at her sanity. "Is that a bad thing?"

"It's not a good thing." Her gaze shifted to the elevator button, then up at him expectantly.

Was he wrong? Had he imagined how this woman

looked at him? How he caught her watching him? He'd bet his Hummer that she wanted him, too. So, why was she playing hard to get? Was there more going on than met the eye?

Grant didn't like games. Lord only knew, he'd played enough of those the past few years with Ashley. But he liked Joni in a way that made him want to know more, that made him unwilling to let this go until he understood her rejection.

Which perhaps made him the world's biggest fool.

Because the right thing to do, what he should do, was lift his finger off the door-closed button, see her to her car, and forget about the pretty little nurse he thought about more often than not.

But that wasn't what he did.

Instead, he took advantage of how close they stood to each other in the elevator and, keeping one finger on the door closed button, with his free hand he lifted her chin.

"Fine. You don't want to date me. I'm not your type. Asking our co-workers about you prior to asking you out was a bad thing. But what about this?" he challenged.

She stared up at him with huge eyes. Her generous chest rose and fell in rapid, heavy breaths.

"If I kissed you, Joni, would that be a bad thing, too? Because I really want to kiss you and have wanted to for weeks. If that's not what you want, if you don't want me to kiss you, tell me to stop now."

Her pulse hammered at her throat. Her breath warmed his skin in fast little pants. She swallowed hard. Her lips parted as if she was going to speak, but not a word came out of her mouth. Instead, her eyelids closed, and a thousand emotions flashed across her lovely face all at once.

Ever so slightly her chin relaxed against his fingertips. Her lips parted another fraction. Her eyes remained
tightly closed. Her breathing deepened.

She wasn't saying no. Her body language screamed,
Yes. Oh, yes. He hadn't been wrong.

She wanted him to kiss her.

Which meant what? That she was playing hard to
get? That she was stringing him along? Toying with
him as Ashley had done?

He started to pull away, to cut his losses and put
Joni out of his mind, or at least try since he hadn't had
much luck up to that point. But her eyes opened and
there was such vulnerability in their sea of green that
he tumbled in.

Tumbled in and covered her mouth with his, not one
bit surprised at the immediate explosion of sensation
weakening his knees.

The moment Grant's lips touched hers, Joni was lost.

Lost in wonder and excitement and awe.

His mouth brushed over hers with a feathery touch
that was soft yet masterful. Gentle yet demanding.
Hungry yet restrained. All Grant.

She didn't understand his interest in her, not really,
but his kiss was so sweet, so tender, so hot that she
couldn't pull away. Couldn't do anything except embrace the emotions flooding through her at the simple
joy of his mouth conquering hers.

Of their own accord her fingers found their way into
the golden brown waves of his hair, pulling his head
closer to deepen the kiss. Her hand flattened against his
cheek, loving the smoothness that was broken only by
the hint of late evening stubble. Loving how his long,

lean body pressed against her, so strong, so capable, so absolutely delicious.

And the way he smelled. Oh, my!

She inhaled deeply, dragging in his masculine scent the way she'd wanted to when she'd bumped into him earlier. Never had a man smelled better. Or tasted better. Never.

She wanted to fill her senses with him, to let his intoxicating presence drug her to all reality.

Which had her taking a dazed step back. Only there was no where to go because she already pushed into the hand railing. Panic clogged her throat, widened her eyes, stiffened her body.

What was she doing? She started to ask herself a thousand questions, but Grant's fingertip covered her lips. The gentle touch sent just as many shockwaves throughout her body as the taste of his lips had, as the feel of his strong body pressed against hers had, as the masculine musk of his scent had.

She wanted him. Right here, right now, in this elevator, she wanted him. That terrified her, made her feel out of control, something she'd sworn she'd never be again.

"Shh, don't."

Don't? her mind screamed. Wasn't it a little late for don't? They had.

Now she knew what she really needed not to know.

That he was everything that cocky smile promised.

That where Grant was concerned, she was going to have to up her guard or she was going to fall for him whether she wanted to or not.

That she might have thought he was like Mark, but she'd been wrong. Grant made Mark look like kid's play and the doctor she'd considered her future had tattered her heart and her whole life, almost pushed her into a well of despair that drowned her.

"Don't over-think what just happened. Just enjoy the moment." He flashed that lethal smile. The one that said he knew exactly what she was thinking, feeling, wanting, all of which involved him touching and kissing her a whole lot more. Enjoy the moment? Who was he kidding?

She geared up to blast him for having kissed her but before she made a single sound, she stopped.

How could she blast him? He hadn't forced her. No, he'd given her opportunity to stop him, and she hadn't. Instead, she'd closed her eyes and waited for him to kiss her.

Why hadn't she stopped him?

He ran his thumb along her jaw, leaving a tingly trail of awareness, reminding her exactly why she hadn't stopped him. Not that she'd known he had magic fingers, exactly, but chemistry had gotten the better of her.

"If not before, I'll see you Friday night."

She blinked, confusion adding to the mix of swirling emotions. "I'm not going out with you." At his fading smile, she rushed on, "I'm sorry if I misled you by not telling you not to kiss me. I should have, but I…" What could she say? That she'd been curious? Full of desire for him? That she had a mile-long masochistic streak and after five years of celibacy he made her want to throw caution to the wind with a single kiss? "But nothing's changed." Everything had changed. His kiss had turned her world upside down and inside out. She'd never look at him again without recalling how he'd curled her toes with his kiss. "I don't want to have a relationship with you outside our professional one at the hospital."

She really didn't want to have that one either. Too dangerous. She needed to stay far away from him. But unless she transferred out of the ICU, she'd have to deal with him on a regular basis. She loved working in ICU. She'd lost one job she loved because of a man, she wouldn't lose another.

"I know." But his eyes said otherwise, that her rejection confused him as much as she confused him. Probably just that he wondered how someone who was such a plain Jane would have the audacity to turn someone like him down. "I meant that I would see you at Hearts for Health on a non-date outing where we will both just happen to be," he pointed out, all apparent innocence.

"Oh." She searched his face for sarcasm, but only saw the ever-present twinkle in his eyes. The one that said he read minds and liked what she was thinking. He probably knew exactly the effect his kiss had had on her. Great.

He grinned and tweaked her nose. "Look, I'm sorry if I pushed more than I should have with the kiss, but I couldn't help myself. You have that effect on me." Another flash of the sexiest smile she'd ever seen. "I'll behave Friday night. Just give me a chance to get you past whatever makes you think you shouldn't go out with me. I promise I can change your mind."

He couldn't help himself? She had that effect on him? Hello, it wasn't as if she was the kind of woman to inspire men to lose all control. If she had been interested in dating, she'd be thrilled at the interest he was showing.

Who was she trying to kid? Deep down, she was thrilled at his interest. She was also terrified. A lot of years had passed since she'd been interested in a man, since she'd been touched, since she'd felt anything for the opposite sex.

Maybe too many years.

She had forgotten how good a man's touch felt.

Maybe she'd never known.

Had it felt that good when Mark had kissed her? Perhaps. She'd blocked the memories of her only lover for so long that she really couldn't recall how she'd felt the first time he'd touched her, kissed her. There was too much pain tied up in those memories to let them flood in now, so she shoved them back wherever they'd been hidden away.

As far as Grant changing her mind, well, that was what worried her. Based on her reaction to his kiss, he could change her mind all too easily, and then what? She'd be left with the fallout, left to pick up the pieces of her broken life. No, thank you. She was in charge of her destiny, not her libido.

"I probably won't even see you," she admitted slowly, not looking at him, not wanting him to see the fear coursing through her veins. Predators sensed fear and used it to their advantage, right? Yet thinking of him as a predator didn't quite fit. He had told her to tell him to stop if she didn't want his kiss. She had wanted him to kiss her. That was the problem. "I'm working the cake walk."

He grinned that smile that said he knew all and liked the power that came with it. She really should censor her thoughts around him—just in case.

"The cake walk? Imagine that. So am I." His eyes sparkling with mischief, he kissed the tip of her nose. "Who says you can't have your cake and eat it too?"

"How did you—?"

The elevator door slid open, interrupting her question.

Joni hadn't even realized he'd removed his finger from the button, hadn't even realized she was moving downward.

Had his kiss dazed her that much? Apparently.

She let him walk her to her car, let him open the door after she'd punched the unlock button on the key fob, let him close the door and watch her leave. All without another word.

All without admitting to herself that she hadn't "let" Grant do a darned thing. He was a man who took what he wanted one way or another. For some crazy reason he wanted her.

Holy water, garlic, and crucifixes warded off vampires, but what did one use when needing to ward off the devil himself? Especially when he kissed as sinfully deliciously as Grant?

Joni held her patient's hand while Grant pulled the tube free from the sixteen-year-old's chest. Casts on his left arm and leg, both in traction, the young man grunted with his pain. He gritted his teeth, wanting to look tough in front of his parents, doctor, and nurse.

The boy had been in a car accident that had resulted in multiple fractures, crush injuries, and a collapsed lung. A surgeon had repaired a few internal bleeds and removed his spleen. An orthopedic surgeon had pinned his broken bones back together. Grant had been following the young man's pulmonary status from the point he'd been admitted to the ICU. If his lung didn't collapse again, he'd be transferred to the medical floor and sent home within a couple of days.

"You did great, Dale," Grant assured the boy, closing the wound as Joni handed Grant a pair of suture scissors. He ran through listening to the boy's lungs and assured himself there were breath sounds in all lung fields.

"Yes," the boy's mother praised, worry and fatigue from the past week's events obvious in her expression and body. "You're so brave."

"Right." Dale rolled his eyes, obviously embarrassed by her compliment.

Laughing, Grant patted the boy on the shoulder. "You are the man, Dale. Have your nurse page me if you get short of breath or have any negative change with your breathing."

He spoke with the boy for a few more minutes, then left the hospital room. The boy's parents followed him out, no doubt to corner him with questions.

Joni ran through another set of vital checks and made sure all the telemetry was still connected correctly. She reminded him what symptoms to watch for regarding his breathing, fractures, and other injuries, then left the room.

She wasn't surprised to find Grant in the hallway.

Distracted by the boy's parents, he seemed oblivious that she'd stepped out of the room. His navy scrubs hung loosely on his frame and he'd obviously raked his fingers through his hair a few times. Although barely seven a.m., he'd already been at the hospital for several hours, having gotten called in to the emergency room when a patient had gone into respiratory distress just prior to daybreak. No doubt he had an office full of patients waiting on him, too. Yet he answered each of the boy's parents' questions with admirable patience and a genuine smile.

He was a good doctor, gorgeous, kind, self-assured.

He'd kissed her.

She'd been fighting the thought from the moment

she'd arrived at the hospital and learned he was already there.

No, truth was, she'd thought of nothing else the whole night. Even attending AA with her mother hadn't distracted her. When she'd finally drifted into sleep, she'd dreamed of him. Dreamed of his lips tasting hers, conquering, taking, mastering. When she'd wakened, she hadn't felt rested at all. She'd only felt restless, on edge, as if she'd been waiting for him, as if his kiss had awakened her and shot her to the precipice of the rest of her life.

Which was crazy.

She was no Sleeping Beauty and Grant was no Prince Charming. He had nothing to do with the rest of her life.

Once upon a time she'd believed in happily-ever-after. She'd been a wide-eyed innocent who'd believed the lies of a powerful man almost twice her age. Lies that had stolen her belief in fairy-tales, her self-respect, and had almost destroyed her life and career.

"Joni?"

She met Grant's gaze, saw the question in his eyes. She shook her head, sent a quick smile to the boys' parents, and went to check on another patient. A twenty-two-year-old who'd been in an MVA two nights before and had yet to regain consciousness.

"You okay?"

Not having realized that he'd followed her into the patient's room, she spun, startled.

"Sorry, I didn't mean to scare you." His fingers brushed over her arm, eliciting thousands of goose-bumps.

Why was he always touching her?

"You don't scare me."

His lips twisted. "Actually, I think I do."

"Oh, get over yourself. Not every woman wants you." Clamping her lips closed, she cast a quick glance at her unconscious patient. She wanted the boy to wake up, to give her a reason to move away from Grant. A reason that he couldn't mistake as fear.

"True," he admitted. "But we're not talking about every woman, are we? We're talking about you."

She glared, not liking him.

"Whether you're willing to admit it or not, you do want me, Joni." He smiled that smile that was really starting to get on her nerves. "And for reasons I don't understand yet, I definitely scare you."

CHAPTER THREE

"So WHAT'S up with you and Dr. Take My Breath Away?"

Joni pretended not to hear Samantha's question, just set down the box of cakes she'd made for the cake walk on the long table in the community room.

"Hello." Samantha snapped her fingers in front of Joni's face. "The man asked me all kinds of questions about you right down to where I thought he was going to have me sign an affidavit stating I was telling the truth, the whole truth, and nothing but the truth, so help me God. I've seen how you two look at each other and thought there was something there, but you never said anything so I thought maybe you just didn't realize yet. Then he walked you to your car the other night and you've been tighter than a clam ever since. Best friend here." She thumped her chest. "I want details. Lotsa details."

Taking a red velvet cake out of the box, Joni found an empty spot on the table, then turned to her friend. "What makes you think there are lotsa details?"

"The fact that you're being so evasive and blushing like the entire football team just saw you in your undies."

"Well, it is a little warm in here." She made a pretense of fanning her face.

"Right." Samantha shivered and glanced around the mostly vacant community room. "I expect to see a group of penguins and a few polar bears go strolling by any moment there's such a heat wave in this place. Brrrr."

Okay, so her friend had a point. Due to expecting such a crowd, the thermostat had been set low to cool the building off prior to hundreds of warm bodies heating up the place.

Joni finished emptying the box and stooped to slide the box beneath the table. "You going to help me set up the cake walk?"

"I thought that was my job."

Grant!

Samantha gave her a "you are so going to tell me everything later" look. "Yeah, I'm pretty sure it is. Besides, I'm needed at the ticket table. A lot of work setting that up, you know."

"You need us to help you?" Grant offered, carefully putting the box he held on an empty spot on the table.

"I've got it covered." Samantha shook her head, made eye contact with Joni and did an "I'm watching you" finger motion before leaving the community room to head towards the front of the building where tickets would be sold.

"This doesn't start for almost an hour, you know," Joni pointed out as she watched her friend bail on her for the second time that week. Some best friend.

"I know. I came to help with set-up." He pulled out several home-made cakes that had Joni's mouth watering. Wow. How many little old ladies had he hit up for that stash?

She eyed him suspiciously. "Did you know I was helping with set-up?"

Not looking one bit ashamed, he grinned. "Would you believe a little birdie told me?"

"Ha. I'd believe a big birdie told you." Her gaze went toward where Samantha had just disappeared through the double doors.

He laughed. "I can't let Samantha take the blame for this one. Brooke in Admissions told me."

"Brooke?" Joni shook her head. Just how many of her friends had he talked to? "Do I have no friends?"

"Oh, you have lots of friends. They all think you are a great nurse, a great person, although a bit of a control freak. You like your privacy and have no romantic life that any of them are aware of."

Joni's jaw dropped. "They told you all that?"

"What can I say? Apparently, they like me."

Good thing she didn't have enemies.

"They don't know you like I do," she quipped.

"True," he admitted, taking the last of the cakes out of the box and arranging it just so on the table. "And you don't know me anywhere near as well as you're going to. Now, where do we start?"

Joni started to argue with him that she didn't want to know him better, but what was the point? He would just flash that smile of his and keep right on going.

"Fine," she acquiesced, just ready to get this enforced time with him done and over with. "Carry this box over to the middle of that section and we'll lay out our cake-walk squares. I checked earlier and all twenty-four squares are there. We just have to get them laid out in an eye-pleasing way."

"Eye-pleasing, eh?"

"Grant—"

"I know, I know, get to work. Such a control-freak slave-driver." He picked up the box and began doing her bidding one cake-walk square at a time while she pretended not to notice how his jeans hugged his behind and thighs in a way that made her want to moan.

Great. Just shoot her now, because tonight was going to be a long, torturous night.

Punching the Play button on the old-fashioned boombox being used for the cake walk's sound system, Grant grinned at his cute assistant who held the container full of numbered cards.

Apparently loving the festivities, Joni had been smiling all evening. Well, all except for when she looked directly at him.

Then she frowned. But only a few times since he'd first arrived and caught her off guard. Good, he liked catching her off guard because then she didn't have time to slide that masked expression into place.

Not that she'd masked her expression much tonight.

Whether she wanted to admit it or not, she was having fun. A lot of fun. With him.

So was he. With her.

How long since he'd felt this attracted to a woman? This relaxed? Years, thanks to Ashley. Why had he let her take over his life so? Well, he knew why. Staying with her had been easier than dealing with the drama of breaking up.

But sometimes love wasn't enough. In Ashley's case that had held true. Or maybe he hadn't been enough. Definitely not enough to keep her away from the demons that drove her.

Grant pulled his mind back to the present, determined not to let the past drag him down, not tonight. Not ever again. He'd moved to Bean's Creek to make a new start. He'd needed to make a fresh start. He had, right down to meeting Joni and knowing he wanted more than just a co-worker relationship with her. Knowing he wanted more than just friendship with her but proceeding with caution because he didn't want to end up right back in a similar relationship he'd been in with Ashley.

What he wanted was to peel off those snug jeans and kiss his way down the curve of Joni's hips, the lushness of her thighs, the tonedness of her calves, right down to the arch of her foot. Was she ticklish? Would she squirm free from his embrace, giggling and retaliating with touches and kisses of her own? Or would she simply moan in pleasure?

He closed his eyes, swallowed. Hard. If he didn't get his mind on the job at hand and off Joni, he was going to be hard. He was about halfway there already. More than halfway.

"Grant?"

His gaze went to Joni's expectant one. She was so beautiful, so full of verve, so tempting. "Hmm?"

Brows drawn tight, she gave him a pointed look. "Don't you think the music has gone long enough this round?"

Grant grimaced. He'd forgotten to stop the music. The cake walkers had been circling around the numbered squares for God only knew how long. He covered his slip with a grin. "I was building the suspense."

"It's built." She sounded breathy, and his gaze dropped to where her sweater hugged her full chest. Never in his life had he been jealous of a shirt, but tonight he'd like to be wrapped around Joni. When he'd first arrived, the room had been cold and she'd been at high attention, had captured his notice and his imagination. Flashes of sliding his hands beneath her sweater, tweaking those taunt peaks, cupping those generous breasts, had been teasing him all evening.

"And," she continued, oblivious to how he wanted to drag her beneath the table full of cakes and nibble his way around her body, "Mrs. Lehew is about to need to replace her portable oxygen tank if she has to make another lap."

If he kept staring at Joni's tight little sweater, he was going to need portable oxygen himself.

"You might be right." He pressed the button to pause the music, pointed to the basket of numbered cards for Joni to draw out a winner. "Have at it."

"Number eleven," she called, casting him another odd look, before smiling sweetly at the seven—or eight-year-old snaggle-toothed boy who was jumping up and down on the number eleven block. Instantly, Grant had visions of Joni jumping up and down on the square, of her sweater outlining her breasts as they bounced and jiggled and beckoned to him. His jeans grew tighter. Too tight. Any moment he was going to lose all circulation in the lower half of his body.

Immediately after the young boy claimed his prize, Joni called for the crowd's attention, again. "Since Dr. Bradley got a little carried away by the music..." she sent him a sugary smile "...stay on your squares, because we're going to pick another winner." She reached into the basket and pulled out another card. "Number fourteen."

"Mrs. Lehew." Despite his uncomfortable jeans, Grant laughed. "You sure you didn't rig that win, Nurse Joni?"

At her impish grin, he realized she'd done exactly that.

"Call it preventative medicine because the poor

woman really can't manage any more trips around the cake walk. I didn't know how she was going to manage to begin with, but then you made her go even longer despite the fact she was slowing down the entire procession."

He really hadn't picked a good time to zone out with thoughts about Joni and leave the cake walkers going round and round. But the smile on Mrs Lehew's face said if she'd minded in the slightest, she no longer did.

"Maybe since she won a cake she'll sit out the remaining walks because if not," Joni mused, "we're going to have to find a designated walker for her."

"Or a wheelchair."

The ecstatic obese woman with severe chronic obstructive pulmonary disease excitedly took Joni's hand. "Oh, thank you. Thank you. I can't believe this. I never win."

"Well, you did tonight. Congratulations. Here's your cake, Mrs. Lehew." She handed the woman a chocolate-frosted cake from the long table still loaded with donated goodies.

"You know," Grant mused, scratching his chin with a feigned thoughtful look, "it's a good thing I'm her pulmonologist and not her endocrinologist or I'd have to protest that cake."

"Good thing," Joni agreed, responding to his teasing with a slight lifting of her mouth at the corners. "Then again, maybe she wanted to win the cake for her grandchildren or maybe she just wanted to do the cake walk to support a really good cause."

"We can tell ourselves that."

Joni's lips twitched. "But you're not buying it?"

"Not after her last hospital admission and seeing how

well controlled her sugar was when she didn't have easy access to snacks and junk food."

Looking as if she might tackle the elderly woman and wrestle the cake from her, Joni glanced toward Mrs. Lehew.

Sorry he'd mentioned the woman's uncontrolled diabetes, Grant touched Joni's hand. "It's okay. I learned a long time ago that you can't control what others do to themselves. You can only encourage them to do the right thing and hope they are paying attention." So maybe saying he'd learned that lesson a long time ago was stretching the truth, but he had learned. Eventually. "If she wants cake, she's going to have cake regardless of whether or not she wins one here." He squeezed Joni's hand, wanting to see her face light up with a smile again, wanting the sense of camaraderie, albeit precarious, they'd shared while doling out cakes to continue. "Besides, that one is for her grandkids."

Nodding resignedly, Joni gave him what appeared to be an appreciative smile. "Sure it is. If she ends up in the emergency room tonight with a five hundred blood sugar, I'm going to feel as if I put her there."

"No need for that. Look." Grant gestured in the direction the woman had headed and Joni's gaze followed suit. Mrs. Lehew was sitting at a table with three small children clamoring to get a better look at her prize. They were calling her Granny and tugging on her sleeves.

"Oh, you're good," she praised with a hint of sarcasm.

"I know." When Joni's gaze met his, he winked. "Oh, you meant because of Mrs. Lehew? What? You mean you didn't believe me?" He tsked. "Shame. Shame."

But rather than correct him or slap him down, she

just gave a resigned sigh and turned back to the cake walkers.

They collected the tickets from the next group in line, then Grant restarted the music and turned to her.

"You'll find that I am many things, Joni, but you can take what I tell you to the bank."

"Meaning?"

"Meaning that when I tell you how I've thought of little else except kissing you again, that I want to kiss you again, you can believe it's the truth."

"I don't doubt that you want to kiss me again."

She didn't sound happy about the prospect, though. Not exactly the reaction he'd hoped for. He wanted her to quit fighting the attraction between them and admit she wanted him too. He wanted whatever had her running scared to fade into the background and for her to embrace the chemistry between them. Still, she wasn't saying no.

"That confident that you were that good?" he teased.

"No, you are the one who just commented about how good you are, remember?" She shook the basket of numbered cards. "I'm just that confident that you see me as a challenge, and that's why you're so determined to pursue me," she countered. "But I'm not a challenge, Grant. I'm a real person with real feelings. I don't want to be hurt."

Grant started to speak, but she leaned over and punched the Pause button, killing the music and effectively drawing all eyes to them. Without another glance his way, she pulled out a card. "Number nineteen."

Why did Grant keep looking at her as if he wanted to peel off her clothes and take a bite? Joni bit the inside of her lip, wondering if she was going to gnaw a hole right through if she didn't stay away from a certain doctor. She'd accused him of seeing her as a challenge because that was what her brain had decided was the logical conclusion. Was that why he kept coming back for more of her pushing him away?

No, truth was, she was beginning to think he really liked her. The more she thought about it, the more likable he was, too. For all his cockiness, he was just as likely to say something self-deprecating to make her smile. Why, oh, why, did he have to be so likeable on top of how completely hunky he was? After all, she was only a mortal woman. How was she supposed to resist his allure when everything about him appealed?

She did her best to ignore him for the rest of their cake-walk stint. Not an easy thing when they were working to keep the cake walk going, but she did manage to avoid any more private talk.

A few minutes prior to the end, Vann and Samantha got into the cakewalk line.

"If I don't win, you are in so-o-o much trouble," Samantha teased, handing Joni her ticket and casting a questioning gaze toward Grant. She gave Joni two thumbs-ups. Puh-leeze. Even her best friend was matchmaking. Spare her.

Besides, she was irked at Samantha for bailing twice. And for telling Grant no telling what.

Ignoring Samantha's go-for-it sign, Joni shrugged. "Sorry, sugarplum." She never used endearments so this got a giggle out of her friend. "But your odds are the same as everyone else's. One out of twenty-four."

"I'll take those odds. Especially since Vann bought our tickets." Samantha patted his arm, keeping her hand on his biceps. Her friend usually insisted on paying her equal share, so the fact she'd let Vann pay was significant. Vann didn't look impressed. Actually, he looked irked, too.

Joni shot a curious gaze back and forth between the two, but Samantha just borrowed one from Joni's book and shrugged.

"Hey, Vann, you expecting special favors, too?" Joni asked, giving her friendliest smile and hoping to ease whatever strain was in the air.

Stepping out of Samantha's hold, he nodded. "Samantha wants cake, so let her eat cake. Lord forbid, she doesn't get everything she wants right when she wants it. To hell with the rest of the world."

Joni forced a laugh at his quip, hoping to ease the tension jetting back and forth between her two dear friends. Unfortunately, Samantha was now glaring at her boyfriend. Surely he hadn't proposed again tonight? Vann proposals were always followed by a fight, which was usually followed by making up and then another few months of the status quo before they repeated the process all over again. Eventually, Vann was going to tire of Samantha's refusals. But, for now, apparently he was hopeful enough that he'd change her mind to keep sticking it out. Either that or he liked their make-up ritual.

As far as Joni was concerned, Dr. Vann Winton was the sole good guy left in the world. Then again, he was a cardiologist so maybe he naturally had more heart.

Having finished collecting the rest of the tickets, Grant joined them.

"Vann." Samantha stepped forward. "This is Dr. Bradley, the pulmonologist I was telling you about. He's a miracle worker in the ICU. I've seen him yank patients back from the other side on more than one occasion. I swear he must have made a pact with God somewhere along the way." Then she waggled her brows and said a bit too brightly, "Or with the someone who hails from down below. Pun intended."

Joni couldn't argue Samantha's point. Hadn't she often wondered if Grant was really the devil himself?

Vann eyed Grant warily, making Joni question just what her friend had said about Grant in private. Still, polite as always, he stuck out his hand. "Dr. Vann Winton. I practice in Winston-Salem. Nice to meet you."

Grant whistled. "I've heard of you. I enjoyed that article you wrote about the promising beneficial effects of Tracynta on the treatment of pulmonary hypertension."

Vann's expression changed and if they'd had time, the two men would have launched into a conversation about whatever the article had said. Interesting. Vann usually took a while to warm up to strangers, but with one comment Grant had won him over to the dark side. Joni almost sighed. Maybe the man's appeal wasn't limited to little old ladies and nurses.

Samantha and Vann took their places on the numbered squares. Using the microphone, Grant briefly explained the rules to this round's walkers. When Joni called out the winning number, Samantha didn't win.

Vann did.

His lips curved in a smile. With wry amusement, he handed the cake over to an ecstatic Samantha, then he looked at Joni. "What did I tell you? If she wants cake, I give the woman cake."

Samantha leaned forward, whispered something in his ear that only he could hear.

His face brightened further, turning his already handsome face into a thing of beauty. "Apparently, I'm going to thoroughly enjoy her having her cake, too."

Giggling, Samantha nodded. "Oh, yeah, you're going to enjoy my…cake."

"I've heard of enjoying pie…" Grant mused, feigning innocence and making Samantha laugh again. Joni just rolled her eyes at them all.

Leaning close, Vann and Samantha obviously were no longer aware that anyone existed other than the two of them.

Unexpected envy shot through Joni. Which didn't make sense. She was happy. She had a great life.

Active, healthy, a sober mother, a job where she made a difference in people's lives. She had the life she had chosen for herself, that she had worked hard to make happen, and she wouldn't let anything, or anyone, threaten it. But when Vann's hand settled low on Samantha's back in a purely possessive move, Joni felt an ache. An ache that something major was missing.

Not that she needed a man to be happy. She didn't. But maybe she'd discounted the benefits of physical contact with an attractive person. Maybe she'd miscalculated when she'd buried herself so effectively behind her protective walls five years ago. Maybe life wasn't so cut and dried.

Maybe she could have her cake and eat it too.

Or at least have a lick of icing every now and again.

Really, she'd let Mark steal much more from her than she'd realized. Let her focus remain on keeping her mother sober to the exclusion of her own life.

She wanted cake.

Beef cake, a perverse little voice taunted from somewhere in her head. Yes, she wanted beefcake.

She wanted Grant.

After Mark she'd promised herself she'd never get involved with another doctor, that she'd never get involved with another playboy, period, no matter what his profession.

In reality, she hadn't gotten involved with anyone.

Not since she'd been a nursing student who'd fallen for a man in power who'd been so brilliant, so suave, so exciting to be around that she'd given him her heart and her body.

In the end, he'd burned her so badly she had only existed for months. For years.

She wanted to do more than exist.

She wanted to live.

Life at its fullest stood just a few feet away, tempting her with the sweetest pleasures. Only…could she?

If he only saw her as a challenge, should she? But how would she know if she just sat on the sidelines of life?

She wanted to know. She wanted Grant. And cake.

Heat fusing through her, Joni's gaze met his. Tension sparked. Was he thinking the same thing she was? Was he envisioning them sharing cake? Her spreading the whipped icing on that marvelous chest of his and licking it off one trace of her tongue over his skin at a time?

When his eyes lowered, settled onto her lips, visions erupted of him feeding her icing off his fingertip and then kissing her to share in the sweetness.

Oh, my. Her breath caught in her throat and she forcibly sucked in a deep breath to stay conscious.

Every cell in her body tingled, cried out for cake.

Her lips parted, then curved into a smile.

If she went in knowing she and Grant were just about chemistry, if she was the one who made the rules and Grant was willing to play by them, why couldn't she have cake?

CHAPTER FOUR

GRANT watched the slideshow of emotions flicker over Joni's face. God, she was beautiful. And tortured. And everything he wanted.

Or maybe she was just intent on torturing him because she was the only thing he wanted?

But despite the heat that burned, she insisted upon keeping those walls between them. Walls so high he wondered if he was ever going to scale them.

So when her expression softened, her lips parted, and her pupils dilated with what appeared to be lust, he took a step back from shock.

Then she smiled.

Full fledged, full force, Joni smiled. At him.

Grant wanted to tell the cake walkers to get lost, that he was going to push Joni down on those numbered squares and feast on the most divine woman's lips, that he was going to help himself to one of the cakes and smear icing on her throat and sup the sticky sweetness off one delectable sup at a time. He'd search out all her sensitive spots and repeat the process until she arched into his touch, until she offered him the sugary goodness of her body, shaming the sweetest of confections.

On cue, their replacements arrived and without a word Grant handed the microphone to Jamie, a phlebotomist he'd seen around the hospital a few times. Taking the basket of numbers from Joni, he handed them to, hell, he had no idea who he handed them to, just that he shoved them towards someone and someone took them.

What he knew was that when he grabbed Joni's hand, her skin was soft and warm against his. Her hand felt right. So right. More importantly, she didn't pull away.

Instead, she squeezed his hand, laced her fingers with his, kept up with him as he wove them out of the room full of people. He didn't pause when spoken to, just nodded an acknowledgement and kept heading toward the door, intent on finding someplace private so he could devour the woman next to him. Escape was only a few feet away when Dr. Abellano, the hospital's medical director, patted him on the shoulder.

"Grant." The man's voice sounded remarkably like Sean Connery's. "There's someone I'd like you to meet."

Would it be rude to say he didn't want to meet anyone? That all he wanted was to get Joni somewhere where they could be alone? His gaze shot to her. He knew his exasperation showed, but she just smiled at him. A knowing little smile that said she wanted out of this room as much as he did.

This had better not take long, otherwise he might be looking for a new job in the near future for ditching the medical director so he could go have his way with an ICU nurse.

"Hello, Dr. Abellano." He managed to hide his impatience.

The man nodded a brief acknowledgement to Joni, then redirected his attention to Grant. He kept talking, but Grant was only catching bits of the man's words. How could he focus on the older gentleman when Joni's pink tongue darted out and licked the corner of her mouth?

Unbelievably, she was teasing him, torturing him in a whole new way. She knew he hadn't wanted to stop, that he was having trouble focusing on what his boss was saying. He buried a growl deep in his chest, wanting to bury himself deep inside her instead. Didn't she know how desperately he wanted to strip off those jeans and sweater, push her against the wall, and make her scream his name?

Actually, he was pretty sure she did know and that she was enjoying herself. Which just made him want to strip her naked and make her enjoy herself all the more in other, more physical ways. To make her lose that tight control she clung to.

No, he needed to slow down, get a handle on the lust surging through him. For their first time he didn't want it to be rushed against a wall. He wanted a big bed and a bunch of hours to prove to her how good a relationship could be between them.

There would be a first time.

Whether tonight or next week or next month, there would be a first time between them. Dozens more. Hundreds even. If ever he had doubted the chemistry between them, staring into her eyes, he no longer did. He saw the stars, the moon, the promise of all the heavens above staring back at him in her green eyes. He wanted every out-of-this world experience she offered and to give them back to her tenfold.

"This is my daughter, Heather," Dr. Abellano introduced.

Grant barely glanced at the woman, greeted her only to keep from being discourteous to his boss and in the hope of quelling his libido enough to take a slow hand with Joni. But when Joni's gaze settled on the woman, her smile disappeared so quickly Grant took another look.

Heather Abellano was an extraordinarily beautiful woman. Tall, statuesque, dark, wavy hair, and almond-shaped brown eyes that popped. But she wasn't the woman whose hand he held. Neither was she the woman he desperately wanted to be alone with.

"Heather is a cardiologist just finishing up residency. She will be at the hospital for a few weeks." The medical director couldn't have sounded more like a proud father if he'd tried. "Make her feel welcome, won't you?"

The newcomer stuck out her hand. Hating to let go of Joni's hand, Grant did and exchanged quick pleasantries with the woman.

When he turned to introduce Joni, she was gone.

Joni slid into the seat next to Samantha, set her barbecue plate on the table, and took a big gulp of her diet soda.

Anything to quell the burn in her throat. Not that the rather flat soda was helping.

"So, what was that all about?" Samantha asked before the liquid even hit Joni's churning stomach.

She met her friend's gaze. "You tell me. Are you and Vann fighting?"

Taking a deep breath, Samantha shook her head. "Earlier, but not any more."

Joni popped a potato chip into her mouth, soaking up the salty goodness on her tongue. "He proposed again, didn't he?"

"At the front ticket desk." Samantha stuck her finger in her throat and made a gagging noise. "He walked up to the table where I sat with Bobbie Jean Evans and he asked me to marry him. How unromantic is that?"

Considering the man had already proposed a dozen times and had just driven in from Winston-Salem, Joni imagined that mustering romance knowing one was likely to be rejected yet again might be difficult. At least Vann was persistent.

What her friend had said hit her.

"Do you want romance?" Had she been misreading Samantha all this time? She'd thought, like her, Samantha didn't believe in happily ever after, but maybe her friend wanted the fairy-tale.

"Of course I want romance," Samantha confirmed, blowing Joni's mind a little. "What woman doesn't want romance?"

It might not be a good time to raise her hand. Especially in light of the fact that she so didn't want the conversation turning back to her and Grant. Not that there had been anything romantic between them, only...no, that had just been chemistry. Chemistry got people into trouble, got her into trouble. Much better to focus on her best friend's love life than her own.

"Does Vann know you want romance?" she asked, popping another chip into her mouth.

"He should. I've told him often enough."

She considered her friend's answer. "But does he know? I mean, really know that's what you want from him?"

Because Joni believed there wasn't much the man wouldn't do to convince Samantha to walk down the aisle.

"I don't know how he couldn't know. I've practically beat him over the head with it. Sometimes I think we've dated too long, we're too comfortable with each other, and that we'd be better off just being friends." She dropped her head to the table and beat her forehead against the molded plastic a couple of times. "Only he's all I've ever known, and I can't imagine my life without him."

Joni tried to imagine what it would have been like if she'd had a Vann, a man who'd been a part of her life from adolescence into womanhood, a man who'd brought her into womanhood, a man who'd held her hand during the hard times rather than turn on her. Yeah, she supposed the idea of letting that safety net go would be terrifying. Especially when that safety net was a man as wonderful as Vann. Still, he was obviously missing the clues her friend was dropping.

"Men can be so dense." Such as the fact she'd been ready to throw caution to the wind with Grant and he'd become distracted by a luscious brunette cardiologist.

"Such as Dr. Bradley?" Samantha echoed her thoughts. "Is he dense?"

"As a brick." Did the man have attention deficit disorder or what? For weeks now he'd been setting the stage to ask her out, had asked her out for this very night. The exact minute she'd decided to give in to the pull between them, he'd gone googly-eyed over another woman. Maybe she'd been dead on the money when she'd decided he just saw her as a challenge. Once she'd mentally acquiesced, she'd lost all appeal.

"A brick, eh?" Samantha laughed, then took a bite of her sandwich. "So, tell me what he did," she said between chews.

"He didn't do anything." Not really. She supposed he'd only been polite. Yet seeing his gaze rake over the brunette had ripped off a scab to a wound she hadn't wanted opened, to a wound that ran deep and left her raw even years later.

"The man walked you to your car the other night,

practically whisked you away from the cake walk, and you're telling me he didn't do anything either time? Not even a kiss?" Samantha's gaze narrowed as if that would give her the power to see right into Joni's head. "Right. I believe that. So, where have you been for the past fifteen minutes?"

"You should believe me. It's true." Joni forked a big bite of meat and poked the whole thing in her mouth. The spicy flavor made her mouth water. "I've been in the bathroom, trying to figure out what I want from Grant."

"The bathroom? What you want from Grant?" Samantha stared at her a moment, pushed her plate back, and turned in her chair to fully face Joni. "Tell me what happened back there."

Vann chose that moment to return to the table and put Samantha's drink in front of her. Samantha pointed towards the table of drinks. A line had formed of folks ordering. "Go get Joni a sweet tea, please."

Glancing back and forth between the two women, he nodded and went to find sweet tea.

"Forget romance. You really should marry him, you know," Joni said between bites. "He's a great catch."

"So am I," Samantha countered without skipping a beat. "You really should tell me what happened between you and Dr. Make Me Breathe Hard a few minutes ago, you know."

"That's an easy one. Nothing happened." Which was the truth because Samantha had asked about a few minutes ago and not about an elevator kiss that had poisoned her mind to all else.

No wonder she'd given in to the silly idea that she could have her cake and eat it too. Grant's kiss had infected her mind.

"But something is going to happen between you, isn't it?"

Was it? Joni sighed. "No." Pause. "Maybe." Another pause. "I think so."

"You think so? Woman, that man is hot and he was looking at you as if he wanted to spread his icing all over your cake, so to speak."

Leave it to Samantha to say something so outlandish, so totally inappropriate, yet that somehow worked. Sticking another potato chip in her mouth, Joni sought the right words to explain to her friend. "There's this thing between us. I don't understand, but it's definitely there."

"It's called chemistry, baby."

Ignoring that her friend had interrupted, Joni went on, "There's this chemistry between us. I don't understand it or even want it, but its there all the same."

"So what are you going to do about it?"

"That's what I spent fifteen minutes in the bathroom trying to figure out."

Samantha stared expectantly. "And?"

"Maybe I'm not going to do anything."

"Maybe you should."

"I...well, there for a minute I thought maybe, but now..."

"But now what? A gorgeous man is attracted to you and guess what? You're attracted to him, too. What could be a more perfect scenario? Life is short. Live a little. Smile. Laugh. Have some fun."

Samantha made it sound so simple. Just two people being attracted to each other and...and then what exactly? What was she so afraid of? "I don't want to get hurt."

Samantha placed her hand on Joni's. "That I understand."

"Vann would never hurt you."

"Not intentionally." She glanced up and smiled at the man they spoke of and who had just rejoined them.

"Thank you," Joni said when he gave her the disposable plastic cup of sweet iced tea.

"I hope you don't mind…" Vann took his seat across from them and pulled his plate toward him "…but I invited Dr. Bradley to join our table."

"Goodie," Samantha said, rubbing her palms together and earning a confused frown from Vann.

Joni was going to elbow her friend, but Grant stepped up to the table, a plate loaded with food in one hand and a drink in the other. "Hope I'm not intruding."

Ha, right. Would he leave if she told him he was?

"Of course you're not," Samantha assured him, gesturing to the empty seat across from Joni. "Have a seat."

"What happened to your new friend?" Joni could have bit her wayward tongue the second the question slipped out.

His brow arched. "Dr. Abellano's daughter?"

"Is that who she was?" Oh, she didn't sound jealous at all. Not one bit. Great. She couldn't look at Samantha because she was pretty sure that if she did her friend would burst out laughing.

"If you'd stuck around you would know that's who she was because I was going to introduce you but you disappeared. And I have no idea where she is now," he said, sliding into the seat next to her rather than into the empty seat next to Vann, leaving Vann alone on the opposite side of the table. "You jealous?" he asked close to her ear.

"Ha." She feigned indifference, wondering if she

was really that easy for the world to read. "Why would I be jealous?"

Why was her face on fire?

"Why indeed?" He grinned, obviously liking the pink tinge to her cheeks.

She was not jealous.

Was she? Yet when she analyzed her reaction, she had been jealous. Very jealous. Great. She hadn't even gone out on a single date with the man and yet she felt possessive about him? Not good. Not good at all. Maybe Dr. Abellano had done her a favor by interrupting, reminding her of another man she'd been attracted to, another man who had led her down a treacherous path. Yes, she owed the beautiful cardiologist a thank you. Obviously, she'd lost her mind there for a few minutes, thinking it would be okay to become involved with a man like Grant.

Being involved with Grant would be like playing Russian roulette. With a fully loaded gun and the devil egging her on.

But she wasn't a coward, was she? As uncomfortable as Grant made her feel, a part of her liked how alive he made her feel.

As long as she didn't fall in love with him, didn't risk her career, what would giving in to chemistry hurt? It wasn't as if she thought there would ever be anything more between them than physical attraction. She didn't even want there to be anything more between them. Actually, she didn't want that either, but apparently her body hadn't gotten the memo.

"You have no reason to be jealous of Heather Abellano or any other woman."

Any moment her cheeks were going to burst into flames. "I realize that."

Of course, she didn't have any rights where he was concerned. So he'd asked her out, told her he wanted her, had looked at her as if he wanted to wallow in cake icing with her. That didn't mean she owned him. She knew that. He could be with anyone he wanted and she had no right to say a single word of protest.

"That's not what I meant." He quickly interrupted her thoughts, giving her an exasperated look. "You always jump to the wrong conclusions where I'm concerned, Joni. Give me a little credit. I meant that from the moment I first saw you I haven't been interested in any woman except you."

Her gaze shot to his.

"Just you," he emphasized.

Grant's words released a thousand butterflies in her stomach at once, made her feel light-headed, and threw her completely off kilter. She hadn't expected his claim. Although perhaps she should have. He constantly threw curve balls her way.

Okay, so, try as she might, resisting the man was futile. He really was the devil in handsome-doctor disguise.

She liked him, was attracted to him, wanted him to touch and kiss her, emotions she hadn't felt since Mark.

"I want you." His words came out a caress, wrapping around her with warmth and desire, drawing her in and making her want to lean toward him. "I want you a lot."

She wanted him a lot, too.

"Why?" she asked, wondering if she should elbow Samantha for eavesdropping because her friend's curiosity coated her as palpably as a blanket. Or maybe that was Samantha's breath on her back from where her friend leaned in so close?

"Honestly?" He shrugged. Taking a bite of his barbecue sandwich, he considered her question. "I don't know. There was something about you that caught my eye from the beginning and made me want to get to know you. I'm not sure how to label that. I just know I haven't been able to stop thinking about you since we met."

"Because you want to have sex with me?" She was pretty sure she'd shocked herself as much as she had him with her bold question. Based on Samantha's gasp, she'd definitely shocked her friend. Good, maybe it was time to shake up her life. No more just existing. No more vanilla. She wanted wild raspberry swirl or some other exotic flavor, even if only a brief lick.

Even if only while playing by a cautious set of rules meant to keep everything tidy and neat, controlled.

Grant's blue gaze met hers. "That's a trick question, Joni. If I say no then that implies I don't want to have sex with you. That would be a lie because we both know I want you in my bed." He paused and gave her a sexy grin. "And in your bed and about a dozen other places."

Joni swallowed, closed her eyes at the images flashing through her mind at his words. Only the jab of Samantha's finger into her back kept her from leaning over and telling Grant to take her to any of those places this very minute. All of those places. Over and over.

"But if I say yes," he continued in a way-too-logical tone of voice, "then it makes me look like a cad just out to bag another babe."

"That's not what this is about?"

He pushed his barely touched plate back and turned to fully face her. "I don't know exactly what this is about. But I would like the opportunity to find out. With the exception of in the elevator, you've shot me down at every turn."

"I don't want to be used. Or hurt. Or made a fool."

"Neither do I."

His softly spoken words sounded so sincere, so heart-felt that Joni reeled. Had he been used in the past? Had someone hurt him as much as Mark had hurt her? Why did that thought make her want to wrap her arms around him and hold him tight? Despite whatever this connection they shared was, she barely knew the man. She shouldn't want to comfort him. No way.

Yet she did.

"I'm not sure what to say," she finally admitted.

"You say, 'My place or yours?'" Samantha advised from beside Joni. "And what the heck happened in the elevator and why haven't I heard all the juicy details?"

Grant grinned at Samantha's advice. Joni rolled her eyes, then shook her head as she found herself smiling, too.

"I have some bids in on the raffles." Where that inane comment came from Joni had no idea. She did have bids in at the raffle but, hello, winning a basketful of gardening supplies or bath and beauty products wasn't the be-all and end-all. Not when the most gorgeous man she'd ever met was telling her that he wanted her in his bed.

"Bids? Seriously?" Samantha elbowed her, echoing her thoughts. "There is no basket here that offers what you need."

It had been a long time since she'd let a man close to her, physically or otherwise. How did she even know what she needed? What she wanted? Grant confused her.

She wanted him. Denying it wouldn't make it less true.

Try as she might to fight the way he affected her, she would be having an affair. But she wasn't a fool. Not any more. Not ever again. If she was going to do this, they'd do so on her terms, by her rules, when she was ready.

Elbowing Samantha, hopefully into silence, she twisted in her seat to where her back was completely to Samantha. She met Grant's amused expression. "When we're through eating, perhaps you'd join my nosy friend and I during the auction and raffle?"

"I heard that," Samantha said from behind her.

"I'd like that," he agreed, giving her the smile that would have Mrs. Sain's heart monitor beep-beep-beeping.

Joni's heart was doing a beep-beep-beeping of its own, but she didn't look away from the intensity in Grant's eyes. Instead she gave what she hoped was a mysterious smile of her own and said, "Me, too."

Grant couldn't drag his gaze away from Joni during the charity auction. Not when she excitedly bid on a spa package, only to lose when the cost ran up beyond what she was willing to pay. Or when she burst out laughing when she won a free eight-by-ten photo during the raffle draw.

"As if I want an eight-by-ten photo of myself."

Grant couldn't help but think he wouldn't mind an eight-by-ten picture of Joni. Although no photo could ever capture the essence of the woman beside him.

He'd seen her relaxed with patients and with her co-workers, but never had she been relaxed around him. Until tonight. Something had changed in her mindset while they'd been eating their barbecue dinner. Something that had put a predatory gleam in her eyes whenever she looked at him.

Not that she needed a predatory gleam when it came to him.

He was more than willing to play mouse to her cat just so long as he got to play with her.

The mere idea had him grinning.

"What are you thinking?"

"That you have a beautiful smile."

"I'm not smiling," she unnecessarily pointed out, focusing on the auctioneer at the front of the crowded room.

"You should be. I like your smile. You should always smile, Joni."

"No one smiles all the time."

"But you usually do keep a smile on your face." She had one on her face this very second. "It's one of the many things I like about you."

She shifted in her chair. "You don't even know me, Grant. Not really."

"I've been trying to get to know you for weeks, but you keep shooting me down."

"I figured you'd lose interest."

"You aren't the kind of woman a man loses interest in, Joni. Not by a long shot."

Her eyes glazed over slightly, as if she was lost in the past, making him wish he could read her mind, know what she was thinking. But shaking off whatever had momentarily clouded her mood, she grinned. "Well, even during the worst of times I've never been accused of being boring, that's for sure."

He'd like to have asked about her worst of times, but didn't want her mind going back to whatever she'd been thinking. Not when she was with him. When she was with him he wanted her to be all smiles. He wanted her to be all smiles all the time.

A hot-air balloon-ride package that a local company had donated came up for bid and an idea hit him. One involving him and Joni floating high in the sky, the feel of her lips much more thrilling than flying.

"You ever been up in a hot-air balloon?"

Surprise lighting her eyes, she shook her head. "No, I'd like to, but it isn't the kind of thing I'd do by myself."

Which was a telling statement. Just how long had she isolated herself? "Why not?"

A flash of confusion crossed her face, then she shrugged. "You're right. It's on my bucket list, so why not? I can take my mom."

She raised her hand to bid, but Grant jerked her arm down and raised his. She attempted to pull his hand down as he'd done hers, but to no avail.

She tugged harder. "What are you doing?"

"Winning that package."

"Why? I was bidding."

The auctioneer rattled off more numbers, found another bidder, but Grant instantly countered.

"The package is for a romantic sunset flight for two. If I win, will you go with me, Joni? I'd say your mom could go with us, but the package is for two." He winked. "Too bad."

Not that he wouldn't like to meet Joni's mother. He would.

Joni didn't smile, but her lips twitched. "Is this your way of asking me out on a date again, Grant?"

"Depends. Is it working? Because so far the more traditional method hasn't proven effective."

"Okay," she agreed on a breathy sigh. "If you win the hot-air balloon package, I'll be your date, go up in the balloon with you and watch the sun go down in a blaze of colors, but only on one condition."

"What would that be?" Please don't say that your mother gets to go too. He'd probably be bad enough to need his hands slapped a few times, but he didn't want Mommy Dearest tagging along to chaperone.

"That you help me mark off another item on my bucket list."

"What would that be?"

Her eyes shone like magic, drawing him under her spell. "To be kissed in a hot-air balloon."

That was on her bucket list?

"Kiss you in a hot-air balloon?" The thought of her mouth pressed to his had him raising his hand higher when someone outbid him yet again. "It would be my pleasure."

Hand on his shoulder to steady herself, she stretched close and whispered into his ear, "Actually, I'm counting on it being my pleasure. You did promise you were really good."

Without hesitation, he stood, called out a bid that silenced the room and even left the auctioneer slack-jawed.

When he was announced the winner, Grant turned to Joni and grinned smugly. "If pleasure is your theme, you should add me to your bucket list."

CHAPTER FIVE

"LET me get this straight." Puckering her lips at herself in the bathroom mirror, Samantha rolled the tube of lip gloss down and slid on the cap. "You were on your way out of here with a man intent on ravaging you and you walked away when his boss stopped him to introduce his daughter?"

Yep, that about summed it up. Staring at her wild-eyed, rosy-cheeked reflection, Joni nodded. The night hadn't been dull, that was for sure.

Meeting her gaze in the mirror, Samantha shook her head in disbelief. "Honey, that's when you were supposed to put your hand around him to get the message across that he was your man."

Right. That was so her style. "But he's not my man."

"Duh." Samantha gave her that look that said she wasn't having her brightest moment. "He won't ever be if you don't get your act together."

"I don't want him to be my man." Joni took the lipstick Samantha handed her and decided why not? She usually didn't wear anything more than balm or gloss, but the shade did look great on Samantha. Of course, everything looked great with Samantha's silky black hair and deep blue eyes. "Not really. I mean, I agreed to go on that hot-air balloon trip with him." And had made

that quip about pleasure. "After all, he paid a small fortune for the bid, so how could I back out?"

Especially when his eyes had promised untold pleasures she ached to sample. Add him to her bucket list.
Ha, he'd top the list. All other adventures would dull
in comparison.

"You can't not go," Samantha agreed. "His bid was
impressive, quite romantic."

"You might want romance, Samantha, but I don't."
She wanted…what? Pleasure? She did want pleasure.
Physical pleasure. But not romance. Romance created
expectations that broke hearts. She didn't want a broken heart again. Stretching her mouth open, she ran
the lipstick over her lips, rubbed her lips together and
inspected the effect. "I just want to use Grant for sex."

"Do what?"

Joni's hand jerked at Samantha's loud exclamation,
smearing lipstick across the corner of her mouth and
causing her to frown.

"You are going to have to repeat what you just said
because I have lost my hearing. Or my mind. You totally
did not just say what I think you just said."

Joni glanced toward the empty stalls to reassure herself there were no eavesdroppers, intentional or otherwise. She took a deep breath, then tried to explain her
comment to her best friend. "I don't want a relationship
with Grant or with any man. Relationships are messy
and stress I don't need. But I am attracted to him. I just
want to have sex with him. Really good, really hot,
blow-my-mind sex."

Did that sound as horrible as she feared? She grimaced and waited for Samantha's verdict, knowing
without doubt her friend wouldn't hold back. Samantha
stared in wide-eyed silence.

"He probably wouldn't be okay with that, would he?" Joni's grimace deepened. "Should I just forget the whole thing? I should, shouldn't I?"

Samantha shook her head slowly. "He's a man. He'll be okay with you wanting to have sex with him. And, no, I don't think you need to forget the whole thing. Far from it."

Joni breathed a mental sigh of relief. If her best friend wasn't telling her she was a fool, then maybe she wasn't. Then again, men did it all the time. Why not her?

Samantha gave a concerned look. "What I need to know is whether or not you're really okay with that because I have trouble believing that you are."

"Of course I'm okay with it," Joni assured her friend. She wanted this. She wanted Grant. What she didn't want was to get hurt. "Relationships are complicated, especially between co-workers. I'm not willing to put my job in jeopardy." Been there, done that. "But if I go into this with my eyes wide open and abide by the rules, everything should be fine."

Looking skeptical, Samantha leaned against the bathroom sink. "Rules are meant to be broken."

Joni frowned. "No, they're not. Rules are meant to keep life orderly, to avoid problems by having a structured set of expectations. If I lay out the rules of our affair and Grant agrees to them, everything will be fine."

Samantha remained quiet a few seconds, then shrugged and smiled. "If it gets you to have a little fun, I say go for it."

Joni wasn't sure how to take Samantha's comment. She wanted her friend's approval, wanted her to think her plan brilliant. Instead, she sounded as if she thought Joni led a boring life. "Boredom has nothing to do with why I want Grant."

Samantha's brow quirked at her claim. "I'm sure it doesn't, but that doesn't mean you aren't ready for a little adventure in your life."

"I do have fun," Joni insisted with perhaps a little too much force. She enjoyed her life. Her calm, stable life that Grant had thrown such a wrench into. But Samantha had a point. Something had been missing. Maybe she hadn't acknowledged it even to herself, but she had begun to experience restlessness even before Grant had arrived on the scene. "But not as much fun as I'm going to have for however long this chemistry thing lasts between Grant and I."

"That's my girl."

Joni gestured to the make-up pouch Samantha was dropping back into her oversized purse. "Do you have something you can do my eyes with? I want to knock that man's socks off."

Samantha handed her the make-up. "Honey, it's not his socks you want to knock off. Let's aim for another, better piece of clothing." Samantha waggled her brows. "Like his boxers."

Grant finished paying for the bid he'd won and collected the raffle basket Joni had won while she'd been in the bathroom. She and Samantha had been gone long enough that Grant was beginning to wonder if Joni had flown the coop. He wouldn't be surprised. Not after the disappearing act she'd pulled while he'd been talking to Dr. Abellano.

He and Vann stood in silence in the hallway along with dozens of others. They'd been making idle chit-chat but Grant sensed the other man's unease at how long the women had been gone, too.

So when Heather came up to him and began asking

questions about the ICU and his practice, Grant welcomed the distraction.

Vann's gaze lit on someone down the hallway and the man sighed with relief. Grant turned to greet the women, but stopped short when he saw Joni. She was always beautiful, but there was something different about her as she made her way toward him. Her gaze locked on his, she didn't look away, just came closer. Make-up, he realized. Joni had put on make-up. Not a lot, but enough to accent her pretty eyes and draw attention to her high cheekbones and plump lips.

Wow. She really was beautiful.

Her big green eyes never wavered as she walked right up to him, so close he could smell the sweet jasmine scent of her. The scent that had forever imprinted into his mind on the day he'd kissed her in the elevator.

Ignoring the others, she touched his shoulder and stretched on tiptoe, leaned close to his ear. "Let's go."

Grant didn't have to be told twice. Balancing the raffle basket on one hip, he absently nodded goodbye to the others, took Joni's hand, and made a bee-line for the closest exit.

"Is your car here?" he asked when they reached the still more than half-full parking lot.

She nodded, pointing out her little silver sedan. "Follow me to my place?"

"Lady, I'd follow you to hell and back."

Glancing up at him from behind thick eyelashes, she smiled with feminine power. "No trip to hell required, although I don't doubt you've been there a time or two. But things may get that hot before the night is over."

"I hope so." He groaned, put the basket into the back seat of her car, then pulled her to him and studied her

pretty upturned face. What had transpired in the bathroom? "I want you, Joni, but if you're not sure…"

"I'm sure." She kissed him to prove her point, but
rather than deepen the kiss she jumped into the driver
seat of her car, spouted off her address in case he got
separated, and gave a little wave. "Keep up if you can."

Grant stood there a moment, blown away by the
woman backing out of her parking spot. After weeks
of running, Joni had finally realized they could be good
together, that a relationship between them could work.

Good, he wanted a relationship with her. He wanted
a lot of things with her, getting hot topping the list.

They sizzled any time they were near each other. He
couldn't wait to get her out of those clothes, to kiss her,
to taste the moist sweetness of her body and have her
cry out his name with bliss, to have her throbbing with
need, exploding with pleasure.

Grant raced to his car and started the engine.

His internal engine was already revved and raring
to go.

Vroom. Vroom.

Grant pulled into Joni's driveway right behind her,
was out of his Hummer before she'd even killed her
ignition.

Taking a deep breath, she reminded herself she was
in control. This was what she wanted.

So why did she feel so awkward? Like what they
were doing was so calculated?

Grant opened her door, extended his hand toward
her.

She hesitated only a second before she put her hand in
his, but her slight pause was enough to raise a red flag.

"Having second thoughts?" he asked as, hand in
hand, they stepped onto her front porch.

Could the man read her mind or what?

"No," she assured him, sounding more confident than perhaps she was. Extracting her hand from his, she unlocked the house door and they stepped just inside the entranceway. "I want you."

"I want you, too. So much, Joni." He pulled her into his arms and kissed her lips, her throat, the hollow of her neck. "I think I've wanted you from the moment I first saw you."

A soft moan escaped her lips as she lost herself in the sweet sensations his every touch elicited. The man's mouth was a phenomenon. So talented. So unreal. So intent on giving her promised pleasure.

His hands weren't anything to scoff at either. Oh, no. When he ran his palms over her arms, she shivered. When his fingers dug into her hair and pulled her closer, she quivered. When he slid his hand beneath her shirt, cupped her breast, tweaked his fingertip over her straining nipple, she almost melted into a puddle on the foyer floor.

"Take me to my bedroom," she ordered. Or had she been begging?

He grunted a response, but Joni couldn't make out his words. He scooped her into his arms and her belly fluttered with excitement. Had she died and gone to heaven? No, Grant hailed from the other direction. With as hot as his kiss burned, she was sure he did. Still...

"Which way?"

Her face pressed against the hard strength of his chest, she pointed towards her bedroom. She rubbed her cheek back and forth over his cotton-blend shirt, breathing in the wonderfully masculine smell of him. "It's the second door on the left."

She squinted when he turned on the overhead light, wanted him to turn it back off, but he refused.

"I want to see you, Joni," he said, stroking his hands over her. "I want to see every reaction to my touch. I want to see you respond."

She wanted to see him, too. Wanted to know if he was as buff as his body hinted at beneath his clothes. As rock solid as he felt against her body right at that very moment.

He whipped her black and white comforter and sheet back in one motion, placed her gently on her bed. Lying on her bed, she watched his every move, mesmerized. He kicked off his shoes. Grabbing the hem of his shirt, he lifted it over his head.

Joni's breath caught at the sight of his broad shoulders and chiseled abdomen. Oh, wow. The man should never wear a shirt. Not ever.

She reached for him, ran her hands over the cut planes, then rose up enough to place a kiss just above his navel.

The muscles beneath her lips tightened. He sucked in a deep breath. The sheer wonder that this beautiful man wanted her, that he was there with her, planned to make love to her, was so affected by her touch, blew her mind.

She needed to tell him her rules, to make sure he was okay to abide by them. But his fingers were in her hair and her mouth was too busy exploring his belly to actually form words.

She liked the growling noise he made when she accidentally brushed against the crotch of his jeans. She liked it so much that she stroked her fingers there again, purposefully, while she traced her tongue beneath his navel to tease just above his waistband.

"Joni," he groaned, his fingers twisting in her hair,

not painfully but almost. Realizing what he was doing, he let go, slid his fingers free from her locks. "Stop."

Her heart fell. Had she done something wrong? Or had he changed his mind? Biting the raw inside of her lower lip, she lifted her head to look at him just as she closed her fingers over his zipper. Didn't he know she didn't want to stop? She wanted to touch him, to taste him, to be the one to give him pleasure, to be the one to whom he gave pleasure.

"You want me to stop?" Did she sound as disappointed as she felt?

"You have me on edge." His voice sounded strained, as if he really was on a high cliff and was about to topple off.

Understanding dawning, she stared at him, stunned. "But we've barely started."

"I know," he said with more than a tad of frustration. "But I've wanted you so long it's not going to take much. I want to be good for you, to give you every iota of pleasure I promised. At the rate we're going it's going to be over before we get started."

Wow. Knowing he was so turned on—by her!—was making this better and better, made her insides melt with definite pleasure.

Slowly and with a determined smile, she lowered his zipper, slid her fingers inside his jeans and tugged the material downwards.

With a groan Grant let Joni strip him, let her take in the sight of his naked body. Damn, he wanted her. Wanted to rip off her clothes and plunge inside her body until they both cried out in ecstasy. He wanted more from Joni than sex. He would force his body under enough control to take his time, to have her on edge as much as he was, to make sure she toppled into orgasmic bliss over and over before he lost his control.

Part of him questioned if they weren't rushing things. But he couldn't stop her, couldn't stop himself.

"You are way overdressed." Something he set about remedying. She reached to pull off her clothes, but Grant placed his hands over hers, staying her. He wanted to do this, to take her clothes off this first time, to enjoy each new inch of her exposed body. This was one journey he wanted to take slowly, to stop, smell the jasmine, and not miss one thing.

He pushed the material of her sweater upwards, exposing the milky flesh of her belly and placing a lingering kiss to her navel. How many times had he fantasized about taking off her sweater? Just the reality that he was actually doing so was enough to make him throb.

His tongue danced in and out of her navel in slow, tantalizing strokes. He cupped her hips, slid his palms around to cup her round bottom, arching her off the bed, trying to pull her closer and closer, his mouth supping on her while he finished undressing her. When he finally removed the last of her clothes and she lay naked beneath him, he rose to take in her loveliness.

Softly moaning, she reached to pull him back, her greedy hands tugging him toward her. Still, he was in no rush, just soaked in the sight of Joni unleashed.

Her curvy little body stretched out on the sheets beckoned for him to run his fingers over every inch of her, to taste every inch of her, burn everything about her into his memory for all time.

"You are beautiful." He barely recognized his voice, could barely vocalize. Yet her beauty deserved poetic words his tongue could never do justice to. She deserved everything he could give and more.

"Thank you." Her cheeks bloomed rosily, her lashes lowering a brief moment before lifting to reveal her desire-filled green eyes. "You're beautiful, too."

Him beautiful? It was enough to make him laugh, but her fingers had begun exploring his body again and the noise that came from his throat sounded more a growl. Touch after touch, kiss after kiss, they explored each other, stroking each other higher and higher until she whimpered with need and he couldn't hold back any longer.

He had to be inside her.

Donning a condom from his wallet, he moved over her. As he spread her creamy thighs, the only sound he could make was a grunt of acknowledgement. No poetry there.

But nothing had ever been written that compared to the desire he saw in Joni's eyes when he pushed into the moist softness of her body, to the gut-wrenching pleasure that shook his body with each thrust inside. Deeper and deeper.

Her fingers dug into his buttocks, gripping him tight, urging him faster, harder, pushing him over that edge he was dangling so close to, that edge he didn't want to fall over quite yet, but couldn't fight any longer.

"Grant," she cried, her body spasming around him, contracting tighter and tighter. "I need you now!"

"Joni," he growled between gritted teeth, giving in to the urgency in his groin, giving in to the feminine call of her body. He spilt himself deep inside her and toppled over into satisfaction he'd never known.

CHAPTER SIX

Despite having her face practically buried in her pillow, Joni winced at the sunlight peeking in around the shades that mostly blocked the brightness from her bedroom.

Morning already?

Urgh. Why did she feel like a truck had run over her?

Because a Grant truck had run over her.

And into her.

What had she done?

Not rising from where she lay on her belly, she prised one eye open slightly, letting her surroundings come into focus. Over the edge of her pillow she saw evidence of exactly what she'd done.

More like whom she'd done.

Sleeping on his belly, too, Grant lay sprawled on her full-sized bed, taking up more than his fair share of mattress real estate. Thank God he was still asleep so she could escape and…and, well, she wasn't quite sure what she was going to do at this point. She'd never had a morning after. Mark had always gone home not long after finishing his business—which had never taken long. Until last night she hadn't had anything to compare Mark's quickies to. Now that she did, well, quickie was the only description that fit.

Grant hadn't been quick. Oh, no. The man had taken

his time and taken her to a whole new plateau of sensations. She was pretty sure that last night in his arms she'd developed a sixth sense. A sexual sense.

Or maybe just a Grant sense.

He'd touched every part of her body, tasted every part of her body, had continued to touch her even afterwards, almost as if he hadn't been able not to.

Memories of all he had done filling her mind, she studied him. His dark lashes fanned over his strong cheek bones. Beautiful and tousled and way too sexy in sleep.

Asleep or awake didn't matter. The man was way too sexy, period.

For some crazy reason he'd found her sexy, too, had told her over and over during the night how much he wanted her, how crazy she drove him, how he'd been fighting the urge to touch her since they'd first met. Even now, he had one hand possessively cupping her bottom.

How many times during the night had he told her how much he liked her bottom? That when he looked at her round curves it was all he could do to keep from pushing her legs apart and thrusting deep inside her body?

Not that he hadn't done that. Multiple times.

He had. Yet each time they'd had sex hadn't been any less urgent, any less heated when they'd come together.

How many times during the long night had they… three…four? Not a quickie amongst them. A smile spread across her face. No wonder she felt like she'd had a head-on collision with an eighteen-wheeler.

Doing her best not to wake him, she wiggled free of his hand, rolled onto her side, and stared at the man who'd done such amazing things to her body throughout the night.

They hadn't been awkward. Had someone asked her if they would have been, she'd have argued they would. Even months into their relationship she'd still felt awkward with Mark, had preferred the lights off when they'd had sex. He hadn't minded, had told her on more than one occasion she should diet.

Grant had minded. Had insisted the lights be on that first time, had taken in every aspect of her nakedness with eager eyes. So how could she possibly not have felt awkward when she'd been so thoroughly inspected by a man as beautiful as Grant with the lights on?

Yet he'd looked at her with such desire, touched her with such reverence and need of his own, that awkwardness just hadn't been an issue. He'd made her feel beautiful, desirable, as if she were the sexiest woman alive.

Or maybe she'd been so consumed with desire that her own need had waylaid any awkwardness that might have arisen.

Regardless, she'd felt divine in his arms. Decadent and desirable and sexy.

Her gaze slid over the defined contours of his body, over the muscles of his back, the dip of his spine just at where her sheet bunched low on his hips, revealing just a glimpse of his tight buttocks.

She'd known he had a great behind.

He had a great everything. From the chiseled planes of his chest and abdomen to the sinewy lines of his thighs to the strong arms that had held her all night. His body was perfect. He was perfect.

He'd been generous, tender, demanding, giving, and had made her feel like the most desirable woman in the world. When he'd looked at her, she'd felt like the only woman in the world. As if he really cared about her.

Which was insane.

She didn't need to go repeating history. She'd made the mistake once of reading more into sex than just sex. Not that sex with Mark had come close to what she'd experienced at the mercy of Grant's talented body.

Try as she might, she couldn't even picture Mark's body, even his face seemed fuzzy in her mind. Odd as once upon a time the man had occupied all her thoughts, had been the center of her world.

Had almost cost her everything. Had he really thought she'd turn her back on her mother? Even if he hadn't cheated on her, she would have stood by her mother always. To add insult to injury, he'd used his professional role at the hospital to raise doubts about her nursing abilities after he'd already tattered her heart with his cheating ways.

No, she wouldn't be making the same mistakes again.

This time she was going to be the one to call the shots, to make the rules.

Perhaps she should have laid them out to Grant before they'd spent the night tangled in her sheets, but better late than never.

Better now than later.

"Wake up." She shook his shoulder. "We need to talk."

One sleepy blue eye popped open, then the other. A lazy, self-satisfied grin slid onto his handsome face. Joni's heart skipped a beat, begging her to forget talking and jump the man's bones instead. Really, how often did she wake up with a gorgeous, smiling hunk in her bed? Never.

"Morning, darling."

Her insides melted to a warm, gushy ooze. A gorgeous, smiling hunk in her bed who called her darling! Pathetic! She was easy if that was all it took to get her juices flowing.

The man had only to exist to make her juices flow.

"We need to talk," she repeated, determined not to be distracted by the warm, gushy oozy flow.

He rolled onto his side, yawned, stretching out his arm high above his body, emphasizing each and every muscle along his ripped ribs and belly.

Oh, me, oh, my! Joni's insides caught fire.

"This the part where you tell me this was a mistake and kick me out?" He looked more amused than worried.

Hardly. "This probably was a mistake and I should kick you out but, no, that's not what we need to talk about."

He gave a mock sigh of relief. "Good, because I'm hungry. Whatcha got that I can rustle us up for breakfast? We can talk while we eat."

Keeping the sheet pulled up over her naked breasts— why hadn't she put on clothes before waking him?—she shook her head. "Breakfast isn't what I want."

His brow lifted. But rather than take her seriously, his eyes twinkled with mischief. "You hungry for something else?"

"Not that either," she quickly assured him, tightening her grip on the sheet. She did want that, had wanted that from the moment she'd awakened and realized he was still in bed with her. Crazy. "Now," she scolded, determined to see this through, "be serious. I need to lay down the ground rules."

"You're what I'd like to lay down." He waggled his

brows at her, scooted up on his pillow. "What ground rules?"

Ignoring how the sheet dipped seriously low over his waist, revealing a happy trail she'd like to walk down, she toughened her resolve. "My ground rules for what happened last night."

She didn't have to tell him to be serious now. His expression grew guarded. "Which are?"

"That this means nothing."

He had the audacity to laugh. "Lady, if you believe that, you're crazy."

She didn't like it that he was laughing at her. "Last night was amazing, but we both know it didn't mean anything." When he started to interrupt, she held up her hand. "It didn't. Not beyond phenomenal sex."

"It meant something to me."

Her heart skipped a beat. Or ten.

"I'm not interested in a serious relationship," she warned, not wanting him to say things he didn't mean just because they were in bed. She'd heard men said what they thought women wanted to hear. Mark certainly had. He'd said all the right things and not meant one. She didn't want false platitudes.

"I'm not interested in casual sex," he countered, so smoothly she could almost believe him. Almost.

"We haven't been out on a single date, haven't had any kind of relationship outside the hospital. How could last night be anything other than casual sex?" See, she could be logical. She sounded logical. Only the wild beating of her heart hinted that more than logic might be at play.

"Only because you refused to go out with me when I asked you out," he reminded her, then sighed. "You're right. We probably should have waited, but last night was a lot more than casual sex. There's powerful chemistry between us."

He shifted toward her, exposing a glimpse of what treasure lay at the end of his particular happy trail. La la la, she so wasn't going to stare…even if she wanted to.

Oh, yeah. Logic. She was supposed to be logical. "Chemistry is just lust, Grant."

Just as her reactions to him were just lust. Nothing more.

He didn't bother pulling up the sheet to cover what he'd partially exposed, just shrugged. "If you say so."

"I say so."

His expression unreadable, he studied her for a few moments, then grinned that half-cocked grin that hinted he knew a lot more than she gave him credit for. "That your only 'rule'? That last night be defined as just chemistry?"

This time she laughed, but partially to hide her discomfort at their conversation. "Hardly."

"You gonna tell me the rest of your rules, Lil Miss Control Freak?" He didn't appear in the slightest nonplussed, just amused, as if she was a child he was humoring.

"Don't mock me, Grant."

"I wouldn't dare." He grinned, doing just that. "You have the good stuff, and I want more." His gaze skimmed over her face, her throat, her shoulders. "Lots more. Tell me what I've got to do to get more."

Joni gulped. Why hadn't she gotten dressed, brushed her teeth, combed her hair, and put on some lip gloss? Anything to help improve her look first thing in the morning.

Then again, Grant didn't seem to mind in the slightest the way she looked all tousled and wild haired.

Actually, if what was peeking out from beneath the sheet was anything to go on, he really liked how she looked. A lot.

"I do," he said, almost with a growl.

Startled, her gaze shot to his. "You do what?"

"Want you."

"I didn't say you wanted me."

"You didn't have to." He brushed a hair away from her temple, cupped her face. "Now, tell me about these rules I have to abide by so I can make love to you."

How was she supposed to tell him her rules when he looked at her like that? When she could see on his face that he was remembering what they'd done throughout the night and he wanted to do all that again? When she wanted him to do all that again?

"I don't want anyone to know," she rushed out.

His fingers stilled. "Huh?"

"I don't want anyone to know we're having an affair. That way when we end there won't be any fuss and muss at work." They'd just stop having sex and that would be the end of it. No worries about any negative impact on her career. No looks of sympathy from her co-workers. Nothing. Just a clean break.

His brow quirked. "Do you really think that's possible after last night?"

Her face burned. "No one knows about last night."

He didn't look convinced. "You think no one saw us leave together?"

He made a good point, but they had taken different vehicles. "That doesn't mean they know you came here or that they know what we did."

"Anyone who saw me look at you knows exactly what we did last night. I wanted you, Joni." He stroked his thumb across her cheek. "I still do."

She wanted him, too, but she was not going to get distracted from her rules. Not again. Because she really should have laid them out prior to them having sex and the longer she delayed the harder it would be to play by them. She needed those rules. Without them she was nothing more than a sitting duck waiting to have her heart trampled on.

"No touching me at work," she said.

"But touching you in private is okay?" His fingers brushed down her throat, touching her in private quite nicely.

"Private is okay." More than okay. "In private, I want you to touch me."

"Good, because I like touching you." His finger traced over her collarbone, over her chest to toy at where she clutched the sheet to her breasts. "I like touching you a lot."

She liked him touching her a lot, too. Wowzers, but the man had magic hands.

"Don't ask me personal things." Never would a man use her mother's alcoholism against her again. Even though her mother had been dry for almost five years, had recently married and was happier than she'd ever been, Joni wouldn't let a man close enough to throw rocks at the fragile glass house protecting her mother.

"As in?"

"Like about my family and past, that kind of thing."

His lips twisted and for a moment she thought he was going to balk, but instead his finger began dancing over her again.

"Any more rules?" he asked, dipping to blow warm breath against the curve of her neck.

Shivers ran up and down her spine.

She took a deep breath and spat out the one that had

hurt her most. False words of love. Words she'd heard once but that had been fabrication. Never did she want to hear such lies again. Never. "Don't tell me you love me."

Grant straightened, his hand falling away from her body. "Pardon?"

"Don't say I love you or things like that. I don't want to hear mushy pleasantries or have you do mushy things like flowers or candy that make implications that this is a relationship leading anywhere other than mutual physical satisfaction."

Not that she thought he would do any of those things, but if she'd laid down the law that he couldn't, then she'd never be disappointed when he didn't.

Grant shook his head as if to clear his thoughts. "Let me get this straight. We're going to have an affair, not let anyone know. I'm not to ask anything personal and can't tell you I love you or do 'mushy' things for you, and I can only touch you in private?"

She nodded.

His brow quirked high. "That it?"

"For now."

His gaze narrowed. "You get to make up new rules as we go?"

She hadn't thought that far ahead, but it sounded good to her. "Is that a problem?"

"Possibly." He shrugged. "Depends on the rule."

"If you don't like the rule, you don't have to play." Did she sound as much like a petulant child as she felt?

He regarded her long moments. "If I opted not to play?"

Her heart squeezed tightly in her chest, but she kept her expression bland. She waved her fingers in a bye-bye motion.

"So, it's your way or the highway?" He made it sound so crass, so unyielding, but he didn't look miffed, just amused as always.

Which annoyed her. And worried her. But she wasn't going to back down. She couldn't. She needed those rules for her own survival. Without them she might fall in love with Grant, might end up with a broken heart again, might end up having to fight to keep her job again.

"Those are my rules for now. Take them or leave them."

Why was she holding her breath? Why did her every cell seem to be anxiously awaiting his response? What if he said no? Then what? Could she really say goodbye after what they'd shared during the night? Could she really deny herself that pleasure, deny herself him?

"Oh, I'm going to take 'em," he assured her, running his finger through his hair. "No doubt about it. I just want to make sure I understand your terms so there's no confusion down the road."

"I will clarify anything you aren't sure about."

"We are having a sex-only relationship?"

Joni thought about it. Pretty much that was what she'd outlined. Their lives would be less entangled when they broke up. Eventually, they would. If he only encompassed one part of her life, moving on would be so much easier. She wouldn't be as devastated as she'd been with Mark's multiple betrayal. Sex-only was a good plan.

"Sex is all I want from you." Why did she feel a bit nauseated at her words? She wasn't a sex-only kind of woman. Well, she hadn't been a sex at all kind of woman for the past five years. After last night she'd realized what she'd been missing out on all these years.

She didn't want to go back to celibacy. No way. "I want sex from you, Grant."

He regarded her as if he couldn't quite believe what he was hearing. "At work we pretend we're, what? Just friends? Nothing at all?"

"Nothing about our relationship at work needs to change. We will go on as we have always gone on. Professionally, but nothing more."

"You really think that's possible?"

Of course. Otherwise he shouldn't be in her bed.

"Why wouldn't it be?"

"Because every time I look at you I'm going to want to touch you."

"You're not allowed to touch me except in private."

"And in my mind," he added. "When I see you at the hospital, I'm going to remember what you look like without those scrubs on and in my mind I'm going to touch."

She would probably be doing some mental touching of her own, but she wasn't going to tell him that.

"I'm allowed to touch you in private?" His expression took on a wicked gleam. Or maybe it was that he was smiling that smile that said he knew her thoughts and liked them. "If we end up alone in a supply closet, I have to keep my hands to myself?"

The man was too much.

"If we end up alone in a supply closet, it'll be because you've pulled me into that supply closet."

His gaze traced over her face, lower. "You think?"

He wasn't even touching her. Why was her skin tingling? Why were her thighs clenching? She held the sheet tighter to her, kept her arms over her breasts.

"I don't go hanging out in hospital supply closets of my own accord." But if doing so meant he would touch her, she just might set up camp. She wanted him touching her. Right now, she wanted him touching her.

He might not physically be touching her, but his gaze was blazing a hot trail down her throat, making her imagine his hands there, making her imagine his mouth there.

His brow arched. "But you might develop the habit?"

This was so unfair. The man was turning her on without laying a finger on her. How did that work? She started to bite her lip, realized what she was doing and wet them instead. "Hasn't been a problem in the past."

"A shame. You've really been missing out." His eyes met hers, held, mesmerized. "Maybe you should try it some time."

She swallowed. "Me? Or we?"

"Well, if you're offering…"

"That would break my own rule before we even got started."

His gaze bored into hers, deep and intense and for once more serious than amused. "Rules are meant to be broken, Joni."

Wasn't that exactly what Samantha had warned?

"No," she quickly denied, not liking his suddenly solemn expression. Although perhaps she should. That meant he was taking her rules under sincere consideration, right? "My rules are to protect us. Both of us."

"I don't need protecting, Joni. Not from you."

"Sure you do." Her tone was light, teasing. Why, she didn't know, because she wanted to be taken seriously, but she wanted his smile back on his face, wanted the intense expression he wore gone. "You don't even know me. Not my likes or dislikes. Not my bad habits. Not my pet peeves. Nothing. Not to mention I'm a crazy mixed-up woman who is laying down rules for our relationship."

"I know enough and the rest I'll learn," he said, scooting further back against the bed's headboard. "At least you're being upfront about where you stand and what you want from me. That's more than most women do."

Had he been hurt in the past? Had some woman not been upfront? Just the thought caused a pinch in her chest that she barely acknowledged, much less attempted to label.

She picked up a pillow, straightened the cotton case around the spongy material, attempting to smooth the wrinkles. "I don't want either of us to get hurt. Rules are to keep people safe."

Grant's hand covered hers, smoothing her palm over the cool cotton. "Everyone gets hurt, Joni." He flipped her hand to lace her fingers with his. "One just has to decide who is worth getting hurt for and who isn't."

His hand felt so good holding hers, so right. Yet his words...

"That's a pessimistic attitude," she accused, wanting to diffuse the conversation, to move to something lighter, more fun.

Taking her cue, he laughed. "This coming from the woman who just laid down rules to clearly draw the lines of our relationship as purely physical because she's afraid to have a real relationship because one of us might get hurt."

He gave a mock sigh and shook his gorgeous head.

"Not wanting a real relationship with you and being afraid to have one are two very different things," she pointed out, wanting to be sure he understood, wanting to be sure she understood. She wasn't afraid. She just didn't want the messy fall-out that would come when they ended. She didn't fool herself that they wouldn't end. She knew they would. Planning ahead was not the same thing as fear.

"You're not afraid of us?"

"No," she denied. Fear had nothing to do with her rules. Prevention was just good medicine. As a doctor, he should know that. Having rules in place to keep either of them from having unrealistic expectations was just smart.

"I am," he surprised her by admitting, lifting her hand to his lips to place a soft kiss against her knuckles. "I'm terrified that I'm in bed with a control freak who wants to talk about rules and relationship boundaries when we are alone and naked and should be giving each other a great deal of pleasure. Scary stuff."

His lips lingered against her hand, rubbing gently back and forth. His caress caused thunder to roar inside her body. Her heart beat wildly in her chest. Her lungs flopped around, forgetting to take in vital oxygen. Her blood quivered through her veins, anticipating what he'd do next.

"That scares you?" she whispered, watching him closely, thinking him the most beautiful man she'd ever seen. Maybe not physically, although perhaps, but there was something about him, something that made him stand out above the crowd.

Then he smiled and her every body function stalled.

Mrs. Sain was right. It was his smile.

The smile that was just for her, Joni. That beautiful smile that made you feel as if you were the center of his universe. That wicked smile that let you know he was thinking something naughty and you were the star of those naughty thoughts. The smile that said he enjoyed life and that for however long he graced you with his presence, you'd enjoy life too.

"Oh, yeah," he said softly. "That scares me."

The tip of his tongue poked into the sensitive skin between her fingers, rubbing in an erotic little motion that had her aching body surging to life, had her other hand twisting the sheet against her breasts.

"What are you going to do to make me not afraid any more?"

His tone was so seductive, so alluring, so full of the promise of pleasure, but she wasn't ready to acquiesce to him. She was the one in control here. He would do well to remember that.

"Turn on the lights?" she suggested, biting back a moan when his teeth nipped at her finger. Oh, heaven, that felt so good.

He shook his head. "Not going to work. It's not dark."

Telling herself not to give in to the pleasure his magical mouth was eliciting, not yet, she let her gaze follow that happy trail. "Tell you what a big gun you have?"

He paused, grinned. "That might distract me for a while."

"But wouldn't make you any less terrified?"

"Nope." He turned her hand palm up and she prepared for an onslaught of sensation as his tongue toyed with her palm. So when his lips supped against the delicate flesh of her wrist instead, sucking gently, she almost came.

"Maybe you should try again." He lifted his head to stare into her eyes. "Come up with something more creative to allay my fears."

He wanted her to try again? He wanted creative? She'd give him creative.

She let go of the sheet, letting the material drop to

her waist and expose her bare chest. His audible sucking in of breath sent a surge of power through her, sent
a thrill of pleasure ricocheting through her body. He
wanted her. This man looked at her, even in the early
morning when she needed a shower and toothbrush, and
he wanted her so completely that the sight of her naked
body had him catching his breath. Wow.

"Maybe…" she leaned forward, traced her fingertip
along the downward path marking his flat belly, liking how his muscles contracted with her touch, liking
how his eyes never left hers "…we shouldn't be talking at all."

CHAPTER SEVEN

"As LONG as you behave, Dr. Bradley plans to transfer you to the regular medical floor today." Joni checked Mrs. Sain's telemetry, happy to see her vitals remained stable.

"Me behave?" The woman cackled with delight. "Since when have I ever behaved?"

"Not since I've known you, that's for sure," Joni agreed, winking at the smiling woman. "But I figure you're probably getting tired of hanging out around this place."

"This place isn't so bad. Around here I have hunky men coming into my room several times a day."

Uh-oh. "Hunky men?"

"Dr. Bradley."

"Ah." She so wasn't going there. Not with Mrs. Sain. Not with anyone. Samantha had already cornered her several times, trying to get her to spill the goods. Not happening. Mostly because what she and Grant shared had been private. Not something she wanted to impart. Not even to her best friend. For now what was between them was her happy little secret.

"You put that man out of his misery yet?"

Joni's gaze shot to her patient's. "What?"

"You know what." Mrs. Sain shook a bony, clubbed finger at her. "I may be old, but I'm not blind."

"That's questionable." Joni attempted to smother a smile and failed horribly. Seriously, how was she supposed to smother a smile when she felt so amazingly happy?

The woman cackled again. "You're going to give that boy a run for his money, aren't you?"

"I'm not going to give that boy—" which seemed like such a wrong descriptive label for Grant when he was definitely all man "—anything."

"That's a pity." Mrs. Sain shook her head as if sorely disappointed. "If I was fifty years younger, I'd give him anything he wanted and then some."

Joni bit back another smile. Yeah, she'd given Grant everything he wanted and then some, too. Or maybe it had been the other way around. He'd given her everything she wanted, amazing sex, agreed to her rules, left with no fuss, and hadn't bothered her since except to send her a few very suggestive text messages that had made her burst out laughing then sigh in giddy remembered pleasure.

Her mother had asked about the texts, but Joni hadn't even told her about Grant. He was her private secret. Sort of.

"No," she contradicted her patient, just to be as ornery as the older woman, mostly because Mrs. Sain liked the sparring. "You wouldn't. Fifty years ago you were happily married to Hickerson and wouldn't have even noticed another man."

"True." The woman nodded, closing her eyes for a moment and smiling at whatever memories floated through her mind. When she met Joni's gaze, she wore a happy expression even if her next words scolded. "But if you don't get busy, fifty years from now you aren't going to have memories to look back on."

Ha, what would Mrs. Sain say if she told her that she'd gotten busy Friday night with the very hunky Dr. Bradley? Very busy. Saturday morning, too, right up until they'd realized they hadn't had any more condoms. They'd improvised and Joni had no complaints about how satisfied he'd left her. No complaints whatsoever. The man could do amazing things with his mouth.

O-mazing things. And his little finger. And his big toe. And everything in between. Oh, yes, he could do O-mazing things.

"That's an odd smile on your face."

Joni didn't meet the woman's eyes, neither did she bother trying to hide the smile on her face. She couldn't have even if she had tried. What could she say? The man made her smile. He made her smile real big in a goofy kind of way.

"Well, you sly little girl." Mrs. Sain sounded pleased, as if she'd played matchmaker and was proud of her meddling ways. "It's about time."

"About time for what?" Grant stepped into the room, pulling his stethoscope from around his neck and flashing a smile at both ladies.

Joni immediately looked away, pretending to be busy. She couldn't look at him. If she did she'd only confirm all the things Mrs. Sain thought she knew.

Unfortunately, she couldn't not look at him either.

How could she not look at him when just hearing his voice sent a jolt of joy through her veins?

She'd not seen him since he'd left her place Saturday afternoon. Not talked to him because she'd told him not to call. AA had taken up most of the day and night but Grant had never been far from her mind. Of course, his silly text messages had made sure he was never far from her mind. Good thing he'd reminded her after the first one that she'd said for him not to call, but hadn't mentioned a thing about texting.

When she'd crawled into bed she'd considered calling him, asking him over, but she figured she shouldn't get used to him in her bed every night. Plus, what if he'd changed his mind? What if once he was away from her he'd realized he didn't have to play by her rules? That there were hundreds of women who'd love to let him set the rules?

But if he'd decided any of those things, he wouldn't have texted her just before midnight to wish her sweet dreams, would he?

Obviously, he'd thought about her as much as she had him, had enjoyed their night together as much as she had. Just the thought made her want to dance around the ICU room.

"Her vitals are stable, Dr. Bradley." But mine aren't. Mine are going nuts because you're in the same room with me and all I can think is how much I'd like to strip those hospital scrubs off you and lick those fantastic abs.

"Thanks." He didn't look up at her, almost appeared to be purposely ignoring her. Then again, maybe he was.

Wow, they sounded out of place, stiff and too formal. Although she understood exactly why he wasn't teasing her as he usually did, she admitted that she missed the attention he usually showered on her.

Insane. He was giving her what she wanted. Sort of.

Mrs. Sain glanced back and forth between them, shaking her head. "Don't know what's wrong with young people these days. Back during my time we had common sense."

"We have common sense," Grant said, patting her hand.

The woman gave a perturbed shake of her head. "Not from where I'm lying."

"Which is what I'm here to discuss with you." Grant winked at his patient. "I'm transferring you to the medical floor this morning. If you remain stable there, I'll send you home in a few days."

"Home." The woman crinkled her already wrinkly nose. "Home is where the heart is. Can you send me there?"

Joni couldn't pull her gaze away from Grant. He still hadn't looked directly at her, just that flash of a smile when he'd come into the room, and then he'd poured all his attention on their patient. But something wistful played on his face, made Joni want to ask about his home, to know everything about him.

"Where would that be?" he asked their patient.

"Not at that assisted living facility, that's for sure. That place is more a prison than a home."

"We've discussed this. Your family moved you there because they believe that's what's best for you. They didn't want you living alone anymore because it just wasn't a safe option."

"I know," she admitted on a resigned sigh. "I agree that they did what they believe is the right thing. I know I'm not a spring chicken anymore and need a little help from time to time and that's why they encouraged me to go there. It's also why I agreed because I didn't want them to feel guilty, because they shouldn't. I'm old and have lived my life. They need to get on with theirs." She stopped, took several deep inhalations through her nasal cannula, letting her oxygen saturation rise where it had fallen from her talking. "But," she continued, "that doesn't mean I have to like it. And that sure ain't where my heart is."

Joni listened to them chat while she entered data into the electronic medical record. Surreptiously, she studied Grant.

He looked great in his navy scrubs, especially now that she knew what those loose scrubs hid. The man had a gorgeous body.

And a killer smile that he was flashing Mrs. Sain's way.

Joni's heart flopped around like a fish out of water.

His mouth had kissed every inch of her, had made her back arch off her bed and her body go into total meltdown. She'd run her fingers over every inch of him, knew what his skin tasted like, knew how it felt to have him stretching her body, knew how it felt to orgasm mindlessly in his arms.

She'd done all that without feeling in the slightest bit embarrassed.

Now fully dressed and in a professional setting, she felt awkward and unsure. What was she supposed to say to him? How was she supposed to act?

Because what she really wanted to do was wrap her arms around him and tell him how happy she was to see him, how much his text messages had meant yesterday.

She'd been the one to lay down the laws of their relationship, but spouting out those rules while lying naked in bed with him had been one thing. Not wanting to have him smile at her and publicly acknowledge that something spectacular had happened between them quite another.

In theory, they were good rules.

But life wasn't theory. Life was real, just as Grant was real. Even if she hated to admit it, she was disappointed that he was ignoring her.

What had she wanted? Him to bombard her with roses and promises of forever after a single night in bed together?

Hardly. She just needed to get her act together, to abide by her own rules. If she couldn't do that, then she couldn't see Grant at all.

"If there's nothing I can do for you, Dr. Bradley, I'm going to go check on another patient." Perhaps her voice inflected a little too much coolness, but she needed to escape, to get away from his over-abundance of pheromones before she gave in to his allure and did something crazy. Like tackle him and drag his sexy behind beneath Mrs. Sain's hospital bed.

"Oh, there's something you can do for me, Nurse Joni. A lot of somethings."

Joni's jaw dropped. Had he really just said what she thought he'd said or had she imagined his words? His implications?

With a devilish grin, he continued, "You can call the medical floor to have them prepare a bed for Mrs. Sain so we can get her transferred."

Mrs. Sain muttered something about him being bad, but Joni couldn't be sure because of the roaring in her ears. Or maybe it was the sizzling heat pouring off her face.

Blast him! He'd done that on purpose.

"Yes, sir," she said with a straight face and a tone that would have fit in perfectly had she clicked her heels together and saluted him.

"And you can..." He gave a couple of other medical orders. The things he said could be twisted into double meanings, but she didn't let on that he'd said anything out of the ordinary.

"Yes, sir," she repeated when he'd finished. She didn't meet his eyes, just stared at his ear and tried not to think about the fact she'd had that earlobe between her teeth not so very long ago. "I'll get right on that."

"Thanks," Grant said, without glancing up from where he'd pulled Mrs. Sain's last portable chest X-ray so he could review the digital film displayed on the computer monitor.

Joni glanced toward her patient, who watched them both curiously but who had thankfully remained gracefully quiet. Good. The last thing she needed was Mrs. Sain to comment on how goofily she'd been smiling earlier, about how totally infatuated she was with a man whom she was only supposed to be having a short-term physical relationship with.

"I'll be back to check on you in a little while," she promised her grinning patient. "And to get you ready for your big move."

Having stared at the lateral image of Mrs. Sain's chest X-ray so long he had commited it to memory, from the corner of his eye Grant watched Joni leave the room. When he turned back towards his patient he found wise old eyes watching him.

"Don't suppose you'd tell me what happened between you two this weekend?"

"Nope."

"Didn't figure you would." Mrs. Sain laughed, then cleared her throat with a cough.

"But you asked all the same."

"I'm old. If I ask or say things I shouldn't, people just put it down to me being senile."

Shaking his head, Grant grinned. "Only a fool would take you for senile. Your mind is sharper than most."

"Too bad this broken-down body can't keep up with what's still in here." She tapped the side of her head. "Up here I don't feel any different than when I was in my twenties."

Grant nodded. He'd heard others say similar things. The mind remained young, but the body wouldn't co-operate. Mind over matter didn't always hold true. Although he certainly gave credit to Mrs. Sain repeat-edly pulling back from death's door to the fact that her attitude was full of gumption.

"You finally convinced her to go out with you?"

Speaking of gumption. "There you go with those se-nile questions again. I may have to order a CT scan of your brain if you keep that up." He winked. "Besides, you know every woman is beating down my doorway to get me to take her out."

"Uh-huh." Mrs. Sain didn't look convinced. Or se-nile. "Except for the one you want, and she's running scared. Although maybe she forgot her tennis shoes this weekend because I don't think she was running."

"Good thing you're not senile."

Mrs. Sain rolled her eyes, then scooted up in her bed. "Stick to your guns and give her time."

"Time?"

"To get past whatever has her running. She likes you and that scares her. Can't say I blame her. You pack a potent punch."

Grant tried not to wince at an eighty-year-old telling him he packed a potent punch.

"She'll come round."

He marked that he'd reviewed the chest X-ray and

closed the radiology program within the EMR system. "That's what I'm hoping for."

He really shouldn't admit that to his patient, was probably being all kinds of unprofessional in doing so. But maybe he needed to talk to someone. Mrs. Sain seemed liked the logical choice regardless of however an unlikely one.

This time it was her bony hand patting his. "I know you are, son. It shows every time you look at her."

Was he that obvious? And why did something in his chest constrict at Mrs. Sain's "son"? Why did her endearment make him long to see his own mother and have her comfort him? Christine would think him crazy if he called her up and told her he wanted a visit. After all, there wasn't a holiday in sight.

"Maybe you should do something nice for her," Mrs. Sain continued, oblivious to his mind's crazy rambling. "Send her flowers or a box of chocolates. Women like that kind of thing so long as you're sincere about your intentions."

"Oh, I'm sincere about my intentions all right." He couldn't help but grin and waggle his eyebrows in his best bad-boy imitation. "But I have strict orders not to."

Mrs. Sain frowned. "She on a diet?"

"You might say that." Did Joni diet? She certainly didn't need to. Her curves were perfect. She had dug into her food at the fundraiser with gusto, but in reality she hadn't eaten much off her plate.

"Well, flowers don't have calories." Mrs. Sain's face crinkled with thought. "Unless she has allergies. She have allergies to flowers?"

"Apparently so." He had no idea. He needed to spend more time with Joni so he knew the answers to questions like these. He needed to spend time with her so they could get to know each other and see where the attraction between them led.

"Hmm." Mrs. Sain became thoughtful. "Maybe you should talk to her friends, find out what she likes, then do something for her that would have special meaning. Women like it when you take the time to make the things you do for them personal."

"Not a senile bone in your body," he teased. "Don't let anyone tell you otherwise." He leaned down and gave the woman a peck on her forehead. "But I think I should stick with your first advice and give Joni time to figure out what she wants."

"It's a plan." Mrs. Sain's expression didn't convey that she thought it was a good plan, just a plan. "Just don't give her too much time or she'll think you aren't interested."

"I'm interested."

"I know." Mrs. Sain's eyes lit with excitement at his admission. "I just wondered if you knew. If she knew. Oh! I do know." She practically sat up in her hospital bed. "You could be a secret admirer. Soften her up by wooing her incognito."

"Wooing her incognito is about the only way she'll let me woo her." He laughed, letting the idea stir. He did want to woo Joni. He wanted to take her into his arms and tell her how amazing Friday night and Saturday morning had been, how he'd picked up his phone a hundred times the day before, wanting to call her, to hear her voice, to beg for an invitation back into her bed, even if just to hold her. Then again, according to Joni, the only invitations into her bed that she'd be issuing wouldn't be for sleeping or cuddling. She wanted action and nothing else. How ironic.

But wooing her incognito? Maybe. Definitely there

would be a perverse satisfaction in rebelling against her ridiculous rules, and, really, could she blame him if she had a secret admirer?

"How'd you get so smart?" he asked the woman who watched him intently and had obviously read his every thought as it flitted across his face.

"You live long enough you learn a thing or two."

"I'll keep that in mind."

"You do that, and I'll keep thinking on a way to help you win her affections."

He didn't ask why his patient would be willing to do that. He figured lying in a hospital bed day and night she probably didn't have a lot of other things to focus on.

Besides, where Joni was concerned, he needed all the help he could get.

CHAPTER EIGHT

TRUE to his word, Grant ignored Joni at the hospital.

At least before, he'd always had a smile for her, always found a reason to accidentally touch her, talk to her.

Now nothing.

Not even a meeting of the eyes.

Four days had passed. Mrs. Sain had been transferred to another unit and Joni heard she'd been discharged from the hospital altogether that morning. She'd meant to say goodbye to the woman, but they'd had a code on the ICU floor and all chaos had broken loose. By the time she'd been able to take a break, Mrs. Sain had already left the hospital with her daughter-in-law.

Grant had been by the ICU several times that day. He'd had two new admissions, two pneumothorax patients, and had about ten others who were there for various problems, mostly related to acute exacerbations of chronic bronchitis.

On Monday night, she'd texted Grant that she wanted him. He'd been on her doorstep in less than an hour and brought her to even higher planes than he had over the weekend.

On Tuesday night, after she'd come home from her mother's, she'd wanted to text him, but had denied herself the pleasure, not wanting to do two nights in a row. Two nights in a row seemed too relationshippy. She hadn't technically listed that as a rule, but she should have. Sex with Grant two nights in a row would just be…fun, wonderful, exactly what she wanted. Which was why she had settled with just texting a "Not tonite" in response to his "Can I C U?". Which made her irritable because she wanted him.

What was that Scarlett O'Hara had once said about tomorrow? About it being another day? Well, tomorrow couldn't arrive fast enough for Joni.

Adrenaline rushing through his veins, Grant slid the tube down his patient's throat, intubating the woman and hooking her to the artificial life support that would keep her breathing. He ran through his checklist to make sure placement was correct, and watched her chest rise and fall with the aid of the ventilator.

The forty-year-old woman had gone into acute respiratory failure when she'd overdosed on her prescription pain medications mixed with alcohol. He'd seen it happen before. Someone in pain popped another pill, took a drink or two, thinking it wouldn't hurt even though they weren't supposed to mix their medications with alcohol, thinking that the combination would ease the ache or at least make them not care.

He'd seen it happen with Ashley, had watched her destroy her life, the life they'd had together, almost destroying him too.

Kathy Conner hadn't cared about much of anything when she'd drifted into sleep and her husband hadn't been able to wake her. Grant felt sorry for the man, felt thankful he had finally extricated himself from Ashley's messed-up life.

"Great job," the emergency room physician praised. Grant had been paged to assist when the woman had lapsed into acute respiratory failure minutes after arriving at the emergency department via ambulance.

"I was afraid we wouldn't be able to save this one," the emergency physician continued, pulling off his latex gloves.

"She's not out of the water yet." Unfortunately.

Just because her breathing had stabilized with the aid of the ventilator, it didn't fool Grant. The woman had suppressed her central nervous system to the point her body functions could shut down at any point. She'd be lucky if she only needed a ventilator to keep her alive. Just as easily her liver or kidneys could fail from the toxins she'd poisoned her body with.

How many times had he watched over Ashley as she'd detoxed, praying that she pulled through? He glanced at his patient, a mixture of disgust and pity filling him. With so many of his patients fighting for every breath, he sometimes struggled to remain compassionate with someone who treated life so carelessly.

"Call ICU and have them get a bed ready," Grant told the nurse who'd been assisting with the procedure. "Ms. Conner is going to need close care over the next twenty-four hours to see her through this one. I'm going to talk to her husband and let him know what's going on, then I've got to see the patients at my office. If anything changes, have me paged."

When Grant finally made it to the ICU wing, the first person he saw was Joni. Instantly, his body tightened. Instantly, he had flashbacks to the previous night. To every other night for the past five weeks.

Why she only called him every other night he could only imagine, and did, but on "their night" she didn't hesitate or dawdle. She called, told him exactly what she wanted, and he came running.

Not exactly what he'd had in mind when he'd agreed to her rules. He wanted more than the hours they spent in bed. Because essentially he was her booty call.

Sure, while they were together, she gave him her all, holding nothing back, letting him hold her afterwards until oftentimes he grew hard again and had to have her a second or third time.

Sure, she laughed and played with him in bed, answered most questions he asked—no, she wasn't allergic to flowers and, yes, she was on a diet, because, *duh*, what woman wasn't perpetually on a diet?—but at no point did she seem interested in changing the status quo of their relationship. At no point would she answer any question about her childhood or her parents or about how she occupied her time on the nights they didn't see each other.

What did she do on the nights she wasn't with him? Who was she with? He didn't believe there was someone else, but he couldn't shake the feeling that on the nights Joni wasn't with him, she was doing something he wouldn't like.

Then again, only five weeks had passed. Maybe he should stick to what he'd told Mrs. Sain. Give Joni time. Or maybe he should try some of the older woman's other suggestions, see how those panned out for him. Flowers, chocolates, or one of those fairy figures he'd noticed around her house.

What woman who collected figurines of such whimsical creatures only wanted a physical relationship with a man? Surely she was a romantic at heart? Surely he just needed to appeal to that love of fantasy and convince her that she should trust in the chemistry between them?

At that moment, she glanced up, saw him. Her full lips began to curve into a smile, but then she caught herself, sobered, and glanced away.

Smiling at him at work was against the rules.

He'd had enough of her rules, enough of her shutting him out, enough of not knowing what she did every other night that she didn't want him to know about.

It was time to break out Plan B.

Let the wooing begin.

Joni came out of her patient room and caught sight of Grant standing near the nurses' station. His head was thrown back and he was laughing at something Samantha had said.

A pang of jealousy shot through her. Red-hot jealousy.

Her entire insides had lit up like a Christmas tree when she'd spotted him earlier in the day. It had been all she could do not to drop everything she was doing and run to him, wrap her arms around him, and tell him how wonderful he looked.

It had taken all her willpower to rein in how he affected her, to damp down her happiness at seeing him, and remain professionally detached.

He hadn't seemed to mind. He'd walked right past her without saying a single word, without an accidental brush against her or even another glance her way, as far as she knew.

But what could she say? She'd been the one to tell him to ignore her at work, that theirs was a sex-only relationship. He'd been true to his promise.

Just because she was feeling the constraints she'd put

on them, it didn't mean she'd been wrong to put them there. Just the opposite. If him ignoring her bothered her this much, she'd been right to keep as much distance between them as possible in her professional life.

If every night she wanted to call him, beg him to come to her, stay with her, then she'd been right to keep their trysts to every other night, to insist he couldn't stay until morning.

Her rules might be a pain in the kisser, but if she wanted to walk away without having to clean up a mess she didn't need, then she had to cling to them, had to make him stick to them.

No problem there. He seemed just fine with their affair the way it was. What did he do on his off night? She never asked and he never told. Sure, he texted her one-liners meant to make her smile—or ache with desire—but he could send those from anywhere.

Even from another woman's bed.

She grimaced. No, Grant wasn't spending time in another woman's bed.

Was he?

Before she could think better of it, she marched over to where he stood.

Enjoying the surprised look on his face a bit too much, she grabbed hold of his scrub top and led him away from the nurses' station, away from a laughing Samantha. But where to?

"Not a word," she ordered when she opened the door to the supply closet and he opened his mouth. "Not a single word about where we are."

Instead he flashed his most wicked smile, shrugged, and didn't utter a single word.

"I forgot to tell you a very important rule."

His brow arched, but he didn't speak, his silence forcing her to go on.

She gulped, then lifted her chin. "While we are involved, neither of us can have sex with anyone else. We're monogamous or not at all."

His eyes widened with surprise, then twinkled with amusement. "I never took you for the jealous type."

"Who said you could talk?" she snapped back, hating it that he read her so clearly.

He grinned. "I have to tell you, I never took you for the bossy type either, but I'm liking it. Liking it a lot."

She rolled her eyes. "I'm not bossy."

"Lady, you are a total control freak, but I'm crazy about you anyway."

"I am not a—" The rest of what he'd said hit her. "You're crazy about me?"

"You think these past few weeks have just been about sex?"

She bit her lip, hard. She needed the pain to dull the euphoria blossoming within her at his words.

No. No. No.

"The past few weeks have just been about sex. Don't say things like you are crazy about me."

He snorted softly, pulled her to him. "If you insist. I won't tell you how crazy I am about you or how good you feel."

Wow, but he felt good pressed against her, too.

"I insist."

"Fine, but for the record we are in the supply closet." His head lowered to within centimeters of hers. "I distinctly recall us discussing this."

Butterflies danced in her belly. "We are at work, Grant."

"We are in a supply closet. Alone." He said the last with great emphasis. "You're mine."

His lips covered hers.

How could she deny him when he was right? They were in a supply closet. Alone.

Joni's face burned hot when Samantha didn't bother covering her laughter. Had her friend been laughing the entire time? Or just had a fresh bout hit her?

"Did I really just see you come out of the supply closet?" Samantha snorted.

Best friends were like that. Thought they had the right to point out the obvious and laugh about it, too.

Joni ignored her friend's laughter and smoothed her wrinkled scrub top. Not that she hadn't straightened the material a dozen times prior to stepping out of the closet. But each time she had, Grant had pulled her back to him and kissed her again.

When he'd slipped his hand under her scrub top and cupped her breast through her bra she'd known she was in danger of pushing Grant against the shelving and having her way with him. She'd wanted to do just that.

Had she lost her mind?

Anyone could have opened that door and caught them. Then what? Would she have been called into the nursing director's office and reprimanded? Would she have been handed her walking papers for inappropriate behavior? Her behavior was inappropriate. She was on the clock, had patients depending on her.

Her behavior was everything Mark had falsely accused her of. Everything she'd had to defend her job and nursing license for. Well, except for the under-the-influence part. She never drank or did any kind of drug. Never had and never would. Too risky.

Needing to escape, she'd run out of the closet, leaving a startled Grant behind her.

"I needed supplies," she explained to her friend, despite the fact she'd come out of the closet breathless and empty-handed.

"Ha." Samantha's gaze went past Joni to where Grant was now stepping out of the closet. "I see exactly what you needed. He must have worked up a sweat helping you find those supplies."

They both watched him disappear into Kathy Conner's room. An odd tug pulled at Joni's heart. Despite all the reasons she shouldn't have been in that closet, she couldn't blame him. She'd been the one to drag him there. It wasn't as if he hadn't warned her about being alone in the supply closet. Had she been tempting fate? Tempting him because she'd been jealous at the thought of him possibly being with someone other than her?

"It's not like that." It was exactly like that. Both in regard to what her friend meant and to her own treacherous thoughts.

"No?" Samantha sighed. "Well, it should be. How many times do I have to tell you that your rules are the craziest things I've ever heard?"

"They're not crazy." The supply-closet incident proved that. Had she stuck to her rules she wouldn't have just risked throwing her career away. Wouldn't be feeling jealousy over a man she was only having a short-term affair with. "You don't understand."

"Then make me understand," Samantha urged. "Because you're right. I don't understand why you have a wonderful man like Grant who is nuts about you and you're holding him at arm's length and refusing to let him in."

Ha. The reason Grant was nuts about her was because they weren't real. Men wanted what they couldn't have.

"Of all the people in the world, you shouldn't be accusing me of not letting him in. Not with the way you keep refusing Vann. I let Grant in."

"Yeah, you let him in all right." Samantha slammed the medication cart drawer closed with more force than necessary. "Every other night you let him in. Then you kick him back to the curb."

Joni winced at her friend's crass words. "Sleeping with him every night would feel too much like a relationship."

Samantha rolled her eyes. "Call it whatever you like, but for you to sleep with a man at all is a relationship, Joni. We both know you aren't a one-night-stand kind of girl."

"You're right." She lifted her chin. "We've had a lot more than just one night."

"And you have a lot more between you than just sex. Admit it."

"No."

"Well, don't look now, but your boy toy is finished in Mrs. Conner's room and is headed this way," Samantha warned. "Better go hide in the break room if you want to maintain your pretense of not having a real relationship with him."

Joni shook her head, but did as her friend suggested and ducked into the break room. She stopped short just inside the doorway.

A square box about the size of a coffee mug sat on the break-room table with a ribbon tied around it and a card propped beside it. "Joni" was written across the envelope in dark nondescript calligraphy.

Had Samantha done this?

Her friend knew she'd been emotionally up and down over the past few weeks. High over how happy she was when she was with Grant. Tense over how much she missed him and thought of him when they weren't together.

Not quite sure what to think, or even what she wanted to think, she picked up the box. Not very heavy, but definitely something inside.

She started to gently shake the box, but an inner voice warned her not to.

Instead, she untied the ribbon and lifted the lid.

A cupcake.

A single beautifully frosted red-velvet cupcake. Its decadent scent wafted from the box and made her breathe in.

Unable to resist, she dipped her fingertip into the icing and licked off the sweet confection. Rich cream-cheese icing melted in her mouth, delighting her taste buds and sending her into sensation overload.

Mmm, but she was going to kill Samantha for doing this.

Getting naked with a man as beautiful as Grant had left her wondering how he could possibly find her desirable when there was nothing tight or sculpted about her body. Samantha knew that, knew she was trying to lose a few pounds, that on the nights she wasn't doing the horizontal mumbo-jumbo with Grant she was sweating to the oldies and every other torturous exercise DVD she'd ever bought but rarely used until three weeks ago. Now she did AA with her mother, then she did FF, Flab to Fab.

Deciding that one more small dollop of icing

wouldn't hurt, she stuck her finger into her mouth, sucked the sugary treat off, then tore open the card.

Because a woman as beautiful as you should never diet

Not from Samantha.

From her Secret Admirer. Ha. Right.

CHAPTER NINE

Joni lay in her bed, beneath her bunched around her comforter. Through the darkness, she stared at the lit screen as she typed her message.

I know what you did today, she wrote.

What's that?

She smiled. Don't play dumb with me.

Playing dumb is not what I want to do with you.

A giggle escaped her lips as she typed her response. Your secret admirer fooled no one.

I have no idea what you are referring to.

Sure you don't.

Is there something you should tell me?

Thank you, but don't let it happen again.

She closed her eyes, anticipating the vibration of her phone signaling that he'd messaged back. When the buzz shook her hand, giddiness whipped through her. She punched the button to display his message. A thousand fighter jets took flight in her belly as she read what he'd written.

Invite me over so you can thank me properly for whatever it is you're giving me credit for doing.

She wanted to. Desperately she wanted to invite him over and feel the onslaught of sensations just being with him always gave her. To feel the pleasure of having all his attention focused on her, on bringing her body to as high as it would go time and again.

I can't.

He made her wait a full minute in the darkness before her phone jarred against her fingers.

You mean you won't.

Same difference.

Hardly.

His disappointment was palpable, made her second-guess her resolve to stick to not being with him two nights in a row. She wanted him so much. Would welcoming him into her bed tonight really be that much of a problem?

The fact she was questioning her resolve said, yes, it would. Sort of like when an alcoholic thought they could have just one drink.

Her phone shook again, startling her as she hadn't yet responded to his text.

Actually, not hard isn't accurate. Tell me what you'd do to thank me if I was there.

Oh, my, she thought, more turned on by his request than she would have believed possible.

What? You want phone gratitude?

Amongst other things.

Excitement surged deep inside her.

You admitting your guilt?

I'm admitting nothing. Now thank me.

Smiling, Joni closed her eyes, let her mind wander. If he were there, if she could thank him any way she liked, what would she do?

I'd take what was left of this naughtily delicious cupcake and I'd smear the icing down your chest.

In her mind she was doing just that, spreading the icing down the groove that cut his six pack in two. She wouldn't lift her finger until she'd left an icing trail all the way down to where his own happy trail disappeared. She loved his chest, loved that happy trail.

Sounds messy. Then what?

Messy? Ha, she'd give him messy. She could picture him lying in his bed, phone in hand, grinning as he'd typed his message.

I'd clean up the mess I made.

Oh, really?

Oh, definitely.

In her mind she already was.

How?

With my tongue.

Through the miles and darkness separating them, she heard him moan when he read her message.

Tell me more, cupcake.

Cupcake? She'd never been into nicknames, but she didn't correct him, just let warmth fill her as she thought about what "more" she wanted to tell him. She closed her eyes, pictured him standing beside her bed, icing streaked down his chest and abdomen. She imagined herself next to him, bent to where her mouth connected with his skin just so. Mmm… Had he heard her moan as she'd heard his?

I'd clean the icing off with little licks, savoring each burst of flavor as the icing melted on my tongue.

You're killing me here, came shooting back immediately.

She giggled in a way too feminine way and punched her reply. It's called cleaning, not killing.

Silence, then, What would you do next?

Smiling, she closed her eyes again, let her mind go back to their fantasy.

Well, it would take me a while to clean all that icing

off, to make sure I didn't leave any stickiness. I like to do a thorough job at anything I do, you know.

I know. Had he just gulped?

I might have gotten some in your navel that would require a lot of tongue action.

Might.

Would be hard work, she teased.

Very hard. But someone has to do it, right?

Right.

What's next?

Next? What was next? If she'd just licked cake icing off Grant's body, what would she do next if he was at her mercy?

Next would be your turn.

I get to rub icing on you and lick it off?

If that's what you want, cupcake. She wasn't sure why she tossed the endearment back at him, but doing so felt right, fun.

I want you, Joni.

I want you, too, Grant.

That an invitation?

Was it?

I… She hesitated, deleted the lone letter and started over. Nite, Grant.

For the longest time she waited for his response. She was just this side of asleep when it finally came, the vibration of her phone startling her awake.

She pushed the button that lit her screen, touched the text icon, and read his message.

Rules are meant to be broken, cupcake. Dream of me.

After way too long, she fell asleep and did just that.

Joni pulled the sticky note off her driver-side window and shook her head at the message. If you could call it that. A hand-drawn smiley face was the only thing on the yellow paper, but had the note contained words of poetry the gesture couldn't have touched her heart more.

She supposed she should be upset about all the little things Grant kept doing. A donut with the word "smile" written in icing. A handful of daisies that just very well may have been picked off the side of the road and left on her doorstep. All sorts of silly little things left at work with a card from her secret admirer.

He'd agreed to her terms. He'd just found a sneaky way around them. He still hadn't admitted that any of the gifts were from him. But she knew.

As did Samantha and several other of her co-workers who had started teasing about all her secret-admirer gifts.

Were they all in on his "secret admirer" act? Helping him pull off the little things he did? Helping him come up with just the right thing to say or do to put a giddy, happy feeling in her chest? To set off fireworks in her belly?

No, she shouldn't be smiling as she pulled the smiley sticky off her car window, but that didn't stop her.

Grant made her smile. A lot.

Hand on the doorhandle, she paused, closed her eyes and let images of Grant into her mind. The man felt so perfect.

"You waiting on someone?" a male voice whispered close to her ear.

"Just you," she replied, spinning to face him and almost wrapping her arms around his neck before she recalled where they were. Since the supply-closet de-bacle they'd pretty much stuck to their "no touching at the hospital" policy, not that she believed they were fooling anyone these days. "Aren't you in the wrong parking lot?"

"Not if this is where you are." His smile warmed her heart, but tension lines marred his expression. "I meant to catch you earlier to find out what time you wanted me over, but I got hung up with Kathy Conner."

Kathy Conner. Joni had spent a lot of time talking with her husband, her teenage son, had given them information on addiction. How could she not have? The woman reminded her of her mother, of sitting in a hospital waiting room not knowing if perhaps this was the time her mother wouldn't be coming home. The nurses she'd met during her mother's overdose hospital stays had influenced her so much and for that she was grateful, wanted to be a positive influence on others.

"I heard she had to be sedated to keep from pulling out her vent tube."

He nodded. "The woman is damned lucky to be alive. She should be ashamed to put her family through this."

Joni cringed at the brusqueness in Grant's voice. "Addiction is a disease, not something someone does because they want to be cruel to their loved ones. She obviously has a lot of problems." She hoped Kathy Conner pulled her life together the way Joni's mother had. Not that the fear of relapse wasn't always present. Each and every sober day was a blessing not to be taken lightly, and Joni didn't. That was why she was so diligent in attending AA with her mother, in her visits to watch for the slightest sign of trouble.

"Obviously."

The bitter way Grant said the words struck Joni as wrong, very unGrant-like. The man had more compassion and heart for his patients than any doctor she'd ever worked with. But she hadn't imagined his earlier brusqueness. His comment had sounded judgmental, lacking in empathy.

"Not everyone's life is cut and dried. You don't know what pushed her down the path she's chosen, what she's dealt with."

"You're right." He didn't meet her eyes.

Warning bells blared. She didn't know why it was so important that Grant not be judgmental the way Mark had, but it was. They were only short term, physical. What he thought didn't matter.

Yet it did matter.

"You don't really believe that, do you?"

He sighed, glanced around the parking lot, raked his fingers through his thick hair. "I believe we shouldn't be having this discussion, because we obviously disagree."

"Obviously." She mimicked his earlier comment with a hefty dose of sarcasm. She knew she was out of line, yet she couldn't contain herself. Couldn't ignore that his quick-to-judge attitude bothered her. "So, if I was like Kathy Conner, you'd not want me any more?"

His face paled. Visibly blanched so white she thought he might pass out. "That isn't funny, Joni."

"My question wasn't meant to be funny. It was meant to glean information."

"You aren't an addict, so it's irrelevant."

"For all you know, I could be."

"Are you?" he asked from between gritted teeth.

"No, I'm not." But wasn't that her greatest fear? That she'd end up becoming what Mark had told the nursing director she was—an addict? "Does whether I am or not matter? We're sex only. Would sleeping with me not be as good if I had problems? Or would you be sleeping with someone else? Heather Abellano perhaps? Or maybe you already want to be sleeping with her and that's what this is about?"

He worked his jaw back and forth. "I agreed to your rules, one of which included that while we were together I wouldn't be with another woman. Not that you had to put that rule into effect anyway. If I wanted to be with another woman I'd end things with you and be with another woman."

Her heart balled up into a tight lump in her chest.

"Is that what you're doing?" Why did she feel like she couldn't breathe? "If so, just get it over with so I can go home."

Go home and cry her eyes out. Hadn't she just minutes before been musing about how happy she was? Ha, she should have known better.

Color splashed his cheeks and his eyes burned blue fire. "Why do you always jump to the worst conclusions where I am concerned?"

"I don't," she denied, fighting tears and failing.

"Yes, you do." Although he kept his volume to a minimum, anger laced his words. "You assumed I'd slept with the women on my golf team, that I sleep around, period, that I want to sleep with Dr. Abellano's daughter. Have I done something that makes you feel I deserve those assumptions?"

Had he? No, Mark had, but she didn't want to discuss Mark.

"Silence," he pointed out. "Which means you just don't want to tell me what the real issues are or you're just waiting for me to slip up so you can point out my many flaws and walk away. Is that it?"

"I don't want you to slip up." Not to mention that she wasn't even sure he had flaws. The man was too perfect. Maybe that was his flaw. Perfection.

"No?"

She shook her head. She didn't.

"But you expect me to?"

He was right. She did expect him to fall off his pedestal, to do something so wrong that her heart would break. She knew he would. It was just a matter of time. Wasn't that why she'd had to have her rules to begin with? So that when things went wrong she had an insurance policy to protect her heart? So she wouldn't let him become tangled with thoughts of the future?

But she didn't want things to end. Not yet.

"I have done this your way, Joni, even though I didn't agree with the sex-only relationship, not that it ever really was sex only for either of us. I thought if I did things your way for long enough, you'd realize I was sincere, that I wanted a real relationship with you, that I want you as part of my life. But I'm wasting my time, aren't I?"

No, she wanted to cry, he wasn't wasting his time. But she'd only be delaying the inevitable. If he stayed, then what? They'd carry on until he realized she came from a messed-up home, until he judged her mother the way he'd judged Kathy Conner? Would she be lessened in his eyes because she was the daughter of an addict? Because she'd never turn her back on her mother?

"You can't even deny it, can you?" He sounded disgusted. She supposed he was. "Is this what you want, Joni?"

How could she answer? She wasn't even sure what he was asking. "Is what what I want?"

"To call an end to this pretense we have going?"

Pretense? Emotions she refused to label shriveled up and died inside her. She should cut her losses now.

The fact she was crying already implied she was more tangled up with him than she should be.

"That would probably be for the best." Embarrassed at the moisture in her eyes, on her cheeks, she met his narrowed gaze head on, hoping she looked tougher than she felt. "But, no, I don't want us to end."

He swore under his breath, took her hands into his. "Tell me what you want and, if I can, I'll give it to you."

What did she want? Great question. One she wished she knew the answer to. All she knew was that she wasn't ready to let him go.

"I want you," she answered honestly, wondering if he could feel how her body shook. "I want you to kiss me until I forget everything, except you."

Grant wanted to scream. Really? He was trying to have a serious conversation with her, to talk about his feelings, and she wanted to bring everything back to physical? Weren't women supposed to want to talk about their feelings? Not his Joni.

"Here?" he asked, testing her and knowing that was what he did. They stood in the employee parking lot. Anyone could see them. Was she ready to acknowledge what was between them?

Grimacing slightly, she shook her head. "You know not here."

Oh, he knew all right. He knew a lot of things. Like that her friends, even Samantha, knew very little about her past, knew very little about what made her tick. Joni had secrets. A lot of secrets, and she wanted to keep it that way.

The question was, why? What was she hiding? Not what Ashley had so effectively hidden during the first year of their relationship. Joni had said she wasn't an addict. Had she seen how he'd been unable to breathe

while he'd waited for her answer? Had she seen the relief wash over him at her denial? But the facts didn't
quite add up.

After years of dealing with Ashley's drug problem,
he'd done his research before asking Joni out. No one
had raised any concerns. Right or wrong, he'd even
taken a peek at her employee file, had seen her repeated
negative random drug screens. He'd thought he'd been
smart, had taken precautions. But she was hiding something.

"Why don't you want me to kiss you right now?"

Her glassy eyes widened. "It's inappropriate and asking for problems."

"Because?"

She glanced away, took too long considering her
reply. "There are things you don't know."

Exactly. There were a lot of things he didn't know.
Mysteries he'd like to unravel.

"Such as?" he pushed.

But rather than open up to him, she shook her head.
"Doesn't matter."

He wanted to throw his hands into the air. "You're
wrong. Everything about you matters." Despite her rules
against touch, he bent enough to kiss her forehead. "You
matter, Joni."

Her big green eyes met his in challenge. "Because
of sex?"

Had a more frustrating woman ever existed?

"If that's what you want to believe, fine, because of
sex." Was that all they'd ever have? Sex? He wanted so
much more, wanted her to be his. The thought that she
might completely shut him out someday had him wrapping his arms around her, hating it that she stiffened

against him, knowing that if he wanted to keep Joni in his life, patience was the name of the game.

Unfortunately he was feeling more and more frustrated and less and less patient.

Grant had planned the day down to a *T.* He and Joni were going to have a real date, spend time together without it revolving around sex.

Not that he didn't like the sex. What wasn't to like about Joni's hunger, which matched his own? About the way his body shredded into a million bits when he came inside her?

But he hadn't started their relationship wanting just sex. He wanted Joni. All of her. Not just her body.

Since she insisted on abiding by her Rules of Affair, as he'd dubbed them, today was his one chance to prove that they would be good together outside the physical realm.

Their hot-air balloon trip. Their first "real" date. Their only "real" date, according to Joni.

He'd had to think outside the box to come up with something to give her since flowers were out of the question. The hot-air balloon refrigerator magnet was corny, but he wasn't allowed to give a more traditional gift. He figured she'd put it on her refrigerator, would hopefully smile and think of him when she saw it.

Truth was, he liked coming up with the silly little things he did for Joni. Because he wanted to make her smile, wanted to brighten her day.

Because he was crazy about her.

He knocked on her front door. Checking his watch, he was glad to see they had plenty of time, could maybe do some sightseeing before arriving at Skyline.

"Come on in," she called from somewhere in her house.

He twisted the knob and went to find her so they could leave. He'd barely gotten the front door shut when he spotted her. His heart fell to his knees and another body part rose to the occasion.

Naked as the day she was born except for a pair of red high heels and a stethoscope dangling around her neck, Joni stood just a few feet inside the doorway. She had obviously been hiding behind the door as he entered her house so he could get the full effect of her outfit—or lack thereof.

"Morning," she offered, her voice low and husky. "Wanna play doctor with me?"

Seeing her always caused a testosterone surge through his veins, but her greeting him wearing nothing but her birthday suit, heels, and a stethoscope? Lord help him. Today was not supposed to be about sex.

"Joni." His jaw hung somewhere near his ankles. Unable to tear his gaze away from the beauty of her exposed body, he held up his wrist and pointed to his watch. "We need to go."

Today was about building a foundation for their relationship. One that didn't involve him playing doctor with his favorite nurse.

"Our flight," he reminded her. His gaze traveled over her. His nostrils flared. His pulse thumped a heavy rapid beat at his throat.

"Come here." She beckoned him to her. "I need to check your heart rate."

His heart rate was on the rise. He would like to think he was strong enough to stick to his plan, to resist the pull of her body for at least a day. Obviously, he wasn't.

When Joni crooked her finger, he was a goner.

"To hell with our flight."

Hands were everywhere. Mouths were everywhere.

He quickly ended up inside her against her living-room wall, on her sofa, in the middle of the hallway floor because somehow they hadn't made it all the way to her bedroom.

So much for keeping his hands to himself.

Okay, so technically Joni wasn't supposed to go on a date with Grant, but she had sort of promised that she would go if he won the hot-air balloon package, hadn't she?

So here she was, in the front seat of a gas-guzzling monster of a vehicle headed out on their late-afternoon adventure. Even sitting here next to him was an adventure. Mostly because every now and then he'd look over at her and give her that grin. The knock her off her feet he was so gorgeous, grin.

Going out with him like this was against the rules she'd set up to keep her heart safe, but just so long as she remembered that none of this was real, all the closeness and smiles and attraction was an illusion, here today and gone tomorrow, she'd be fine. Really, she would.

So just for today she was going to relax and enjoy being with this man who stole her breath with just a half-cocked smile.

"What are you thinking?"

She cut her gaze to him, her breath catching in her throat. The way he looked at her had made her feel like the most beautiful girl in the world.

"About how much fun we are going to have today."

He flashed a naughty grin and waggled his brows. "Don't know about you, but I already had some fun today." His eyes twinkling with merriment, he drew his brows together. "Let me rephrase that. I do know about you. Lots about you. We both already had some fun today."

He was right. They had both had fun.

Because the second he'd stepped into her house his clothes had begun flying every which way in a frenzied strip-fest. She leaned back against the Hummer's passenger seat, relived the memories. Oh, yeah, they'd had fun.

Hot, sweaty, orgasmic fun.

Just remembering had her shifting in her seat, her panties dampening between her legs. Again. How did he do that? Make her so physically aware of him? Make her want him so much?

She'd never considered herself an overly sexual person—if anything, quite the opposite. But with Grant she couldn't get enough.

"I recognize that look," he warned from the driver's seat.

This time she was the one flashing a naughty grin. "What look would that be?"

"Uh-uh, not again, Joni Thompson." He winced, shook his head as if to clear his thoughts. "I can't believe I'm saying that, that I'm not pulling off the road and giving you exactly what you want, but we don't have time. Not after this morning." He took a deep breath, met her eyes for a brief moment. "I want to take this balloon ride with you."

She sighed with great exaggeration. If she pushed even slightly, he would pull off the road. The realization was quite heady and a big turn-on. She wanted him.

"Get those thoughts out of your head."

She smiled, not bothering to mask her thoughts, not bothering to pretend she couldn't see exactly the effect her thoughts were having on him. She liked the effect she had on him. He made her feel beautiful, sexy, as if looking on her body was a cherished gift. When he looked at her she could see the desire in his eyes.

For whatever crazy wonderful reason, Grant wanted her.

Sure, it wasn't happily-ever-after, but since they were just physical, what did that matter? She didn't want happily-ever-after. She wanted Grant. She was going to ride this gravy train for all it was worth. Ride him for all she was worth until the attraction between them played out.

She twisted in her seat so she could more readily see him. Reaching out, she traced her finger down the clingy blue cotton of his T-shirt, lower and lower until she hit the waistband of his jeans.

His very tight jeans.

"Joni," he groaned. "Don't."

"Don't what?" She almost moaned at the pleasure hidden away behind the faded denim. The man did amazing things for a pair of jeans. But what he did when he was out of those jeans...wow was all she could think to describe how his body felt inside hers. Wow. Wow. Wow.

Her fingers toyed at his waistband, dipped into his navel, undid his snap.

"Joni." Her name came out half warning, half moan.

"What? You don't think you're up for a quickie?" she teased.

"Oh, I'm definitely up for a quickie." The bulge behind his zipper left no doubt. "Only problem is we have to be at Skyline in thirty minutes or we might miss our ride."

She scraped her nails over where his jeans strained. "Might be worth it."

"I'm sure it would be," he rushed out. "You always are. But I'm not pulling over."

"Who said anything about pulling over?"

With a daring she hadn't possessed prior to him, she unhooked her seat belt, shifted in her seat, and lifted the hem of her T-shirt, exposing a new silk and lace bra showcasing her heavy breasts.

He'd watched her dress when they'd finished that morning, had commented on how fantastic she looked in her underwear and how just looking at her made him want to take them off her again.

"Joni," he groaned, not taking his eyes off the road. She knew he could see her in his peripheral vision, though. The way he white-knuckled the steering-wheel was proof enough.

Knowing he was attuned to her every movement, she knelt on the floor of the vehicle and kissed where her hand had been moments before.

His abdominal muscles clenched against his T-shirt, his tension palpable as she ran her hands over him, down his muscular thighs. He made a noise that sounded like more of a growl than a word.

"Hmm?" she murmured as she struggled with his zipper, finally parting his jeans. She lowered her face, nuzzling against the soft cotton of his boxer briefs, breathing in his musky scent.

The man gave off some serious pheromones.

Just the smell of his body made her want to rip off his clothes and drag him between the seats so she could lick him all over.

Actually, she was going to lick and have her way with him right now. Without him pulling over.

With his hands occupied on the steering-wheel, she could explore his body without getting distracted by what he was doing to her body. Normally, if she was touching him, he was touching back. She'd soon lose all thought except...well, the man was turning her into a sex fiend.

"I should have tied you to your seat."

She laughed, glancing up at his handsome face. "I can think of a few things I'd like you to do to me if I were tied to the seat."

He audibly swallowed, placed his hand over hers on his thigh, keeping her palm locked against him. "You drive me crazy."

"You want me to stop?" She pressed her lips to where the tip of him jutted out of the top of his underwear.

"Yes." He gritted his teeth together when she licked him.

"Yes, you want me to stop?" She ran her tongue along the groove of his head, now fully exposed.

"No," he growled, his knuckles popping he gripped the steering-wheel so tightly. "I don't want you to stop, Joni. Not ever."

The need in his voice about undid her, made her want to give him pleasure, lots of pleasure.

"Good, 'cause I didn't plan to." She shoved his underwear out of her way, exposing the hard length of him, and didn't stop.

Not when he cursed and drove the Hummer off the road to a quick stop.

Not when he buried his hands in her hair, urging her on, telling her how amazing she made him feel and how he wanted to be inside her.

Not when he cried out her name and exploded.

CHAPTER TEN

TAKING a deep breath of fresh mountain air, Grant squeezed Joni's hand, lifted it to his lips and kissed her fingertips.

Her eyes bright, she smiled at him.

God, he loved her smile, loved doing things he knew would put a smile on her face.

"This is amazing." She gestured to the view beyond the hot-air balloon basket they floated in high above the ground. "Thank you for bringing me."

He agreed that the view of the mountains in the distance was spectacular, but she was amazing. Completely and totally amazing.

Everything about her. The way she cared for her patients, the way her eyes would meet his and he'd know exactly what she was thinking without either of them speaking a word, the way she came around him without holding back and felt so perfect in his arms afterwards.

The way she pushed him over the brink time and again, making him go a little crazy with need for her.

The only thing that wasn't amazing was her ridiculous rules.

Which she reminded him of quite frequently.

When she refused to actually go out on a date with him.

When she made him go home in the middle of the night because she didn't want to wake up beside him.

When she refused to tell him what she did on the nights they weren't together, even acted oddly when he asked, as if whatever she was doing, she didn't want him to know.

When she refused to acknowledge to anyone that she was his despite the fact that they weren't fooling anyone who knew them.

She was his. In every sense of the word, Joni belonged to him.

Only she refused to admit it. Refused to acknowledge that there was something very special between the two of them.

Only sex, she'd say. Only chemistry, she'd insist. Only physical, she'd explain. He'd had sex before. He'd had chemistry before. He'd had only physical before.

Joni wasn't only anything.

She was everything.

Only she wouldn't allow him inside the wall she'd erected. A wall full of rules and regulations meant to keep distance between them.

He wanted more.

Had always wanted more with her, he realized.

Only every time he tried to make their relationship about something more than physical attraction, she'd either spout rules at him or blindside him with lust and he'd end up inside her.

Not that he was complaining. They were phenomenal together. Their bodies were so in tune with each other. But today was his chance to show her how other aspects of their lives would merge just as well, that they weren't just about physical pleasure.

Not that he was doing such a great job proving a

thing. They'd had sex at her place, and then again in his Hummer.

Or did his pit stop even count as sex as she hadn't got to orgasm?

He'd been intent on keeping his eyes on the road, on not letting her get to him. Then he'd glanced over, seen her creamy cleavage on display beneath that lacy concoction she called a bra. He'd about busted free of his jeans. He'd been a goner before she'd ever put her plump lips against him and had no idea how he'd lasted the few minutes he had.

Never had he felt so out of control of his own body. Only with Joni.

"You're thinking about the Hummer, aren't you?" she asked close to his ear so the balloonist couldn't hear.

"It's not my vehicle I'm thinking of."

She giggled, looking happy. Really happy. More than anything he wanted her to hang onto that feeling. Wanted to be the one to give her that feeling, to make her happy.

Because he'd begun to suspect Joni hadn't had a happy life. That something or someone had hurt her and caused her to think she needed all those rigid rules.

"I want to date you. For us to be real in every sense. For the world to know that you are mine, Joni, because I think I'm falling in love with you." Where the words came from, he didn't know. Only that he couldn't take them back, neither could he deny them.

Had he wanted to kill her happiness, he'd achieved it in spades.

She stepped away from him, glancing desperately around them, over the basket edge, obviously needing space, much more space than the balloon basket offered.

Much more than the vast open sky around them offered.

For a brief, scary moment he thought she considered bailing out of the basket despite the hundreds of feet they floated above the ground.

He stepped closer, reached for her, but she shook her head.

"Don't say that." She wrapped her arms around herself, rubbed her palms back and forth over her upper arms as if she were cold. Maybe she was.

Maybe he was a fool.

Taking a deep breath, he handed her the jacket they'd been instructed to bring. "Here, put this on and forget I said anything."

Not that he would be able to forget.

"Joni?" he prompted, when she didn't take the light coat he held out.

Without glancing at him, she slipped the jacket on.

Then she stood there, looking lost, as if she didn't know what she was supposed to do next, as if she were trapped in this balloon with him and was afraid.

He hadn't meant to say what he had, but he couldn't take back his words, couldn't erase them. But today was his day, the day she'd promised him on the night they'd first made love, and she owed him this chance.

"Come here."

She hesitated.

"Come here, Joni."

Head down, she did. He wrapped his arms around her, held her close, kissed the top of her head. He repositioned her to where she was close to the edge of the basket, her back pressed tightly against his front, and he wrapped his arms around her. She remained stiff in his arms, and he bit back a sigh. He held her close, breathing in her sweet jasmine scent. Together they took in the beautiful scenery around them. Slowly, she relaxed against him and began pointing out different things below them.

Fine, he would play by her rules for a little while longer. Whether he liked them or not.

Joni smiled at the man who handed her a glass of champagne. Champagne. Ha.

He'd said he thought he was falling in love with her.

Not the most flattering of declarations.

Not even a confident one.

How could Grant be falling in love with her when their relationship was only based on physical fulfillment? When he didn't even know her or else he would never have handed her the champagne?

Besides, he couldn't be falling in love with her.

Because if he was then that meant her rules didn't offer protection and she could be falling in love with him too. No way would she allow that to happen.

No way would she risk such pain and humiliation again.

If it was happening, she'd have to change her rules pronto. Would have to add a rule that they couldn't see each other any more. Not under any circumstances outside work. Even work would be difficult. But she couldn't allow herself to be so vulnerable to a man ever again.

"To new beginnings."

New beginnings? She wondered, clinking her glass with his. Ha, Bean's Creek had been her new beginning. Now she played by the stringent rules that kept her on the straight and narrow life path she'd chosen for herself.

Only with Grant had she ever questioned her direction.

She'd thought she could play and not pay a price. What she hadn't counted on was that in their game she wasn't the only player.

"And to playing by the rules," she added. Maybe it was perverse to say so. Certainly the look on Grant's face said her toast wasn't one that made him happy.

But she needed protecting from herself because he was so irresistible. Because she couldn't see him if she couldn't abide by her rules. More and more she was beginning to wonder. That scared her, made her think maybe she couldn't continue to see Grant.

Hating the cold hard truth, she pretended to be entranced by their surroundings. The moment the balloonist distracted Grant by pointing something out, she tossed the contents of her champagne glass over the side of the basket without having taken an actual sip. The balloonist stared at her as if she was a lunatic, but he didn't say anything, and when Grant turned to see what the man was looking at, Joni just shrugged.

She could have just told Grant she didn't drink, except then he'd have asked why and that wasn't something she intended to get into with him. Ever.

The balloon landed near a predestined spot and another Skyline worker met them and helped them out while the balloonist made adjustments inside the basket.

"Wow, this place is magnificent," she breathed, looking around them. Lush, tree-covered mountains in the distance, deep blue sky above them, soft green meadow beneath their feet.

If not for the fear that this was going to be her last day with Grant, she might think the setting just about perfect. Instead, the beauty of the place just seemed to mock her.

Still, she had today. One last day with Grant.

She'd been quiet way too long, Grant thought, holding Joni's hand as they walked several yards away from the balloon and watched the employees tie the basket down.

"Come on," he ordered, tugging her towards where he'd arranged for a romantic picnic. According to the person he'd talked to, they would have an hour of total privacy to eat and enjoy each other's company in the beauty of the North Carolina countryside. An hour where he and Joni could talk without any distractions.

"Where are we going?"

"Just over that rise there's a stream. Our dinner is there." He waggled his brows. "I worked up a hunger on the drive over."

She looked toward the rise, then gave him a mischievous grin. "I must have missed that. I don't remember you doing much work."

If she thought keeping his concentration on the road, keeping his hands on the steering-wheel rather than on her, had been easy, she needed to think again.

"You're right," he admitted, wrapping his arm around her waist. "I owe you one."

Acting nonchalant, she batted her lashes. "You owe me more than one."

Yes, he did. Lots more.

"Dozens," he promised, kissing the tip of her nose. Which was a mistake because putting his lips anywhere on her body just made him want to taste her all over.

"Dozens?" She looked impressed. "That's better."

"I can think of better."

Her gaze met his and all teasing ceased. "Me, too."

Grant fought the urge to toss her over his shoulder, carry her over the rise, and do better. Lots better.

He'd like to do better.

Their bodies were perfect. But them? He and her? They needed a chance she refused to give them.

He tugged on her hand, determined to see this through.

"Wow!" she exclaimed, coming to a complete stop when they came on the prepared picnic. "That was some prize package you won. This is amazing."

He wouldn't tell her he'd upgraded his package, put in custom requests, paid a small fortune for the additions. There wasn't any reason to. Seeing the excited look in her eyes made everything worthwhile.

She made everything worthwhile.

"Just as requested, your picnic dinner awaits," the Skyline employee named Kyle informed them, having finished at the balloon and having joined them.

A picturesque picnic complete with red and white checked blanket had been spread out on a grassy area a hundred yards or so from where they were. A large basket overflowing with goodies sat on one corner. A smaller basket rested on the other corner.

"You have an hour before we have to be back up in the air," the man continued. "There's a cabin down that way." He pointed in the direction he meant. "To give our customers privacy, we'll be at the cabin until about five minutes prior to take-off. If you need a bathroom break or anything, you can head in that direction. We want you to enjoy your Skyline experience."

"Thank you," both Joni and Grant replied at the same time.

"You folks enjoy, and if you need anything, just give a holler."

"Will do," Grant agreed, watching as the man disappeared over the rise.

Joni squeezed his hand, her gaze eating him up as it raked down his body. "I'm starved. You?"

Oh, he was hungry all right. But not just for food. Or for her body for once, although the way she was looking at him was rapidly getting him there.

What he was starved for was answers to the dozens of questions running through his head, not the least of which was her reaction to him telling her he was falling in love with her.

There was probably a rule she'd forgotten to tell him about him wanting answers, but today wasn't about rules.

Today he was going to prise apart whatever held her back from a relationship with him.

CHAPTER ELEVEN

GRANT insisted on catering to Joni, made her sit while he examined the contents of the basket.

She started to argue, to insist on helping, but she'd realized he wanted to do this. That she wanted to let him. If today was her last day with him then she would have the full fantasy. Let a gorgeous man wait on her. Truth was, part of her still couldn't believe he wanted to, that he'd said what he had about wanting a real relationship with her.

"Looks good," he said when he had the food out of the basket and arranged on the blanket between them.

"Smells good, too." Joni inhaled deeply, eyeing the food with real appreciation. "I didn't realize how hungry I was."

"Flying works up an appetite."

Flying wasn't what had worked up her appetite.

"Or something like that."

Meeting her gaze, Grant grinned. "Right. Let's eat."

The basket had been stuffed with the meal that Grant had pre-ordered. Fruit, cheese, grilled chicken, steamed vegetables, a chocolate dessert to die for—at least that was what Grant said the menu had stated.

Later, she agreed with the menu's claim. "Okay, this is phenomenal." She licked her spoon to make sure she didn't miss a trace of the chocolate delicacy. "We're in the middle of nowhere, and this is better than most restaurants. How did they do this?"

"I imagine they helicoptered the food in. Wouldn't take but a few minutes to get it here by 'copter. Although they could have driven it in." He proffered his laden with dessert spoon to her, smiling when she closed her mouth around the treat and moaned. "Regardless, we took the scenic route."

"That is so good," she said, shaking her head when he offered his last bite to her. "You eat it, please. The balloon may not be able to lift me to get us home as it is."

"You didn't eat that much. Here." He stuck the spoon in her mouth again, causing another meltdown of chocolate deliciousness.

"I ate more than my share. Thank you. Everything was wonderful." She lay back on the over-sized blanket, stared at the blue, blue sky, wondering how nature had so perfectly replicated the hue of Grant's eye color. If she would ever look at the sky on a perfect cloudless day and not think of him.

No, she wouldn't think of that. Not now.

"I'm so stuffed I may never move again." Glancing at him, she pointed her finger in a mock scold. "Don't even say it."

"What?"

"Whatever you were thinking." Her smile killed the effect of her words.

"I'm innocent, I tell you." Despite his claim, he didn't look any more innocent than he sounded—which wasn't at all.

"Right."

He lay back next to her, clasped her hand in his.

"Whatever shall we do for the next thirty minutes?" Despite her full belly, Joni started to roll over and kiss him, to spend the remaining time with her body entangled with his. After all, the workers had ensured their privacy and they'd never made love in the wide open countryside. Neither would they ever have opportunity after today because she really couldn't risk continuing their affair.

Her heart squeezed, skipping a beat. Desperate to feel his body against hers, she leaned towards him.

But rather than accept her kiss, he shook his head. "Talk to me, Joni."

Huh?

She was offering herself to him in the middle of paradise, and he wanted to talk? Really?

Okay, so they had already made love twice, but... Unsure what to think, she attempted to disentangle her fingers from his. He held on tight enough that she couldn't free her hand, yet not once did his grip hurt.

"Don't do that."

"Do what?" she asked, because she really didn't understand.

"Pull away from me. I don't mean from my hand. I mean you shutting me out."

"I don't shut you out."

"Sure you do," he countered, squeezing her hand. "Every time I try to move our relationship beyond the physical, you shut me out."

"You shouldn't attempt to move our relationship beyond physical. Let's be real, you and I are only physical. Once the chemistry fizzes, poof, we're gone like a puff of smoke."

"Do you really believe that?" He looked stunned and she found herself questioning so much. But even if he wanted more, how could she ever risk her career again? She couldn't. When they ended, who was to say he wouldn't turn on her the way Mark had? She liked her life in Bean's Creek, didn't want to start over somewhere else.

"Why wouldn't I?"

He lifted their twined hands and placed them on his chest just above his heart. "Because of this."

She shook her head. "I don't want to have this conversation."

"I'm sure you don't, but this conversation is overdue."

She didn't want to ever have this conversation. "Aren't you listening? You and I are just sex."

"If you believe that, you're lying to yourself. You and I have never just been about sex."

She started to deny his claim, but she couldn't. He was right. No matter how she wanted to label what was between them, no matter how she wanted to cling to a bunch of rules that had only served as a ruse for her to hide behind, she and Grant were about more than just sex.

"What is it you want from me?"

He gave her hand another gentle squeeze. "For you to talk to me."

"About?"

"About why you refuse to acknowledge that you and I are in a relationship together. About why we are so perfect together, yet you insist we are only physically attracted to each other. About whatever it is you're hiding from me. About whatever happened to you to make you not believe in love."

Emotions flooded through her. She didn't want to talk about the past. "Don't."

"Don't what?" he asked, his voice so gentle moisture stung her eyes.

"Don't ruin today," she pleaded.

Confusion shone in his blue eyes. "Talking to me about our relationship will ruin our day?"

"Yes."

"Why?"

"Because it's against the rules."

"Screw your rules, Joni. They were only words all along."

She swallowed hard. "You were just humoring me?"

"I was waiting for you to realize you were wrong."

"I'm not wrong." Her throat pinched tight, making breathing difficult.

"Which would mean that I am wrong to believe there is more between us than just sex?"

Joni closed her eyes, bit into her lower lip, then winced. Was he wrong? The wild thumping in her chest implied he was, but if that were the case then she'd only been fooling herself from the very beginning. Had she set herself up for heartache? Had she possibly jeopardized her career by becoming involved with another doctor? Someone the hospital would value much more than her if push came to shove?

What had she been thinking?

She hadn't been thinking. She'd been feeling.

Lust. That was all this was. Physical attraction. Yes, Grant was a good man. He was a responsible doctor who provided good care to his patients. He treated all the hospital staff with respect and courtesy. So of course she liked him.

Liking him didn't mean she loved him.

She wasn't in love with him.

She just wasn't. Love had hurt so much.

She glared at him, hardened her voice. "Not every woman is waiting for Prince Charming to come swooping into her life and carry her off on a white horse."

Not that such a creature even existed. Prince Charmings were as fictional as the fairies she collected.

"I don't believe they are. Just as not every man wants to settle down and marry someday. But most people do want someone to share their life with. Someone to talk to and discuss the day's events with. Someone to listen and hold your hand." He stroked his thumb across hers as if to stress his point. "Someone who cares what happens."

"You want that?" she gulped out, barely able to breathe.

"Yes, Joni, I want that." He inhaled sharply. "With you."

Why was her throat closing off? Why was her head spinning? Why was her heart racing a mile a minute? Why couldn't she just tell him to forget her rules and have that with her?

A fuzzy image of Mark's face danced through her mind. He'd told her he loved her, that he wanted to spend his life with her, that they'd marry and have babies together, that they'd grow old together. Instead, he'd cheated on her, wanted her to turn her back on her mother, and tried to destroy her career.

"If what we have isn't enough, we end right now."

Grant stared at Joni in disbelief. Seriously, she'd let them end before she'd admit that what they had was much more than just sex?

Was he so wrong?

He wanted to take her in his arms and kiss her until she admitted she needed him.

But, then, that was the problem, wasn't it?

Joni did admit to needing him physically. Elsewhere in her life was where she wouldn't budge. She wanted their relationship in a neat little box that she could label as only sex.

He signed in frustration. "You haven't enjoyed today?"

"You know I did. But today is about sex."

Yeah, he hadn't meant for that to happen. Unfortunately he had trouble remembering that when she'd started touching him. Or met him at the door naked.

"We didn't have sex in the balloon." So he was reaching with that one, but they hadn't and not because he hadn't thought about it. A lot.

Apparently wanting to lighten their conversation, she gave him an impish grin. "Yet."

Her one little word sent his libido into hyperdrive, sent visions through his mind of him behind her, inside her, as they floated through the sky.

"Joni," he began, not wanting their conversation to turn sexual.

She rolled onto her side, ran her finger over his chest in a slow tease. "Face it, Grant. You and I are all about this right here." Her finger made an erotic sweep down his mid-section. "This powerful, magic pull between us that makes me want you inside me right now."

"Right now?" He gulped, wondering if she was trying to kill him.

"Oh, yeah." Her fingers were walking again. Lower and lower. She pushed against his chest, laying him flat on his back. Crawling on top of him, she smiled down at him. "I want you inside me."

A stronger man might resist her. Grant couldn't. Not when she rubbed herself against him and kissed him as if she needed him more than her next breath. Hell, he was only human.

And she was really hot.

"Dr. Bradley?" a voice called from way off in the distance. The balloonist. So much for guaranteed privacy. Probably wise the man was giving them warning way before they could see him. Very wise.

Joni quit moving, slid off him and back onto the blanket next to him. "You were saved by the bell."

"You think I wanted to be saved by the bell?"

She shook her head. "No, I think you wanted the same thing I wanted."

"What gave you that idea?"

She glanced at his jeans.

"You make a good point."

"Grant?"

He didn't like the seriousness in the way she said his name.

"On my rules…"

Neither did he like the word "rules" or that she felt she needed them with him.

"You do still agree to them, right?"

Had he ever really agreed to them?

"Because if you don't, I can't see you any more," she continued. "Not outside the hospital, I mean."

He hated this. Hated that she wouldn't let him inside those walls she'd hidden behind. Maybe with time he'd scale them. Or knock them down completely. But he was tired of Joni's damned rules.

"Dr. Bradley?" the balloonist called again, this time from much closer. After promising complete privacy, Grant was a little irked that they were being interrupted.

"Over here. Where the picnic was set up," he called

back, although surely the man knew exactly where he and Joni would be.

When the balloonist rushed over the rise, rosy cheeked and out of breath, Grant instantly knew something was wrong, that their privacy wasn't just idly being disturbed. He jumped to his feet and headed toward the man.

"Kyle was messing around outside the cabin and reached for something and was bit by a rattler," the man exclaimed breathlessly before Grant could ask.

"A snake?" Joni asked, also now on her feet.

The balloonist nodded. "He's at the cabin. I hated to leave him, but I didn't know what to do other than to come get you, Dr. Bradley."

"For the record," Grant said as they hurried toward the cabin, "I'm a pulmonologist."

"You still know what to do, though, right?" The man sounded worried, like he would somehow have to know if Grant didn't.

"I know." He'd never worked an actual snakebite case, but he did know the basics.

"Me, too," Joni piped up from where she ran beside them. "I worked the emergency room before I moved to Bean's Creek. We saw several snakebites during my time there."

Something else Grant hadn't known about her. That she'd worked in the emergency department at a hospital other than Bean's Creek. Where? he wondered. And why had she left? Did that have something to do with her need to try to put their relationship in a tidy box with boundaries and rules?

When they came upon the cabin, the man was half sitting, half lying on a rugged-looking leather sofa. Pale, he held a dish towel over his left hand. There was more blood on the towel than Grant would have expected from a snakebite.

"I feel like such a fool," he said when they rushed into the room.

"How long ago did the bite happen?" Joni asked, immediately taking the man's hand with care and elevating it. "You need to keep your hand elevated to the level of your heart."

Careful not to touch any of the bloody areas, Grant lifted the towel away from the man's hand.

"Maybe fifteen minutes ago." The man glanced toward his left hand and winced. "I didn't know I was supposed to have my hand elevated."

"Having the bite site elevated to the level of the heart helps to slow down envenomation." Grant began checking the bite site. There were two deep puncture wounds. Blood oozed from the man's hand. The snake had definitely been poisonous. Only poisonous snakes had fangs. Non-poisonous snake bites would show a row of teeth marks, not the fang punctures.

"Am I dying? I watch those television shows about people who shouldn't have survived and stuff." The man's voice cracked, sounding panicky. "I'm going to die, aren't I?"

"Those television shows show the dramatic cases because that's what makes people tune in. Snakebites are serious business, but death from a snakebite, even a poisonous snakebite, is rare," Grant assured him, although the truth was the man's bite was serious. They were in the middle of nowhere with limited medical supplies and who knew how long it would take for the emergency helicopter to get to them to transport the patient to the hospital. He continued to assess the bite. Redness had begun spreading around the area. The man's entire hand was swollen.

Not seeing anything he could readily use to bind around the man's arm to also help slow down envenomation, Grant stripped off his T-shirt, took his keys out of his jeans, and jabbed a hole into the material. Using the hole as a starting point, he tore the material into a strip, then jerked it apart.

"I need to take your ring and watch off you. We don't want any jewelry cutting off circulation if you continue to swell," Joni told the man as she attempted to do so. With his hand and fingers already swollen, removing his wedding band wasn't easy. It took her squirting hand sanitizer on the area to add lubrication before the gold would budge.

While Joni's fingers remained on the bite victim's wrist, taking his pulse, Grant turned to the other Skyline employee. "Is there a first-aid kit? We need to see if there is a snakebite kit." Or anything else they could use to suction the wound.

The nervous man, who'd been standing just beyond the sofa, watching, pale faced, nodded and went to grab the first-aid kit.

Grant tied the material from his shirt around the man's forearm, not tight enough to cut off circulation but enough to slow down the spread of the venom.

"I feel really dizzy." Kyle shifted, sounding frightened. His movement caused a fresh wave of blood to ooze from the wound. The only good thing about the blood was that maybe some of the venom was being forced out along with the blood.

"Try to stay still, calm," Grant advised, because the man becoming excited, moving around a lot, would increase his circulation and speed up the spread of the venom.

Joni's gaze met his. "Heart rate is one hundred thirty. Respirations twenty."

Tachycardic and tachapneic. Not good. Most snakebites didn't cause the victim to go into shock, but it could happen, depending upon the amount of venom injected.

"Here's the first-aid kit." The balloonist almost tripped over his feet trying to get the kit to them.

"Go get him something to drink," Joni ordered the balloonist, taking the kit and opening it. She handed Grant a pair of latex gloves and donned a pair herself. "Preferably bottled water. We need to push fluid."

"I feel like I can't breathe."

Panic, shock, or a reaction to the venom?

"It's okay," Joni soothed after leaning in, listening closely to the man's chest then digging through the kit again. "Dr. Bradley's specialty is breathing. He's the best, and we're going to take good care of you." She turned to Grant and held up a small plastic package. "Look what I found."

A snakebite kit.

Handing him a disinfectant packet so he could clean the wound site, she tore open the sealed snakebite kit. She removed the extractor and handed the suction device to Grant while she began talking to their patient again, trying to calm him, carefully continuing to assess his breathing status.

Grant couldn't help but think how glad he was that Joni was there with him, for many reasons. She was a great nurse. A great woman. And they couldn't see each other any more if he didn't play by her rules?

He wanted to scream and rant and rave about how

unfair she was being, that he was not a glorified booty call, that he wanted a real relationship, to make her see reason. Now wasn't the time, though. A man's life rested in their hands.

So he suctioned the wound, letting Joni's calm voice help calm him, too. The man was going into shock. They were in the middle of nowhere. The first-aid kit was basic. No epinephrine. Nothing to intubate the man if his airways closed. Not much of anything other than basic run-of-the-mill first-aid bandages and creams. He supposed he should be grateful someone had had the foresight to purchase a snakebite kit.

"Here's water. I got one for you and Doc, too."

Joni smiled at the balloonist, took the water, opened the lid, and encouraged the bite victim to start drinking. "You feel light-headed because your blood pressure is starting to drop. You need to take in fluid. As much fluid as you can stand. Drink up."

The man took the bottled water in his good hand and took a drink.

"Is there a defibrillator on the premises?" Joni asked the question as if it were no big deal, as if she was making casual conversation, but Grant knew better. She was wanting to be as prepared as possible for anything that came up with their patient.

The balloonist pointed toward a far wall. "That's what that is. We were trained, but I don't know that I could do it."

"Not a problem." She flashed a reassuring smile. "Dr. Bradley and I are more than qualified should need arise. Which isn't likely," she added for the victim's benefit.

The man had downed about half the bottled water. "My hand is twitching."

Yes, Grant had noticed the muscle spasms. A sign of neurotoxicity.

"That sometimes happens," Joni assured the man, patting his arm. "Do you have any other health problems? Are you on any medications?"

"I'm a walking pharmacy." Kyle took another swig of the water. "But I can't remember all the names. I have about ten different ones."

"Do you know what you take them for?"

"Diabetic problems, blood-pressure problems, my heart, and my blood."

"Your blood?" Grant wondered if Joni's stomach had clenched the way his just had.

"I have to take some of that rat-poison stuff because I've had blood clots in my legs in the past."

He was on anti-coagulation therapy to prevent the reoccurrence of clots. Not good.

"When was your last protime and INR test to see how thin your blood is?"

"A couple of months ago. I'm supposed to go every month. But it's always good. I missed last month." His gaze dropped to his swollen hand. "Didn't figure it would be a problem."

"You really need to have that checked every month as so many things affect the level of medication in your system. It's easy for the blood to get too thin or too thick if your levels aren't monitored properly."

"Yeah, they told me that I can't eat greens any more because of that."

That explained why there'd been more bleeding than Grant would have expected. The man was on a blood-thinning agent. Great. One of the mechanisms of venom was to thin the blood.

The bite victim's risk of internal bleeding went way up.

So did Grant's heart rate.

They needed to get the man to the hospital Stat.

"How long did they say it would be before the 'copter got here?"

"Probably about twenty minutes."

"Twenty minutes?" Surely twenty minutes had already come and gone from the time the man would have made the call. Just fetching him and Joni and their trip back to the cabin probably had taken longer.

"Maybe there was another call or something," the balloonist offered.

"Maybe." Grant shook his head at the irony of it. He'd wanted time with Joni, time for them to get to know each other besides physically, and instead the romantic day he'd planned had turned into a crisis.

"How much of this do I have to drink?" The patient held up the water bottle. "Its making me feel like I want to throw up."

Between Joni's ultimatum and the guy's increasing symptoms and risk factors, Grant knew just how he felt.

Wondering how she and Grant's fabulous hot-air balloon trip had turned into wilderness medicine, Joni got up to search for something the man could use as a sick basin. She found a small white plastic trash bin and carried it next to the sofa.

She knelt next to Grant and reassessed Kyle's vitals. "Heart rate is one forty. Respirations still at twenty. Pulse is a little thready."

"Blood pressure is low." Grant spoke her thoughts out loud as he turned to the man. "Drink the rest of that water. Now."

The man nodded, his eyelids drooping.

"Drink," Joni ordered in a voice Grant would probably say was her bossy voice. The man did so, finishing off what remained in his plastic bottle. She handed him one of the bottles the balloonist had brought for her and Grant. "Here's another. Drink."

The man grimaced. "I'll puke if I do."

"Puke into the garbage container, then, because you need to be drinking."

"I've suctioned out everything I can get."

Joni looked at him. Something she'd been trying not to do. Grant was always potent. She always wanted him. But Grant shirtless? Oh, my. Even in a crisis she wasn't immune enough not to notice that the man had a beautiful body. Her body wasn't strong enough not to be aware that he was so close.

Crazy. Not only were they in a crisis but they were also sort of in the middle of a fight. Why was she noticing how hot he was when he hadn't agreed to keep playing by her rules? When she didn't know where things stood with them?

"Then we just keep him stable until the rescue crew arrives," she said, looking directly into Grant's blue eyes and having a flashback to when they had been lying on the blanket, staring up at the sky, not having a care in the world except each other.

"Joni." His one word conveyed so much, conveyed all that she was thinking because she knew he was right back in that meadow with her. How did that work? That connection between them that allowed them to so readily read each other?

Her gaze went back to her patient and her heart almost stopped. Blood was trickling from the man's nose.

Not wanting to alarm him, her gaze went back to Grant's.

"Why is his nose bleeding?" the balloonist asked.

So much for not alarming their patient. The man wiped his nose, saw the blood, and became agitated. "I'm dying, aren't I? That's why you were asking about my medications."

"You're blood is just a little too thin, that's all," Joni assured him at the same time as Grant tried to get the man to lie back down.

"You've got to stay calm," Grant advised. "If you're up moving around, any venom I couldn't get out will spread faster."

"If my nose is bleeding, I'd say it's already spread."

"Is he dying?" the balloonist asked, looking paler and paler.

Joni gave him a "get it together and be quiet" look, then pointed to a chair across the room. "Sit down, and be ready to help."

The last thing they needed was for him to pass out and give himself a concussion. One patient was more than enough.

When the balloonist had done as ordered, she turned back to her patient, whom Grant was talking to and assessing.

"There are different aspects of what the snake's venom does. One is to thin the blood, another is to suppress your central nervous system, which is why you're having that little muscle twitch in your hand. The third is to cause breakdown of tissue." Grant's voice was calm, steady. He talked to distract the man from his panic more than to actually educate him on snakebites.

"I feel really light-headed."

Joni wished she had a way to measure Kyle's blood pressure. She knew the readings would be low, that his body was in shock.

She packed his nostril with gauze from the first-aid kit in the hope of stopping the bleeding. Help would arrive soon so the man could be transported to the hospital and anti-venom could be administered.

As if her prayers were answered, a low buzz could be heard in the distance.

"Thank God," she breathed as the sound grew louder and louder.

"Amen," Grant seconded.

Once aboard the rescue helicopter, Joni had nothing to do except sit on her hands.

The paramedics had taken over Kyle's care, so really even Grant was unnecessary at this point. He sat next to her with nothing more to do than to observe as well.

"So much for our romantic sunset flight, eh?"

Joni glanced out the helicopter's window. The sun was beginning to settle behind the mountains. Brilliant oranges, reds, blues, pinks, and yellows streaked the sky.

"For whatever its worth, the sunset is gorgeous."

He grinned. The noise from the helicopter made further conversation difficult, so they sat in silence during the trip to the closest emergency department.

When they arrived at the hospital, everything blurred. Joni and Grant both offered to help any way they could, but the emergency room doctor had taken over and they were superfluous.

"Dr. Bradley, we admitted a patient to ICU earlier. While you're here you may want to peek in on them," Cindy, the emergency department nurse, told him, glancing curiously back and forth between Grant and Joni.

Joni didn't meet the woman's eyes, wanted to go and

hide, but, really, what was the point? Word would be all over the hospital that she and Grant had been out on a balloon ride together. Great.

Grant asked the woman a few questions about the admitted patient, then turned to Joni. "You okay waiting for a few minutes?"

"Of course, Dr. Bradley."

She spoke so formally that Grant winced. Still, what had he expected? That she'd bat her lashes at him and say, "Sure, honey, anything you want"? Hardly. The entire emergency department probably thought something was going on between them now. Ugh. Why hadn't she thought of this earlier when they'd climbed aboard the rescue helicopter? Then again, it wasn't as if they could have flown the balloon back themselves and the balloonist was all shaken up. No way would she have wanted to float through the sky at his mercy.

"Joni?"

Shocked, Joni glanced up to see an older version of herself in the closest curtain-partitioned bay. "Mom? What are you doing here? Is everything okay?"

She glanced back and forth between the tired-appearing woman lying on the hospital bed and her stepfather, who held his wife's hand.

"I'm fine. I tripped and fell off the porch. Chris thought I might have broken something."

Tripped? Fell off the porch? Warning bells blared in Joni's head. "You weren't...?" She couldn't finish her question. Not with her so aware that Grant had followed her into her mother's bay, that he listened to every word being said. She didn't want him to know, didn't want to risk a repeat of history.

Her mother's face paled.

"No, she wasn't drinking," Joni's stepfather assured

her, lifting his wife's hand to his lips and pressing a kiss to skin. "You'd be proud and can tell everyone at your next AA meeting that she even told the E.R. doctor that if her ankle was broken, she didn't want any narcotic pain medications because she was a recovering alcoholic and an addict."

There it was. Those awful words. That awful truth from her past. Out in the open for Grant to hear and know. Out in the open for her fellow hospital co-workers to hear and know.

Joni Thompson's mother was an alcoholic and an addict.

Her whole life she'd dealt with that fact, loved her mother, and had forgiven her years ago for the pain and anguish she'd suffered as a child and teen with a parent who'd stayed intoxicated more often than not.

For the briefest moment she resented the public announcement of her mother's past sins. But only for the briefest of moments. Then she met Grant's startled blue eyes head on, took in the disgust that settled onto his face. She'd known, hadn't she? That he would have no compassion or sympathy for her mother? Fine. Who needed him, anyway? She lifted her chin high, daring him to say a single derogatory word, because if he so much as uttered a single one she was liable to hit him.

He didn't. He just stared at Joni, her mother, then shook his head as if he couldn't take another moment, and walked away without a word.

Joni knew she talked to her mother and stepfather for several more minutes, that she didn't leave until the X-ray films showed that her mother had just severely sprained her ankle, not sustained any fractures, until she knew her stepfather didn't need her help getting her mother home and settled.

She also knew she and Grant wouldn't be picking up where they'd left their conversation at their picnic.

There was no need.

He wouldn't be playing by any rules.

He wouldn't be playing at all.

Thank goodness she'd had her rules to protect her or she'd swear that ache in her chest was her heart breaking.

CHAPTER TWELVE

Using all her might, Joni pressed against her patient's chest in repetitive motions, giving two breaths via the CPR bag to every thirty compressions.

Samantha had gone after the crash cart and to call the code. Her friend couldn't have been gone more than a few seconds, but already time seemed to have stopped.

Yet every second that passed that she couldn't get Mr. Gold's heart to jump-start increased the odds that he wouldn't come back.

Her arms wobbled, feeling like water had replaced her muscles. She'd done CPR before, never failed to be amazed at how much energy was required to perform the chest compressions correctly. No matter, Samantha would be back in the room soon, would inject Mr. Gold with medication and together they'd defibrillate the man in the hope they weren't too late.

Seconds later whoever was on call as code physician would arrive, would take charge of the code, and Joni could react to orders rather than have a man's life in her hands, literally.

Please let his heart beat. Please let him take a breath.

She leaned down, listened and felt for a breath. Nothing. She checked for a heartbeat. No pulse.

She started another set of compressions, wondering why her workout routine hadn't prepared her in the slightest for this because surely if it had, her arms wouldn't be aching so.

"Here, let me."

Relief and a million other emotions washed over her as Grant moved to the other side of the patient and took over compressions while she continued respirations.

"Tell me what happened." His chest compressions were perfect, perfect depth, perfect rhythm, seemingly effortless from his strong arms.

"I was doing neuro checks when his eyes rolled back. His telemetry went off. No heartbeat. No respirations. I called for help and started CPR." She squeezed the bag to give the man a puff of air in perfect sync with Grant's sets of compressions. "Samantha was in the next room, came to check, and she's gone to call the code and get the crash cart."

On cue, the code announcement came over the hospital intercom system. Samantha rushed back into the room. Altogether her friend hadn't been out of the room a full minute, but Joni was so relieved to see her friend that weeks could have passed.

Grant began issuing orders while Samantha injected epinephrine into Mr. Gold and hooked him to the defibrillator.

"All clear. Now."

Samantha set off the charge. Mr. Gold's body jumped, but no heartbeat. Nothing.

"All clear. Again."

Over and over they tried to revive their patient, but nothing. After long, exhausting minutes Grant called the code to an end.

Joni dealt with death routinely. Working in ICU, how could she not? But never did she lose a patient that her own heart didn't ache over the loss. Each patient was someone's mother or father, someone's brother or sister, someone's son or daughter, was the person someone's heart was most connected to. Each death marked a life that had affected many people's lives.

She'd fought tears the last few minutes of their efforts to save Mr. Gold. Only she wasn't sure if the moisture stinging her eyes was just for the man's life that had slipped away or for the loss of Grant from her life.

They might not have had a real relationship, but somehow every aspect of her life had gotten all tangled up with him and she missed him. Missed him so fiercely that each night for the past two weeks she'd cried herself to sleep and woken up with her pillow damp from even more tears.

She imagined she looked a wreck. Definitely, Samantha, Brooke, and several others commented on how worried they were about her. But what could she say? That she'd lost someone she'd never really had? That Grant had learned of her mother's problems and hightailed it out of her life?

As soon as she could sneak away from Mr. Gold's room, she did. Finding an empty patient room, she let the tears fall, not trying to stop them.

She cried for Mr. Gold, for his family, for his friends. She cried for herself and the hospital staff that hadn't been able to save him. She wanted to save every patient.

Impossible, she knew. Death was inevitable for every person. But with each patient she lost she felt disappointment, a sense of failure, had a moment of what if she'd gotten to the person earlier, realized what was happening sooner, somehow have done something that might have brought on a different, better result.

Life was full of what-ifs.

What if she'd met Grant first, hadn't had the scars of her relationship with Mark? What if she'd trusted in him and been willing to risk a real relationship with him? What if she went to him and begged him to let her back into his life because she only felt half-alive without him by her side?

"You okay?"

"I'm fine." Joni immediately sat up straighter, swiped at her tears. Why had Grant followed her? For two weeks he'd not said a word to her, or sent a single text, or left any "secret admirer" gifts or notes. Nothing. So why was he here now when she felt so weak? When she wanted nothing more than to lay her head on his shoulder and breathe in the scent of him?

Grant stared at her, shook his head. "No, you're not. Come here."

She didn't move, couldn't seem to get her legs to co-operate with the mixed signals her brain and heart were sending. Don't budge, her brain urged. Lean on him, her heart pleaded.

When she didn't move, Grant took her hand, pulled her up from the chair and into his arms and held her.

Tight. As if she mattered. As if he hadn't walked out of that emergency room and her life.

Fresh tears began to flow.

She loved him. Loved this wonderful, beautiful man who was holding her so close, comforting her, even though he didn't want her any more.

Even though he'd walked away from her. How could she love someone so intolerant of other's flaws? What right did he have to judge her mother?

She pulled away. "No, really, I'm fine. Just leave me alone."

Lips tightening into a fine line, he stared at her. "Joni?"

Knowing she had to put some space between them, she shook her head. "I just needed a minute to compose myself. Sometimes I have to do that after losing a patient."

"Understandable," he said slowly, studying her so intently she wanted to squirm. "You're a great nurse, care about your patients."

She nodded. "I can't do this, Grant."

His jaw worked back and forth as he silently regarded her. She'd expected him to say something but he just stood staring at her, waiting for her to elaborate. Sometimes she'd swear the man had the patience of Job.

"This has been fun, but..." But what? She didn't want more? Ha, she wanted lots more. That was the problem. She wanted more from him but had been too scared to admit it even to herself until he'd walked away. "I can't pretend we're friends when we're not. I can't pretend nothing happened between us when it did. Please just go away and leave me alone."

Grant stepped back, looking at her as if she carried the plague.

"Fine." He shrugged, sounding as if he didn't really care one way or the other. "If that's what you want, that's what I'll give you. This whole relationship has been about what you want anyway."

His words stung. Stung painfully sharp. Her pride kicked in.

"I didn't hear you complaining about not getting what you wanted when we were in bed. Not once did I hear a single complaint."

"Take note, Joni." His eyes bored into her, glittering with anger. "I'm complaining now. I'm complaining that you are the most selfishly independent woman I've ever met. I'm complaining that when I was willing to give us a real chance, you put stupid rules in place that prevented us from ever having a chance at anything more. I'm complaining that you never let me in, never told me about your problems."

His voice grew angrier and angrier with each new complaint, searing into Joni's chest with icy coldness. "I'm complaining that you would hide something as major as addiction from me. How could you do that, knowing how I felt? How could you have deceived me about something so horrible?"

His words shredded the tattered remains of Joni's heart.

She wanted to scream at him, wanted to demand how he could have professed to be falling in love with her and later that same day to have turned your back on her because of her mother's problems? What did he expect? For her to turn her back on her mother? Why would she do that after her mother had been sober for almost five years? Not that she would even if her mother fell back into the same habits. You didn't turn your back on people you loved no matter what their problems were. Not ever.

Grant didn't love her. He'd just been caught up in the fantasy of their attraction to each other. Ha, for once she could honestly say just the sight of him disgusted her.

"Complaints duly noted." Body stiff, she stared back at him, watching as more and more angry color stained his face. "Aren't you lucky you don't have to ever deal with my silly rules ever again? Goodbye, Grant."

With that, she marched out of the room, head held high, proud that this time she'd been the one to walk away.

Later she'd deal with the doubts burning in her chest. Much later.

Or maybe never, because she didn't want to examine too closely the thought of Grant not being a part of her life, that maybe she was wrong, that she should have opened up to him, talked to him, told him her fears and vulnerabilities.

At least she still had her career this time. Because as angry as Grant was at her, she didn't believe he'd turn on her, lie to her boss and try to get her fired.

Then again, she'd been wrong before.

"So how's your love life?"

Joni grimaced at Mrs. Sain's question. She so didn't want to have this conversation, but had known when she'd seen Mrs. Sain's name on the schedule that she wouldn't be able to avoid questions about Grant. "Not that it's any of your business, but I don't have a love life."

What was she saying? She'd never had a love life. A sex life, yes. Love life, no.

"What happened with you and Doc?"

Really, the woman was too much. Didn't she know asking such questions just wasn't polite? Or did such things not matter so much once you reached a certain age in life?

Maybe not, because Mrs. Sain didn't look in the slightest apologetic or embarrassed, just curious.

"Well? Don't even tell me that you blew it with my hunky doctor. Surely you're smarter than that."

"Surely," Joni agreed, finishing the woman's morning vitals.

"You blew it, didn't you? So what did you do?"

"Nothing much. Just told him to leave me alone."

"What?" The woman looked appalled. "He listened?"

"Yes. He listened. Why wouldn't he?"

The older woman shook her head, obviously disgusted with both of them. Good, maybe the older lady would quit asking questions and reminding her of what she fought really hard not to think of—Grant. Not that she succeeded much. Odd how not trying to think of something meant constantly thinking of that something.

Mrs. Sain gave a disgusted grunt, mumbled something under her breath.

Joni sighed, knowing she was going to regret her next words. "Go ahead. Say whatever it is you're thinking. I know you want to so don't start holding back now."

"You're an idiot."

Joni didn't know whether to laugh or cry at the woman's observation. "Probably."

"No probably to it. You are," Mrs. Sain declared, matter-of-factly. "That man is crazy about you and has been trying to win your heart for weeks."

"That's just sexual attraction." Why was she admitting this out loud? Really, she had lost her mind.

"Lucky you."

Yeah, lucky her. She plopped down into the chair next to Mrs. Sain's bed. Only she wasn't having sex with Grant any more. Instead, she was spending a lot of time recalling all the wonderful times she'd had with Grant. Times she'd classified as just sex but they hadn't been. Just sex would have been Grant leaving the moment they'd finished. Instead he'd held her for hours, talking, stroking her hair, her skin, kissing her so gently that he might have thought her fragile.

Her rules had been a joke, hadn't protected a thing, especially not her heart.

Wait! She wasn't supposed to be thinking about Grant.

Don't think about Grant. Don't think about Grant. Don't think about Grant... Oh! What was the use? She thought about him all the time whether she wanted to or not.

She missed him, deep down as if she'd lost a vital part of herself missed him.

"Now that you've told him to leave you alone, and he is, how are you going to win him back?"

Win him back? "I didn't say I wanted him back."

"I may be old, but I'm not blind."

"Or mute."

The older woman cackled with laughter, which triggered a coughing spell. Joni beat on her back, trying to help clear the mucus. Finally, Mrs. Sain was breathing semi-regularly again.

"Let's not do that again," Joni advised, assessing the woman's breathing pattern and oxygen saturation.

"Agreed."

"I'll have the respiratory therapist come do your breathing treatment, see if we can't get your airways cleared."

"Maybe you should just put a call in to my lung doctor. Pretty sure he could clear my airways better than any therapist. Maybe he could clear a few things for you, too."

Joni smiled at the older woman's gumption. "You do realize you're my patient, not my shrink, right?"

"Do you need a shrink?"

Did she? Goodness knew, her mind had been everywhere since she'd walked away from Grant.

She'd only caught rare glimpses of him at the hospital. Which meant he was avoiding her, just as she was avoiding him.

Which was for the best. Having to see him all the time and knowing she'd never touch him again would be so much worse. At least she figured it would be. At the moment she did long to see him. To put her eyeballs on him and soak in his features.

She missed him.

Missed everything about him.

Especially his smile. The smile he reserved just for her.

"It really is his smile, you know," she said with a wistful sigh.

"I know," Mrs. Sain agreed. "The man's smile is positively lethal. You going to woo him back?"

"Woo him?" Joni grimaced, plopping back down in the chair she'd occupied prior to Mrs. Sain's coughing spell. "I wouldn't know where to begin."

Mrs. Sain's white eyebrows lifted. "You've never wooed a man?"

Before she'd learned that he'd been sleeping around for most of their relationship, she'd wanted to hang on to Mark, but she hadn't ever wooed him, had she? Perhaps she'd tried, but, if so, she'd failed.

She'd loved him, but now she knew better. He'd used her. As if shattering her heart hadn't been enough, he'd undermined her job, reporting her for supposed patient negligence, for supposed use of narcotics while on duty, leaving her utterly devastated personally and professionally.

Professionally, she'd recovered as the claims hadn't been true. Still, by the time the investigation had ended, she'd lost all joy in her job, all respect for the hospital board that had stood behind the acclaimed doctor who'd made the claims rather than a mere nurse. She'd needed a change, had moved to Bean's Creek, taken her mother with her, and started over.

Personally, she'd thought she had recovered, too. She'd thought she'd put all the pieces back together. But what she'd done was piece together a brick wall to hide behind. For the past five years she'd been hiding, afraid to live. No one had even tempted her to step out from behind her protective shield until she'd met the devil himself—Grant. Only he hadn't been a devil at all. Far from it.

He'd been her saving grace and she'd been too blind to see the truth. She'd attempted to shield herself with rules. Rules meant to provide a barrier to protect her heart.

Rules that hadn't barricaded a thing.

"Tell him the truth," a crotchety old voice broke into her thoughts and advised.

"The truth?" She stared at Mrs. Sain in confusion.

"That you love him and want him back."

"He wants nothing to do with me." He didn't. He'd made no effort to see her, had accepted her request to leave her alone quite easily. She might have been the one to say goodbye, but he'd been the first to walk away that night at the E.R. Even if she'd doubted herself a thousand times since, he'd let her go, let her say goodbye. Then again, had she given him a choice? Had she even listened to anything he'd said or had she only been trying to scramble back behind her protective walls? "I pushed him away."

Mrs. Sain adjusted her nasal cannula, taking a deep breath. "Tell him you made a mistake. Ask him for his forgiveness."

"Why would he forgive me?"

Even with her wrinkled face it wasn't difficult to decipher Mrs. Sain's "duh" expression. "Because he loves you and wants you back?"

If only.

"I wish he did," Joni admitted on a wistful sigh. She rose to her feet because she'd dallied long enough and needed to get back to check on her other patient. Wishes were a waste of time.

"Do you?"

Joni's heart stopped. She turned slowly toward the door. Grant stood there, looking wonderful in his blue hospital scrubs that so perfectly matched his eyes. His beautiful eyes that she had missed looking into so much.

How long had he been standing there? Had Mrs. Sain seen him and not said anything? Probably, the wily old woman thought she knew best.

Joni opened her mouth to speak, but nothing came out. Not a single sound. If she admitted that she really did wish he loved her and wanted her back, he'd probably laugh at her, remind her that she'd been the one to insist that they have a sex-only relationship. He'd probably tell her that he couldn't deal with her attending AA with her mother regularly and being her mother's number-one support system—although, honestly, she wasn't so sure about that one any more as her stepfather seemed to have a happy handle on things. He'd probably tell her that it served her right that she wanted him to love her because he'd tried to have a relationship with her and she'd been too scared to risk it. She'd stopped him at every turn, insisting they abide by her rules. Because she'd been afraid to risk love.

Now she'd lost him.

"What purpose would it serve if I loved you and wanted a woman back who only wants me for sex?"

"I never said that."

His brow lifted. "Didn't you?"

"Not in so many words, but yes," she admitted, face on fire. "I guess I did essentially say that."

Joni glanced toward Mrs. Sain, who was practically rubbing her hands together in glee. They shouldn't be having this conversation in front of her. Maybe they shouldn't be having this conversation at all.

Yet her heart wouldn't let her walk away. Not this time.

Sure, she'd be made a fool, just as she had been with Mark. Sure, Grant would probably laugh at her. But at least she'd know that she put her heart out there, that she had breathed life back into her body and lived.

And loved.

And risked everything for that love.

This time she knew that despite the fact that she truly loved Grant, she wouldn't bury herself away the way she had after the demise of her relationship with Mark.

Loving Grant had made her stronger, more capable of facing the rest of her life with arms open wide.

Yes, she'd lost her mind right along with her heart, but she loved this man and she wouldn't cower. Not ever again.

"Yes." She held her head high. "I wish you loved me and wanted me back."

Grant almost slid to the hospital floor in a surprised heap. He couldn't believe his ears. Was Joni really saying words he'd dreamed of her saying for weeks?

Then again, maybe she just missed the sex.

Definitely, he could understand that. Their bodies did phenomenal things together. Just being near her had every cell in his body standing at attention.

But they had bigger problems than just whether or not she'd realized there was more between them than sex. She was an addict. For weeks now he'd lain awake trying to come up with a solution to Joni's problem, to come up with a way for her not to end up as Ashley had. Apparently, she and her mother were in Alcoholics Anonymous together, perhaps even other rehab programs as well. How long had she been clean? How long had her mother? Back and forth he'd battled whether or not he could risk another Ashley. At times he knew he was strong enough to stand by Joni, to encourage her to make the right choices. At others he wondered if he could watch another woman he loved destroy herself.

"This is better than any soap opera I ever watched."

Grant glanced away from Joni at Mrs. Sain's observation. The woman's face glowed with excitement, but this was a conversation better done in private. He and Joni couldn't discuss the real issues with another person privy to the private details.

"Come with me," he ordered Joni, then told his patient, "I'll be back to check on you later."

"No rush, Doc. Take your time. Ain't as if I have anywhere to go."

Without waiting to see if Joni followed, Grant turned, left the room, and waited in the hallway.

"Grant, I…" She stopped next to him, stared at her feet, took a deep breath, and met his eyes. "I want you in my life."

"As your lover?"

"Yes," she immediately answered, her gaze searching his.

"If that's the only way you'll have me, then, yes, be my lover, Grant," she whispered, taking his hand and lacing their fingers. "But you should know that

I'll spend every moment of the rest of my life trying to make you love me."

Grant's heart quickened, pumped hard against his ribcage. "There's no need."

Her hand fell from his, her face tightening. "Then I've lost you for ever?"

"You misunderstand." He lifted her chin, forced her to meet his gaze. "There's no need for you to try to make me love you, because I already do."

Gaze lifting to his, her eyes glittered with moisture. "You do?"

He brushed his fingertip across her cheek, catching a single teardrop that had trickled down her face. "I tried telling you on the day of our Skyline trip, but you didn't want to hear what I was saying."

"I thought… Never mind what I thought. I wasn't ready to hear."

"I noticed. But that didn't make my words any less true." He cupped her face, stared straight into her eyes. "I love you, Joni Thompson. Now and for ever. I love you, but I'm not sure love is enough."

Joni's heart swelled, threatening to burst out of her chest, then careened at his final words.

"I lived with a woman before moving here. I loved her, planned to marry her, but about a year into our relationship I started noticing things, how much she drank, how many pills she popped. Unfortunately, I didn't see the half of it. I should have gotten out then, but I thought I could cure her."

He'd lived with an addict? That was why he'd felt the way he had about Kathy Conner? Why he'd walked away when he'd learned about her mother? Not because he hadn't loved her but because he hadn't been able to deal with having another addict in his life.

"I couldn't cure her, just as I wouldn't be able to cure you, Joni, and I don't know that I could bear watching you destroy yourself, but I can't not try, because I need you in my life."

"I won't turn my back on my mother," she interrupted, knowing she was sealing her fate but also knowing she had to lay all the facts on the line. "She doesn't need as much from me these days as she's been sober for almost five years, and especially not since she met and married my stepfather. But if she relapsed, if she needed me, I'd be at her side without question. Always." What he'd last said sank in. "Me?"

"Your mother?" he asked at the same time.

"I do not and neither have I ever used drugs of any kind. I was falsely accused once by someone I loved, but he was wrong."

"He was a fool," Grant said with such conviction Joni laughed.

"He was an esteemed doctor I had an affair with and it cost me my self-respect and my job."

"Like I said, he was a fool." He cupped her face. "I love you, Joni."

She'd heard the words before, heard them from Mark, but never had she heard them sincerely, never had she heard them from one heart to her own.

Grant loved her.

She could see the truth in his eyes, in the sweetness of the way he wiped away her tear.

"I love you, too." Joy filled her body and without thought she flung her arms around his neck, kissed him. "I've missed you! Oh, Grant, I've missed you so much."

"I've missed you, too." Grant seemed a bit stunned at her show of public affection, but kissed her back with a quick kiss to her mouth.

Embarrassed by her unprofessional act right in the middle of the ICU hallway, knowing she'd probably embarrassed him, too, Joni bowed her head.

"I'm sorry. I shouldn't have done that," she apologized, wondering at her crazy zig-zagging emotions.

"Look at me," he ordered her, lifting her face to his.

She did so.

"Don't ever be sorry for that. Not ever. Because I'm not." He closed his eyes, took a deep breath. "I'm yours, Joni. All of me. Any time you want me, I'm yours. Just yours."

She nodded, becoming more and more aware of their surroundings. They stood in the open hallway of the ICU. Anyone could see them. Everyone could see them.

"But I…"

"But you are mine, too." As if to prove his point, he cupped her face again, stared into her eyes. "Mine to touch. Just mine. No supply closet required."

Unable to find the power to speak, she nodded again.

"And, Joni?"

She met his gaze.

"This time I'm making the rules."

Not believing the sheer happiness jolting through her, she bit back a smile. "Oh? What kind of rules?"

"Rules of engagement, because I want you to be mine for ever."

Joni's eyes widened. Her jaw dropped. Was he?

"I may be rushing things, but I don't want to wait. Neither do I want there to be any question about what it is I want from you. I want everything. My first rule is that we go tomorrow and buy you the biggest, gaudiest diamond we can find so no one can miss that you are taken."

"But I don't need—"

He shook his head at her, interrupting. "My second rule is that we don't have sex again until your last name is the same as mine."

"I don't think—"

"No worries, Joni, love. I'm just ensuring that we have a really short engagement."

"I still don't—"

"And my third rule," he continued, not letting her finish, "is that you introduce me to your mother. Tonight. After we get off work, we'll go, tell her our news."

Joni stared at him in amazement.

"And my fourth rule, the most important rule of all, is that we love each other for ever."

No longer caring that they stood in the hallway, Joni wrapped her arms around his neck. "Are those all your rules, Dr. Bradley, or do you get to make more up along the way?"

"Depends." His mouth hovered close to hers.

"On?"

"Whether or not you agree to the first four rules of our engagement."

"And if I don't?"

"You have to. Not agreeing is against the rules and I know how you feel about rules."

"That they are meant to be broken?" she teased, loving the way he looked at her, the way his eyes danced.

"Not my rules." His lips met hers, kissing her until she was breathless, until clapping sounded all around her.

Joni pulled back, smiled at Samantha and her other co-workers.

"Well, answer the poor man," Samantha ordered. "And you are not allowed to say no."

Joni started to point out that her friend was a good

one to talk but, unlike Samantha, Joni didn't want to say no. She wanted Grant. For ever.

She looked straight into his sky-blue eyes. "It's your smile, you know."

"My smile?"

She nodded. "Oh, yes. Your smile is why I accept your rules of engagement."

"And here I thought it was because you loved me."

"I do love you, Grant, but it's your smile, the one you reserve just for me, that takes my breath away."

Grant smiled.

* * * * *

So you think you can write?

Mills & Boon® and Harlequin® have joined forces in a global search for new authors.

It's our biggest contest yet—with the prize of being published by the world's leader in romance fiction.

In September join us for our unique Five Day Online Writing Conference
www.soyouthinkyoucanwrite.com

Meet 50+ romance editors who want to buy your book and get ready to submit your manuscript!

So you think you can write?
Show us!

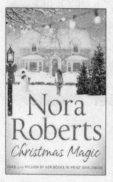

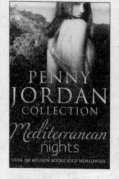